Previously Creative Director at RDF Television, Beth Morrey
now writes full time. Her debut novel, *Saving Missy*, was a
Sunday Times bestseller and longlisted for the Authors' Club
First Novel Award.

Beth lives in London with her husband, two sons and a St
Berdoodle named Phoebe.

@BethMorrey
/BethMorreyWriter
@bethmorrey

Also by Beth Morrey

Saving Missy

BETH MORREY

HarperCollinsPublishers

HarperCollins*Publishers* Ltd
1 London Bridge Street
London SE1 9GF

www.harpercollins.co.uk

HarperCollins*Publishers* Ltd
Macken House, 39/40 Mayor Street Upper,
Dublin 1, D01 C9W8, Ireland

First published by HarperCollins*Publishers* 2022
This edition published 2023
1

A catalogue record for this book is available from the British Library

ISBN: 978-0-00-833411-6 (PB)

Typeset in Adobe Caslon by
Palimpsest Book Production Ltd, Falkirk, Stirlingshire

Printed and bound in the UK using 100% Renewable Electricity
by CPI Group (UK) Ltd

This book is produced from independently certified FSC™ paper
to ensure responsible forest management.

For more information visit: www.harpercollins.co.uk/green

For Wilfred and Edmund

A wise woman once said to me:
'There are only two lasting bequests
we can hope to give our children.
One of these is roots; the other, wings.'

Hodding Carter,
Where Main Street Meets the River

Autumn Term

Chapter 1

*E*very morning, Maman used to fling open the curtains, calling, '*C'est le premier jour!*' Every day was the first day, a new beginning. That was how I remembered her: turning with a smile, the sun streaming through her hair, alight with expectation and possibility.

Pressed up against a cold wall, as dawn broke, I lay staring at the mould on the ceiling, pretending I hadn't done it a thousand times before. It crept across a crack that ran along the corner above us, a blooming sphere amidst a crescent of smaller blue-black circles; my own little Rorschach test. There was a time when I loved tests. Was it a waxing moon, an apostrophe, or a bass clef? The body beside me shifted uneasily, pushing me further against the damp Anaglypta. A sickle, a fish hook . . . An elbow jabbed me in the rib as I eased myself out of bed. When it came down to it, it was just mould – mould I didn't have the time, money or energy to get rid of. Pulling on a jumper, I heard a murmur from the ruffled head buried in its pillow.

'Go back to sleep,' I said, and headed for the kitchen.

There was a pot soaking in the sink and, after putting the kettle on, I plunged my hands into the congealed water, nails scraping at the softened pasta that clung to the sides. Outside, the sun was coming up, but it hadn't yet reached our basement flat, never really did any more. The house I dreamed of was always perched up high, in the trees, light pouring through the windows. But that was like the pictures in the mould, existing only in my head. Dad didn't stir when I tiptoed in to give him his tea, and when I went back to our bedroom, the body was barely visible under the duvet. Grabbing my clothes, I edged towards the door, but the head emerged, round eyes fixed on me.

'Don't be late for school,' I said, and backed out. No need to worry; she never was.

Le premier jour. It was mid-September, which still felt like the beginning of the year to me, even though I left school twelve years ago. On the bus to work, I squared my shoulders, ready to take the day by the scruff of its neck. That mould was a beckoning finger, a call to arms, to new beginnings.

Gio clicked his tongue in irritation when I arrived at the café, although I was never late either.

'*Andiamo! Dai!* Giddy-up!'

'Sorry.'

He picked up his *Daily Mail* and shook it, as I hurried to unload the dishwasher, tying my apron behind my back. The radio was playing, Elton John belting out 'Tiny Dancer', and my hips swayed involuntarily as I riffled through the cutlery tray, thinking of my daughter's nightly gyration around our bed, poking and kicking me as she turned. Picturing her tousled head, pirate smile peeking over the covers, my heart

4

squeezed a little, the sudden lurch of love that unbalanced me, even as I was staring at my distorted face in the back of a spoon. She was getting too big, our bed too small, but, like the mould, I didn't really know what to do about it.

The day disappeared in a blur, frothing like milk around a steam wand. Grinding, stirring, chopping, spreading, wrapping, dashing. Morning rush, followed by mid-morning rush, followed by lunch rush, then a lull that made me long to slump at one of the tables and squeeze my aching feet. But Gio hated to see inactivity, so I propped myself on the counter to polish the cutlery again, surreptitiously easing my toes out of my shoes to flex them. He wouldn't let me wear trainers, said it looked sloppy. If only I could get through the rest of the day, then go home to Em for hot chocolate, and maybe a bath if there was enough hot water, and—

'Delphine Jones!'

A woman stood before me, vaguely familiar. About my age, but with the glow of good fortune draped around her like a fur stole. She had the kind of buttery highlights that can't be achieved with a packet dye, skin as shiny as the stainless steel I was holding, glacé nails clutching a leather purse she definitely didn't buy at a market stall. Staring at her, my mind did a rewind, and freeze-framed on her aged sixteen, spraying her hair and rolling up her skirt in the school toilets.

'Lexy?'

'Fancy seeing you.' She put her purse on the counter between us. 'You . . . *work* here?'

That much was obvious, and it seemed stupid to deny it, standing there in an apron, holding a tea towel. What was also

5

stupid was that I felt the need to, to claim I was just passing through on the way to my skyrise corner office overlooking Canary Wharf.

'It pays the bills.' It didn't even manage that, entirely.

'How funny.' She raked a hand through ramrod-straight hair. 'I always imagined you doing something a bit more . . . scholarly. And here you are, a coffee-maker.'

'Barista,' I said. 'Do you want anything?'

'Decaf latte with soy milk.'

I kept my back to her, yanking the filters, pretending I couldn't hear over the noise of the radio, Freddie Mercury singing about rage, the flame that burns, secret harmonies . . .

'You were always such a swot at school, I thought you'd be running the country by now, but of course you had a *baby*, didn't you. What a shame.'

My hands stilled around the hot cup, head bent to inhale the bitter scent of the beans as I pictured my crooked-toothed friend sobbing after Lexy called her Metal Marni. It seemed the years hadn't mellowed her.

'Why you dilly-dally about? Lickety-split!' Gio's voice roused me, and I turned, holding the coffee.

'Your latte. Sorry about the wait.'

She smiled, but her eyes were ice chips. What had gone wrong in her life that made her this way? There were rumours about her dad having a nasty temper. As I pushed the mug towards her, she leaned forwards and lightly circled my wrist in a chummy, confidential grasp. Up close, she smelled of jasmine and something woody. She'd need a lot of perfume, to mask the polecat.

'Do you see Adam at all?'

I swallowed. 'No.'

She gave a sympathetic tut. 'What a shame. Still, I suppose at least *he* went on to bigger and better things.'

The cluster of carpal bones are what make wrists particularly flexible. Em told me that, once, after she spent an evening committing them to memory. Not an evening, really, not even half an hour; when Em sees something it shoots into her brain and lodges there instantly. I remembered them only because she taught me the mnemonic: Sally Left The Party To Take Cathy Home. Scaphoid, Lunate, Triquetrum, Pisiform, Trapezium, Trapezoid, Capitate, Hamate. The hamate is hook-shaped, like the mould on the ceiling. Keeping my expression neutral, the bones moved together in perfect formation, strong and supple.

'Arrrrrrgh!' Lexy's scream brought Gio running. Grabbing a stack of napkins, he began swabbing her steaming crotch, leaving white shreds of tissue on her designer jeans. What a shame.

'I'm sorry, it was an accident.'

Gio grabbed more napkins to dab on the wet patch, as Lexy raised her snarling face to mine.

'She did it on purpose,' she hissed.

My boss looked from his employee to his customer. Me, Delphine Jones, in my apron, scraped-back frizzy hair, red-raw knuckles, bitten nails. Her, Alexa Marshall, Shellacs curled to claws, white teeth bared, her tiny, pale-blue leather bag still on the counter. It was quilted, with two interlocking 'C's on the catch. Gio saw how it was. He was annoyed with her forcing him into it, but of course he couldn't show it. So he turned his anger on me, his punchbag barista.

'Why you act like a crazy woman? After all I do for you! Always causing trouble, *pigro*, this is enough! *Basta!* Go at once.'

Once he'd got into his performance, Gio started enjoying himself, reading the riot act, while I let my mind drift to a climate change protester in the street the other day, holding a placard: 'TOO HOT TO HANDLE'. Such a scorching summer, still burning itself out, everything heating up, bubbling and spitting until it boiled over . . . I could tell Gio was already having second thoughts, even as I collected my stuff, but Ms Marshall would have considered it a personal insult if he went back on his word. So he stood, holding the door open, waiting for me to leave, and I squeezed awkwardly past him, head down, out into the dense heat of that sultry September.

Standing on the step, I found I was holding the long-handled silver spoon I'd been polishing, plucked from the apron pocket. It glinted as I rotated it, the inside of the bowl battered dull and grey, but the curved outer side shooting off sparks, fired up by the sun. I thought of my mother – Maman recounting how the father of one of her pupils had ordered her about like a minion; how at the time she said nothing – '*Rien de tout!*' – and only afterwards thought of the perfect retort. '*L'esprit de l'escalier, ma chérie.*' Staircase wit – you only ever think of the thing you should have said on the way out, and by then it's too late.

Gio was still standing in the doorway, accepting tearful thanks from Lexy, neither of them expecting my sudden return, brandishing my shiny talisman.

'Just so you know, Gio, *tesoro*, I wouldn't work another

minute in this sub-Starbucks shack, even if you offered me a raise. Which you would never do, because you're a tight-fisted hand at the grindstone – a squeezing, wrenching, grasping, scraping, clutching, covetous, old sinner!' *Thank you, Miss Challoner, for schooling me in Dickens.* Lexy's turn. 'And *you*. You liked Adam, didn't you? What a shame he didn't like you.' Back to Gio. 'Just in case I didn't make myself clear, you can take your job, and your crappy espresso-maker and *ficcatelo su per il culo.*' Back to Lexy. 'That means shove it up your ass. Which is what you can do with your Chanel.'

It's one thing to think of it, another to act. The spirit was willing, had the speech ready, but the flesh was weak, my legs trembling at the image, the audacity. The Lexys of this world said what they liked and left the mess behind, but I kept my head down, and cleared up. What had I *done*? Throwing away my job, the job I needed to keep our house of cards from falling, was insane, unhinged. But underneath it all, somehow, the bones had been flexing, pushing me forwards, before the rot set in.

I pivoted on the step and pushed open the door. Gio and Lexy looked at me in silent astonishment as I threw the spoon on the floor that still bore the marks of my mopping.

'Shine your own silver.'

Not much, but better than nothing. I turned and exited once more, out into the sunshine, squinting against the light, shading my eyes against my future.

Le premier jour.

Chapter 2

With nothing else to do, I went to pick up Em from school. Hadn't been back since the first day she started, earlier that month – a shift, or shopping, or some other task had always got in the way. The truth was, I didn't want to go to her school, because it used to be mine. Brownswood High, a scruffy, sprawling state secondary run by Gerald Haynes, an ex-army officer who would have been happier running a workhouse. Now it was an Academy, with a new library and a super-head called Mrs Boleyn, who believed in something called 'co-operative learning', so Em told me. I shivered as I saw the red brick looming ahead, the scene of several crimes.

Would Em want to see me there? It was probably really shaming to be picked up by your mum, particularly one with mascara tracks down her cheeks. I thought about sneaking off, but caught sight of her talking to a woman with piled-up blonde hair and Biro marks on her cheek. My daughter's eyes widened when she noticed me, drawing a hundred conclusions, probably the right ones. She whispered something to the woman, who turned and smiled, sparking a flicker of recognition. She had a Bic stuck in her messy bun, and what looked like a seed in the gap between her front teeth.

'Hi, Mum, what are you doing here? I've got my first fast-track class.'

In the official letter, emailed by the head just a week after she started, they'd said Em was extraordinary: 'A special class for special students.' Extraordinary and special. It wasn't that I disagreed, but sometimes it was better – easier – to be ordinary and normal.

'Sorry, I forgot.'

'Mrs Jones! Lovely to meet you. We haven't met, have we? I'm Mrs Gill, Emily's English teacher.'

The famous Mrs Gill, who Em went on about. She'd sent me an email, too, about a theatre trip, and I fobbed her off because I hadn't got the money together yet. How would I get it, now? I blinked back fresh tears, because Em was desperate to go, but had made out it didn't matter. Just last night, standing in the kitchen running hot water into the pasta pan, shrugging her skinny shoulders. '*If there are any issues with payment, maybe the school could help?*' Mrs Gill had written. '*That won't be necessary,*' I'd replied. An extra shift, sell something on eBay, scrape coins off the pavement rather than admit it was a problem.

'I'd better be going . . .' I stepped away, but she barrelled on.

'Emily is doing brilliantly, she's very well-read for her age. For any age, really! We're so glad she's joining our new group, she'll really benefit from a bit of extra pushing.'

She was pushy, hassling me at the school gates, gabbling

11

away. I was overwhelmed by the day, the looming horror of job-hunting, and the memory-deluge just being here had unleashed.

'Well, it was her decision . . .' I dashed away a rogue tear and her eyes narrowed.

'Of course, but if the parents are on board it's such a . . . Are you OK?'

A tissue appeared under my nose.

'Thank you,' I mumbled, taking it. 'Sorry . . . don't know what made me . . .'

'Emily, Mr Davidson is taking the class today – you'd better get going or you'll be late. I'll show your mum round for a bit. Off you go.'

Mrs Gill nodded at Em, who trailed off, throwing us suspicious glances.

'Come with me.' She led me through a revamped reception, along various bright corridors, both new and weirdly familiar, chatting the whole way, as I tried to ignore the influx. There was the classroom where Marni and Sheba plaited their hair together and spent the day lurching around like Siamese twins until Miss Kornack threatened them with a pair of scissors – unprofessional but effective. The dining hall where Leroy Ellis had an allergic reaction to fish, and Mr Wilsden had to give him an EpiPen injection in the middle of lunch. The science lab where Sally Barclay . . . *No. Stop it.* It was Em's school now, everyone else had moved on.

'I can't tell you how brilliant Emily is. I'm sure you already know – I knew from the very first lesson. We were reading *Much Ado*, Benedick and Beatrice arguing, and I asked for other examples of couples who argue. Of course, I was getting *nothing* – someone said Ant and Dec – I mean, I *ask* you – and then Emily pipes up from the back: "Kate and Petruchio." Then her *Twelfth Night* speech! So, when Mrs Boleyn asked me who should join the fast-track class, I said immediately – "Emily Jones."' She opened the door to an empty unlit classroom and beckoned me in. 'Take a seat.'

The classroom didn't have any particular associations, and even in the dim light it was clear what a vibrant space it was – colours and thoughts and effort everywhere. There was a Word Wall between the windows, a display of paper butterflies emerging from an open book, each wing covered in synonyms for the word that spanned its thorax. *Rich: wealthy, prosperous, abundant, bountiful, productive, fertile . . .* Mrs Gill handed me another tissue, and for a second was silent as I calmed myself down. When I looked up, she smiled and picked at the seed between her teeth.

'It's almost impossible to cry on camera, you know. They use these drops, and some make-up artists have a tear stick they use. Sometimes they blow menthol air in your eyes. Dangerous really, because if you got any of the actual oil in your eye you could damage it. Which would mess up the scene completely, continuity-wise.' She reached into the drawer of her desk and produced a pretty pink box. 'Have a macaron.'

Having read the list of staff in the school prospectus, I'd been relieved to see few from my era had survived. Mrs R Gill (BA) was one of the new wave, and Em had researched her thoroughly when she found out who she was. She was still recognizable when she smiled – that famous gap between her teeth. More than twenty years before, as a teenager, Miss

Rosalind Cartwright played Rosalie Murray in the Oscar-nominated movie *Agnes Grey*, dancing round the schoolroom, reeling in Sir Thomas Ashby with her ringlets. It seemed impossible to imagine, in this Hackney classroom. I watched the film with my dad, twelve years ago, when I'd just found out I was pregnant. Sitting in our cold living room with a dinner tray, angry because, although I was watching it with Dad, he wasn't really there; angry because I'd just given up my A levels, and would never be able to do the things I wanted to do with books like *Agnes Grey*. The anger never really disappeared, just lingered, dormant, with nowhere to go.

Rosalind Cartwright must have made a fortune, so what was Mrs R Gill doing teaching at Brownswood? Surely that kind of past was a deadly weapon for students to taunt her with. Unless Em was the only one who knew – my daughter harvested information like other children stockpiled conkers. She'd told me her teacher had married a rock guitarist and for a while they'd been one of those couples in magazines, but gradually things had petered out. Apart from some crime drama a couple of years ago, Roz Gill hadn't been in anything for a while and, in her new incarnation, she certainly didn't look like a famous person. Burnt-blonde hair greying at the roots, a network of fine lines around the startling blue eyes – an older, messier, chattier version of the screen persona. Both of us were fallen stars.

'So, is something the matter? You looked upset back there.' My daughter's teacher bit into a macaron, using her cupped hands to catch the falling crumbs and cram them into her mouth.

'Just had a rough day. Lost my job.'

'Oh, no. How come?' Resting her chin on her hand, she fixed me with an intense stare. There were sugary specks on her lips.

'It was . . . a misunderstanding.' It was true in a way. Gio didn't understand that Lexy deserved to be drenched in coffee.

'Can you explain? Get your job back?'

'There's no point.' I traced the subtle pink ridges of the macaron with the tip of my finger. 'Besides, I hated it. My boss was awful and the pay was terrible.' I'd put up with two years of it, because terrible pay was better than no pay, an awful boss was better than no boss. On the wall behind the desk someone had written on the whiteboard: 'Can you be rich and poor at the same time?' *Poor: impoverished, needy, broke, substandard, faulty, pitiful.*

'Well, maybe it's for the best. Can you get another job? What is it that you do?'

'Waitress. And cleaner.'

'I used to do bar shifts when I was studying for my teaching diploma – it's hard work, isn't it. I could ask around if you like? Still got a few contacts.'

'Thanks, but it's fine. I've got my cleaning job.' It wasn't fine but, like the money for the Shakespeare play, there was no way I would accept help. As soon as you did that, it opened the floodgates. Questions, forms, social workers, reports. Help became interference. Best just get on with it, keep your head down.

'Is there a Mr Jones?' She immediately checked herself. 'Sorry, that's none of my business.'

I thought of Sid, my most recent ex, and Dad, the only

Mr Jones in my life, and shook my head. She looked about to say more but thought better of it, squeezing my shoulder. 'Sure you'll find something.' She got to her feet, brushing off biscuit crumbs. 'Now, I'm going to have to escort you out of school, because if anyone catches you wandering round without a pass you'll probably get arrested.'

Trying to laugh, I stood up, still holding my uneaten macaron. But as we moved towards the door, someone else opened it, flicking a switch and flooding the room with light. My watery eyes adjusting, it was a second before I could focus.

'Delphine Jones!'

Another older version of a woman I remembered. But the same piercing gaze, same mannish suit, same short brushed-back hair – greyer now. So many hours spent watching her, listening to her, writing down the words she said, hanging onto every one. Until I walked away from it all.

'Miss Challoner.'

Eyes wide with surprise, she extended a hand. 'Mrs Boleyn now,' she said.

So Miss Challoner was the super-head. When she'd taught me, she'd been a lowly English teacher, struggling to get funding to refurbish the library. The library where Adam and I . . . Stuffing the biscuit in my mouth, I took her hand, hoping she wouldn't feel mine shaking.

'Delphine was my star pupil, once upon a time.' Miss Challoner – Mrs Boleyn – nodded to Mrs Gill.

'Really?' Mrs Gill looked delighted. 'And now her daughter is mine!'

Mrs Boleyn shot me a sharp glance and I tried to meet her eye. 'Daughter? You're a parent here?'

'Em Jones,' I mumbled, swallowing. How much would she guess? She taught English; how was her maths? 'She's . . . eleven. Just started in Year Seven.'

She frowned for a second, before her brow cleared. 'Ah yes, Emily. Roz mentioned her. Quoting Shakespeare. Extraordinary. Chip off the old block, eh? She joining the fast-track class?'

'Yes,' I said. 'She's very excited.'

Mrs Boleyn nodded in approval. 'Excellent. Just like you!'

But I was determined that Em would be nothing like me. She would succeed where I failed.

Chapter 3

*Y*ou never forget a good teacher. They stay with you, kindly ghosts at your shoulder reminding you you're worth something. I remember the teacher who taught me to read and write, who told me my story of Icarus was excellent: 'What wings you gave him!' she said, as I beamed brighter than the sun. That bond between teacher and student is precious and profound, the knowledge teachers possess as rosy and tempting as a newly plucked apple. They're the gateway to a new life, a *better* life – or at least, that's what I believed, once upon a time. Miss Challoner was one of those teachers who could open up a whole world and, in my case, that world turned out to have Adam Terris in it. He was another apple I couldn't resist.

Adam joined Brownswood at the beginning of Year Ten. His dad had some posh job in the civil service, had transferred from Brussels to London, so there was already glamour attached to him. Straight away he established himself as brainy, and chilled out about it. Miss Challoner ran a book club at lunch-time on Wednesdays, and when

Adam joined it suddenly became well-attended, everyone coming to gaze at him, lounging in his chair, making the paperbacks look small in his big hands. I went because of her, not him. To listen to her talk about Thomas Hardy, and Charlotte Brontë, hear her read Elizabeth Bishop. But gradually I started listening to him, too, noticing the way a lock of his copper hair fell over his face when he read aloud; a stirring as potent as the fieriest villanelle.

The only time I felt properly warm was deep in a book, escaping to another world where I wasn't Delphine Jones. I spent hours at the local library because it was cosier than our flat; the dank basement with Dad slumped in his chair, pulling me down when I wanted to soar. Another English teacher, Mr North, started bringing in books for us, so I devoured them too. The only time I felt properly seen and heard was when I was talking about what I'd just read, Adam watching me, waiting for my teacher's approval.

Outside school, it was like a light switched off. It *was* a light switched off – to save the electricity. Keep food in the fridge, fix the leak, find the money and, above all, stop anyone guessing what was going on. Floodgates closed. I started waiting on tables at weekends to pay bills Dad couldn't manage, eating dry rolls from the café for dinner, reading into the night by torchlight. In the beginning, keeping up with schoolwork was just a way of fending people off, making them believe everything was fine. But necessity became a pleasure. What started as a flirtation became something much, much more.

School was the beacon – the bright, warm rooms; the noise and colour, the hot lunches. Teachers like Miss Challoner, pushing us to be the best we could be. Books, offering an escape route. And Adam, in class, listening to me and looking at me, *noticing* me in a way that Dad couldn't manage any more. Since Maman had gone, all I'd wanted was to be overlooked, for no one to see the mess we were in, but Adam was different. He was the sun, and I wanted him to shine on me, flying higher and higher until I could feel the warmth on my wings.

Chapter 4

After her fast-track class, Em and I wound down the best way we knew, with hot chocolate and chess. The old wooden set belonged to Dad, who taught me to play. I was six and it was a rainy afternoon; we sat on the floor with the board between us as he explained the rules. My favourite was that a pawn could become a queen if it reached the other side. He called me his queen after that, and we had a match every weekend. Now Em and I played on the little fold-down table, while Dad sat in stalemate beside us, eyes glued to the TV.

'Why did you come to pick me up today?' Em opened with her pawn.

I winced, thinking of the showdown at the café, and pushed my own piece forwards. 'Just wanted to see you.' That wouldn't pass muster. 'Wanted to see if you skipped school to go on climate strike.' Em had read about a young girl protesting outside the Swedish Parliament, and was considering making her own stand.

She frowned at the board. 'Thought about it. But I didn't want to miss my new class.'

'How was it?' I brought a knight out, feeling reckless. Em would win anyway.

'It was cool. We're doing more on *Twelfth Night*.'

That trip. I had to find the money somehow. 'That's great. Given that you've pretty much memorized it already.'

Em released a bishop with a wry smile. 'Still got Act Five to go. How was work?'

My hand hovered. 'What do you mean?'

'You were out early. And you were crying.'

'I . . . handed in my notice.'

Em took a sip of chocolate, checking it was cool enough to drink. 'Good. Act Five, the resolution. You can get a better job.'

'I'm not exactly inundated with offers.'

'Anything's better than Giovanni.' The few times Em had dropped by the café, Gio had not been welcoming, and she'd noticed him giving the wrong change to customers too many times for it to be accidental.

Anything was better than Giovanni, but I didn't have anything. If I got a better job, then we could move out of Dad's flat, get a place of our own, rooms of our own, begin the life I wanted to build for Em. But how could I possibly help with Dad's rent, and pay mine, leave him to fend for himself, find a job with a decent wage, when I had no qualifications, no prospects? Once, in the park, there had been a kind of travelling fair, and right in the centre of all the rides was a bungee run. People climbed on and ran like hell, only to be pulled back at the last moment. I'd had no money for a go but, in many ways, I didn't need any to feel that sensation. My whole life was that run.

'*Thou must untangle this.*' Em shifted her queen.

I stared at the board. '*It is too hard a knot for me t'untie.*'

'Checkmate,' she said, with her pirate smile.

So many permutations, and Em had them all figured out. Getting to my feet, I began putting the pieces away. 'I'll start dinner. Why don't you get your homework done?'

'Did it on the bus on the way home.'

'Of course you did. Go and sit with Granddad while I sort us out.'

Three fish fingers, two tubs of Pot Noodle, mixed with tinned sweetcorn, bread and margarine on the side. There was satisfaction in arranging the jigsaw pieces of our kitchen cupboards. I could see Em through the serving hatch, curling her way around her grandfather's armchair, the only one who could stir a morsel of delight in him. He was watching *Back to the Future*, the scorches of the DeLorean burning on the road. Every week, I went to the library to borrow something. He particularly liked sci-fi and fantasy – I guess the further away from reality the better. After putting the fish fingers in the oven, I flicked the kettle on and went into the living room to perch on the other arm of his chair.

He was quiet for a minute or so, then said, 'Eighty-eight miles per hour.'

'That's right.'

'It's not that fast.'

'No.' The film made time travel look easy, like anyone could cobble together a machine in their garage, and that appealed to Dad, who was always looking for a way out. Maybe the past was within reach, if he could just get up to speed.

Hearing the click of the kettle, I went back to pour it

over the noodles, and we ate watching Marty McFly find his way back to a future he could live with. When the film finished, I took the DVD out of the machine and gathered up the others to return to the library. Dad examined the latest offerings – *I, Robot*, *All About Eve*, *The Truman Show*, turning them over in his hands, lips moving as he read the blurbs. Em made him a cup of tea while I cleared up and did a stocktake for tomorrow's dinner. As Em waited for the tea to brew, she looked out of the window, at the steep grass verge that sloped up to the communal garden beyond. A garden Dad didn't visit any more.

'Tell me about JoJo,' she said.

My daughter often asked about her grandmother, and I didn't like to deny her, though it was painful to dredge it up, to supplement her bank of knowledge with my precious memories.

'When she was down, her favourite thing to play was "But Not for Me".' I rested my hands either side of the sink. 'She'd pick it out, just a couple of notes, slowly, so you could hardly hear the tune. But when she was happy, she'd play "On the Sunny Side of the Street", thumping on the keys, humming, sometimes breaking into song. But she still sang with her accent: *"Leave your wureez on ze doorstep . . ."*' I sang, softly, so Dad couldn't hear.

'When was she happy?' Em took the tea bag out of the mug and went to the fridge for milk.

'Most of the time. Didn't take much to put her in a good mood. Your granddad bringing back daffodils. My drawings – she'd thread them into a kind of bunting across the living room. Cooking. She liked making things from home – crêpes, onion soup, clafoutis, that sort of thing. Sometimes she'd make an afternoon tea, if we were celebrating.'

'When was she sad?'

Running the hot tap to wash the plates, steam rose around me, and I batted it away.

'When we ran out of money,' I said. 'When she thought we might have to sell the piano.'

We both looked back towards the living room to the piano, a dusty altar, untuned and unplayed, but unsold.

'Well, at least it never got that bad,' said Em, carrying the tea through. I laughed, though of course it wasn't funny. The piano was still there, but Maman wasn't, and neither was Dad, really. He was in the DeLorean, trying to scorch his way back to a time before things went wrong.

Once upon a time, Dad told stories and Maman sang songs. He didn't read much, but they were all in his head, somehow, and he was always ready to tuck me up and weave a new world. He told me Greek myths, ghost stories, brutal fairy tales, tender love stories. They worried about me being an only child, but I grew up surrounded by the magical characters he created – my imaginary friend a cheetah called Yara who had travelled the Hindu Kush mountains to carry an enchanted amber stone back to its ancient cave. Maman once left food out for her – a dish of oat biscuits sprinkled with hundreds and thousands. I went to bed thrilled at the thought of it, and the next morning the plate was clean.

I tried to make magical worlds for Em over the years, but it was hard on my own, jingling bells out the window on Christmas Eve, writing a card from the tooth fairy, without another parent to be my partner in crime. Dad and Maman used to chuckle in corners, tell each other the things I'd said, meet each other's eyes before they answered my questions. When his stories finished, her songs would start, a beautiful flourish at the end of the tale. We danced from story to song and song to story until my thirteenth birthday, when the music stopped, and the stories ended, and from then on it was just silence, me sitting on my bed with my arms around my knees, my father in his chair, both of us talking to the shadows.

The past was done, and there was nothing you could do but carry on, leaving the wreckage behind. I thought about the day Em was born, that miraculous bundle handed to me – Emily Josephine Jones; how her tiny fingers reached out, and in that moment everything shifted. Seventeen years old, alone in a hospital room, torn and bleeding, but somehow, looking down at her, I felt settled into new grooves that would carry us away from the mess I'd made. Before she arrived, I thought I might have her adopted, that she could have a better life away from me, but the moment her hand held mine, I knew she was my future, and all that mattered was making sure hers was the best I could provide. Like the queen who wishes for a daughter with lips as red as blood, skin as white as snow and hair as dark as ebony, I vowed I'd make a home for us with a red roaring fire, a white picket fence and a bank account that was finally in the black.

But that night, as we wriggled down together in the bed we shared, in the damp, narrow room I'd slept in since child-hood, it didn't seem like I'd made good on that birth-day promise. Instead, I felt like Snow White in the casket, waiting for someone to rock up and knock out the poisoned apple.

Chapter 5

*A*dam spoke French. His family had lived in Brussels, and he'd learnt at the international schools, used to drop it into conversation. His accent wasn't bad, tipping towards American, which made it even sexier. By the spring term, all the girls were mad about him, hoicking up their skirts whenever he walked past, giggling and flicking him eyelined glances. He didn't encourage it, but he liked it, a red setter lolling as he was fussed.

In book club, we had a bit of a Beatrice and Benedick thing going, sparring over DH Lawrence's poems, locking swords over Edgar Allan Poe's 'The Tell-Tale Heart', cheered on by Miss Challoner, or Mr North, who was fond of literary props. One day Mr North threw a doorknob and a handkerchief on a desk, challenging us to name the author of the story. I got there first – 'Ray Bradbury!' – smiling at his approving nod and Adam's chagrin.

'"The Fruit at the Bottom of the Bowl",' said Mr North. 'Can you tell us what's the connection with "The Tell-Tale Heart"?'

'Guilt,' I said. 'And covering your tracks.'

'Exactly,' he replied. 'The print-outs are on my desk – I want you all to read it, and we'll discuss these themes at our next session. Ms Jones can take the week off.'

Afterwards, Adam stopped me in the corridor – the first time we'd spoken outside the classroom. His hand on my shoulder made me quiver but I turned casually, as if I hadn't waited for this moment.

'You a sci-fi fan then?' It was hard to tell if he was interested or teasing.

'I guess. Since I watched *Fahrenheit 451* with my dad.'

'I've read that. And a couple of his short stories. But not that one, that one about the fruit.'

'It's wax fruit,' I replied. 'It's not real.' Couldn't think of anything else to say, so we just stared at each other.

'"Dark They Were and Golden-Eyed",' he said, reaching to gently tweak my hair out of my face. 'Have you read it?'

It was a story about humans moving to Mars and slowly evolving into Martians. My bones were quaking at the sea-change between us, blowing in on an unearthly wind.

'Yes,' I said. 'It's strange, but beautiful.'

'You look like you could be in it.' He leaned forwards, lips barely moving as he whispered in my ear. '*J'ai trouvé l'or dans tes yeux.*'

I've found the gold in your eyes . . . It was cheesy, but I could feel my cheeks growing hot. '*J'espère que je ne suis pas en train de devenir une extra-terrestre.*'

He reared back, laughing. '*Touché.* I didn't know you spoke French.'

My throat felt tight. 'My mum was French.'

'Was?'

I nodded, smiling before the tears could get going. 'Sorry.'

'I'm sorry.'

We both said it at the same time. I'd messed up – we were flirty and fifteen, full of glorious pretensions, like the wax fruit in the bowl, but I'd gone and ruined it with my tragedy. Now he would pity me, and I just wanted him to fancy me.

But then he reached out again and traced my cheek, the lightest brush, with one finger.

'You're so clever,' he said softly. 'The cleverest of them all.'

Chapter 6

*O*n Sunday, after church, we stopped on the way home to buy milk and bread with money saved not contributing to the collection. I figured God would forgive us, even if the reverend didn't. The flat was dark and chilly as usual, the flickering screen in the living room, Dad in his armchair, a blanket over his knees. It was still warm outside, but winter in here. He was wearing a grubby cardigan over his shirt, flakes of dandruff on his hunched shoulders, but his lean lined face lifted when he saw us come in, and he held out his bony hands.

'Hi, FiFi,' he murmured, as I bent to kiss him. 'And my baby girl!' he added, as Em curved around his chair.

'We went to church,' I said, and he nodded absently. He and Maman used to go every Sunday, because she sang in the choir, and Em and I carried on the tradition, though there didn't seem to be much point, professing a faith I felt only as a faint echo. On some level, I just wanted to keep a candle burning.

That evening, with another fast-track class approaching,

Em carted her copy of *Animal Farm* around, trying to get me to talk to her about it.

'Have you read it?' Flopping on her beanbag, she waved the book at me.

I was staring at my laptop (a chugger of a machine, bought second-hand off eBay), trying to update my pitiful CV. It was unlikely Gio would give me a reference.

'Can't remember.' Kept my eyes on the screen, typing things and immediately deleting them.

'Freedom is worth more than ribbons,' she said, twirling a pencil round her fingers.

'Liberty.'

'What?' She looked up at me expectantly.

'Liberty is worth more than ribbons,' I said, tapping impatiently.

'Really?' Em turned back to the book as if to check, but of course she already knew. She had this habit of drawing me into whatever she was reading, despite my reluctance.

Giving up on my CV, I looked on my Instagram feed, which was pretty pointless because I hardly posted anything or followed anyone. I'd been tagged in an old photo – me and another teenage girl, arms spread wide, pouting ridiculously. My breath caught as I remembered that moment, with Sheba Hughes, ready for the school prom, snapped by Marni, yelling at us to stay still. So much excitement and expectation in that image. Underneath the photo, Sheba had written, *'Hey stranger, want to catch up sometime?'* We'd met for coffee a couple of times since she'd moved back to London after university, but the conversation was stilted, and I usually made an excuse to leave early. For a second I imagined us, meeting in a bar for a gossip, but the idea was embarrassing. I still lived at home with my dad, sharing a room with my daughter, waiting tables for a living. Didn't even do that any more. What would I have to say to her?

I sighed and closed my laptop. 'Go on then.'

Em flicked the pages. 'What's it all about?'

'What do *you* think it's about?'

'Power, and how it corrupts.'

'OK.'

'What do you think it's about?'

There was a moth bashing against the overhead bulb. It wasn't getting anywhere, just shredding its wings as it aimed for the light.

'Change. It's not always a good thing. You can end up worse than you started. Sometimes you're better staying put.'

She looked sceptical. 'Better the devil you know?'

I reopened my screen. 'Better not to know any devils.'

Em huffed. 'Well, you're no help. Mrs Gill says we have to think of other allegories. I wondered about *Watership Down*, but everyone will suggest that.'

'So, suddenly you want to be different? Get noticed?' I smiled at her, nestled in the reading beanbag I bought for her eleventh birthday. Eleven candles on a Miss Havisham bride cake, as requested. Em was nothing if not original. I spent ages decorating it with deadheaded roses and cobwebs made out of melted marshmallows.

'Maybe.'

Only a few weeks into secondary school, and already Em was branching out, thanks to Mrs Gill. I was tired, and hungry. That night we'd had beans on toast, with no margarine left, and I just wanted to go to bed because, at least when I was asleep, I could forget my empty stomach and my bank account, which was heading the same way. But there was Em, with her round golden eyes and ravenous brain.

I ruffled her hair. 'What about *The Tiger Who Came to Tea*? No one will suggest that.'

She wrinkled her nose. 'Because it's a baby book.'

'You'll be a maverick.'

'I'll be a freak.' She got to her feet, heading towards our room. 'I'm not even sure it's an allegory.'

'Then that'll be a good discussion to have, won't it.'

Sometimes a tiger is just a tiger. Sometimes it's something else entirely. Just the threat of a tiger at your door, clearing you out.

The next morning, after my weekly cleaning gig in Bloomsbury, I headed back to Finsbury Park and spent the rest of the day traipsing round cafés, pubs and bars, trying to find work. Some were closed down, handwritten signs in the window apologizing to their customers, stacked cups gathering dust inside. The establishments that were still open weren't keen on recruiting. 'We're laying off.' A bar manager shrugged, as he haphazardly sliced lemons. In one pub, the proprietor looked me over, before saying flatly that he preferred to hire men: 'They can deal with the arseholes.' As the day wore on, I got more and more desperate, straying further and further from home. I'd do anything – wash pots, clean tables, collect glasses. 'You've got ten GCSEs,' observed a woman who ran an organic wine bar in Stoke Newington. 'But I need a minimum WSET Level 1.' 'Sorry, I don't know what that is,' I said. 'Then I'm afraid there's no job for you here,' she replied.

I'd printed my CV in the photocopying shop on Blackstock

Road, but by four-thirty still had nearly all the copies left, a waste of 20p per sheet. Our rent was due the following week and we had an electricity bill coming. The cleaning job wasn't enough. Not nearly enough, never enough. I walked home, feet aching, tears prickling, panic setting in. As I opened the door to the flat, inhaling the stale smell that always seemed to linger, there was the usual low rumble of the television.

'Hi, Dad.' I took off my jacket and looked around for signs of Em, but there was just a Post-it note on the table next to the serving hatch. It said, 'Meet me at Merhaba, 5.30', followed by an address.

'What's this?' Picking it up between my thumb and forefinger, I waved it in front of Dad. He blinked and refocused, struggling to recall. Like a scratchy signal, my father flickered in and out, occasionally losing connection.

'Em,' he said finally. 'Said you should meet her.'

'Why?'

He frowned. 'Something about a library.'

I was tired and sweaty, just wanted to lie down and plan my next job hunt. Now I had to go out again. The address was some la-di-da bit near Upper Street – a trek, particularly when I couldn't waste money on the bus. What was behind this summons? My daughter's mysterious ways often stumped me. Like my father, she sometimes operated in a different dimension – a higher dimension. I shouldered my bag with a sigh and set off again.

Fretting over our finances, I walked past the place three times without noticing it. So scruffy and unassuming, tucked away on a side street between narrow Georgian townhouses. The sign above the door read 'Merhaba', its faded blue and gold paint peeling but still legible in the autumn sunshine. Cushions in vivid colours had been pressed up against the bay window seat and, peering through the glass, I saw a wine bottle with a candle crammed in its neck, set on a round table with a base made of woven straw.

Inside, it was a mish-mash – a thousand cultures and ideas mulched together in a long room that stretched back into the gloom. Books and knick-knacks stuffed onto shelves that lined the walls, a higgledy-piggledy tiled floor in ochre and blue and black, Turkish lanterns hanging from the ceiling, tiny succulents in cracked turquoise pots, the smell of coffee, cinnamon, Billie Holiday playing softly in the background. A few tables were occupied – an elderly couple at one who appeared to be playing cards, a young man reading at another, two women laughing together at a third.

That clutter. The luxury of being able to afford *things* to litter a place with. Our flat was mostly drab and bare, bar Em's books. It had been different in Maman's day – she was always good at making things – but after she went, when anything got broken or lost, it was never replaced. When you spent your money on rent and food and fuel, there was nothing left for decoration.

'Hi, Mum.'

There was Em, sitting in a dimly lit corner, swinging her legs, a glass of lemonade in front of her.

'How did you get that? Have you paid for it?'

She looked affronted. 'Of course! I did Keziah Slack's maths homework and she gave me a fiver.'

I put my bag down and sat beside her. 'You've got to stop doing that. It's not right.'

'I explained to her how I did it, after. So it was more of a lesson than a cheat. It's not my fault if she didn't understand.'

Reaching for her glass, I took a sip. It was home-made, sharp and sweet at the same time. 'Are you going to tell me why we're here?'

'They need a new waitress, and I think it could be you.'

I choked on the drink. 'What?'

'Their last one went back to Poland to go to university. Selassie is desperate.'

'How do you know all this?'

Em reached into her rucksack and produced a little card. 'They put this on the noticeboard at the library. I took it so no one else could go for the job. It's perfect for you.'

She handed me the card: 'WELL-READ WAITRESS WANTED'.

'Selassie likes people who like books,' continued Em. 'Says you can trust them. His last waitress, Zofia, always carried a copy of *Anna Karenina*. That's how he knew she would do well.'

'How do you know all this?' I repeated.

'He's chatty. You'll like him.'

I looked at the note again. 'I'm not well-read,' I mumbled, feeling ashamed.

For a second, Em's face fell. 'But you were. Once upon a time.'

Our eyes met. That beloved little face with its pointed chin and barn-owl eyes – everything I'd dreaded, and everything I'd ever wanted, all in one frizzy-haired package.

I pulled myself together. 'Where's this Selassie, then?'

'In the kitchen. His coffee grinder broke, and he's trying to fix it.'

'Well, while we wait, you can tell me about your special class. Did you go for *The Tiger Who Came to Tea*, in the end?'

Em shook her head. 'Too babyish. I remembered one of Granddad's films, *2001: A Space Odyssey*. The monoliths, representing change, even though they always look the same.'

We'd watched that film together. The bone flying up in the air, and the blank stone looming, waiting for someone to absorb its energy and make a leap.

'Did Mrs Gill like that?'

'Yes. Better than Lenny Mitchell's. He came up with *Dick Whittington*, just so he could keep saying it. Pathetic.'

'My apologies for the delay, now what can I get for you? Some lemonade, like your little *fiori* here?'

We both turned to see a short, elderly man standing before us, rubbing his hands. This was evidently Selassie, who could possibly be my new boss, if I could persuade him I matched his unusual job description. Remembering what Em told me, I smiled. 'Could I have a cup of coffee?' In my purse, there was around £2 in change. If that didn't cover it, I could raid my daughter's underhand homework earnings.

'My apologies, again. The grinder is broken,' grumbled Selassie, looking fretful.

Em gave me a nudge, and I got to my feet. 'Let me have a look.' He frowned at me, perplexed. 'I've known a few coffee machines.'

'OK,' said Selassie, leading me to the back of the café. He bustled between tables, replacing books on their shelves, twitching chairs back into place, relighting a candle. He was busy and neat. He reminded me of Dad, before he stopped being busy, stopped caring if anything was neat.

The kitchen was the opposite of the space it catered to, bright and pristine, with gleaming stainless steel and sharp knives. Industry and enterprise. An old lady as short as Selassie was stirring a steaming pot; she smiled at me as we entered, seemingly unsurprised by my appearance.

'My wife, Abrihet,' said Selassie. 'The best cook in Asmara.'

We headed for the coffee machine. It was a good one – Rancilio – and the only problem with the grinder was that it was blocked and overheated.

'Have you got a wet towel? Could you put it in the freezer for a minute?'

He rushed off, while I set about emptying the grinder, pushing out the tightly packed beans. When it was clear, and Selassie had returned with the cold towel, I wrapped it round the base.

'Got to cool it down.'

We stood waiting in silence for a second, listening to the gentle warble of Abrihet's pot.

'It's good coffee,' I said, breathing in the earthy aroma.

Selassie beamed. 'The best. Yirgacheffe.'

'Garden coffee.'

'Yes.' He looked searchingly at me. 'How do you know this?'

Unwrapping the towel, I set the grinder back in place. 'I've worked in cafés. I like coffee. When it's made properly.'

Selassie's gaze flicked between his working grinder and me. 'What book did you last read?'

I thought back, to those days at Brownswood, lying in

the park with Adam, him tickling my neck with a blade of grass. '*The Mill on the Floss.*'

'Good.' He eyed me beadily. 'And you are Maggie, yes?'

'Without the drowning, hopefully.'

He chuckled. 'Do you want a job?'

He said it like a joke, but it was too important for me to laugh. We stared at each other, the standing stone of the grinder between us.

'Do you have one?' I braced myself against the hope. What if someone else had seen the library advert?

'Yes. My last waitress, she went back to Poland, to university. She was excellent. You look excellent too.'

Breathing out in relief, I smoothed my hair with shaking hands. 'I am excellent.'

'Then you start next Monday, Maggie.'

We could pay the rent. We could go and do a big shop at the supermarket. Em could have a new pair of shoes. She could go on that theatre trip. I had to repress the twinge of joy as we shook on it; it didn't do to celebrate, to take pleasure in the rare bones life threw.

Back in the café, Em was draining the last of her lemonade.

'I got the job,' I said, a note of triumph trembling in my voice.

'Did you?' returned my daughter, studiously examining her empty glass. 'You should tell him to use paper straws. These ones kill the turtles.' She looked up and smiled her pirate smile. 'Well done.'

'Well done, you. You found the monolith.'

She fingered the notecard. 'Libraries are very useful places.'

'Yes,' I said, thinking of Maggie Tulliver. 'They are.'

Chapter 7

The next morning when I got up, Em was already in the living room, on her beanbag, *Animal Farm* propped against her knees. She was eating a bowl of cereal, glued to the book.

'Thought you were going to school early, to meet your friend Halima?'

She nodded, not taking her eyes off the page. 'Getting the bus in a minute. Just wanted to finish this. I used the last of the milk.'

Taking a handful of bran flakes from the packet, I began to eat them. 'You might have to look after Granddad a bit more now I've got this new job. There'll be a few evening shifts. I'm sorry.'

Em raised her head and studied me with an inscrutable expression, and I shifted uncomfortably. I didn't want Em to become Dad's carer, as I had been. It was too much for a little girl. On the other hand, someone had to keep an eye on him, and at least I'd be earning money in the meantime.

'That's OK,' she said, eventually. 'It's nice being with him. I'm trying to make him play chess with me.'

That seemed unlikely, but I didn't want to dash her hopes. 'Have you got another of your classes?'

She nodded. 'Mrs Gill is going to tell us about Stalinist Russia, and the revolution, modern parallels, class mobility. Four legs good, two legs bad!'

'Great.' The bran flakes were too dry, and wouldn't go down my throat.

'Mrs Gill thinks I'm a genius.'

'Oh, right.' I filled my glass from the tap and swallowed. 'She said that?'

'Not exactly. She said I have great potential, and she wants to fulfil it. Maybe she thinks I'm like Matilda and my brain will explode if it's not channelled properly.' Suddenly, she looked troubled. 'Do you think that might be true?'

I put my glass down. 'What, you'll develop powers of telekinesis?'

She glared at me. 'Don't be silly. Just . . . do you think I'm . . . *weird*?'

'What? What are you talking about?' I sat down on the floor next to the beanbag and tried to take her hand, but she pulled away.

'Sometimes I answer a question in class and even Halima looks at me like I've said the wrong thing. Like that day when Mrs Gill asked us to quote Shakespeare. I started the willow cabin speech and just went on and on. Afterwards, everyone was quiet, and I felt like I'd gone too far.'

That question scrawled on the whiteboard in the class-room: '*Can you be rich and poor at the same time?*' I was always clever. And sometimes, unbelievably stupid. But there was a different kind of cleverness – not academic. The kind of cleverness that looked into a dear worried face and knew exactly what to say. The truth was, sometimes even I was unnerved by Em. Did her cleverness come from me, or . . . her father?

I reached out and tweaked a lock of her hair. 'People can be afraid of intelligence. It's not your fault, or theirs. You just have to decide how you use it. For good . . .' I moved my hand to her shoulder and made a gruesome face. 'Or for eeeeeevil.'

She smiled, but the worry still tugged at her brow, and I felt that, unlike Em, I hadn't gone far enough. Nevertheless, her eyes were already wandering back to her book. That irresistible pull, the urge to keep reading, oblivious to the rest of the world. I hadn't experienced that for years, wanted to lose myself in a story, swept away like when Dad used to beckon me to the foot of his chair: 'Come closer, FiFi, and let me tell you a thing.' But real life – stark, mundane, brutal real life – kept intruding. Sometimes a tiger was just a tiger. And sometimes it was a bill on the doormat, or a body in the road.

Once upon a time, I was the cleverest of them all. But now it was Em's turn, and it was up to me to keep the road clear for her.

Chapter 8

I was in a Year Eight science class, leaning over a Bunsen burner, when they came to get me. Sally Barclay had just singed her fringe and everyone was holding their noses and tittering as she wept, while Miss Oliver tried to clip the remaining burnt straw to one side of her face. I was leaning forwards into the flame, wondering how close you had to get to do any damage. A science experiment of a kind.

Through the clamour of crying, shouting and Miss Oliver clapping for attention, a voice cut through.

'Is Delphine Jones here?'

The flame was blue in the middle, fierce and potent, but when you twisted the valve you could enjoy a more leisurely, undulating orange flame. Backwards and forwards, tightening and slackening, cheeks flushed, eyes watering in the heat. I sensed in that moment everything was about to change, going from the leisurely glow to the fierce burn. Someone above, twisting a valve to unleash the furies. The moment I looked up, I'd know. So I kept my eyes down, until someone tapped me on the shoulder and I turned to see the set face of Mrs Abraham, the school welfare officer, a muscle in her jaw flickering.

'Would you come with me, please, Delphine?'

When she beckoned, the class cacophony immediately simmered to a whisper, and I was almost glad to leave the room as the glare of the group transferred from Sally and her fringe to me. Following Mrs Abraham along the corridors, my shoulders were tight in anticipation of the blow that was surely coming. You didn't just get taken out of class. With each step my heart seemed to get a little higher in my chest, riffling through possibilities, remembering the time Dad was tuning a customer's piano and sliced his forehead open with a pair of pliers trying to get a wire into a tuning pin. I didn't get out of class then, just went home to find Dad with his wound skin-glued shut. So this must be worse than that.

By the time we got to the headteacher's office, there was a drumbeat in my head, a signal to war. He got up hastily as we came in, and his knitted brow told me everything. Much worse than pliers to the forehead. My whole world was about to be ripped apart.

That morning when I'd arrived at school, the sun had been shining on my first teenage day. My friends Sheba and Marni had clubbed together to buy me a leather bracelet from Camden Market. Mr North said the latest Harry Potter had arrived in the library and he'd asked them to save it for me. There'd been lasagne for lunch, and apple crumble. I was wearing my new hoop earrings and had so far got away with them. Sheba and Marni were coming over after school and we were going to get Thai food and dye our hair and listen to *Justified* until Dad banged on the wall.

That was all I could think as I met Mr Haynes's sliding eyes: we weren't going to get Thai food. My hair wouldn't have red streaks. And I'd never be able to listen to that album again. His gaze flicked to my earrings and for a second his mouth opened as if he was about to mention it, tick me off for not conforming to the regulation uniform. But then he closed it again, and gestured for me to sit. I found I couldn't – my legs wouldn't obey me, stiffening and hardening like clay in a kiln. I stared at him, willing him to say something cheery and anodyne, or just tell me off for the hoops and send me on my way, back to my Bunsen burner and sympathizing with Sally's burnt fringe.

'Won't you sit down, Delphine?' Mrs Abraham put her hand on my arm and I flinched, making her jump.

'Sorry. I can't.' It was barely a whisper. 'What's going on?' Why did I ask? I didn't want to know. Wanted to stay in that limbo state where they hadn't told me, and therefore it hadn't happened. It might still all be OK, if we could only look the other way.

'Afraid there's been an accident.'

There it was, the valve open, the burn. I caught my breath, my legs gave way and I sank onto the chair.

'What . . . who?'

Mr Haynes cleared his throat. 'Um . . . your father – the hospital called. Your mother appears to have been involved in an accident. They think you should go over there right away. You can go in a taxi, it won't take long.'

'Try not to worry,' said Mrs Abraham, squeezing my arm.

'Is she badly hurt?' My voice sounded thin and cracked as if it was coming down a bad telephone line.

Mr Haynes shuffled some papers. 'We don't have many details at present. It's best you get over there and see your father.'

Mrs Abraham helped me to my feet and began to lead me out of the office.

'Oh, and Delphine?'

I turned, brushing the tears from my face, Mr Haynes a blur behind his desk.

'Those earrings. Not acceptable for the classroom. Leave them at home tomorrow, would you.'

I don't recall much about the cab journey with Mrs Abraham, or arriving at the hospital, but I remember Dad's expression, finding him slumped outside the hospital room. His eyes were dark caves underground, the ones that lie untouched for thousands of years. There might be paintings on the walls, but no one will ever find them or raise a torch to see the pictures. I tried to hug him, to curl into his arms and make them hold me, but they were limp at his sides. It was a nurse who told me, tears in her own eyes as she clasped my hands round a paper cup of sugary tea.

Maman had gone to get the cake. I was thinking about the Thai food, had forgotten all about it, but she'd got on her bike and gone out to buy her daughter a vanilla sponge. It had been resting in the basket of her bicycle when the car hit her. And although the bike was mangled in the crash, for some reason the cake had stayed put in its little box and was intact when they found her. Sunshine-yellow icing, just like I'd asked for.

How did the nurse know all this? Dad told her, as he held Maman's hand just after the doctor pronounced her, before he shut himself down. The nurse sat with him; he told her and she told me. She thought it would help, to know my mother was thinking of me in her last moments, happily planning our afternoon tea, wondering whether the nice knives needed a polish.

We'd had a conversation that morning and Maman had suggested a trifle, but I said no; I wanted a cake. A proper shop-bought cake with yellow icing, and cream cheese frosting inside. My friends were coming over, and Maman's trifles always looked a little out of place, haphazard, with their wayward scattering of sprinkles and unevenly whipped cream. Whereas a cake from a shop would look smart and birthdayish and was nothing to be ashamed of.

Now it was something to be ashamed of. My ridiculous teenage demands, indulged by her, with unthinkable consequences. Did Dad know? He never said, and obviously I never told him. It was terrible, but I hoped my mother said it was her idea, before she went. I couldn't bear to picture him, holding her hand, contemplating his own series of if-onlys, with my request at the end.

But maybe he'd always known. Maybe that was why he shut me out. Since then, I'd had only a part of him, the measliest slice. The rest he kept for JoJo, intact in the box, waiting for her to come home and set the table.

Chapter 9

Despite a sleepless night before, restless with nerves, my first day at Merhaba was everything I hoped it would be. Busy, industrious but not hyped-up, like Gio had to be to get anything done. As the days passed, I battled with the unpredictable coffee machine, got to know the regulars, discovered that I loved Eritrean food, and my new employers. Abrihet was teaching me how to make injera, the sour and spongy flatbread they served with their stews. She had nodded at my latest batch. Hadn't progressed to an actual adjective yet, but a nod was a start. With every drink I delivered, every crumb swept, every tip received, I felt a tiny unwinding of the tightly coiled spring inside me. '*Merhaba*' is a greeting in Arabic, but more than a hello; a welcome, and a sense of peace.

The café was occupied by an eclectic bunch of customers. Two old men who came to play backgammon – intensely, silently, companionably, shaking hands at the end of the game. A book club who met every Thursday, enthusiastically disagreeing with each other's readings, and sinking several bottles of red in the process. A student doing her PhD, who drank coffee as she put the finishing touches to her thesis. She would sit oblivious, hunched in the corner, tapping away on her laptop, and I would refill her cup slowly, eyeing the screen as if there might be a secret I could stumble on and take home along with my pay packet.

There were two new mothers, who met twice a week, after some sort of massage class. One of them seemed depressed and would cry quietly while the other jiggled her baby and tried to cheer her up. One morning, I gave both women a leftover slice of himbasha, the sweet celebration bread Abrihet made. Shortly after Em was born, I burst into tears in the clinic after a health visitor told me she wasn't gaining weight fast enough. 'You have to work harder,' she said, briskly rubbing down the scales with disinfectant and tracing my baby's downward spiral on a graph. As I cried outside in reception, Em picked up on my distress, wailing against my chest as I frantically soothed and sobbed. Another mum who was passing stopped, putting one hand on my shoulder and another on Em's downy head. 'Don't worry,' she said, 'your best is good enough. It's all she needs.' Everyone could do with a crumb of comfort occasionally.

Another regular turned out to be Rosalind Gill, Em's English teacher. Merhaba wasn't far from Brownswood, and she came in one day after school, to do her marking.

'Hello, Mrs Gill.'

'Call me Roz, please. Could you be an angel and bring me my own body weight in caffeine? Then I've got something to show you.'

'It's unbelievable,' Roz continued, when I returned with her coffee. She was riffling through her bag, bringing out a pile of books, papers, and a bottle of Vamousse. Seeing my gaze linger on it, she grimaced. 'One of my Year Sevens has nits, doesn't want to worry her mum 'cos she's lost her benefits. Anyway,' she shook several sheets in my face and I recognized Em's weird adult scrawl, 'we're doing gothic fiction. I asked the class to write their own story. The boys did slasher stuff, people cutting off each other's heads. Bloody idiots. The girls mostly did mopey witches falling in love. But not Emily. You know "The Tell-Tale Heart"? Edgar Allan Poe?'

The tray I was holding nearly slipped from my grasp, and my own heart jumped in my chest. The same story Adam and I read in our book club. Guilt, and covering your tracks. I put down my glasses and wiped clammy hands on my skirt. No matter how much I tried to avoid it, history kept repeating itself.

'Yes. I know it.'

'Em's done a prequel. She's called it "Beating as One", and it's incredible. Here.'

She held out the papers for me to read, and I stood, skimming at first, before slowing down to savour the story. Em had taken the unnamed narrator of 'The Tell-Tale Heart', given him a piercing and pitch-perfect history that led to the killing of the vulture-eyed old man in Poe's story. I felt a tingle of revulsion and excitement – it *was* unbelievable that an eleven-year-old girl could produce something so monstrously clever and coldly logical. The pace of the prose was rhythmic, incessant, thumping away to its heart-stopping conclusion.

'A-plus isn't enough,' mumbled Roz, taking a sip of her

coffee. 'It's magical and horrible and quite brilliant. She's got such talent.'

Handing her the story, I had to blink back a well of tears in my eyes, and wasn't quite sure why they were there. Pride, certainly, but also a sense of loss. Em must be free to use her talent, exploit it, enjoy it. Unlike me. Still lost in my thoughts, it was a second before I noticed Roz fixing me with an intense stare, like a journalist mid-interview, wondering if they were being lied to. It made me uncomfortable, as if she could see all my secrets.

'Emily gets it from you, of course,' she said, picking up a napkin and rolling it between her fingers. 'Sarah Boleyn said you left school after your GCSEs. Why did you never go back, do your A levels?'

I reached for my tray. 'It would have been impossible to go back to Brownswood with a baby.' My voice sounded high and unnatural.

Roz shook her head. 'I mean after that, when she was in primary school.'

'Studying for exams doesn't pay the bills.'

'You could do it part-time.'

People like Roz, with their received pronunciation and assumption that all you needed to get through life was a stiff upper lip and a daily grind, would never get it. Who was she to lecture me about what I could and couldn't do? I disappeared back into the kitchen to wash the pots, savagely scrubbing at them and thinking of that sentence on the whiteboard: 'Can you be rich and poor at the same time?' People like Roz were just rich, whatever they did. By the time I went out again, she'd gone, back to the Highbury house Em had told me she lived in; the kind of house we could only dream of. Knocking back her Pinot Grigio in a kitchen with one of those glass extensions, I'd bet. I cleared her table and wiped it down.

The next day Em skipped into the café after school, bag and ponytail swinging, looking unusually pleased with herself.

'Hi, Em-Jo.' I wiped and repositioned the candle. 'Don't take up the space if someone wants it.'

'I won't,' promised Em, settling herself and opening her bag. She'd brought *The Bell Jar* from the library, which wasn't a particularly upbeat read for an eleven-year-old. Deep in the book, Em nonetheless looked up and beamed as Selassie set a chilled glass in front of her. Selassie and Abrihet had run a famous jazz club, Tesfay's, in Eritrea, but left in the turbulent years following the war with Ethiopia. Their son Jamal went back, and now owned a restaurant in Asmara. They were waiting for him to get married and give them grandchildren, but he showed no sign of getting on with it, so Selassie gave all the affection he was saving up to the young ones who came into his café. He tickled the babies, had shoot-outs with little boys and provided an endless supply of home-made lemonade for Em.

I started sweeping the floor, which had been the target of a particularly messy boy. Em put her book down to watch me.

'Mrs Gill gave me an A-plus for my story,' she announced. 'We had a chat after class. You know she dropped out of university to do that film, *Agnes Grey*?'

My broom stilled. So many opportunities seemed to have come Roz's way. 'Did she?'

'Yes,' said Em, sucking at the corners of her glass. 'Selassie got paper straws, like I told him.'

'Lift your legs,' I instructed, thrusting the broom under her feet. 'So . . . how did she get her degree?'

'What degree?' asked Em, innocently.

I pushed the bristles at her feet again, and she giggled. 'Someone wants to order.' She indicated a couple who'd just arrived.

'Sorry, coming!' Propping the handle against the wall, I hurried over.

When I got back, Em was buried in her book. *The Bell Jar*, Snow White's casket, it was one and the same thing. The thing that trapped you, held you down, left you struggling to breathe. We had to get out somehow, me and Em. I jabbed the broom at a piece of cake that was sticking stubbornly to the floor, to dislodge it. At the end of my shift, on my way back through the kitchen, Abrihet intercepted me, pressing a warm aluminium container into my hands.

'For you,' she said. 'Zigni berbere. Beef stew. To build you up. And the little one.'

I opened my mouth to protest, but Abrihet held a finger against my lips. 'No. It is your gift to me to enjoy it. Then I show you how to make it.'

Looking down at the nodding, smiling, glowing face, I leaned forward and kissed her wrinkled cheek. Then drew back, embarrassed, because that wasn't the kind of thing I did. Maybe I was branching out, like Em.

Abrihet held her hand against the place where the kiss had been. '*Tebarek!*' she chuckled, and pushed me away. 'Go.'

Striding back through the café, I put the container in my

bag and poked Em on the shoulder. 'Come on, let's go home.'

Em reluctantly closed her book and put it in her rucksack, and together we walked towards the bus stop.

'She did her degree after, you know.'

My pace slowed. 'Who?'

Em looked up at me, limpid and deadly. 'Mrs Gill. She dropped out of university to do that film, but she did her degree later, part-time. In between acting jobs.'

'Good for her.' The bus arrived, distracting us both, but as we swayed and juddered our way home, my mind crept towards my favourite daydream. Us two, in our own place, building a better life together. A *bigger* life, full of opportunity and adventure. There were so many things in the way – so many barriers, bills, poisonous apples – could it ever be anything but a dream? I should stop thinking about it, and trudge on.

But the idea was sticking, stubbornly, like the piece of cake on the floor, and wouldn't be dislodged.

Chapter 10

*A*t lunchtimes, particularly during that hot summer term of Year Ten, everyone at Brownswood used to escape to the park to soak up the sunshine, texting, smoking, sitting on logs doing each other's make-up. I didn't join in any of that – couldn't afford a phone, cigarettes or mascara – but went too, to circle the lakes and read on one of the benches. Each had a plaque, a rusty testament to those loved and lost, and perhaps that was why it was nice to sit there, to remind myself I wasn't the only one bereft.

One day, I was working my way through *Richard III* in preparation for that afternoon's class when the page darkened and I looked up to see Adam grinning down at me.

'*Now is the winter of our discontent . . .*' he intoned.

'*Made glorious summer.*' I smiled and closed the book, ready for sportive tricks.

He sat down next to me and for a while we just looked at the lake, the fountain bubbling merrily, swans dipping and ducking into the depths, the reeds that ranged the banks blowing in the breeze. The perfect June day. About to get more so.

He crossed his legs at the ankle and leaned back against the plaque. 'So, fancy crashing the prom with me?'

I went absolutely still. GCSE students had their post-exam party in the school hall at the beginning of July, a massive bash that was making the whole year group twitchily precoital. Though Year Tens regularly slunk in to line the walls, I wasn't particularly keen on going, until now. Now, it had just become the high point of my year, possibly life.

'Sure,' I managed, pulling the book against my chest so it wasn't obvious my hands were shaking.

'Cool,' he said. When we got up to go back to school, he slung an arm round my shoulders, which made us *officially* a Thing, and it was a huge effort to look unconcerned, not to grin like a jackass at Marni mouthing in the corridor. Brows bound with victorious wreaths, we wandered into class together, him squeezing my fingers as we went to our separate desks. Sheba, eyes on stalks, reached across and stabbed me with her pen.

'What the actual fuck?' she hissed, as I cupped my chin in my hand to hide my smile. She leaned forwards again, but Miss Challoner marched in, flinging her jacket over the back of her chair and sitting astride it.

'Right,' she barked. 'Which of you buggers has actually read it?'

We slid into Shakespeare, debating Richard's courtship of Lady Anne, but throughout I was sneaking glances at Adam, thinking of our own, and rolling my eyes at Sheba, who was touching herself suggestively like Meg Ryan in *When Harry Met Sally*.

'Ms Hughes. Is there something you would like to share with us?'

Sheba sat up abruptly, knocking her pen to the floor. 'No, miss.'

I sniggered under my hand, surreptitiously watching Adam through my lashes. He was lolling in his chair, twiddling his pen round his fingers; so completely at ease, so comfortable in his own skin, that I held my breath, transfixed. What on earth did he see in me? What on earth would I wear to the prom?

'Delphine. What do you make of it?'

'Uh . . . sorry?' Jerking upright, heat flooded my face as I gazed at Miss Challoner, who was looking down at me with growing irritation.

'Back in the room, Jones. Why would Anne take Richard's ring? When she believes he killed her husband and father-in-law? Come on.'

Shifting in my seat, I pulled myself together. 'Because she's frightened, and thinks that's her only option. That she doesn't have the hope of anything better. Even a murderous hunchback's better than nothing.'

'Better than nothing?'

'Nothing is being unmarried, unprotected. She can see how determined he is, how powerful he could be. Better to have that on her side, than fight against it.'

'So, she's being pragmatic?'

'I guess so. She ended up with a ring, right? And she didn't promise anything. She's hedging her bets. That's what women have to do.'

'Huh.' Miss Challoner stared at me for a second, before turning to the rest of the room. 'Anyone want to add to Delphine's take?'

Having survived that encounter, I let myself daydream for the rest of the class, wondering if Sheba would lend me an outfit. When the bell went, I grabbed my books and prepared to rush out to huddle in a corner and squeal, but was stopped by Miss Challoner's curt voice calling me back.

'Delphine Jones, Adam Terris, Lorenzo Ricci. Could you stay a moment, please?'

We eyed each other uncertainly. Usually this sort of thing meant trouble, but Lorenzo was super-serious, gunning for a place at medical school, and didn't mess about, approaching his education like a miner tackling a vertical shaft. We stood waiting as Miss Challoner stacked papers. Finally, she stopped and glared at us.

'Next year,' she said. 'GCSEs coming. Big year. You guys are on track for the highest grades. But we'd like to make sure of it. Mr North and I are running an extra English group, Monday evenings and Thursday lunchtimes. Six of you from across the year. We'll study the texts in more depth, push you all a bit more. Help you be the best you can be. What do you think?'

'Sounds great,' said Adam casually, hunching his rucksack on his shoulders.

Lorenzo nodded, his mouth a flat line.

All I could think was that it would push Adam and me together even more, and was having trouble stopping the smile spreading across my face. But I knew better than to express enthusiasm, so when Miss Challoner's gaze fell on

me, I dipped my head and murmured 'Cool.' As we sauntered out of class, Adam briefly interlinked his fingers with
mine again, and I thought I might pass out with the thrill
of it. He went off to his next class and Sheba met me in
the corridor, arms folded.

'Jones! You dark fucking horse. You need to spill.' She
frogmarched me up to 'the hill', more of a mound, which
was where everyone congregated outside class.

'We'll be late!' I protested, laughing. We were five minutes
late for our history class and Mr Waites, kept waiting, was
not impressed. But it was worth it, to sit on the grass for a
moment and confide something lovely and ordinary – the
kind of secret I *wanted* to divulge. In the two years since
Maman had gone, I'd got used to hiding what was going on
at home, making sure no one guessed how bad things were
with Dad. So I was willing to bend the rules, let someone
stare at me in awe, tease me and agree to lend me their Diesel
dress in return for me sharing '*every single detail*' after the
event. That's what your life turns on, isn't it? Single details;
the choices and moments that change everything.

Chapter 11

'So,' said Roz, briskly forking up beef stew. 'I wondered if you'd do me a massive favour?'

She was marking at her usual table, but had ended up ordering a glass of wine to get her through it, then stew to soak up the wine. I'd been too busy to speak to her as Merhaba was unusually crowded that day, a late lunch of office workers followed by the boozy book group, and various other customers keeping me coming and going from the kitchen. After delivering Roz her early dinner, I had to take someone else's order, and by the time I got back to her she was halfway through her meal, wiping injera round her plate and sucking her fingers. She did everything with gusto. It might have been a thespian thing, playing to the fourth wall, giving it her all.

Roz nodded at me to sit down, but I didn't want to while I was working. Selassie wasn't a *stronzo* like Gio, but he was my boss and might not appreciate me socializing on the job, so I hovered over her table while she talked with her mouth full.

'I've got this friend, Sylvie, who lives in Canonbury. Gorgeous woman, we met at a life-drawing class in Stoke

Newington and she couldn't stop giggling. Anyway, her mother's just moved in. Hurt her hip in a fall, in France, so she's come to live with her. She's quite old, in her eighties, and filthy rich. She's worried about going senile, and Sylvie's worried about her being lonely, so they're looking for someone to come and sit with her, talk to her. In French. You speak French, right? Sarah Boleyn said she remembers you were fluent at school.'

I felt uneasy, wondering what else Sarah Boleyn remembered about my time at Brownswood. It was intriguing, all the same.

'*Used* to speak French. Haven't spoken it in years.'

'It's like riding a bike, isn't it? You don't forget.'

I wasn't sure about that, but sometimes I dreamed in French, and it was my mother's voice I heard, telling me to get ready for school: '*Maintenant! Allons-y, ma chérie! Nous sommes en retard!*' Or I remembered her singing 'La Vie en Rose', sitting at the piano with her hair tumbling down her back. Or making yoghurt cake with her, begging to lick the bowl – '*S'il te plaît, Maman.*' For a moment, the deluge swept me away, and I wondered if I could ever speak French again, to someone other than my mother.

'They want someone twice a week. One of the language teachers at Brownswood said she'd do it, but then she went and got engaged.'

If there was a choice to be made, it was probably preferable to get engaged rather than go and speak French to some doolally old lady. Fleetingly, I thought of Adam, but that ship had sailed. Then I thought of Sid, my last boyfriend, and decided that maybe the old lady was a better option. But it wasn't a tempting prospect.

'I haven't really got time. What with my café shifts and my cleaning job.' Once a week, I went to clean for an old friend of Maman's, who owned a flat in Fitzrovia. She didn't even live there; just wafted in now and again from the Cotswolds when she felt like going shopping on Bond Street. But she paid me fifty pounds to dust, water her plants and change the sheets. The extra money was very welcome – sometimes essential – and although initially I'd felt guilty about the lightness of my duties, occasionally I had to clear up after her son stayed over, and the mess he made more than outweighed the mess she didn't.

'Well, she *might* pay you. Her daughter Sylvie didn't really say one way or the other. To be honest, I can't remember, we were too drunk. But I'm sure I promised her I'd find someone. You'd be perfect. Go on, pleeeese, for meeeee . . . ?' Roz clasped her hands together as if in prayer.

I laughed and wiped the ring of red wine on her table. 'I'll think about it. When do they want this person to start?'

'*Toot de sweet.*' She reached over to her bag and fished out a piece of paper. 'Here's her number. She's old and also quite odd. But good value.'

'OK.' I fingered the paper. The number was written in a French hand, with horizontal lines struck through the sevens, like Maman used to do. The germ of an idea was stealing in, and I shook my head, to clear it.

'What?' Roz was staring at me searchingly, her head on one side. 'You looked like you were about to say something.'

'No.' I picked up my tea towel. 'It was nothing.'

Chapter 12

Back at the flat after my shift, I hung up my jacket, stripped off my skirt and T-shirt, and got into my running gear. A half-hour spent pounding the streets and park paths allowed my mind to unravel, stretch and flex just as my body did, weights and worries streaking out behind me until they eventually detached, like a child letting go of a balloon. It was freeing and, more importantly, it was free. So I put my trainers on and set off, settling into a regular rhythm and allowing my subconscious to take control.

Thoughts and notions sidled along like passing clouds: long-forgotten memories, random acquaintances, shopping lists – my tumbled head giving itself a good hard rinse. I thought about making injera at Merhaba, heating the skillet, adding the batter and watching the bubbles form on the surface, then covering it and waiting for the precise moment to scoop it out. Too soon and it wouldn't be cooked; too late and it would go gummy. Was it too late for me, or was it the right time to try again?

It was mild for October, but a breeze was ruffling the

trees above as I entered the park and headed up towards the deer enclosure, feet hitting the tarmac in steady thuds, like a relaxed heartbeat. The animals were nibbling the grass and meandering round their little patch. I admired their velvety antlers, the sprouting roots grown, and shed, and regrown, in a cycle of renewal. They could always start over.

Then I was gone, past them, on to the playground where I used to take Em all those years ago, pushing her on the swings and watching, heart in mouth, as she climbed and gripped her way across the frames and ropes towards the slide. Little Em, her tubby legs stomping round the sandpit, the sands of time sliding through so quickly that you could blink and a decade had gone by. Time, waste of time, back in time . . . I brushed the sweat out of my eyes and carried on, round the lakes where Adam had asked me out, twinkling as their ripples caught the rays, the occasional fish bubble popping like the injera on the skillet.

When *was* the right time? Was it eighteen, when everyone did it – everyone who hadn't ruined it for themselves? Or was it twenty-eight, when I'd made my mistakes and was ready to move on? But I was afraid, because I'd tried before, when I was twenty, and it hadn't worked. I remembered creeping into that college open day, thinking I might enrol, thinking maybe I could do it, now Em was a bit older. My daughter's pudgy hand was clasped in mine, but while I was reading the forms, she wandered off. I was absorbed in the course details: *18–21 hours per week, coursework, classroom and workshops, fees £2,980 . . . fees £2,980 . . . fees £2,980*. As the figures swam and refocused, there was a harsh voice in my ear, shattering the drum along with my dreams.

'Are you this child's mother?'

Turning, still clutching the papers. 'Sorry?'

'I believe this is your daughter. Could you take her, please? We found her riffling through our books. Not an appropriate place for a child.'

As we crept out of the building, Em raised her puzzled face to mine. 'But I was reading them, Mummy. I like reading.'

'I know, sweetie,' I said. 'I know.'

Eight years later, I was still afraid. But there was also that shred of hope, a tiny bubble that hadn't yet popped. Past the lakes and up the hill, my heart pumping harder with the effort. All that *effort*. What was it for, in the end? Just for a grade on a piece of paper. But suddenly my mind slid back to that dream of mine, the safe space for me and Em, a room of my own – something truly mine. It was as if it was right in front of me: a flat with sloping ceilings, sunlight streaming through the windows, the door open, inviting us in. Qualifications, a career, security – everything I'd ever wanted. I had to start somewhere. Forget the past, forget the future: why not *now*?

When I was eleven, my mother opened a bank account in my name. A college fund. '*Pour l'éducation de Delphine Jones*,' she announced, and we had a trifle to celebrate. Of course, the contributions stopped abruptly after my thirteenth birthday but, years later, I found the card and checked the balance. Before she died, she'd managed to pay in nearly four hundred pounds, more money than I'd ever seen in my life. But I never touched it, even when things were really bad, because I felt the weight of her intent. It wasn't meant for paying gas bills or buying bread. That money was important and, even though my education had been abandoned, the account was sacrosanct. But maybe it was finally time to make a withdrawal . . .

It was as if a valve had opened and now all these longings were creeping out like a gas, overwhelming me. Once upon a time, I'd had such grand ambitions, but I'd had to stopper the bottle, tuck it away on the highest shelf to gather dust. I kept running, out of the park and back towards Finsbury Park to our flat, and as I pounded, the vision gradually faded until it was just a sepia echo. Stopping outside our block, breathing heavily, I looked up at the bland brick that bore no resemblance to my white picket fence. Trudging down the path, sweat was pooling in the hollow of my back, making it itch.

In the flat, Dad was watching *The King's Speech* while Em was curled up on her beanbag reading *Flowers for Algernon*. It was a book from the library I'd tried to read weeks ago, but the words had blurred before my eyes, refusing to sink in. She must have renewed it.

'Sorry I'm late,' I gasped. 'Are you hungry?'

She looked up. 'A bit. That container in the fridge. Did Abrihet give you more stew?'

'Tsebhi Dorho. Chicken. I'll put it in the oven.'

'Brilliant!' She put down her book.

We ate at the table, steam billowing from the stew. Dad had his plate on his knees, staring at the screen. Em chattered away, full of her English class and what Mrs Gill had said about satire, and I let her enthusiasm nourish me along with the food, doting on that pointed little face with its frizzy halo, praying that every one of her grand ambitions would be fulfilled.

'What about you?' Em asked, pulling a piece of chicken from the bone. 'Did Mrs Gill talk to you?'

'About what?'

She chewed and mumbled through the mouthful. 'That French woman.'

'She spoke to you about it?'

'I spoke to *her*. Overheard her talking to Mrs Boleyn. And then just happened to remind her that you speak French.'

'What?' I put down my knife and fork, dumbfounded. 'This came from *you*?'

My devious daughter shrugged.

I gaped at her for a second, before picking up my cutlery again. 'Well, it doesn't matter. I'm not doing it.'

She shrugged again. 'It's your decision. Just an opportunity, that's all.'

'An unpaid opportunity.'

'I meant, an opportunity to help someone.'

'Oh.'

'Hmm. Well, I'd better do my homework.' Em began to gather and stack our dishes.

'I'll take that. You go and do your work.' Nudging her away, I took over, feeling shamefaced, like I'd been rebuked in class. When everything was tidied up, I went back into the living room and found Dad shuffling towards me, clutching his empty plate.

'Who's the French woman?'

I stopped in my tracks, staring at him. Dad rarely showed interest in anything, and then only fleetingly, so a direct question from him was unexpected.

'I'm not sure she's French,' I replied, taking the plate from him. 'She just wants to speak it. To help her . . . not forget.'

He nodded. 'You should do it,' he said, putting his hand briefly on my arm. 'To help you . . . not forget.'

I reached with my free hand to clasp his. 'You think so?'

'You got a good brain, FiFi. You got to use it.'

This was the longest conversation we'd had in months, and I wanted to keep it going.

'Daddy,' I began. 'I wanted to ask you if you thought it was a good idea—'

'Off to bed,' he murmured, and shuffled down the corridor to the space he used to share with Maman. When Em was born, he offered to swap and give us the larger room. I was so shocked by the suggestion – it was so unusual – that I said no, we would manage together in mine. We did, for a while, but when Em got bigger and I changed my mind, I couldn't find a way to ask him. He kept the room as a shrine to Maman, her perfume bottle on the chest of drawers, her dressing gown hanging on the door, a book she was reading – *Bonjour Tristesse* – splayed open on the bedside table. Us occupying it would have felt like a violation after all those years, and staying as we were seemed easier.

After he'd gone, I picked up Em's *Flowers for Algernon* from the beanbag. It was open at the first page. Settling myself on the sofa, I began to read, tucking my feet underneath me, breathing in the distinctive and familiar smell of well-thumbed leaves. I expected the words to swim as usual, the information curdling in my brain and seeping away before I'd had a chance to absorb it. But, in the blessed silence and semi-solitude, I found myself sinking into the text, swept away in the story of Charlie Gordon and the mouse called

Algernon, their fates intertwined. A science experiment helps them both increase their intelligence dramatically but, in the end, is proven to be flawed, killing the mouse and leaving Charlie to face his own regression.

I read the book in one sitting, ignoring Em coming out in search of hot chocolate, finally emerging, gritty-eyed and shellshocked by Charlie's terrible fall, after midnight. Flicking back to the epigraph, from Plato's *Republic*, about bewilderments of the eye, I couldn't decide if it was worse going into the light, or coming out of it. Either way, both of them messed you up. I got to my feet, legs stiff and unyielding, and put the book back down on the beanbag, open at the first page, as Em had left it. Was it better to unlock your mind like that, with the possibility of it being shuttered again, or was it preferable to stay in darkness? You could leave things exactly as they were, or be bold enough to make a change, but I was wary of making that leap. Roz Gill might be another monolith, but I was afraid to find out.

Chapter 13

It was an unfamiliar bit of Canonbury – a posh bit – where Georgian houses with wrought-iron balconies overlooked private squares and the front doors were solid black, glossy and forbidding. Recalling the bracing conversation when I'd arranged this first meeting, I couldn't help feeling daunted.

'I told you before, I don't even have a computer, so you can bloody well stop phoning me!'

The woman on the other end of the line had sounded like the queen, but fruitier and angrier.

'Um, is this Letty Riche? Roz Gill gave me your number. It's Delphine Jones.'

'*Ah, Delphine! Formidable. J'attendais votre appel, Rosalind m'a tout raconté sur vous et votre fille Emily . . .*'

This flood of information was hard to follow, as the last person to speak to me like that was my mother.

'Sorry,' I said, in halting French. 'You're speaking too quickly for me to understand you.'

Letty switched to English. 'In that case, you must come over immediately and we can get you up to speed.'

So here I was, trailing round leafy squares in search of Letty's flat. She lived below her daughter, and had told me to go to the basement. Reaching the address, I paused in front of the parterre front garden, hedges rigorously pruned, flagstones lined with shingle. The communal gardens of our block grew wild until someone from the council came twice a year to mow and take away the abandoned beer cans. Making my way round the back, I found stone steps leading to a tiny courtyard lined with potted plants. Tapping tentatively at the door, I waited.

It was opened by a diminutive elderly lady, leaning heavily on a walking stick. On closer inspection, the head of the stick was carved into a bird of prey, and there was definitely something hawkish about the wrinkled face staring up at me. Letty had a mass of grey hair drawn up into an Edwardian bun, a beaky nose and the sharpest eyes I'd ever seen. Her nails were painted a defiant scarlet.

She peered at me impassively for a second. 'Well, Rosalind never mentioned you were a looker. That's interesting. I like good-looking people, and was one myself about fifty years ago. You'd better come in.'

Edging past her into a small, cluttered kitchen, I was greeted by a fluffy black and white cat who wove around my ankles, purring.

'That's Aphra,' said Letty, nudging her with the stick. 'She belongs to my daughter but seems to prefer me. Cats are terrible sodomites. No, I don't mean sodomites, I mean parasites. Would you like some tea?'

Speechless with shyness, I nodded, and was pointed through to Letty's sitting room, which was crammed with antique furniture, books piled on every surface.

'I've got to bring them in one by one, bloody hip,' shouted Letty, as she shuffled back in holding a delicate china saucer and cup with one hand, her stick in the other.

'Sorry, let me get the other one.' I jumped up and rushed into the kitchen to collect the second cup. When I returned, Letty was sitting dwarfed in the largest of the armchairs, Aphra already curled in her lap. Setting the tea in front of her, I returned to my own place on the sofa. It was covered in cat hairs.

'So,' said Letty, dropping a cube of sugar in her tea and stirring vigorously. 'Rosalind has told you, presumably, that I'm a dotty old bat who needs looking after? My daughter Sylvie is a ridiculous fusspot, she practically put an advert in *The Times*.'

'N-no, not at all,' I stammered, stirring my tea for something to do.

'I don't want company. I've got Aphra. But she can't speak French. That's what I want. *Me souvenir*. To remember.'

Then she started gabbling away in rapid-fire French, and I had no idea what she was saying. There was a word here and there, but she was so fast, I couldn't possibly keep up. I nodded occasionally, managed a weak '*Oui*' at one point when she appeared to want an answer. But it was becoming more and more obvious that I was out of my depth. I felt I'd deceived her, there under false pretences, but was also full of despair – Roz said you didn't forget, but I *had* forgotten. This was supposedly something my mother gave me, and somehow it was missing. A link between us, severed.

Eventually, Letty stopped, glaring at me. 'You didn't get a word of that, did you?'

'It was just a bit quick. If you could slow down . . .'

'I'm eighty-four,' she snapped. 'If I slow down, I'll die. *You* need to speed up.'

'Sorry, maybe—'

She rapped her stick on the floor like Nanny McPhee. '*Non. Ça ne va pas marcher.* I'll tell Rosalind you won't do. You can let yourself out.'

Utterly defeated, I'd moved to heave myself out of the squashy sofa when the cat suddenly leapt off Letty and up onto my knee, kneading my leg with her claws, purring loudly. After staring intently into my face, she curled delicately onto my lap, rumbling contentedly. I looked across at Letty.

'Shall I, um . . .' I mimed pushing her off, and Letty clicked her tongue irritably.

'Well, you'll have to stay there now, won't you? Damned cat. I'll fetch some biscuits.' She hauled herself up with her stick and hobbled off to the kitchen while I sat, rigid under the eggshell weight. Aphra gazed at me, the sharp slash of her pupils hypnotic. Don't waste this opportunity, she seemed to be saying. But I already had. She flicked her tail, and tucked her head underneath her body like she didn't want anything more to do with me. I was just a convenient mattress.

Letty came back with a tin as I watched, wide-eyed, trapped under my jailer. She settled herself again and we sat in silence for a moment, eating Florentines. When she spoke again, it was in French, but slower, like she was speaking to a child.

'Who taught you to speak the language?'

I hesitated, reluctant. 'My mother. She was French.'

Letty shot me a keen glance and rapped her stick. 'Was? Or *is*?'

'Was,' I repeated the past participle.

'When did she die?'

There was a long pause. The grandfather clock in the corner ticked laboriously.

'When I was thirteen.' I stumbled over the sentence, eyes on the cat's halo of fur.

The clock ticked twice before Letty replied. 'That's why you are *rouillée*.'

'*Rouillée?*'

She reached over and patted me on the hand. 'Rusty. Out of practice. But don't worry, we'll get there.'

Evidently, there had been some sort of shift; perhaps Aphra had conveyed approval, or she just felt sorry for me. Haltingly, we talked about Emmanuel Macron, who Letty thought was marvellous, and very '*craquant*'.

'*Craquant* means dishy,' she translated. 'You'll have to throw in words like that if you want people to think you're a native. I defy any Parisian to suspect I was born in Chelmsford.'

At the end of the hour, I felt washed out, like I'd been on a run. When she tapped her stick to signal the time, Aphra leapt off my knee and wheedled round her legs.

'Damned cat,' said Letty, pushing her away. 'I suppose you'll be wanting *l'argent*,' she added, struggling to her feet and shuffling over to a wooden box on the dining table.

Torn between elation and discomfort, I began to protest, because even though Roz had suggested money might be involved, the arrangement felt suddenly awkward – being paid for providing companionship, chatting. Besides, as Dad

had suggested, it felt like she had helped me 'not forget', nudging me back to my mother tongue. But Letty brushed away my objections.

'Pish,' she said. 'What's money? I lived in Provence for twenty years and, let me tell you, no one cares about it over there. It's just melons and the mistral, and they're both free, pretty much.' She took a key out of her pocket and put it in the lock of the box. When she opened it, my eyes nearly fell out of my head. It was completely full of cash – there must have been thousands in there. Easy not to worry about it when you had it.

'Why did you come back?' I asked, watching her count out the notes. Twenty-five pounds. Twice what I earned at Merhaba.

Letty looked up, her gimlet eyes filling with tears, one gnarled hand resting on the lid of the box.

'Bloody hip,' she said. 'And Brexit. Dash it all.'

'I'm sorry.'

Letty brushed at her tears, angrily. 'No need. I'll be dead soon, it's young folk like you who'll bear the brunt of it.' She gave me the money and gestured towards the kitchen with her stick. 'Go on then, *au revoir*. I'll see you on Friday.'

'*Au revoir*.' I skipped up the steps, wondering if we could treat ourselves to a takeaway pizza. A Neapolitan with extra olives, Em's favourite.

Rouillée. Maybe, but I'd get there.

Chapter 14

On the night of the Brownswood School prom, my friends Marni and Sheba came over to the flat so we could get dressed together. They arrived armed with clothes, make-up and hair tongs, and we shut ourselves in my room while Dad watched *Peggy Sue Got Married*.

'Is he picking you up?' Marni plugged in the irons and began arranging her stash, her face set and stern. Getting ready was a serious business.

'Of course not,' I scoffed, wriggling and fastening. 'I'd die. We're meeting there.'

'Maybe he'll be waiting outside with a red rose between his teeth.' Sheba's voice was muffled, her head in my wardrobe. She backed out holding a pair of black sandals. 'These'll have to do though they're not very sexy. Have you painted your nails?'

I wiggled my toes at her. Marni had given me some fuchsia-pink polish that she subsequently admitted she'd stolen from Boots, but by then it had already been used for a practice session so there wasn't much we could do about it. Marni's

shoplifting habit wasn't great, but her parents were divorcing, and her dentist was refusing to take her braces off, so we tried to cut her some slack while she worked through her issues. She'd been asked to the prom by a guy in Year Eleven but had said no because he wore aligners, which Marni felt was a shaming thing to have in common. 'Two metal-heads,' she'd said. 'Imagine what people would say.' 'They're not proper braces,' Sheba had soothed. 'It's not the same.' 'But they were there before,' replied Marni bitterly. 'People will remember.' No one had asked Sheba because she was too tall – five foot ten and still growing. That was her own particular tragedy, although she made up for it with long straight blonde hair and equally straight teeth.

That night, we were the Weird Sisters, peering into the cauldron of Marni's make-up bag, plotting the prom takeover. Sheba's dress – nobly lent to me – was black, buttons all the way down and a kind of bustle at the back. It was quite plain and restrained, but somehow sultry. At least, that was how it had looked when she wore it to Annabel Lloyd's Christmas party, though of course it was shorter on her.

'You should wear a Wonderbra.'

'I don't have a Wonderbra.'

Marni's head emerged from her own dress – a purple satin slip with a slit skirt. 'Sellotape?'

Sheba giggled. 'What if he unbuttons the dress?'

I felt myself go livid red. 'Sorry, but he's so *not* going to unbutton the dress.'

'He might. And if your tits are covered in tape that'll be a turn-off.'

None of us had had sex, which was unusual in Year Ten

girls at Brownswood, or at least appeared to be. Sheba was impeded by her height, Marni by her teeth and me by my reputation as a swot, along with the protective shell built up since the day of Sally Barclay and the Bunsen burner. Sheba and Marni talked about it a lot (the lack of sex, not my lack of a parent) and were desperate to get it over with, every party a potential opportunity. They weren't looking to do it with anyone they particularly liked or fancied; just someone acceptable who wasn't likely to shit-talk them afterwards. But when it came to it – when there *was* an opportunity, like Dan Edwards and his aligners, they always found something wrong, and put it off. At the beginning of Year Ten, Sheba had been asked out by a looming boy, Elliott Wragg, and had sent him packing. 'What's wrong with him?' I asked, watching him slink down the corridor, shoulders bowed. 'He's too tall,' she said.

I wasn't sure if I wanted to have sex with Adam, just that him putting his arm around my shoulder set off volts down my spine, that being in the same room as him made my skin prickle. As Marni started attacking my hair with the tongs, taming wild curls into something silkier, I wondered what I would do if he *did* unbutton the dress. But that was a bit premature given we hadn't even kissed. And the buttons were really small and difficult to undo, so maybe it wasn't worth worrying about. Would I have wanted to confide in Maman if she'd been there? Maybe not – teenagers are more inclined to skulk, mumble, avoid, sneak off. But I would have liked to have someone to sneak off from. My father didn't notice either way – when I went out, he never asked where I was going or how late I'd be. He just murmured, 'All right, FiFi, you enjoy yourself.'

With my make-up half-done and bare feet, I went through to check on Dad's dinner. Tiptoeing past the living room, I caught sight of his rapt face bathed in the light of the TV, as Peggy Sue wandered round her childhood home. In the kitchen, I switched the oven off, but left the chicken Kiev in to keep warm, before dashing back to the buzz and industry of my bedroom. Marni had turned her attention to her own hair now, steamrolling it flat, black fingernails glinting with each pass. She nodded at me in the mirror as I went in. 'Do your other eye, you look mad.'

I stuck my tongue out at her and grabbed the mascara, simultaneously slipping on the sandals, which were a little too scuffed for seduction. When we were all ready, we surveyed each other, tweaking and adjusting, heads to one side, mouths pursed.

'There's lipstick on your teeth.'

'Your bra is showing, you tart.'

'Fuck's sake, Jones, show some flesh, or people will think you're a Mormon.'

Ready and restless, I plated up Dad's food and we left, catching the bus partway to the school, falling out of it and tottering off down the road, the sun warm on our glittered shoulders. As we neared our destination, I slowed up, skin prickling again, from nerves or excitement, maybe both.

'Come on, you slags! Look sexy.' Marni whipped out her phone and Sheba and I immediately arranged our faces into suggestive pouts, wobbling in our heels. 'Stop pissing about or it'll come out blurry.'

What if Adam wasn't waiting? Everyone knew he had asked me, so if he didn't show up it would be the ultimate diss, a truly catastrophic let-down. If he wasn't there, I would leave Brownswood and enrol in another school where no one knew me. I'd cut my hair off and wear glasses in a self-imposed witness protection programme. Perhaps a name change: Fi Colbert, my mother's maiden name. I turned to Marni and Sheba to share this resolution, but they were both clutching each other, rictus grins splitting their faces.

'Prince Charming awaits,' hissed Sheba, pushing me forwards.

He was waiting outside the school gates. He didn't have a rose between his teeth, but the sun on his copper crown and the smile in his eyes as he looked at me made this Cinderella moment pulse and sparkle with possibility. The cackling witches I'd arrived with melted away in search of new spells to weave, leaving Adam and me gazing at each other, both twitching to the throb of the music indoors.

'You look amazing,' he said, holding out his hand. 'Shall we see what's going on in there?'

The hall had been dressed with balloons and streamers, bunting and banners everywhere for the post-GCSE send-off. It was about them, the Year Elevens, but really it was about us, Adam and Delphine, our First Date. We talked in the corner, putting our mouths to each other's ears to be heard over the music. When he went off to get me a drink, Mr North walked past and I cowered, wondering if he would tell me off for being there – teachers tended to turn a blind eye to the gatecrashers as long as they behaved themselves, but you never knew. He caught my eye and nodded, saying, 'Evening, Delphine, you look lovely,' and I breathed out in relief because I *did* and everything *was*.

Later, we danced together, swaying under the banners, and I thought Adam might kiss me then, but he didn't, just brushed a lock of hair out of my eyes and said, 'Do you want to go outside?' Hands entwined, we walked out to the hill where a Year Ten crowd, including Sheba and Marni, had congregated. They played it cool and ignored me, though Marni briefly mimed undoing buttons behind Adam's back. We all lay down on the grass as Stevie Richards sloppily rolled a joint, then passed it between us, inhaling and concealing our coughs. Lexy Marshall's flowing skirt was rucked up round her thighs, attracting glazed, admiring glances from several boys. As the wave hit, I relaxed into it, gazing up at the amber midsummer sky, feeling the parched grass crackle under my shoulders. When Adam took my hand again and led me away from the group, I turned back to see Marni and Sheba, who managed to be both drug-addled and agog, writhing on the ground like upended beetles.

Outside the library – the library Miss Challoner wanted to renovate because it had a leaking roof and gouged parquet – Adam stopped and turned me round, hooking one finger under my chin to bring my face to his.

'I've wanted to do this ever since you said you were a sci-fi fan,' he whispered.

'It's the future,' I breathed.

Our laughing lips met, then we both stopped laughing and sank into the kiss, one of his hands at my waist, the other buried in my hair, to the counterpoint of the hall's heart-thumping soundtrack. I wanted the moment to go on and on, and when it finished, I wanted to relive it a thousand times, analyse every undulation, every languorous flicker of his tongue, the feather-brush of his fingertips at my temples.

We walked back indoors together, my mussed head against his shoulder, and for me the evening had hit its peak and could not be improved upon. We drank some more but someone had spiked it with something sickly alcoholic, we danced some more but by then the floor was sticky underfoot, and I didn't want him to walk me home because I was ashamed of our shabby basement flat when he lived in a big house on the edge of the park. But none of that mattered, when I could lie in bed later, winding a snaky curl around my finger, glorying in the image of us trussed together in the shadow of the library.

Teenagers sneak and mumble and avoid, but there was always a moment when you just wanted to cast off the cloak and be seen and heard. I really wanted to tell someone about that night, that perfect night, when everything went right. Not Sheba or Marni, because my interactions with them were always laced with sarcasm, loaded with studied nonchalance. Someone who would really listen, squeeze my hand tight and say, 'It sounds like he's really into you!' but follow it up with 'You will be careful, won't you?' There was no one to say it, which was maybe why I wasn't careful at all, why I thought the golden glow would last, and cocoon me. So I didn't shade my eyes, checking for pitfalls. I just blundered into the light, not looking where I was going, dazzled and entirely blind.

Chapter 15

*A*t my second session with Letty, thighs needled by Aphra's claws, she introduced me to her husband, Jean-Luc. Or at least, she introduced me to his book, *Les Carottes Sont Cuites*, a sort of culinary memoir looking back on his career as a food critic. Jean-Luc himself was long gone, having passed away in Provence over a decade ago. But Letty assured me his book was considered a classic, reprinted many times, earning her a fortune in royalties.

'We were rich anyway,' she rasped, 'because Jean-Luc had a famous column in *Le Figaro*. He was marvellously scathing about everything, and the more offensive he was, the more people liked it. The perspective shifted, you see, so if he said a dish was tepid and unsavoury, that meant he thought it was tolerable, and if he said an establishment was adequate, that was a rave review. He was notorious for being snide. So when he published *Les Carottes*, it was a complete surprise, a revelation. It was enchanting.'

Jean-Luc's memoir was a love letter to French cuisine,

Letty said – nostalgic, sentimental, eulogizing his favourite restaurants and dishes, recipes recreated in lavish detail.

'Where languages are concerned, you have to get stuck in. Read this, look at a recipe. Cook it. Make the dishes, tell me how they tasted, how they made you feel.'

On the flyleaf, I traced the spidery ink: *'Mon petit chou – un billet-doux.'* A love letter. Flicking through a few of the pages, I caught sight of a recipe for *soupe à l'oignon*, accompanied by a picture of a hearty bowl with the familiar French bread floating on top. Maman used to make it in the autumn, singing 'A Foggy Day' as she chopped and stirred, serving it up on the little fold-down table in our living room, laid for three by Dad. We ate so well when she was alive; after that, it was just frozen potato waffles in the toaster. I looked back up at Letty, my eyes misting, and she nodded.

'Yes,' she said. 'That's what it *should* do. Do you know what the title means?'

Taking out my phone, I took a photo of the recipe, and the front page. 'The carrots are cooked?'

She rapped her stick on the floor. 'They're done. No turning back. *C'est une blague* – a joke,' she added, seeing my frown. 'Because, of course, he *was* turning back. Though in the end it turned out his carrots *were* cooked because he had diabetes and did nothing about it. I'll never forgive him for dying.'

'Désolée,' I began, risking a touch of her hand, but she waved me away.

'It was his own fault, silly man. *En marche!* Now tell me about this restaurant that you work in.'

In my stumbling French, I told her about Merhaba, about

Selassie and Abrihet, how they wanted to renovate the waste-land behind the building, turn it into a courtyard, open it up to diners in the summer. I told her about learning to make Eritrean stews, and the jebena coffee pot they brought out for special occasions. The two mums who met up had brought a new mother with them this week, and now it was her turn to weep and wince as she tried to breastfeed, while they both jollied her and fed her himbasha.

Letty nodded approvingly. 'It all sounds splendid. Some-where Jean-Luc would have described as unremarkable and instantly doubled its takings. I must visit one day and try the injera.'

Walking towards Merhaba, another £25 nestling in my bag, I thought about the carrots being cooked, how you couldn't go back, only forward. There was a fearsome inev-itability to it, everything determined, stuck in grooves you couldn't get out of. Were our paths set, our fates so fixed?

In the café, Roz was sitting in her usual corner marking and absent-mindedly eating popcorn.

'How's Letty?' she asked, through a mouthful.

'Rich and acerbic,' I replied, taking off my coat and going to hang it in the back room. Roz being there seemed like an opportunity – like the gods were telling me to get on with it, seize the moment, brandish the fiery side of the spoon. But walking back to her table, I felt the same leaden, tingling sensation in my leg muscles that I'd felt that day in the college, looking up course details.

'Can I ask you something?'

She put her pen down, instantly alert, fixing me with her stare. 'Of course, what is it?'

I twisted my skirt between damp fingers. 'Do you think you could . . . I mean, I was thinking . . . wondering, if it would be possible . . .'

Her eyes widened. 'Get to the point, why don't you.'

Seeing a family of four arrive and wait expectantly in the doorway, I took a deep breath. 'You asked me for a favour, and I wondered if you would do me one in return.'

'Go on.'

'I want . . .' The man in the family waved in my direction. 'I want to take an A level. Get the qualification I meant to get before I . . . before I had Em.'

Roz sat back, crossing her legs, the hint of a smile playing about her lips. 'Reeeeally. What subject?'

I waved back at the man, and held up my notepad as if I was taking Roz's order. 'English. English Literature.'

'Why an A level, and why English?'

I wrote the word '*Because*' on the pad, and tapped my pen on it. 'I would need it if I was ever going to . . .' I could hardly bring myself to say it, voice the dream, '. . . if I was ever going to go to university, to get a degree. And I thought, perhaps you could enrol me through the school and maybe . . . help me with the course?' The tingling in my legs was getting worse, and the man was starting to look impatient. 'Sorry, it's probably a crazy idea – must go and sort these guys.'

Scurrying towards the family, I showed them to a free table, gave them menus and took their drinks order, my cheeks burning as I wondered what Roz had made of that exchange. Was it completely inappropriate to ask my daughter's teacher to teach me? But ever since I'd had the idea, it had been gnawing away inside, and the only way to stop it was to ask, find out once and for all. Part of me hoped she would say no; it was impossible, couldn't be done. Like the woman in college that day, slapping me down, showing me the door. Back in your bell jar, Esther. But when I went back, under the pretext of lighting her candle, Roz's own pen was poised, a white sheet of paper in front of her.

'Right,' she said. 'Usually it would take two years to do an A level but, from what Sarah Boleyn tells me, you could do it in one.'

Was that a yes? My hands shook slightly as I held the match to the wick. 'If we started now, could I do the exams next year?' If I was going to do it, I wanted to do it quickly, stop the sands of time running out.

'Let's see . . . November.' She started counting on her fingers, noting down months and deadlines. 'I'd need to register you, get you started on coursework. You'd have to get stuck in, right now. It would be hard work.'

The flame ignited and flickered before catching properly, settling into a steady burn.

'Hard work for you, too,' I replied. 'Are you sure you're OK with it? You must be really busy with school and your own kids.'

Her face glowed in the candlelight, making her look younger – Rosalie Murray again, beguiling Sir Thomas in *Agnes Grey*. 'Teaching a bunch of rowdy Year Sevens the difference between concrete and abstract nouns is hard work. You'd be a walk in the park.' Roz grinned. 'And frankly, leaving my husband to do a bit more childcare would do him the power of good.'

'You're sure it's not too much for you?' Her enthusiasm made me nervous, my hazily hatched scheme becoming a reality.

To my surprise, she reached for my hand across the table. I flinched, but let her take it. 'This is why I went into teaching,' she said. 'To pass it on, to someone like you. You'll do brilliantly, then I can bask in your glory, be a footnote in your memoirs.'

She laughed at her own joke, but I didn't join in. I wanted this so badly, but I was scared, a caged animal let out of its enclosure, unsure what to do with the freedom.

'Well?' Roz demanded. 'You could do it. Do you want to?'

'I don't know. Maybe.' I moved to the next table, feeling her eyes on me as I lit another candle. Was I ready to make the leap? 'I'll let you know, if that's OK?'

'You'd better get a move on,' she called. 'I'll send you a list of set texts. In case Emily hasn't told you, I'm a really good teacher.'

I blew the match out. 'Em did tell me.'

She was Miss Challoner, all over again.

Chapter 16

Once upon a time, there was a day when everything went wrong in a thousand little ways, my tiny world tangling until I was dizzy and enraged. About eight or nine, I think, snagged by a series of childhood woes. My friend Becki had sat with another girl at lunch, their bent blonde heads blocking me out. There had been a spelling test and I'd got the word 'vegetable' wrong, cringing at Miss Riggott's sorrowful shake of the head, cursing my carelessness, that rogue 'd' taunting me. There was a talk on the upcoming school camping trip, and I'd fidgeted and fretted through it, wondering how my parents could possibly find the money. I was pretty sure we didn't own a sleeping bag. On the way home it rained, sending my hair into a demented frizz, and then, back home, throwing my rucksack into the hallway corner with unnecessary force, I discovered that the mood ring Becki had given me was no longer on my finger. Racking my useless d-for-dunce brain to think when I'd taken it off, where I'd put it down, whether the fact I'd lost it was a sign our friendship was forever severed. But I didn't need it to know I was feeling stormy and out of sorts, and, at dinner, the torrent of emotions whipped up into a tornado that veered into my mother, who'd made macaroni cheese, when I wanted spaghetti. We argued, in French, because cross words between us tended to slide into the mother tongue, and it ended in her suggesting I calm down – '*Sois sage!*'

After my outburst, lip wobbling at Dad's frown, we sat in silence for a while and eventually I felt guilty and hungry enough to eat the macaroni. It was delicious, which made me even more ashamed. When Maman had eaten her own, she put down her fork and said, so gently: 'What is really wrong? It is not the pasta, *n'est-ce pas?*' I burst into tears and told them about Becki and 'vegetable' and the mood ring. I didn't mention the camping trip, though the letter was in my bag. Maman stood up and held out her hand and said, '*Viens.*' And off we went.

She led me outside, and it was still raining and neither of us had our coats on, but she ignored my protests, saying it was more fun this way. We marched down the sodden streets together, getting wetter and wetter, and the further we went the funnier it became, so by the time we reached the park I was laughing, squelching along in my school shoes. She carried on, across a large stretch of grass to the edge of one of the lakes, where a gnarled old oak tree loomed, and *then*, to my astonishment, she grabbed the lowest branch and started to climb. She nodded down at me – '*Suis-moi*' – so I grabbed the branch and followed. It was surprisingly easy to swing our way up, and in a trice we were sitting together, nestled against the trunk, surveying the park below. The leaves above kept off the worst of the wet, and it felt like we were in a little fronded cocoon, safe from outside concerns. And then, there in the greenery, Maman began to sing about how, whenever it rains, it rains pennies from heaven. You couldn't have flowers without the showers, mood rings without the moods.

That might be my happiest memory, sitting there in the tree with my mother, turning my umbrella upside down. When she'd finished the song, we climbed down again, and the rain had stopped, and we walked slowly home in the emerging sunshine, hand in hand. Just before we reached our flat, Maman said: 'Hortense called Papa today; she needs her piano tuned.' And I understood that meant we would be able to afford the camping trip, it would all be OK. The next day I found my ring on the windowsill in the girls' toilets, Becki sat with me again, I got ten out of ten on the spelling test, and everything untangled perfectly; a shower of heavenly pennies.

Afterwards, whenever I had a bad day, I would think of our tree; how a little perspective could help clear the skies; how sometimes it was hard to work out which cloud on your horizon was the one really bothering you. When Maman went, I thought one day I might go back to that tree, sit in it and feel a little closer to her, creep closer to that memory. But I never did.

Chapter 17

*O*n Sunday, after our regular church visit, it was time to try *soupe à l'oignon*. On the way back, I'd bought onions, cheese and a baguette. Selassie had given me the dregs of a bottle of white wine, and I scraped together the few remaining ingredients from our cupboards. If the carrots were cooked, you just had to get stuck into making something new.

With my phone propped up on the worktop, I painstakingly deciphered the recipe, toasting flour to add a nutty flavour, caramelizing the onions *'de manière tranquille'*, stirring in the wine and whisking to prevent coagulation. There was a whole tangent devoted to preventing *'les grumeaux'*, lumps, the sworn enemy of the sauce. Jean-Luc's tone was droll and flippant, with an undercurrent of melancholy that occasionally swelled into sentiment. I could see why Letty had adored him.

As I cooked, I sang. Not humming under my breath, but full-throated crooning, recalling the times when my mother used to sway and stir and sing of foggy days in London

Town. She always sang that song to Dad, saying that when he arrived at her flat that day to tune the piano, she'd been tired of London and life, wondering whether to go back to Paris. But her F sharp was flat. But for that one little thing, she would have gone. But for that one little thing – what it led to – she wouldn't *be* gone. The tiny details fate hinged on – a pinch here, a pinch there, the spice of life. As the savoury smells swirled and filled the kitchen, Em wandered in, munching pretzels.

'What's going on?'

'Nothing. I'm making lunch. So stop eating those.'

Her eyes roved across to the propped-up phone. 'What's with the singing?'

'Just felt like it.'

Stirring and pushing at the bits of burnt onion stuck to the bottom of the pot, I could feel her eyes on my back, weighing up, selecting and rejecting information, brain clicking and whirring. It was an uncomfortable sensation, wondering what conclusions she might draw.

'I came to ask if I can take *Flowers for Algernon* back to the library.'

My wooden spoon stilled. 'No reason why not.' I thought about that night, the blessed oblivion, sinking into it and emerging like a miner from a cave, bewildered by the light.

'Did you enjoy it?'

'Yes.' I added half a teaspoon of salt. 'It was . . . very interesting.'

'Good.' She lobbed a final pretzel into her mouth, left the bag on the table and turned to go, as I began to sing again:

'*For suddenly* . . . Em.'

She turned back enquiringly.

'When you go to the library, could you get me a book?'

'What?'

'Just . . . anything. Something you think I might like. Could you do that?'

The pirate smile flickered across her face. 'Yes. I could do that.'

I turned back to my pot, bubbling away. 'Thank you.'

Adding grated cheese to the sliced baguette, I slid it into the oven, watching it melt and sizzle on the bread. When it was browned, I let it subside on the worktop while I ladled the soup into three bowls. Balancing the bread on top, I checked the corresponding photo from Jean-Luc's book. Our bowls were thin and chipped, not quite as rustic, but other than that it was a good match. I called through to Em in her room – our room, the one we shared, tucked together in one bed because the space was too small for anything more. We were outgrowing this flat, overflowing and spilling over the sides.

'Lunch is ready!'

We ate on the sofa, and the living room felt cosy for once. Dad was watching *Guardians of the Galaxy*, not reacting to any of the jokes, just staring, the frantic action reflected on his glassy eyeballs. But at least he was eating. Em picked up my phone and scrolled through the photos I'd taken from the recipe book.

'He's funny,' she said. 'This guy, Jean-Luc. He your old lady's husband?'

'He was. He's dead.'

'Right.' She nodded. 'But he was famous, wasn't he? So

this is his legacy. That's what Mrs Gill is always talking about. Making a difference. Making your mark.'

I said nothing, the soup hot on my tongue. The bread was soaking it up like a sponge, absorbing all the flavours, growing heavier and richer in the bowl.

'Imagine, writing a book. It's there forever, isn't it. Not just the physical thing, but all the ideas out there, shared, enriching the world!'

Em prattled on, and I ate the bread, relishing the moist-ness and crustiness, the saltiness of the cheese alongside the sweetness of the onions. It was as good as my mother's, and brought back those cold autumn nights when our flat was a home because she was in it, stirring and singing, describing how one of her pupils had finally mastered chromatic scales. 'It's all in the fingering,' she said. 'You have to practise and practise until it becomes second nature. Then you don't have to think about it at all.' Maybe her legacy was all those young pianists, going off into the world, enriching it with their music.

'I'm going to do my homework,' said Em. 'Writing about Greta Thunberg. How, to make big changes, you have to start with a small change.'

Sometimes Em wasn't subtle, but she was always effective. I went over to Dad to collect his tray and, when I lifted it from his hands, he looked away from the screen, tapping me gently on the arm.

'That soup was good,' he said. 'The singing too.'

My fingers tightened on the melamine. Dad often thanked me for the food I made – 'That was nice, FiFi, you're a good girl' – but there was always an absent-mindedness to his tone. There was something direct about this comment, a specific reference to the dish, a light in his eye that hinted what – or who – it reminded him of. A spark of recognition.

I held the tray as carefully as a baby bird. 'Thank you. I'm glad you liked it.' I didn't mention Maman, guessing it would be a step too far. Sometimes big changes started with a small change.

Later on, I called Roz Gill.

'Yes?' she said. I could hear screaming children in the background.

'Hi, um . . . It's Delphine Jones. Is this a bad time?'

'Delphine! Put that down right away! Right away! Five . . . four . . . three . . . two . . . Good. Now go upstairs and take your clothes off.'

'I'm sorry, shall I—'

'No! That was just Izzy kicking off. She's in the bath now. What can I do for you?'

I took a deep breath. 'I just wanted to say . . . if the offer's still there, I'd like to do it. To do the English exam. If you think I can.'

There was the sound of a cork popping at the other end. 'Oh Delphine, you definitely can. If we get stuck in right away.'

'Then let's do it,' I said.

Chapter 18

*W*hen Roz and I had our first 'lesson' in her kitchen, I kept thinking back to that special study group session at Brownswood in the autumn term of Year Eleven, most of us slouching into the room, heads down, trying to pretend we weren't there. Miss Challoner had given us the unfortunate name of 'The Quick Lit Class', quickly abbreviated to Clit Class, people asking where it was, if we could find it. So we were already embarrassed by the whole thing – marked out as swots, or 'slickers' (short for arse-lickers). All except Adam, of course, confident as ever, strolling in and taking a seat like he was waiting to have a massage. And Lorenzo, who didn't express emotion of any kind.

Mr North took that class, waving a copy of *Othello* and telling us we were about to go up a gear. He spent about half an hour on just one line – Desdemona saying, '*Do you know, sirrah, where Lieutenant Cassio lies?*' – my brain creaking and stretching as I forced myself to concentrate in a new way, focusing minutely. When he asked me to read a speech aloud, I was so engaged, engrossed, that I forgot to be embarrassed and stood, beginning, '*My noble father, I do perceive here a divided duty* . . .' delivering the lines with deliberation and commitment. When I finished and looked up, Adam was smiling at me and I barely noticed Mr North saying, 'Thank you, Delphine, that was something special. You would make a wonderful Desdemona.'

I hadn't felt that kind of focus in so long, yet Roz demanded it from me as soon as we were sitting at her kitchen table with its tomato-splattered oilcloth. She and her husband Sanjay lived in a bedraggled Highbury house that she complained was riddled with damp and in need of a revamp. When she met me at the door with her son Joe in his pyjamas, she apologized for its scruffiness, saying they were rewilding the front garden. Joe looked about eight years old, with sweetly oversized front teeth and floppy brown hair still wet from the bath. As we walked down the corridor and into the kitchen, I noticed the clutter of kids' toys, books, manuscript paper scattered about, a music stand in the corner, the guitar propped against the sofa in the living room. Education came easily to them; it was all around, the walls steeped in it. Joe sloped off upstairs while Roz swept a space on the table.

'Good night, darling! Right, here you go. This is a summary of the syllabus and a list of set texts. I'll register you this week. Um . . . there's the issue of the exam fee. I'm not sure of the exact figure, but it's a couple of hundred pounds . . .' Roz tailed off, twirling her pen between her fingers.

I felt my face grow hot, but thought of Maman's bank account. Finally, I was going to use it. 'I can get you the money.'

Roz looked visibly relieved. 'Great. You'll need some ID, a driver's licence or passport.'

'I don't drive, and my passport's out of date.'

'Renew it then, and we'll get started on your non-exam assessment as soon as possible. Now—'

'Sorry, what's a "non-exam assessment"?'

'Coursework. You have to write an essay. Usually a linked essay comparing two different works. We'll get to that. You'll have two exams, first is Shakespeare, Drama and Poetry, second is Contextual Study, and . . .'

She rabbited on, and, like that first day with Letty, it was hard to follow what she was saying, impossible to absorb and process all that information. I started to panic, breathing unevenly, thinking that perhaps this had been a terrible idea, that I'd never be able to manage it, and then would fail and be back where I started, only worse, because like Charlie Gordon I'd have had a *taste* of it, know what I was missing . . .

'Delphine,' said Roz, gently, and I opened my eyes. She was smiling at me. 'That was a bit much, wasn't it? I got carried away. Let's start again.'

She reached across the table and handed me a single sheet with a poem printed on it. The first line bloomed on the page: *'My mistress's eyes are nothing like the sun.'*

'Do you recognize it?'

'Shakespeare.'

'Great. Let's look at it in a little more detail, shall we?'

That's what we did, for the next forty minutes, going over the text minutely, examining it from all angles, talking about Petrarch and the Dark Lady, and notions of ideal beauty.

I was so preoccupied, I hardly noticed the front door opening and scuffling in the corridor, the sound of a dog barking. But I sensed Roz's growing irritation, the set of her jaw as she continued pointing and underlining. And then music – live music – started coming from the living room. Someone playing the piano, and a guitar. Roz clicked her tongue.

'It's Jay and Dylan. They've been in the pub all afternoon. They're going to wake the kids. Just a sec while I go and shut them up.'

She marched off down the corridor and I sat for a second, listening. They were playing 'That Ole Devil Called Love' and, although they might be drunk, they were good, me-andering around the tune, lazily adding flourishes. Drawn by the song and the last person I'd heard sing it, playing our own upright with the same flair and vim, I stepped cautiously into the hallway, leaning on the doorframe of the living room. Roz was standing with her arms folded, waiting for them to finish, but they were oblivious, caught up in their collaboration, just like she and I had been, minutes earlier.

Two men – one, who must be Sanjay, Roz's husband, strumming the guitar, eyes closed. I knew he used to be in a band, quite a famous one. The other, at the piano, had his head bent, so I couldn't see his face. Here in Roz's clut-tered, casually well-to-do house were two genuine musicians, talented in a way that seemed more suited to a dingy Harlem jazz club than Highbury. And in that moment, everything my mother taught me came rolling back, both of us at the piano, singing, turning the pages together, absorbed and enriched by the music, everything glowing and in tune. Almost in a trance, I moved forwards, tugged by an unseen presence, pierced by a thousand memories and secret harmonies, opening my mouth to sing the next line.

As one, their heads flicked up and around, Roz's jaw dropping in astonishment, but by then I'd started and couldn't stop; for once I just wanted to sing, to remind myself I had a voice, find my *l'esprit de l'escalier*, before it was too late. So they played, and I sang, sinking into a beloved, well-worn tune that was still second nature, even after all those years.

'Jeeeeeeez,' said Roz, when we finished, and the last mournful note had died away. 'I didn't know I'd invited Amy Winehouse round.'

The pianist pivoted on the stool, staring at me, squinting slightly. He was lean and wiry, a kind of restlessness about him. Like Roz's house, he was scruffy, wearing ripped jeans and a greying T-shirt, his curly dark hair in disarray. Somewhere inside me, a hammer struck a string. Tucked against the piano next to him was a smallish black dog, panting slightly, head cocked to one side. The man picked his beer off the top of the piano with one hand and gestured towards the dog with his other, snapping his long fingers.

'This is Bernadette,' he said, in a strong Welsh accent. 'I'm Dylan. Will you sing something else?'

But the moment had passed, and I felt foolish for barging in, singing like that with two strangers. I began to back away, shaking my head.

'Sorry, it's getting late, I'd better head off . . .'

Shooting her husband an exasperated glance, which he ignored, Roz came towards me, ushering me back towards the kitchen.

'They're so pissed,' she complained. 'Jay is maddening. I told him to get back for bedtime, but once again he left me to it, the useless sod. And then stumbling in, wasted, bashing away. But you were amazing, I had no idea you could sing like that, who taught you?'

I shook my head, mortified, gathering up my bag and coat and heading towards the front door, anxious to escape.

'They'll carry on now, ordering pizza and messing about till three a.m., and once again it'll be me getting up with the kids at God knows what hour while knobchops snores away upstairs. Honestly . . .'

We got to the door and she put her hand on my arm.

'Listen to me, I'm a sour old cow. You were great today, what a brilliant start. Same time next week, yes? I'll call you.'

She kissed me on the cheek, and it was all so cosy and middle-class that it felt like we were in a Richard Curtis film. I wasn't sure I belonged here, amongst all the *Guardian*s and wine bottles.

Walking down their quiet, tree-lined road, I heard the door open again and turned back. Dylan was standing there, swaying, bathed in the light of the hallway.

'Oi!' he yelled. 'Will you be in our band?'

'For God's sake!' Roz appeared behind him, pulling him back. 'Leave the poor woman alone!'

I laughed and waved, shouting, 'Good night!' as the door slammed shut. Not bad for a first lesson.

Chapter 19

The next day at Merhaba, Roz didn't turn up, but her husband's friend Dylan did, sidling in looking hungover to the teeth. Rather than take a table, he stood in front of me with a shamefaced expression.

'Roz has sent me to apologize,' he said. 'Sorry we interrupted you. I feel like my dog shat in my head. Can you get me something to make me feel less crap, and I'll leave you a massive tip?'

I was feeling equally embarrassed, picturing myself warbling in Roz's living room when I should have been focusing on Shakespeare. Plus, there was a twitchy intensity about Dylan that made me uneasy. I fetched him some of Abrihet's stew and injera, which he inhaled in about thirty seconds, wiping his plate clean with the bread and washing it all down with a glass of their lemonade. Seeing his empty plate pushed forwards, I went to collect it.

'Has that improved the headache?'

He nodded, wiping his mouth on a napkin. 'They should

advertise the healing properties of that dish. Might even be able to drink again one day.'

As I collected the plate, cutlery and glass into a pile to carry back to the kitchen, he leaned towards his satchel and started rooting about in it.

'Listen,' he said. 'I was pissed when I shouted down the street at you, but I meant it.'

'Meant what?'

He pulled out a shiny sheet of paper which unfolded on the table. 'This.'

It was a flyer, amateurish in design, with 'Brownswood's Got Talent' written across the top in Comic Sans font.

'Brownswood as in . . . ?'

Dylan nodded. 'Your daughter's school, right? I teach music there. It happens every year. Fundraising thing. Jay and I thought we'd, you know, take part.'

'Why?'

'Why not?' He sounded defensive.

I set the dirty crockery back down on the table. 'Isn't it just for students?' Em hadn't mentioned it, but if it was a music thing then that made sense – she was about as musical as Selassie's coffee grinder.

He shrugged. 'Not particularly. They've had teachers and guests in the past. Anyone who wants to perform. They're not fussy. Jay agreed to do it with me yesterday when he was drunk. But we both thought we needed a singer. Then you showed up.'

His keen grey eyes met mine, and I looked down at the smeared plate. 'Well, thanks for asking, but I'm afraid I'm not a singer.' I picked up my pile again and prepared to go back to the kitchen.

'You're wrong.'

'I'm sorry?'

'Of course you're a singer. We all knew it as soon as you opened your mouth. Seems a shame to waste that kind of talent. May as well use it. Particularly raising money for your daughter's education.'

I flushed, partly at the compliment and partly the reprimand. 'Thanks, but no thanks. Can I get you anything else?'

He shook his head, looking dejected, and I experienced a spike of guilt, as if I'd let him down. Taking everything to the kitchen, I dumped it in the huge industrial sink, feeling rattled. Abrihet smiled at me as she added a pinch of spice to her pot. She was such a restful presence, unfazed by all the hustle and bustle. She just made her stews, and her himbasha, and let the world fret and fidget around her. Like that poem we learnt in school: '*Go placidly amid the noise and the haste* . . .' I wanted a crumb of that contentment for myself, not to feel so pummelled by life; to go with the flow.

When I returned to Dylan's table with the bill on a saucer, he was fastening his bag, ready to go. For a second, I allowed myself to imagine joining his and Sanjay's 'band', taking refuge in those familiar songs, rediscovering my musical roots, getting money for Em's school . . . But it was a stupid idea. I was used to humming under my breath in cafés, not belting out ballads to hundreds of people. Leaving the bill with him, I went off to clear another table. When I got back, he'd gone, and on the saucer was a twenty-pound note – a hefty tip as promised. I took it, feeling guilty again, and saw that he'd left the flyer, tucked underneath the plate. I smoothed it out: 'Brownswood's Got Talent'. A top hat was hanging off the 'T' of 'Talent' and it was raining musical notes. Pennies from heaven.

After wiping the table down, I pinned the flyer to the wall next to a picture of Billie Holiday. It would have been a shame to waste it.

Chapter 20

*I*n Canonbury later that week, when we'd sat down with our tea and Aphra had climbed onto her lap, Letty's eyes narrowed and she banged her stick.

'What's happened?'

I jumped, nearly spilling my drink. 'What do you mean?'

'You've an air about you. Like you've got a secret.'

'I haven't got a secret.' I rubbed at a drop of tea on the arm of my chair.

'Let me be the judge of that,' she replied, settling herself back. 'What have you been up to?'

I told her about my first lesson with Roz, how we'd started on the reading list, talking about the theme of 'Love Through the Ages'. She listened and barked a few questions at me but I sensed a dissatisfaction in her, so moved on to my week at Merhaba, learning to make panettone, a popular Eritrean treat, thanks to the country's colonial past. Abrihet had dismissed my dough, which didn't rise overnight. Letty didn't even compliment me on my use of the verb *'gonfler'*, so I embarked on a more ambitious story about a customer who turned out to be an old friend of Selassie's from Asmara who—

'Never mind all that,' she snapped, waving a hand. Today her nails were painted a vivid purple. 'What have you really been up to? It's not unleavened bread making you dance around like that. Flibbertigibbet.'

I gaped at her. 'Dance around?'

She pointed her stick at me. 'Yes, dance around! You're sizzling like a sausage in a pan. Are you on that drug young folk take nowadays? DMDA?'

'It's MDMA.'

She sat back in triumph. 'So you are!'

'No! Of course not. I just . . . I had a nice week, that's all.'

'Why?'

'I told you why.'

She shook her head. 'No, you didn't; you told me what happened but you left out the best part.'

'What part?'

Her eyes gleamed. 'The part that made you sizzle.'

I sighed, deflating like my panettone. Letty was a witch, with her scary cat and stick and sixth sense for gossip. 'I was asked to join a band.'

She leaned forwards, both hands clutching her cane. 'Elaborate.'

After Dylan came to Merhaba and left the note, I started to regret my decision but didn't do anything because I was embarrassed and decided that he hadn't meant it, was only being kind.

'What utter claptrap!' scoffed Letty, when I told her. 'I can't abide self-deprecation, it's deathly dull. Just say you're good and get on with it.'

'I said no. But now . . . I'm wondering if I was wrong.'

'Marvellous. And this Dylan, he is *craquant*, yes?'

'No!' I spluttered, mid-sip. 'He's . . . kind of weird, actually.'

'Intriguing. Do go on . . .'

'He's . . . a bit intense.' Those grey eyes, the energy that snapped and fused around him. It made me uncomfortable, and yet . . . I remembered a game that was popular in school when we were younger. Shocking Roulette. It was a little electronic device for four players. You each put a finger in one of the four sockets, and a shock was delivered to one of the players at random. We all used to gather round it, shrieking whether we got the shock or not. But, the more I played it, the more I found I was looking forward to the buzz, the pleasure-pain hit it delivered, the anticipation of it. I felt something like that when I saw Dylan.

'Classic angry young man. Like John Osborne. He tried to chat me up once, the cad. I sent him packing.'

'The playwright?' I stared at Letty, who twinkled at me, birdlike and mischievous. 'When?'

She rapped her cane. '1961, on holiday in France. Awful bounder, and a vegetarian. I gave him a very firm *non*. But of course, I was in love with someone else at the time. Or in lust, at least.'

'Jean-Luc?'

'Dear me, no!' she cackled. 'I was stepping out with a very principled poet from Berlin. He was terribly dreary but devastatingly attractive. It didn't last, of course. The dreariness outweighed the attraction, in the end. Then I met Jean-Luc, who wasn't particularly good-looking, but had something else that was far more interesting.'

'What?'

'*Je ne sais quoi.*'

Since we were speaking French, I couldn't decide if she meant the phrase literally or metaphorically. Both, perhaps. Dylan had *je ne sais quoi* and, as I walked home from Letty's that afternoon, I felt more and more that I'd passed up on an opportunity that should have been snatched with both hands – even if it gave me an almighty shock.

The next afternoon, I'd finished my shift and was doing a last clear-up, when Sanjay came in, closely followed by Dylan. As his gaze swept the room, I felt that electric surge of anticipation before his eyes came to rest on me. He'd brought his dog; I couldn't remember her name other than it was something silly. I checked to see if Selassie was around, as I wasn't sure if Merhaba was dog-friendly, but it turned out he had the same attitude to them as he did to little boys, and was soon on his hands and knees trying to tempt her with bits of injera. While my boss tried to entice Dylan's dog, they did the same with me, without the use of Eritrean treats.

'We've come back to convince you.' Sanjay pointed at the flyer, still stuck to the wall.

I hesitated, balancing my tray of mugs and glasses. 'I've never sung in public before.'

Dylan gave me a little smile. 'It's the same as in private – you just pretend you're singing in the shower.'

Blushing, I shifted my tray. 'It's not though, is it.'

He ran a hand through his unruly hair, making it stand

on end. 'Don't you want to help raise money for the school?'

'Of course. It's just . . .' I studied the smudged glasses. Getting up there, in front of all those people. In front of Dylan, who had a way of looking at me that made me taut as piano wire.

Sanjay butted in. 'After my band broke up, I didn't perform for ages. The last gig I did was in 2015. In a pub in Shoreditch. Six people came, and it turned out one of them thought she was there for the psychic night the following Tuesday.'

I smothered a laugh. 'Oh no, I'm sorry!'

Dylan picked up again. 'I cut down on teaching last year to concentrate on playing, try and make a go of it. Got booked for a wedding this summer. I was halfway through "When I Fall in Love" when one of the bridesmaids was sick into the open lid of the piano.'

I bit my lip to stop myself smiling.

'Sometimes you've just got to put yourself out there,' he said. 'Even if it all goes tits-up.'

'So, will you do it?' Sanjay had somehow found himself a slice of himbasha, which he was munching on enthusiastically, scattering it all down his jumper.

They were a mess, getting drunk, shouting in the street, turning up unannounced, dragging that dog around. But when they'd played together there had been a discipline and dignity to them both. They'd created something beautiful that night and, for a brief moment, I'd been part of it. I should put myself out there, raise money for Em's school, get back to my musical roots . . . but the truth was, looking at them standing in front of me, shedding crumbs and dog hairs everywhere, I just wanted to be in their gang.

I put down the tray and held out my hand. 'OK,' I said, and when Dylan took it, it felt like all my fingers were in the roulette socket. We exchanged numbers and agreed to get together for a first rehearsal, and then they left, arguing about which pub to go to, while I went to the kitchen, unloading the glasses, and worrying I'd made the wrong decision. I'd never done anything like this before. Did I really have time for it, with my jobs, and studying, and looking after Em and Dad? Was it a stupid idea to play this game?

I fretted about it for the rest of the week, but when I updated Letty at our next session, she took a more robust view.

'What arrant nonsense. One must broaden one's horizons, open one's mind, enrich one's soul – and meet as many men as possible,' she said firmly. 'That has always been my motto, and it's served me well. So now you are in a *ménage à trois* . . .' She winked at me, and I put my face in my hands.

'It is a trio,' I said firmly, when I emerged. 'A jazz trio.'

'Playing music together is very sexy,' she replied, using her stick to push herself out of her seat and shuffling slowly towards the money box. 'Jean-Luc and I used to frequent a very sordid jazz club in Paris and it was all *un partie de jambes en l'air.*' She cackled at my lack of comprehension. 'Bonking!'

I used the money to fan my face on the way out, thinking what a rich, buoyant romantic history Letty had, compared to my own. She viewed her encounters nonchalantly, jubilantly, whereas, when I looked back, it just seemed like a measly shortlist of disasters and bad decisions. My last relationship, with Sid, felt like it had put the sealant on my glass casket, locking me down forever. I didn't know how to be with anyone, how to make it work.

There had been a moment with Dylan just before he left the café. Sanjay had taken his plate back to Abrihet to thank her for the free cake, and Dylan was waiting for him. For a second, there was an awkward silence, him rocking on his heels as I went round wiping tables, just for something to do. But as I leaned across with my cloth, there was a cold, wet sensation against the back of my leg. Looking down, I saw the dog's face gazing up at me, tail wagging, and tentatively leaned down to pat her head.

'Hi, there,' I said politely. She licked my hand and nuzzled against it, tipping it up over her head so I could scratch her again.

'She likes you,' said Dylan.

I felt pleased, though up till then my interaction with dogs had been limited to stepping over our neighbour Mrs Munroe's chihuahua when she took it out in the morning.

'Not sure I like dogs,' I found myself saying. That wasn't what I meant at all, but I was confused by the fact I couldn't remember her name. Dylan looked surprised, and cast down, and I cursed myself for being so lame. Letty would have had them both eating out of her hand.

Sanjay had returned carrying a cardboard box, and they left, saying they'd text me the details of our first rehearsal. Dylan didn't look back, clicking his fingers at the dog, who scampered after him.

'Bernadette, *dewch yma*. Jay, there's a jukebox in the Barnsbury Tavern, we could—'

'No way, it only serves wanky craft beer . . .'

They faded away as the door closed behind them. Bernadette. That was it. I'd remember next time. And do better.

Chapter 21

*F*alling in love with Adam was ridiculously easy. Everything about him was easy. Like a lilting jazz standard you know so well, you could sing it in your sleep.

During the summer holidays we hadn't really seen each other, because he'd been off with his family in Europe, visiting friends in Brussels and Tuscany. I moped at home, lovelorn and bored, fetching Dad increasingly romantic DVDs from the library, daydreaming in the café where I was working, living for the odd email Adam sent, updating me on his travels. When the new school year started, we made up for lost time, learning each other all over again. In addition to our regular lessons and extra classes, we spent all the time we could together, lying on the hill reading, the autumn sun warm on our backs; wandering down the corridors, fingers interlaced; frantically kissing in the shade of a willow tree in the park; lingering goodbyes at the school gates.

But that time was limited to school hours, with little leeway either side. Adam's parents always seemed to be hosting dinner parties, or heading off to their cottage in

Norfolk for the weekend. There were tennis lessons, rounds of golf with his dad, trips to the theatre, extended family lunches in Hampstead. He lived in a world where people went skiing every February, had a junior minister as a god-father, sloped off for Sunday brunches at their private club, booked a summer in Siena. I only remembered going on holiday once, to a hotel in Whitstable, where they were baffled when my mother asked for the wine list. We could only afford three nights.

Although aware that Adam and I were from households not exactly alike in dignity, it didn't matter when we were together because we matched in every other possible way. It was a meeting of minds, a glorious symposium, and every time I answered a question in class, had an 'A' scrawled by Miss Challoner, or an approving comment from Mr North, I felt the heat of his appreciative gaze. To be admired for my mind was a heady and wonderful thing, keeping my wits sharp and supple and making me branch out in ways I'd never imagined.

But the question of a meeting of bodies arose. At the beginning of September, we both turned sixteen within days of each other, so it was inevitable it would come up. The sessions under the willow tree were becoming more heated, but the weather had other ideas, often forcing us indoors, where a hand was less likely to slip under a shirt. This became a source of frustration and, one day, huddled on our bench by the lake, Adam proposed a solution.

'My mum and dad are going away on Friday night,' he said.

There was the issue of Dad to deal with, but I'd stayed over at Marni's or Sheba's before and knew he would never check. When I kissed his cheek as I left for school on Friday morning, he gave me his usual 'You have a good day now, FiFi.' When I reminded him I wouldn't be back till the following morning, he simply nodded and said, 'Don't you worry about me,' which of course made me panic that something would happen while I was away, and it would be the punishment for my wanton lust. But I went anyway, toothbrush and condom secreted in my school bag, and, rather than loiter at the gates after school, Adam and I clasped hands and slipped away through the park, grinning like idiots.

'Are you sure no one will be there?' I asked, when we arrived at the smart redbrick Victorian house with bay windows that I'd already walked past half a dozen times, scoping it out.

'No one,' he assured me, producing his key.

'Why didn't you go to Norfolk with them?'

'Because I wanted to stay with you.' His smile widened. 'And I told them I had to finish my Virginia Woolf essay . . .'

I laughed as he led me in. 'We'd better get straight to it then . . .'

Inside it was all blonde wood and beige walls, abstract art and political cartoons on the walls, muddy boots lining the high skirting board. I glimpsed a huge living room on the right, a marble fireplace and velvet chaise longue, but he whisked me through to the kitchen at the back, a vast space with a granite-topped peninsula in the middle, an enormous oak table, and floor-to-ceiling sliding doors that led out into the garden. No one else I knew had a garden that big, much less one with an actual pond and a terrace with another table under a tarpaulin cover.

For a while I wandered round, touching things, flicking

through the newspapers and books that littered every surface, while Adam started opening cupboards, taking out jars and packets, getting food ready. They had a whole shelf of recipe books – Delia Smith and Ken Hom, Nigella Lawson and Madhur Jaffrey, the *Reader's Digest Cookery Year*, *The Silver Spoon*, *Larousse Gastronomique*. Every one was sticky to the touch. I thought of our own tiny kitchen, an old lined notebook Maman used to stick recipes from magazines in, with added scribbles – '*pas trop longtemps!*' and '*plus, plus d'ail*'. Our fold-down table that took up half the lounge when it was up. The hatch she used to pass the bowls through: 'Dinner is served, *mes chéries.*'

'Here you go,' said Adam, rousing me from the pages of Elizabeth David. 'Pasta arrabbiata.'

I was bowled over by the knowledge that my boyfriend cooked Mediterranean dishes, casually, like he was throwing out a chromatic scale, the fingering second nature. It was spicy, garlicky – *plus, plus d'ail* – and I was glad I'd brought my toothbrush for later.

After dinner, he showed me round the house – the first editions lining the walls in his dad's study on the first floor, the roll-top bath with claw feet in the 'family' bathroom, his mum's walk-in closet, the enormous bureau on the landing 'inherited from Granny Leonard'. We made our way up and up to his bedroom in the converted loft, sweetly neat and tidy in preparation for my stay. He had a double bed – an unimaginable luxury – his cello on a stand in the corner, our chaperone. In the little en suite, I brushed my teeth, checking them in the mirror for tomato skin, then went back to find him standing with his head sticking out of the

VELUX window, his hands in his pockets. I joined him on tiptoe to look out. We could see across the park, like that day in the tree with Maman, and I felt that same shift in perspective, getting the lie of the land.

Adam kissed me there under the skylight, and we carefully took off each other's clothes, layer by layer, until we were both shivering by the open window. I looked down at the goose bumps on my arms, thinking that not all of them were because of the cold. He led me to the bed, and we rubbed each other warm, then the rubbing turned to stroking, which turned into other things, and one thing led to another thing, until everything was a kind of delirious blur. Locked together, a brief flash of pain I ignored, trying to adjust to these new sensations and respond as I ought. And then it was all over, and I felt sore but euphoric.

That was the power of the mind, I suppose, that anything Adam did was a blessed caress, the whole thing a consecration. Looking back, I was so naïve, but at least I wasn't Posy Allan. So we lay together afterwards, giggling and arguing about who was going to get up to close the window, and in the end he did, strutting over to pull it shut, simultaneously swatting a fly out at the same time.

'My hero,' I said, as he got back into bed.

He grinned down at me, propped up on his elbow. 'Are you OK?'

'Yes,' I said. And, for a while, I was.

For a long time after Em was born – years and years – I didn't have sex with anyone. How could I? With a young child, and my father the way he was, in a flat like ours? I didn't *meet* anyone, let alone sleep with them. In the end, I did it because I was sick of waiting. Sick of waiting to be attracted to someone again, sick of feeling sick when someone touched me. So I figured I'd just get it over with, lay the ghost. There was a guy, Sid, who used to come into the café where I was working. He hung round enough to make it clear it wasn't just coffee he was interested in.

Philip Sidney. 'Like the poet,' he said when we met, as if he'd read him. I was twenty-four, stuck in Starbucks, writing people's names on paper cups. 'What's a girl like you doing working here?' he said. 'You should be a model.' As if that was what I yearned for. Maman always called me beautiful, and I liked it coming from her. It *came* from her – the crazy hair, wide-apart Americano eyes, thin ankles. But when she went, I wished she'd taken it with her. It felt awkward, like holding up an expensive dress in the mirror, knowing you couldn't afford it. So, biting my truant pen, I wrote, 'Sir Philip Sidney' on his cup, but said no when he asked me for a drink. He came back and asked again, and again, and I guess his enthusiasm was flattering. If we went out, I'd have something to look forward to other than perching on Dad's chair to check whether the film was making him cry, or quietly taking an open album from his lap as he dozed. We could see a film in a cinema, eat at a restaurant, go bowling or something – things normal people did. Maybe that way I could move on. Move on, and be someone new.

One evening, Sid took me back to his flat in Stroud Green. 'You're beautiful,' he murmured against my throat. In the past, I'd been clever; now I was beautiful. I would focus on that, make it work. As he pushed me down on the bed, and his hands slipped lower, I thought about Philip Sidney, his namesake; his creations Astrophil and Stella; the distant star: '*Bend hitherward your wit.*' It was fine as long as I held my mind at arm's length, didn't think too hard about any of it.

But eventually, after the second and third and fourth times, and every time after that, I realized that keeping that gap between my mind and body was exhausting; that I hadn't laid the ghost at all, just thrown soil over it so when it rose up again it was even murkier and more disturbing than before.

Falling in love with a boy like Adam was incredibly easy. Falling in love with a man like Sid was impossible. The bookends of my romantic life, boxing me in. And in between them was someone else entirely; someone I didn't want to remember, but couldn't forget. No matter how hard I tried to focus on the future, the past kept catching up with me.

Chapter 22

Sanjay, Dylan and I had our first rehearsal at a pub in Highbury. The landlord, Frank, was a friend of Dylan's, and he had a room at the back, dismally dressed in limp tinsel although it was only mid-November. He didn't mind us making noise, and even chucked us a few bags of crisps and pork crackling, which both men fell on as though Christmas had come early. They were so busy munching their way through the snacks and discussing Arsenal's defence that it seemed unlikely we'd ever get started, but Sanjay suddenly scrunched his bag, saying, 'Let's do this,' and they both began moving tables around to make a space for us, sending Bernadette running for cover, claws skittering on the wooden floor.

There was a bashed-about upright in the corner, and Sanjay had brought his guitar, but there was no microphone. Dylan said that didn't matter; the idea was for us to get the measure of each other, work out how we 'gelled'. They'd asked me to prepare a song, which was easy since I knew dozens, and sang them all the time, even if it was only under my breath at work. But knowing a song, and singing it for Dylan and Sanjay, were two totally different things. In church, although my voice didn't exactly blend in with the congregation, at least I was one of a crowd. Here I felt very visible, standing in this dingy room watched by two men who a week ago had been strangers.

'Do you have a song?' asked Dylan, settling himself at the piano stool.

'Yes. Should I have told you what it is? How will you accompany me?'

He shook his head. 'No worries, we'll manage.'

I took a deep breath. '"But Not for Me"?'

Where did that come from? It wasn't the song I'd planned on singing. That had been a Leonard Cohen number but, when it came to it, another title slid out of my mouth, like this was what my subconscious had decided on. My mother's song – the one she sang when she was down, when she was worried the piano would have to be sold.

Dylan nodded. 'OK. Why don't you do the first bit, and we'll join you when it kicks in?'

Worse still, *a cappella*. Truly on my own. I took another shaky breath. 'Could you give me a B flat?'

He gave me the note and I stood with my hands pressed together, more self-conscious and exposed than I'd ever felt. Dylan must have seen the terror in my eyes, because his expression softened and he said, 'Take your time. No rush. Just breathe.' He gave me the note again, and sat back on the stool, arms folded.

Casting around wildly for a diversion, I found it in Bernadette, who was watching me, head on one side, panting slightly. Singing to her seemed marginally easier, so I focused on the wet black nose, and opened my mouth.

Scratchy at first, but at least on pitch, I muddled through the first few lines of 'But Not For Me', concentrating on Bernadette's panting as a kind of metronome, keeping me ticking over. And then Dylan picked up, just as Maman would have; a few desultory notes, segueing into a chord, and we were off, writing songs of love.

Sanjay joined us, gently strumming, and they both played so well, such a joy to be singing with this kind of meandering, lazy accompaniment, that I forgot where I was, as I'd sometimes forgotten at Gio's, belting out Beyoncé and ducking when he threw a tea towel at me. The memory made me smile, because he didn't matter any more, and the smile opened me up, allowing my voice to soar into the rafters of that weird room, with the weird dog gazing at me, as her weird owner played those yellowing old keys as if they were the finest ivory.

Delivering the mournful last line, Dylan and Sanjay tailing off their accompaniment before the final three words, I ground to a halt, feeling unsettled by the silence that followed. Bernadette coughed, her long ears grazing the floor, and the moment shattered.

'Well, you can hold a tune,' Dylan said, closing the lid of the keyboard to roll a cigarette on it.

His muted reaction was a let-down. Maybe he hadn't experienced the same kind of rapport, maybe it had all been in my imagination. But at least it hadn't been a disaster.

'That was fucking great,' said Sanjay, opening another bag of crisps. 'Ignore him – he's never satisfied.'

We went through the song again, working on the phrasing,

allowing for more improvisation, tightening some of the rhythms. I felt my brain flexing and uncoiling like it did with Roz at her kitchen table; like it did talking to Letty; like it had in class with Adam. Now they'd committed to the rehearsal, Dylan and Sanjay were completely focused, deep in discussion, occasionally asking me to repeat a line, hold a note a little longer, and I became so caught up in the process that it didn't occur to me to feel self-conscious. It wasn't about me; it was about the song, making it the best it could be.

When we'd finished, I walked to Letty's house, slowly, savouring the crisp, smoky air. It wasn't our usual time, but she had asked me to let her know how it all went, and I felt like dropping by.

She opened the door wearing a quilted dressing gown, holding a tiny glass of burgundy-coloured liquid, and scowling.

'What are you doing here?'

'Oh, I'm sorry,' I stammered. 'Just thought . . . you might want a chat.'

'It's late,' she grumbled. Her hair wasn't in its usual bun, but in a long plait trailing over her shoulder.

'I'll come another time.' I began to back towards the steps, but she beckoned me in.

'No, you may as well stay. You can feed Aphra – I hate bending down.'

I gave Aphra her food, and, hoping to placate Letty, made her a cup of tea, carrying it into the living room where she was waiting in her usual chair. As I entered, her frown deepened.

'What were you thinking of, girl? Who drinks tea at this time of day? After six o'clock, I only drink beverages of an alcoholic nature. Get me *un petit porto.*'

Hastily, I put the cup down and went over to the dusty decanter to pour her a glass. She took it, knotty fingers closing round the stem, shooting me another irritable glance.

'Aren't you having one?'

Glancing at the cabinet, I gave an apologetic shrug. 'I don't drink.' I was shifting nervously from one foot to the other, and she gestured for me to sit.

'It might do you good. *Il faut se détendre.*'

'*Détendre?*'

'Relax, girl! Let your hair down. Well, what is it?'

Feeling sheepish, I grabbed the passing Aphra and arranged her on my lap as a kind of protection against Letty's gimlet eye. The cat's tail flicked, but she settled herself on my knees, tucking her paws underneath her.

'I had my first—'

'*En français, s'il te plaît!*'

'*Désolée . . .*' I began, in my fitful French, to tell her about our rehearsal, and gradually, she unbent, her mouth twitching when I described singing to Bernadette. Finally, repeating Sanjay's compliment, she gave a bark of laughter that made me sag with relief.

'Well,' she said, when I'd finished. 'That seems like an auspicious start, though those two sound like reprobates. What is this concert you're preparing for?'

I told her about the school and the fundraiser, and she huffed in disapproval. 'In all the years I taught in France, we never had one of those. The parents would have been far too busy. Whatever happened to children being seen and not heard?'

'They have to find the money somehow.'

Something seemed to switch off again, her brow darkening. She was looking tired and frail, her wrists birdlike, blue shadows under her eyes. 'Letty, have you eaten?'

She waved a bony hand. 'You fuss as much as my daughter; she's always arranging grocery deliveries. I'm perfectly all right. I had some cereal earlier.'

I jumped to my feet, pushing Aphra off. 'That's not enough. Let me make you something.'

She looked about to protest, then slumped in the chair, closing her eyes. 'Oh, do what you like,' she muttered.

Entering the kitchen, I eyed the cupboards dubiously, assuming they were full of ancient spices and tins from the Blitz. But they were well-stocked with oils and pastas, ham in the fridge, fresh bread and cheese. Seeing the copy of *Les Carottes* on the worktop, I set about making a croque monsieur, humming 'But Not for Me', spreading Dijon mustard on the untoasted sides of the bread, as Jean-Luc directed. In no time at all, I'd set a plate on a tray and carried it back to the living room. Letty was dozing, Aphra sitting bolt upright next to her chair, tail twitching.

'Letty, *c'est prêt.*' She opened her eyes as I set the tray on the little coffee table in front of her. For a second, she looked at the plate in silence, before turning to me with an odd expression.

'*C'est la recette,*' she said, and there was a wonder in her voice, not quite a question but something near it.

'*Oui,*' I replied. '*Une recette de Jean-Luc. Voulez-vous goûter?*'

She shot me a sideways glance as she picked up her knife and fork. '*Tu peux me tutoyer, tu sais.*'

An evolution; permission to move from the formal *vous* to the friendlier *tu*. '*Merci.*'

Letty ate, mopping her chin with a piece of kitchen roll, while I sat scratching Aphra's neck. After she'd finished, I collected the tray and took it back to the kitchen, washing up and returning everything to its place. When I went in to say good night, she was leaning on her stick by the money box, holding out a roll of notes with her other hand.

I backed away, shaking my head. 'It's not one of our days.'

She hobbled towards me. 'You may as well take it, I've got plenty.'

'That's not the point. I didn't come round for that. I came round . . . *pour discuter.*'

'That's what I pay you for,' she rasped, waving the notes.

'Give it to the school,' I found myself saying.

'What?'

I stopped moving away. 'Give it to Brownswood. Come to the concert. Come and see me, and Sanjay and Dylan.'

Her fingers curled around the notes. 'Your *ménage*?' Her mouth was twitching again.

'Why not? You said your daughter's always telling you to get out more.'

She sniffed. 'Will there be any alcoholic beverages on offer?'

'If Rosalind Gill has anything to do with it, then yes.'

Letty straightened up, her wrinkled face lifting in a devilish grin. 'Go on, then. I could do with *une sortie*.'

I held out my hand. 'It's a date.'

She threw the notes on the table, and gripped my fingers. 'I prefer to think of it as an assignation,' she said, and I could still hear her cackling as I climbed the stone steps back up to the street.

Chapter 23

$\mathcal{M}$y second rehearsal wasn't as successful as the first. Dylan suggested meeting at his flat in Stoke Newington, but Sanjay couldn't make it – he was teaching guitar at a private school in Hampstead and told us to get on without him. So it was just me and Dylan, which for some reason made me feel uncomfortable. *Il faut se détendre*, I told myself. *Relax, babe.* That was what Sid always said whenever he encouraged me to wear something more revealing. But thinking about Sid didn't help me relax.

Dylan's flat was supposedly above a music shop on the high street but, although I found the shop, there didn't seem to be any kind of entrance, and I started to think that maybe it was like Diagon Alley and you could only get in if you stroked the right bit of wall. Where was number 146? Where was Flat 9? There were no numbers on any doors, no buzzers to press. Eventually I had to ring him from the street.

'You're late.'

'Sorry, I'm outside, how do I get in?'

'Go into the shop and through to the back,' he said, and hung up.

I pushed open the door, which trilled merrily, announcing my entrance, but the premises seemed unoccupied apart from a few cellos leaning against chairs in a half-circle, as if a chamber group had upped sticks like the crew of the *Mary Celeste* abandoning ship. At the back, a doorway with a bead curtain led to a concrete staircase. On the first floor was Flat 9, with no sign of Flats 1 to 8. I knocked, feeling the heat building in my face.

Dylan opened the door, a mug of black coffee in his hand. He was as scruffy as ever, curly hair on end, wearing a pair of ripped jeans and a red fisherman's sweater that looked moth-eaten, with a greying white T-shirt underneath.

'Come in.' He stepped to one side, giving me a slightly mocking salute. Edging past him into a tatty living room dominated by a grand piano, I felt a thrill seeing the golden 'Bechstein' on the lid. But looking around, I suspected Dylan had spent all his money on the instrument and had none left for anything else. He seemed to have improvised all his furniture. Wooden crates for tables, what looked like a garden bench covered with cushions in place of a sofa, a bookcase made of planks of wood propped on more books. Bare floors that had seen better days, and beyond a bedroom that was simply a mattress on the floor covered with a rumpled duvet, and Bernadette, who was stretched out, snoring loudly. I looked away hastily.

'Welcome to Taylor Towers,' said Dylan. 'Do you want a coffee?'

'Thank you.'

He went through to a kitchenette separated from the living room by another bead curtain and returned bearing a second mug, which I took and sipped, pleased to discover it wasn't instant. There was an empty red wine bottle on a crate side table, and what looked like a photo of a couple embracing, but, moving closer, I was distracted by the dog, who'd realized there was a guest and had come through to investigate. She trotted over and sniffed me, wagging her tail, and I bent to pat her.

'Get out of it, Bernie,' said Dylan, cuffing her gently. He turned to me. 'Shall we get going?'

He sat down at the piano and we began some vocal warm-ups. I tried to open my throat, but it felt constricted.

'Right,' he said, when we'd ploughed through the exercises. 'Let's try one of the songs.'

He gave me the intro for 'Bewitched, Bothered and Bewildered', and I launched into it, but could feel my chest tightening as we went on. Eventually I dried completely, croaking my way to a halt at '*on the blink*'. I am on the blink, I thought, as Dylan stopped playing and raised his eyebrows.

'You need to loosen up,' he said, pulling over his bag of tobacco and some Rizlas. 'That was more like "Stiff, Stilted and Self-Conscious".'

'Sorry.' I wiped my hands on my jeans, feeling all of those things. 'Just a bit tired, that's all.'

Dylan shook his head as he packed and rolled. 'You've got to give your all to the interpretation – it's in the phrasing, the emotion. I can hear your throat closing up.'

'I'm doing my best.'

'That's the problem. You're not.' Dylan got to his feet and came round the piano to stand in front of me. 'You've got the voice, and you're relying on it to carry you through. But you need the heart as well.'

For a second, I stared at him, letting the implications of that sink in. Of course I wasn't giving my heart. It had been wrapped up and put away long ago, like a long-forgotten memento, and there was no way I could dig it out now. He was right though. How could I carry on, when my heart wasn't in it?

'Let's try again,' said Dylan, going back to the piano.

But it wasn't working. That stubborn nugget in my throat, closing me down. It was like going through one of Dylan's bead curtains, expecting an open space, but just discovering more and more bead curtains. I started to panic, trying to push through, not finding anything. There was nothing there. No open space, just . . . nothing.

'Come on,' shouted Dylan over the music. 'Let go! Open up!'

I tried, but my voice was thin and cold, covered in tissue paper, packed away. I stopped, so did Dylan, and we both stared at each other in mutual disappointment. He closed the lid of the piano.

'Sorry,' I said again.

'So am I,' replied Dylan. 'You're really good, but it feels like something's missing.' He bent to scratch Bernadette behind the ear; she had dried mud on her gleaming flank, tongue lolling, eyes closing at the caress. Nothing half-hearted about her.

Feeling deflated, I said goodbye and went back downstairs again, pushing my way through the clicking curtain into the empty shop, where the cellos sat waiting to be played. They were probably out of tune, like Dad's piano. That was what happened when you didn't use something; it stopped working.

Il faut se détendre. Somehow, I had to find a way.

Chapter 24

$\mathcal{S}$uddenly life seemed incredibly busy, my time taken up by shifts at Merhaba, my cleaning job, lessons with Roz, visiting Letty and trying not to neglect Em or Dad. Sometimes when I came home late, I'd find them watching TV together, her perched on the arm of his chair, holding his hand. One night, they'd left the chess set assembled on the table, a game half finished. She told me he'd got tired, but had taught her the French Defence. When I put away the pieces, I felt his eyes on me and looked up. Dad was in his dressing gown, on his way to bed, but he nodded at the box. 'It's a good opening,' he said, and it seemed to me there was something sprightly in his step as he went off to his room.

I asked Em to help me with my English notes, partly to spend time with her, and partly because she was as good a study partner as it was possible to find. When I looked at her frizzy head bent over my texts, I marvelled at this creature I had produced, who felt both fully mine, and a changeling. Interrogative and thorough, she pushed me almost as hard as

Roz, and I was touched by her enthusiasm for my studies, heard her telling Halima on the phone one day: 'My mum is doing an A level . . . Yes, as well as everything else.'

'Everything else' included rehearsals with Sanjay and Dylan, where I battled to loosen up, to find the depth of emotion in my delivery they were looking for. We didn't have long to prepare for the school show, which they both treated like a residency in Vegas.

'A performance is a performance,' said Sanjay. 'Whether you're in front of hundreds of thousands at Glastonbury, or just singing to your cat. That's what marks out a star – you give your all to both.' He sighed nostalgically, as if remembering that time, though he'd never played to hundreds of thousands at Glastonbury – a few thousand at most. Roz was pretty scathing about his old band, Four Thousand Holes, describing them as a one-hit wonder. But at least they had a hit. 'Once Bitten' was still played on the radio, and Roz had let slip that he earned royalties from it even now. Strange to be paid for something you didn't do any more.

One afternoon in early December, after a morning shift, I took the long back route for our rehearsal, wandering down the grander streets, wondering if the people inside those houses were happy. I never wanted to be rich; just wanted not to have to think about it. Presumably rich people would have to think about it, just from a different angle, whereas I wanted to occupy a sweet spot where we had neither too much nor too little, all the time. Somehow Roz and Sanjay managed to seem both rich *and* poor. They had their house, but it was a bit of a wreck, and Roz must have made a fortune as an actress, but now struggled on a teacher's salary.

Sanjay moaned that they hadn't had a holiday in years, but I'd glimpsed professional-looking recording equipment in their study on my way to the bathroom. No holidays, but recording equipment, and a *study*. Once again, I pictured me and Em in our own place, with space for a desk that looked out of a window onto trees. Taking my exams was supposed to bring us a step closer, but it still felt like an impossible dream.

Dylan, Sanjay and I met in the back room of the pub as usual. After rehearsing our tiny playlist, we tried out a new piece called 'Fine and Mellow', written by Billie Holiday – a bluesy torch song. Sanjay and Dylan couldn't agree on their approach; Dylan wanted to slow it right down and play it mournful, while Sanjay wanted to make it more upbeat.

'She's not really upset,' he said. 'She's just taking the piss.'

'How do you know?' returned Dylan. 'You used to hang out with Billie and Lester at the Trouville?'

'She goes on about his trousers, it's obviously not serious.'

'That's rich, coming from you.' Sanjay was wearing black harem pants with a black polo-neck. Roz had complained the other day that he dressed like a puppeteer.

'It'll be more interesting if we do something different, rather than going all moany. Have some fun.'

'What do you think?'

I was so busy enjoying their squabble, scratching Bernadette's neck, that I didn't realize they were talking to me. Flushing, I brushed dog hairs from my fingers and took a sip of water to buy some time.

'Delphine?' They were both looking at me so expectantly that I froze, unsure what to say. No one apart from Em had looked at me like that, wanting to hear my opinion, in so long. Not since those days in Clit Class, when Miss Challoner would point at me, eyebrows raised, while Adam leaned back in his chair, lazily smiling in my direction.

'Um . . . I think it's a bit of both. She's subverting a trope.'

Dylan swung round on the piano stool. 'What do you mean?'

'She's gaslighting him, saying it's his fault that she's behaving so badly. Which is a thing men usually do. Mentioning his trousers is the same – reducing him to what he's wearing. So, it sounds sad, but it's actually an accusation.'

'Right. So how do we play it?' Dylan's expression was intent, Sanjay nodding; it seemed I'd become the expert.

'I guess . . . sing it like a threat, but with a knowing wink.'

'Can you do that?'

'I can try.'

It didn't work in the end – too low-key for a school show, which demanded a foot-stomping beat and lyrics everyone knew. But in that moment, in that dingy pub room, singing a song in a new way, I experienced a feeling of satisfaction, my heart and mind in tune, fine and mellow. At the end, Dylan gave me a nod, and it was as if Miss Challoner had scrawled one of her 'A's on my essay. 'You're getting there,' he said.

'We should write a song together,' said Sanjay, through a mouthful of crisps. 'Subvert a few tripes of our own.'

'*Tropes*, dumbo.' Dylan whipped the crisp packet off him. 'He's right though.' He nodded at me. 'You do the lyrics, we'll do the tune.'

I felt like I might as well read my teenage diary out loud,

but it was sweet of them to suggest it. When we'd finished, they headed to the bar, summoning Frank and arguing over who was buying the round. Despite his royalties, Sanjay wasn't particularly eager to stump up and, as I pushed open the door, blasted by cold air, I turned to see him patting the pockets of his baggy pants as if he'd lost his wallet. Dylan caught my eye and grinned, before giving Sanjay the finger. I wished I could stay.

Instead, I'd agreed to go to Elise de Trafford's flat in Fitzrovia to do an extra clean. Her son had been staying, and she wanted it spick and span so she could come down to do her Christmas shopping. I caught the bus most of the way there, and walked the rest as darkness began to fall, admiring the festive lights that lined the streets and wondering if I could stretch to a new winter coat. The flat was in a portered block, but they knew me there, and the concierge nodded as I walked towards the lift. As ever, I felt a twinge of envy and resentment that anyone could own a flat in a building like this, let alone one they only used occasionally. Everything reeked of wealth and privilege – thick carpets that bounced underfoot; high, arching ceilings with ornate cornicing; the pure vanilla scent of regular maintenance.

But Elise had been a good friend of Maman's, and many of my mother's piano students had come via Mrs de Trafford's recommendation. Elise was one of the few people who knew what a state Dad was in, but didn't say anything about it, just handed me the keys to her pied-à-terre one day when she came to visit, saying that it would benefit from the odd going-over, and she'd happily pay for it. I'd been cleaning for her since I was seventeen, carrying Em in a sling and leaving her gurgling on one of the rugs I hoovered. In all that time, I'd rarely seen anyone there – occasionally Elise would breeze past on her way out, murmuring, 'Darling, must dash, thanks ever so' – but mostly it was just the occasional gushingly grateful text, and the relics of her activities. A silk scarf left on the rumpled bed, long blonde hairs in the bath, an inch of white wine in a bottle in the fridge. When Albert, her son, stayed over, the place was a tip – furniture upended, the kitchen sink full of dirty crockery, suspicious stains on the upholstery. I once found a faint dotted white line on the glass coffee table and wiped it quickly with a squirt of Mr Muscle. Fifty pounds a week meant I was willing to overlook a few misdemeanours.

That evening was different. I could tell as soon as I walked in, sensing a presence – and smelling it too. Booze, mostly, with an undercurrent of expensive cologne. But I didn't trust my instincts, as the flat was usually empty, so carried on through, to the bedroom, where I always started. There was a man in the bed, the broad expanse of his back bare, a shock of thick blond hair flopping on the pillow. I jumped back in alarm, stumbling against the wall, and he smiled sleepily, rolling over and not bothering to pull up the covers.

'Hi, sweetheart,' he murmured. 'You must be the divine Delphine. Enchanted. Albert de Trafford, at your service.'

'Sorry.' I backed away. 'I didn't know anyone was here.'

'Not to worry,' he said, heaving himself out of bed, slowly stretching and reaching for a towelling robe. 'Don't mind me, you get on. Do your . . . dusting, or whatever it is.'

I left the room and headed to the kitchen, rooting under the sink for the sprays and cloths. Scrubbing at the hob, I noted the empty bottles littering the marble worktops. No doubt there would be more white lines to wipe away. Maman never liked Albert: 'That boy is the kind who will catapult a cat.' She blamed Hugo, Elise's husband – they were now divorced, and she'd done very well out of the settlement; her own payment for his misdemeanours.

There were the Hugos and Alberts of this world, and there were the Sanjays and Dylans. I'd felt so comfortable in the pub with them earlier; now I felt threatened in a way I couldn't define. What was I afraid of? Albert wasn't going to do anything, was he? Just . . . look at me in that way. Speak to me in that way. The same way Sid had spoken to me that day in his flat, when he asked me to move in with him. Recalling that time made me scrub harder, as if to scour away the memory. I couldn't do this, couldn't stay a moment longer. Ripping off my rubber gloves, I whirled around to find Albert standing there, a lopsided grin on his face.

'Do you mind if I watch?' he said. 'I'll be no bother.'

'Sorry.' I edged past him. 'Got to go.'

'But you haven't finished!' He indicated the bottles disapprovingly. 'It's still all . . . *dirty*.' Running a finger along the worktop, he licked it. 'Filthy.'

I grabbed my coat and bag, and hurried towards the door. 'Sorry, I don't feel well.'

'I could rub it better.'

'I'll be back next week,' I muttered, pulling the door shut behind me.

On the bus on the way home, still breathing hard, I held my phone in my hand trying to pluck up the courage to text Elise and say I wouldn't work for her any more. But I couldn't do it, I still needed that job, even if it involved dealing with Albert. I wasn't rich enough not to think about it. Christmas was coming up, we had bills to pay. I put my phone in my bag and stared out the window, letting the lights and bustling crowds bring my heart rate back to normal. At least I'd be home by the time Em got back from her fast-track class.

Fifty pounds a week. I'd just have to scrub the incident from my mind, and carry on.

Chapter 25

'I want to go to Cambridge,' said Em, when we were having breakfast before school.

Chewing on a piece of toast, I stared at her. 'Right. Well, you can do anything you want to, honey. If Mrs Gill thinks you could apply there one day, that's great. We could—'

'No,' said Em. 'I mean, there's a school trip. To see the colleges.'

'OK.' I swallowed a mouthful. 'But . . . aren't you a bit young for that? You've got a while before you need to think about that sort of thing.' Maybe Roz thought Em was some sort of child prodigy, the ones you read about in *The Times* who went to study maths at Balliol aged thirteen, before an inevitable nervous breakdown.

'Yeah,' agreed Em. 'But I asked Mrs Gill if I could go and she said it was fine as long as you gave permission. You need to sign a form, and pay for a train ticket.'

'*Why* do you want to go?'

She gazed at me innocently. 'To further my education and enrich my soul.'

'If it doesn't clash with work, then I could come with you.' Her mouth twisted. 'If you want to.'

Em's lack of enthusiasm strengthened my resolve. We could stretch to two train tickets. Maybe I should see some of those oak-panelled libraries for myself. And – another sly image slid in – an office in King's College, with the name 'Dr Adam Terris' on it . . . I stood abruptly, picking up my plate and going to rinse it under the tap, letting the water get too hot as a penance. I should go with Em, for no other reason than making sure she didn't try to find that office. We never talked about him, but her curiosity and detective work would have led her to various conclusions, not always good ones.

After work, where Selassie gave his enthusiastic approval to my shift-swap – '*Shikor'ay*, of course! One day I will open a Merhaba there!' – I texted Roz:

Can I come to Cambridge with Em?

She responded instantly: Why, thinking of applying?

Those libraries, the blessed silence of industry and en-deavour. Maybe.

Maman went to the Sorbonne. Letty went to Oxford. Dad didn't go anywhere. I caught the bus back home, thinking about Letty and my father. Both widowed, adored their spouses, left behind with their daughters. And the French connection, of course. But while Letty had somehow retained her *joie de vivre*, her internal fire, my father had allowed himself to be put out, not even a spark of joy in the embers. He'd always been a quiet, gentle man, but when Maman was around he'd had so much swing about him – rhythm and vitality oozing from every pore. Now you could click your fingers in his face and he'd barely register. I wouldn't even have described it as depression, exactly; just an absence of any emotion at all, like it had drained out of him and left nothing behind. Perhaps some people's grasp on happiness was fragile, easily shaken, while others had sturdier roots.

Unlocking the door, I fished that week's DVDs out of my bag and went through to the living room. I'd got Dad *The Theory of Everything*, a film about Stephen Hawking, because long ago he used to tell me a story about black holes; a boy called Zenvo who used them to time travel and have intergalactic adventures. It made me think that at one time my father must have been interested in physics. After dinner – sausage and potato gratin, inspired by Jean-Luc's book – Em went to do her homework and I sat on the arm of Dad's chair to watch the film with him. Seeing the Cambridge colleges in the background, I pointed to the television.

'Em and I are going there on a school trip.'

He nodded. I didn't expect a reply; it was just something to say. But then, eyes fixed on the screen, he said: 'We went there, didn't we? You, me . . . and JoJo.'

It was so unexpected that it was a second before I could reply. Dad *never* mentioned my mother. It was too painful for him, too much to say her name, as if the very utterance could suck him further into his black hole and shred him to spaghetti. Also, I didn't remember us ever going to Cambridge.

'Did we? When?' I held my breath, wondering if the brief flash of attention would wane, wanting to cup my hands around the candle, keep it aflame.

One finger tapped the arm of his chair, like he was counting. 'You'd have been . . . six or seven. We had a day trip.'

I said, very softly: 'What did we do?'

But the memory seemed to stall; he blinked and sank a little in the chair. 'I don't remember. It was a long time ago.' And he was gone again, back to the film, back to his other dimension. I watched the rest of it with him, and when I squeezed into bed with Em, I was still thinking about Professor Hawking's rousing speech: 'However bad life may seem, there is always something you can do.'

Maybe there was something. A tiny, flickering star in the cosmos that hadn't yet been swallowed into the black. We just had to work out how to keep it burning.

Chapter 26

'So, the question remains: why would Margaret consider marrying someone like Henry? Anyone?'

Year Eleven Clit Class was deep in *Howards End*, mostly united in hatred of the Wilcoxes and admiration for the Schlegels – apart from Adam, who had a weird fondness for Henry Wilcox and kept defending him. I was finding myself despising Margaret Schlegel more and more – for accepting the proposal, denying Leonard a job, overlooking her sister. Henry was just an upper-class fool, but Margaret should have known better. Mr North was looking towards me, but I didn't feel like responding, as I'd get slapped down by Isabelle Saint, who had decided she *was* Margaret and would defend her to the death.

Several months into the class, we'd cleaved into a kind of unit – me, Adam, Lorenzo, Isabelle and the twins, Charlie and Alfie, who were relentlessly flippant, which lulled you into thinking they were thick. Now resigned to the swot label, we tended to hang out in the park at lunchtimes, having self-consciously intellectual conversations. Occasionally

Sheba and Marni would sweep past, flicking us slightly hostile glances, and I'd immediately peel off and catch up with them, trying to clutch the threads of our friendship. But my relationship with Adam had unbalanced everything; somehow four was an odd number, and we'd divided. When I reached them, they'd make a snide remark about love's young dream, but it was a different kind of sarcasm now; there was steel in it. I'd wander back, hoping I wasn't wrong to put all my eggs in this basket, hoping this new group was the beginning of something, rather than the end.

The class was better when Miss Challoner taught it – she was brusque, impatient but, when you arrived at the point she wanted, her nod was like a benediction. Her praise was hard to come by, so I valued it more, whereas Mr North seemed to throw out compliments all over the place, to the extent that sometimes I didn't answer his questions, to dodge the inevitable accolade. He was still looking at me, though, so reluctantly I offered a tepid reading.

'Maybe she's insecure.'

He raised his eyebrows. 'In what way?'

'There's that thing, isn't there, to tell beautiful people they're clever and clever people they're beautiful. Margaret's clever, but she knows Henry doesn't care about that. His proposal suggests she's beautiful.'

'How does she know he doesn't care about her being clever?'

'Because she's a woman. Her cleverness doesn't count for him.'

He nodded, a smile hovering about his mouth.

145

'A persuasive argument. Which would you rather be: clever or beautiful?'

I wrinkled my nose. 'I'd rather be rich.'

Everyone laughed, including Mr North, so I could ignore the fact I didn't feel comfortable answering the question. Only the Schlegels and Wilcoxes got to debate that sort of thing, while the Basts starved. When the bell went, I gathered my books and prepared to leave with Adam, heading to the park to hang out at our bench and whisper our plans for another night together, but Mr North called me back.

'Delphine, a moment?'

I stopped in front of him, signalling to Adam that I'd join him later, and waited to hear what my teacher had to say.

'Your last essay, on *Othello*, was excellent. Really outstanding. I just wanted to ask: you're planning on taking English Literature for A level, aren't you?'

Clasping my books to my chest, I nodded.

He looked down, steepling his fingers on the desk. 'Well, in that case, I really think we should be planning for Oxbridge entrance. Better to get started early. Do you have a preference for either university?'

My breathing slowed, a shaft of sunlight falling between us onto the scuffed parquet. Oxbridge. Another thing that only Schlegels and Wilcoxes discussed. Adam talked about it all the time, was planning on applying to King's; his mum and dad were talking to a specialist tutor who prepped you for interviews.

'I . . . I don't know. Never really thought about it.'

He cleared his throat. 'Well, you should. I can help you, if you like. I'm an Oxford alumnus, as it happens, but I have contacts at both places.'

'Right. I'll . . . think about it, then.'

'Do. And why don't you have this, I think you might like it.'

He held out a copy of *A Room of One's Own* and I took it, pressing it to my chest along with the others.

'Thank you.'

He smiled. 'For what it's worth, you're both.'

I walked to the park, shivering in the shifting winds.

Chapter 27

*O*n the day of Brownswood's talent show, I woke with the beginnings of a cold, probably due to spending a day earlier that week in the school, using one of their music rooms for a final rehearsal. We recruited a couple of brass players, a Year Ten drummer called Dom Seddon who was the Ringo Starr of Stoke Newington, and a backing singer called Michelle who never stopped chewing gum, but had a decent voice. All those teenagers milling around with their germs and half-hearted hygiene; I kept sneezing as I made myself a coffee, trying to ignore the prickle in my throat and the deeper, darker one in my spine. Now the day had come, I was terrified.

Roz hadn't helped. We'd met the previous afternoon for a lesson in Merhaba, and she'd torn my first essay to shreds.

'It may as well be bullet points,' she said, waving it in my face. 'Where's the development of your argument? You just say one thing after another without building on anything. And there's no conclusion – you just tail off.'

We'd come a long way since Mr North used to describe my

essays as 'outstanding'. A long way backwards. I'd obviously lost all powers of perception in the intervening years, along with other things.

'Sorry.' Feeling crushed, I retrieved the papers she'd thrown on the table, folding them to hide the pitiful content. 'I'll try again.' The essay had been finished late at night, after a shift, and the next one would be, too. It was hard to dredge up compelling literary arguments when your eyes felt like they were full of grit and the heating had long since gone off. But Roz had moved on and was attacking a slice of panettone – made by me, now my dough always rose. At least my kneading skills had improved.

'So,' Roz continued, through a mouthful. 'How's this band of yours going? Jay won't tell me anything, just says it's all fine. Which doesn't fill me with confidence – his "fine" usually means he hasn't thought about it at all.'

'It's going OK. Sanjay's been writing songs.'

She swallowed and stared at me. 'Really? For the show?'

I shook my head. 'We're doing covers for the show. But Jay and I have been throwing around some ideas.' Initially I'd been embarrassed, but Dylan and Sanjay had been so encouraging, and it had been fun, writing lyrics, watching them play around with a tune. Now, with Roz's wide eyes on me, I felt silly. What had we been thinking, trying to write a song?

'That's . . . great,' she said eventually. 'He hasn't written anything in ages. He must be feeling better.'

'What do you mean?'

She didn't answer for a second, picking up a rogue raisin and eating it. 'Jay was really gutted when his band fell apart.

Wanted to keep going, didn't want to give up on it. He got very depressed.'

'*Sanjay?*' He'd always seemed so cheery to me, everything very much 'fine'.

'Yeah. There were days when he wouldn't get out of bed.' She sounded faintly disapproving. When you were the one holding it all together, sometimes it was hard to have sympathy for the one who had let go. 'So this is a good sign. As long as they're not crap songs, of course.'

As I got dressed for my shift that morning, I wondered if I would only ever write crap essays, Jay would write crap songs, and if the whole thing had been a crap idea.

'Good luck, Mum,' said Em, poking her head round the door on her way out.

'Thanks,' I said, ruffling her hair. 'Will you be in the audience?'

'Yeah,' she said. 'Halima and I are going. We're helping set up beforehand. But if you're rubbish, then I'll pretend I don't know you.'

'Right.'

We *were* going to be rubbish. I'd never sung in public before; we'd had only a few weeks to prepare, and, as the day wore on and my cold took hold, I started to feel rough, full of snot and foreboding. Selassie sent me home early, telling me to gargle hot lemon and honey: 'We need you well, not coughing into the zigni.'

After going back to the flat to lie down for an hour, I wearily got myself out of bed and dressed in my performance gear – black jeans and a sparkly black top. It was wide-necked, falling off at the shoulder, and I kept hearing Sid, my ex's, voice in my head: '*Relax, babe.*' I couldn't relax; part of me wished I was back at Gio's, before all this began, when my sphere was smaller and simpler. '*Sometimes, you've just got to put yourself out there, even if it all goes tits-up,*' Dylan had said. But what if it *did* go tits-up? My hands shook as I put on my mascara, for once layering on make-up as if it could mask my fear.

When I went to deliver Dad an early dinner, he looked up and took in my outfit.

'You got your show tonight,' he said. 'Your band.'

He remembered. I felt tears starting, and dabbed at them with my tissue. 'Yes,' I whispered. 'At the school.'

'Nervous?'

I nodded, a lump in my sore throat.

Dad reached for the tray and settled it on his lap. 'Thank you, FiFi. You have a good time now.' He took a bite of his chicken goujon. 'Remember what Billie Holiday said: "You have to smile to keep from throwing up."'

It was a dark, drizzly December night, but the school was all lit up, a hive of activity, everyone bustling around. Roz was painting a backdrop laid out on the floor, hair pinned up with a pen, jeans covered in splodges, a half-eaten bacon sandwich on the chair next to her. I approached her warily, still stung by her criticism of my essay. 'I'm so hungover,' she said, reaching for the sandwich. 'Drank a bottle of wine when I got home last night. Inhaled it. It didn't touch the sides.'

'On your own?'

She chewed and said thickly, 'No, Jay joined me.'

'Does that mean he's ill as well?' If one of us was sick and another hungover, it didn't bode too well for our performance.

But Sanjay appeared, looking as chipper as ever, his guitar slung over his back. 'We need a name!'

'A what?'

'A name for the band. So far I've got "Delf and the Dee-Jays". Dylan – Dee, Sanjay – Jay. And you're Delf. Geddit?'

'Just about,' I murmured.

'No.' We all turned to see Dylan wander in, as dishevelled as ever. 'That's *rwtsh*.' I didn't know what that meant, but it didn't sound good. His eyes rested on me for a second, and I pulled up the shoulder of my top.

'Got any better ideas?' snapped Sanjay.

He stroked his chin. 'No,' he said, eventually.

'The Tiny Pennies,' I found myself saying. One of those moments when something slid out of my mouth, unbidden. Dylan frowned. 'Why?'

I shifted uneasily, rubbing my bare shoulder. 'It's an Amy Winehouse lyric. Don't know why I thought of it.' My voice sounded weak and croaky.

'I like it. It's different.'

'It's not as good as Delf and the Dee-Jays,' began Sanjay, but Roz cut him off, standing up and poking him in the midriff.

'It'll do,' she said crisply. 'Just go backstage and get yourselves ready. I don't want you milling round here.'

We trooped up the steps to the stage, dodging scenery, and made our way to the back, where various students were having last-minute rehearsals. A girl was sobbing as one of the teachers patted her shoulder awkwardly. Roz had followed us and was now up a ladder, hanging the still-drying backdrop, shouting at people to help her. I cleared my throat and blew my nose, hoping the tissue wouldn't rub off my make-up.

'Here.' Sanjay held out his hand. Cupped in his palm were two little pills. I looked up at him in alarm. 'Relax, it's paracetamol,' he said, rolling his eyes and pulling a hip flask from his back pocket. 'But I've got a little sharpener, if you want.' He took a swig and offered it to me.

'No, thanks.' I took the painkillers and chucked them down my throat.

Peeking out from the wings, I noticed the lights in the hall had dimmed and parents were filing in. I caught a glimpse of Letty arriving with her daughter and ducked out again before she could see me. She'd come, just as she'd said she would. My hands were shaking so much I had no idea how I would hold the microphone.

'Hey.' Miss Challoner – Mrs Boleyn – appeared in front of me, dressed in a smart black suit with a sprig of heather in her lapel. Heather for luck. It still made me feel strange to see her after all these years, like being a teenager again.

'Hi.'

'Thanks for doing this. It's so great to have parents supporting the school. And teachers.' She nodded at Dylan, who elbowed Sanjay to put away his hip flask.

'Right, I'd better get out there and announce this bloody thing,' she continued, moving past us towards the stage.

I watched her walk out, to whistles and whoops, and thought back to the pep talk she'd given us before we'd taken our GCSEs. All through Clit Class, we'd got used to her faint praise, coming to expect nothing more. She was the Jean-Luc Riche of the academic world, and from her an 'adequate' was like getting an A grade. But the day before our first exam, she got us together and sat on her desk, leaning into a speech I've never forgotten:

'Let me tell you something. Teaching is like a relay race. Knowledge is the baton, and it's your job to pass it on to the next runner. But you have to trust they'll know what to do with it. And guess what? I trust you guys. You've got this. It has been my joy and privilege to teach you all over the last two years. Whatever happens in those exams, you should know that each and every one of you is a star. I'm rooting for you and, no matter what the outcome, I'm proud to be in the race with you.'

Everyone needs a teacher who says that; who trusts you to take the baton. I carried it, and it carried me through those exams, and, in the end, when I got straight A grades, none of them mattered as much as those words. By the time I got my results, I was ruined, already planning my escape, so it made me uneasy to see her again, but it also reminded me that, once upon a time, I'd been part of that golden group, a constellation of stars. Could I be a star again?

Standing there in the wings, I heard Dylan's voice in my ear. 'You OK?'

I nodded, and we stood, side by side, watching Mrs Boleyn finish her welcome speech. As she introduced the first act, he leaned towards me and whispered: 'Don't worry, if it all goes tits-up, we can move to New Zealand and let Bernadette forage for scraps. We'll be fine. Just breathe.'

The lights went down, the audience started to clap, and the show began.

Chapter 28

There were several acts on before us. I checked the running order pinned to a wall backstage, counting them off, getting more anxious as we worked our way down the list. Despite telling myself this was just a school show, not *Britain's Got Talent*, the image of stony-faced teenagers and their parents in the audience made me dizzy with nerves. Somewhere out there, Letty was in the crowd. Would The Tiny Pennies raise one of her devilish smiles? Could I make her proud?

Trying to control my breathing and ignore the tickle in my throat, I watched the other performances. There was a girl from Year Twelve who Em had told me was in the semi-final of Young Musician of the Year. She played a violin solo with huge verve, attacking each note, long hair flicking with every jerk of her arm. Then Brownswood's very own barbershop quartet shuffled out, four teachers in boaters who sang with tremendous enthusiasm but very little ability. Dylan and Sanjay were weeping with laughter, holding each other up. I hissed at them to shut up, and gave myself a coughing fit.

The girl who'd been sobbing backstage earlier was now gargling and rolling her neck, watched by a boy leaning on a broom. They sauntered on stage together and sang 'Why Can't You Behave?' from *Kiss Me, Kate*. At least, the girl sang, while the boy swept the floor and looked sulky. At one point, he jabbed the handle of his broom into the backdrop, which was a painted city skyline.

'Bella and Jake,' whispered Roz. 'I've been helping them with their routine. Bella's got the co-ordination of a baby giraffe. She's overdone the fake tan, looks like Donald Trump under those lights. Jake wanted to split up with her just before the show, I had to bung him a tenner not to dump her.'

'It's a performance worthy of Broadway,' said Dylan, deadpan. 'Hammersmith Broadway.'

'Screw you, Bootleg Blues Brothers,' returned Roz. 'Right, I'm going to lose myself in the crowds. Don't be shit.' But as she passed Sanjay, she stroked his arm in a little gesture that made my eyes fill with tears.

We then had to sit through the school orchestra murdering Tchaikovsky's 'Russian Dance', valiantly conducted by the Head of Music, Mr Griffiths. They couldn't manage a cracking pace, more of a walking one, and Dylan and Sanjay started to giggle again, shoving each other and attempting a Cossack dance. They got into such a state that I had to shush them, and we didn't notice the performance finishing, Mrs Boleyn marching on again for another announcement, as the team of stagehands noisily moved chairs, bashing Roz's backdrop, which had now come loose at one side.

'And now, for one night only, we have a treat for you all.

Brownswood's very own house band featuring one of our teachers, Mr Taylor, the mother of one of our students and former student herself, Delphine Jones, and finally Mrs Gill's husband, the famous Jay Gill! Ladies and gentlemen, and variations thereupon, I give you . . . The Tinny Pennies!'

'Fuck, that's us,' yelped Sanjay, taking another swig and hastily picking up his guitar.

'TINY Pennies,' said Dylan. 'Tiny.' He shot me a smile and I tried to return it, remembering Dad's advice. Smile, so you don't throw up.

We walked on stage to dutiful applause, Roz in the audience, clapping frantically, her hair falling down from its topknot in her forced enthusiasm. Along the row, Em, her hand over her face as other students leaned towards her, shoving her and laughing. Her friend Halima was in hysterics next to her. I reached the microphone, fumbling with it and flinching at the feedback, as someone wolf-whistled in the crowd. Dylan settled at the piano, scowling as he cracked his knuckles. Dom sat down at his drums casually – he was quite cool for a fifteen-year-old – and Michelle stood behind me, chewing. The brass players looked completely terrified, their instruments far too big for them.

I adjusted the microphone with shaking hands, glancing towards Sanjay for guidance. He leaned towards his own mic. You could tell he'd done this for a living, or perhaps he'd just been sharpened by whatever was in his hip flask.

'Yo, Hackney!' he yelled, and was met with a muted cheer. 'This first song is called "Rolling in the Deep". You might know it.'

A couple of whoops suggested people did, but the jury was still out, the audience regarding us with faint distrust and, in Roz's case, high anxiety. What were we doing? That sea of blank faces, all expecting something from me, and, for a second, I couldn't remember the opening line. I turned back, caught Sanjay's eye and he winked, Dylan nodded, and I took a deep breath, feeling that bond of rehearsals, of creating something, being in a gang.

Sanjay began to strum, and I tapped my foot to the beat, ready to show them what we were made of . . . My big moment, the culmination of a corner turned – new job, new studies, new friends, new band. A fire starting in my heart, bringing me out of the dark. It was all coming together. I opened my mouth . . .

And nothing came out. Just a croak, not even a recognizable word. I took another breath, feeling a strange whistle in my throat, like it had divided in two. Sanjay's fingers stilled for a second, then began the riff again – the insistent, driving rhythm that opened the song. We'd chosen a foot-stomper to get everyone going. It was fine, just a hiccup, we could do this. I opened my mouth.

Nothing. Just the rasp of a voice that had given up. That coughing fit, earlier. '*There's a fire,*' I whispered. But there wasn't. Not even a spark.

My head began to pound, lights to dance in front of my eyes. I blinked and swayed behind the microphone, grabbing hold of it to stop myself falling. An uneasy rustle ran through the audience, people shifting in their seats, exchanging glances. I caught sight of Em, her face fixed in horror, Halima next to her looking appalled, then turned to see Dylan staring up at me from the piano.

'What's wrong?' he mouthed. I shook my head, setting

off a meteor shower across my temples. Pinching the throbbing bridge of my nose, I smiled bitterly. At least I wasn't throwing up.

There was a disturbance off stage, and one of the teachers ran on with a glass of water. Grabbing it gratefully, I gulped, as Sanjay stepped forward again.

'Be right with you, Hackney!'

But now we'd lost them. Most of the audience were chatting and laughing; some of them had got up and wandered over to the makeshift bar in the corner, manned by two sixth-formers who were doing a roaring trade. Putting the glass down on top of the piano, I gave a hacking cough and winced apologetically at Dylan.

He shrugged. 'Let's give it another go.'

The cough seemed to have loosened something, so I turned back to the crowd, my face bright red with embarrassment and the effort of not losing it completely. Sanjay began to strum, and we started again.

We got through most of it. That was the best anyone could say. I managed to croak out the words of the song in roughly the right order, some of the parents deigned to leave the bar and sit back down, our drummer kept the beat going, the brass players did their thing. But it was a pale approximation of the performance we'd produced in rehearsals and it was hard not to burst into tears when I saw Roz in the audience, desperately trying to jig along like she was enjoying herself. I didn't dare look at Em, or Letty.

As we got to the last chorus, and I thought that at least it was nearly over and I could escape and maybe drain Sanjay's hip flask, I felt a thistle build in my throat.

A huge, mucus-filled cough coming, nothing I could do about it. Waving frantically at Michelle, I gestured her to come forwards and take my place. With a bound, she snatched the microphone and took over the lead vocals, as I stepped back, hunched over and heaved up my guts. Not throwing up, exactly, but not far off. I staggered towards the wings, my vision blurring and refocusing, while Michelle bellowed out the last line and Roz's backdrop finally gave up the ghost, fluttering gently to the floor to reveal two students passionately snogging behind us. Dom the drummer gave a final crash of the cymbals, Michelle punched the air, spitting her chewing gum to the floor, and Dylan bent forwards to rest his head gently on the piano keys, producing a jangled discord. Sanjay took a huge swig from his flask and leaned towards his microphone as Mrs Boleyn angrily chivvied her wanton pupils out of sight.

'We've been The Tinny Pennies,' he said, in the sombre tone of an undertaker. 'You've been . . . Hackney. Thank you and good night.'

Chapter 29

*T*he bungee rope always pulled you back, no matter how hard you tried. Just when you thought you were getting somewhere – *whoosh*. Back where you started.

With my father barely communicating, arguments were rare, but during the time when I was going out with Sid, there was a day when it all boiled over. All because I threw away Dad's daffodils. *My* daffodils.

I'd found them, wilting and half-price, resting limply in a bucket in the supermarket up from Giovanni's. I was working there by then, already regretting it. Out of the Starbucks frying pan into Gio's fire, but there was nothing to be done, because it wasn't as if there were any other options. I'd taken to passing through the shop on my way home to see what was on offer, and had bought daffodils to cheer myself up, because they reminded me of my mother. Dad used to bring them home and she would put them in jam jars everywhere. Once, she danced round the kitchen with him, one tucked behind her ear.

Dad didn't comment when I arranged them in our chipped

vase, and gradually they withered on the fold-down table. That morning, clearing up the breakfast while Em got ready for school, I casually chucked them in the bin along with an empty cereal packet, and when I went back into the living room, he was staring at me from his chair, his eyes unusually bright.

'Delphine,' he said. I should have known then that he was annoyed because he usually only ever called me FiFi.

'What is it?'

'Why did you throw them away?' He pointed towards the table, the vase filled with sludge-green water.

'They were dead,' I said.

His brow darkened. 'Don't say that. They were good. You could have left them.' His bony fingers gripped the arms of his chair.

It was baffling, because he never really showed any emotion, never cared about anything, and here we were arguing over some old daffodils.

'Sorry,' I said. 'But they would have started to smell.'

Then he did the weirdest thing. He got to his feet, walked across the room and knocked over the vase, sending stagnant water pouring across the table. We both stared at it for a second, as it dripped between the slats and onto the threadbare carpet underneath.

'What did you do that for?' I reached for a tea towel on the back of the chair and began to mop up.

He seemed to shrink into himself, hands shaking, a sheen of sweat on his forehead. 'You shouldn't have got rid of them,' he muttered, shuffling off to his chair. 'You shouldn't have done it.'

'I bought them, they were mine to throw away.' Still

swabbing, my back to him. When I turned around again, he was crying, one hand over his eyes. 'Oh, Daddy.'

He sank into his chair, head bowed, and I went over to him, but didn't know what to do or say. All I could think was that I had to get out, into the fresh air, away from this pit of decay. There was the smell of putrid flower water on my fingers, the wet stain still soaking the carpet. Eventually, he fished in his pocket for a handkerchief, blew his nose and arranged his blanket over his knees. Gone again.

'Would you like a cup of tea?' I twisted my fingers in the towel, glancing between him and the upturned vessel.

He nodded absently. 'That'd be nice, FiFi. If you've got time.'

On my way to the kitchen, I silently swiped the vase to clear the crime scene, then tidied up and made him some tea, trying to think how I could make it all better. Pouring the milk, I had an idea and, without thinking about it, went through to hand him the cup, carrying on towards the piano. Sitting down, I lifted the lid and began to play the first thing that came into my head, which – of all things – was 'Solitude'. *Why?* It was the worst song I could have chosen. I didn't sing, but of course he knew the words, and would be hearing them in his head as I played those tinny keys – '*sit in my chair, filled with despair . . .*' Maybe I didn't want to make it better at all. Maybe there was part of me that wanted to rile him, push him over the edge so that in turn he would push me. I was only a few bars in when he started to shout.

'No, no, no!'

I turned, the notes faltering, and saw he had his hands over his ears.

'You don't play! Get out, get out!'

Em came out of our room with her school bag over her shoulder, and I got up from the piano, closing the lid with a bang.

'What's going on?'

'Come on, let's go.'

As we left, I didn't feel any sympathy for him, just rage. How dare he stop me throwing away the flowers I'd bought, bloody well cleaning up after him like I had for the past thirteen years? Half my life spent caring for him, tiptoeing round, preserving his still waters so he could rot in them. And what did I get in return? He was never there for me, when Maman died, or when all the stuff with Adam happened, or when I found myself pregnant aged sixteen and had to leave school, forget all my dreams and ambitions. No one to turn to, no hope. It wasn't good for Em to grow up in this environment. I hustled her out of the flat, stonewalling her questions, simmering all the way to her primary school.

By that point, Sid and I had been together a while and he'd recently given me the keys to his flat in Stroud Green. Said he was hardly ever around and I could crash there when I felt like it. He knew that living with Dad sometimes got me down. There was no way I'd take him up on it, of course, but the fact he'd offered was touching, and made me feel like our relationship had gone up a level. In the end, I did go round occasionally, after a long shift, or if Dad was particularly bad, just to clear my head for a couple of hours. Sitting up there on my own, looking out onto the treetops, it felt like I'd escaped my life for a moment. Sometimes I'd do a bit of cleaning, or leave some flowers when Sid was coming down. But mostly I just sat there, in my own space, dreaming of a place like that for me and Em.

We carried on for a while, with me staying over when he was in town, occasionally going to a club with him. Sid ran an agency that provided security services – hired out bouncers, basically. His agency was called Musclebound, which struck me as cartoonish, but Sid was very proud of his business and liked to talk about it. When we first went out, he used to take me to one of his Dalston clubs, Omega, which he pronounced 'Oo-MEE-gah'. It was very cold, and the music always seemed to hover around one note.

Hanging out there occasionally, I'd got to know some of the bouncers who nodded me in. They were a nice bunch, and I tried not to think about the fact that they so obviously disliked their boss. He didn't seem like a bad employer, maybe a bit gruff sometimes, but I didn't understand the flared nostrils, narrowed eyes and grimaces behind his back. Perhaps it was the general rough and tumble of club life – security wasn't exactly a civilized profession, anything but secure. One of the guys – Tony – told me that a bouncer who had to use his fists was a poor one, but they often seemed to come out, if only as a threat. Was that why I was interested in Sid, seeing him as protection? He didn't use his fists, but he had them at his disposal, and everyone knew it. Whenever we were out, he was attentive, vigilant; no one dared approach. It was like having a bodyguard and still, after all those years, I felt I needed one. To protect me from others, and myself.

But when we were alone, things changed. Then I felt exposed, vulnerable. I tried to work through it, thinking it would get better as we got to know each other, but every time we were together there was something inside me hardening, little by little. I fought against it – this was natural after what had happened, I just had to '*Relax, babe*' and wait for the thaw – but it didn't come. So often I was on the point of telling him it wasn't working, but something stopped me. Every now and then he'd wrongfoot me, do something wonderful and thoughtful that made me second-guess myself. Like the keys, or the copy of *Astrophil and Stella* he bought me, to remind me of him.

It wasn't just gifts, him spending money on me. Another time, we had dinner at the club before it opened and he arranged for different music to be played. Instead of the usual thumping drum and bass, it was Ella Fitzgerald singing – then Louis Armstrong, Billie, Dinah, Frank, Nina. All my old friends, come to serenade me. I looked at him across the table, and he smiled and raised his glass, and, in that moment, it felt like he could be, if not The One, then The Nearly. And really, what more could I hope for, considering everything that had gone before? Afterwards Tony told me that he'd made the playlist, but it had been Sid's idea, at least. Sid knew me, what I liked, what I needed. So, we struggled on, a step forward, two steps back, and sometimes it was OK – fun, even – and sometimes it wasn't, but I would muddle through it, sit in Sid's flat on my own in the afternoons to clear my head until it was empty again. It became a place of refuge, an escape, and although it was his, I began to think of it as mine.

The evening after my row with Dad, we were having dinner there, our wine glasses glinting in the candlelight. Sid's was empty, and mine was full – I poured a glass to keep him company, and would discreetly tip it back into the bottle when he wasn't looking. We were eating pork chops, cooked just the way he liked, and he'd eaten it all, smacking his lips, in between telling me about his new plan to start a women's wing of his agency, providing female bouncers for discerning establishments. He was saying something about them having to be attractive, but I wasn't really listening, because I was thinking about the argument, those stupid daffodils. I swilled the wine around in my glass. It smelled sour and vinegary.

'What's wrong, doll? You seem down.'

'Just a fight with my dad.' I rarely talked about my home life, as Sid never seemed that interested. But that night he reached for my hand across the table.

'Babe. Anything I can do?'

'Nothing. It'll be fine.'

He leaned back, pushing his plate away. 'You know, you could always move in here.'

Laughing, I got to my feet to clear the table.

'I'm serious.' He lit a cigarette, shaking the match and blowing out a long plume of smoke. 'You need your own place.'

'This is *your* place.' I stacked the plates and the cutlery and carried them to the sink. 'And I have Em to think of.' He hardly ever mentioned her, and I sometimes felt I had to remind him of her existence, though at least he didn't call her Milly any more.

'It could be yours,' he said. 'Yours and Em's.'

My hands stilled in the washing-up water. 'What do you mean?'

He smiled through the smoke. 'You could have it. Both of

you. There are two bedrooms. What's that book you like? *A Room of One's Own.*' He said it in a kind of mocking, half-embarrassed way. 'You could have a room of your own.' I'd told him that Em and I had to share my bedroom in Dad's flat. He remembered that, and he remembered I liked Virginia Woolf.

'But this is your flat.'

He flicked ash onto a saucer. 'I can stay here, can't I? When I'm around. The rest of the time it's empty. May as well use it.'

Those afternoons I'd spent, an hour here and there, watching the sun streaming through the fourth-floor window, the trees shifting in the breeze. My respite.

'I'm sorry. It's a lovely offer, but we couldn't afford it.' A two-bedroom flat round there would cost a fortune in rent, and there was no way I could find that kind of money – not on the salary Gio paid me.

'No need to pay market value. We could come to . . . an arrangement.' He winked, and I felt my stomach churn, but also something else – a twinge of excitement. A flat of our own. Just me, and my daughter. And Sid, occasionally. Not often. Now and then.

I forced myself to laugh. 'Would you need a deposit?'

He shook his head, smiling. 'But I might need something . . .' Standing up, he jerked his head towards the bedroom. His bedroom. My bedroom?

As he pulled me through the flat – my flat, my refuge, a room of my own – I told myself that this was a good development, an evolution. But as his mouth met mine and my lips parted, open to this new opportunity, I felt a sudden, heaving nausea that I could ever consider such an idea. I didn't love him; didn't even like him that much. He wasn't offering me a way out of my glass casket, just providing another for me to lie down in. Wrenching away from his embrace, I wiped my lips with the back of my hand, panting.

'Sorry,' I gasped. 'I can't do this.'

He looked totally perplexed. 'What?'

'Can't . . .' Gesturing vaguely around the flat, my hand ended up raking its way through my hair, and I sank onto the bed in defeat. 'Any of this. The flat. You.'

To my surprise, his lip curled and he folded his arms. 'Oh, come on. You knew the score.'

'What?'

He chuckled. 'A girl like you? Why are you coming on all innocent *now*? You've been waiting for this set-up for a while.'

'A girl like me? What does that mean?'

'Well, it's not like you've got any other offers. Single mum, no prospects, not getting any younger. You should be grateful.'

Now I saw why his bouncers looked at him that way. The colours were emerging, and they were garish, clashing, ugly. He'd smelled my desperation when we first met, preyed on it, lassoed me in, and was expecting his return. A market stall trade, furtively made, both participants knowing they were being duped.

There were so many things I could have said to him, but I didn't utter a word. Just gathered my bag and coat, and left, the bungee rope yanking me back. My father's flat, with nowhere else to go. On my way home, I stopped at a supermarket that was still open and bought some daffodils from the bargain bin. They were waiting in the vase when Dad got up the next morning.

Chapter 30

*A*fter the school show, I went to ground. Em said it was fine, but wouldn't meet my eyes, and I worried that the other kids at school were teasing her, couldn't bear to think of her ashamed of me; the sad, dumb single mum. I skipped my next lesson with Roz, and when she called to tell me off, I told her I was having second thoughts; that with my other jobs, and my family to think of, I didn't have time for exams.

'But I've registered you!' she complained. 'Don't be a quitter!'

'Em is my priority,' I said. 'I should be helping her with her schoolwork, not doing my own.'

'You don't get it at all,' she replied. 'She was so proud of you.'

I said I was late for a shift and hung up. Selassie and Abrihet didn't help, asking how it all went and refusing to believe me when I said it was a disaster. Selassie, who often talked about his jazz club in Asmara, said he was thinking of setting up a regular gig in the café and that we should come and do a turn, but he was only being kind; the idea was ridiculous. Singing for paying customers? I'd put them out of business. The only thing I was good for was making coffee and sweeping up.

Seeing Letty again would be a trial. She'd been in the audience that night with her daughter, though I hadn't seen either of them afterwards, since I'd scurried out and lurked in the bushes at the school gates, waiting for Em to appear so I could scoop her up and head home. I felt guilty that I'd invited Letty then let her down and not even apologized, but when I turned up at her little courtyard flat, she opened the door, her face alight with mischief.

'It's Adele!' she whooped, waving her stick.

I slunk past her through the kitchen into the living room, my face burning, as she hobbled after me, cackling.

'What a night,' she said, in French. 'I haven't had so much fun since a certain evening at the Folies Bergère involving two showgirls and a snake. Marvellous stuff. Why did you dash off?'

'I wasn't well,' I mumbled, arranging Aphra on my lap.

'Young folk today are so feeble,' she grumbled. 'You should have brazened it out and done an encore. What was wrong with you?'

'A cold.' I coughed, to prove it, and she sniffed dismissively.

'Why are you looking like such a misery-guts?' she demanded. 'I don't pay you to sit here with a face like thunder. Entertain me!'

I heaved a sigh. 'Em and I are going to Cambridge tomorrow.' I felt unenthused by the trip, but we'd bought the tickets and she was still keen to go, for whatever reason, so I had to keep an eye on her.

Letty was scandalized. 'Cambridge is full of homosexuals.

Not that I don't adore them, of course. But you'll never find a man there who's interested in *you*.'

'I'm not going there to find a man,' I explained, stroking the cat.

'Aren't you?' replied Letty, amazed. 'Then why do you want to go?'

I hesitated, trying to find the right word. '*Pour m'impregner.*'

Her stick fell to the floor. 'I thought you said you *weren't* going to find a man?' she crowed.

'*De culture*,' I clarified, blushing furiously. But I'd set her off and she wouldn't shut up. To distract her, I suggested we make madeleines, another recipe from Jean-Luc's book. We ate them, too hot from the oven, but, rather than have a Proustian moment, she just moaned.

'These are awful. Why are they so salty? They're burnt at the edges and too dry. Jean-Luc would have said they were disgusting, like eating charred socks.'

But when she gave me my money at the end of our session, she patted my hand, hot-pink nails gleaming. '*Merci*, my dear. I enjoyed that enormously. Go and soak yourself in Cantabrigian culture, then come back and tell me about it. And don't worry about your show – worse things happen at sea, and in the Folies Bergère.'

As I walked home, pinched by the darkening evening air, the rocks in my heart felt a little lighter. The show hadn't been great, certainly, but after what Letty told me happened with the showgirls and the snake, it hadn't been that bad. I could put it behind me, focus on Em and Dad, try to be happy with what I had.

That was enough, I told myself. Just about.

Chapter 31

*E*m and I made our way to Finsbury Park station the next morning, wrapped up warm for the day, our breath making faint puffs in the frosty air on the platform. Roz was waiting for us, along with another English teacher called Mr Bishop, seven serious-looking sixth-form students and one Year Nine boy who already had his maths GCSE.

'Sorry about the exam thing,' I mumbled, as we boarded the train and settled ourselves in our seats.

'You're an idiot,' Roz said, putting her coffee on the floor and taking off her coat. She pointed at Em, sitting across from us, talking to one of the sixth-formers with a starstruck look on her face. 'You say you're giving it up for her, but you should be *doing* it for her. To show her.'

'To show her what?'

'That it's *possible*,' she replied, sweeping her hair back and jamming it up with a wooden coffee stirrer.

I buried my face in my own coffee to avoid answering. The train pulled out of the station and began to gather pace as we trundled out of London.

'Do you know Cambridge?' I said, to change the subject.

'A bit.' Roz took a sip of her coffee. 'Did a play there once. Masha in *Three Sisters* at the Arts Theatre. Terrible production, we should all have pushed off back to Moscow. And I had a teacher friend I used to visit occasionally, but she moved to Winchester. Haven't been back in years. Bagel?' She dug into her enormous bag and produced a dozen rolls for everyone. I munched, watching the grey landscape gradually turn greener as we squeezed our way out of the capital, the rhythmic clatter of the train soothing my jangled nerves.

So, this was not my first trip to Cambridge. I'd been once before, with my parents, but didn't remember it. Or did I? We'd had a day trip, Dad said, and I couldn't recall anything about that. But I did have a vague memory, one I didn't even associate with Cambridge, but it must have been there. More of an echo, really, and it hadn't seemed real until he'd mentioned it. A choral service in a college chapel, my hand creeping into Maman's of its own accord as we listened to pure voices soaring into a fan-vaulted ceiling. Her answering squeeze, and the film of tears in her eyes as she looked down to smile at me, Dad just along from us in the row, his own eyes closed in ecstasy.

Reliving it, I felt an aching sense of loss for my childhood self, sitting there in that nave with no idea what was to come. My future ahead of me, before it was snatched and whirled away, like the landscape flickering past the train. When Roz asked if I'd been to the city before, I didn't mention it; the memory faded as we arrived at the station and queued for a bus to take us into the centre of town. For one thing, the buildings looked very modern, almost futuristic – at odds with my vision of dreaming spires. It wasn't what I'd expected and, not for the first time, I felt inexperienced and unsophisticated. North London was my bell jar, and I'd barely broken out of it.

Cambridge was *cold*, far colder than London. I shivered in my old coat as we all piled on the bus, which began its trundle towards St Andrew's Street, past pubs and coffee houses, bicycles zipping in and out of the traffic. Em had her face pressed to the glass, and when her breath left dew on the pane, she drew – not a smiley face, but the omega sign, which bled into the surrounding condensation. Oo-mee-gah. The last letter of the Greek alphabet, the name of my ex-boyfriend Sid's club. In the grey winter light, the letter looked like a tombstone, and I shivered again, from something other than cold. The last letter, the end of things, death.

'Next stop,' said Roz, as the reassuring glow of John Lewis's Christmas windows appeared ahead, shoppers weaving around each other with their loaded bags. We disembarked and stood, hunched against the crowds. The other teacher got a clipboard out of his rucksack and started handing out leaflets to the students.

'Right,' said Roz. 'Mr Bishop and I are taking this motley crew to Trinity. You're welcome to join us. We're going to run around the Great Court like we're in *Chariots of Fire.*'

The students stared at her like she'd just suggested boiling her head.

'Chill out, guys,' she said. 'I promise we'll unlock the dark secrets of Cambridge. It might even be fun.'

They looked like they'd rather it wasn't, and I thought perhaps we'd be better off on our own. We watched them go, Mr Bishop holding his clipboard in one hand, waving a red umbrella in the other, Roz craning back at us, grimacing. 'Meet you here at five!'

'I might head off,' said Em.

'Where?'

'Around and about.' She shrugged. 'I like exploring.'

'We *are* exploring. That's what this is about.'

'I meant, on my own,' she replied, kicking a cobblestone.

'You're too young to wander on your own,' I began, but tailed off at a look from my daughter, who cheerfully wandered round Hackney's roughest streets. Cambridge's quaint alleyways held no fears for her, and she would already have a map of the city in her head.

'I just want to spend some time with you.' I resorted to emotional blackmail, and bribery, handing her a five-pound note. 'Here, some spending money.'

Em stared at the note, then me. 'Thanks. Guess I'd better spend it.'

We strode around the city together, winding down narrow streets and soaking up the atmosphere, as Letty had instructed. Roz had given us a school pass, so we crept into a few colleges, admiring the compact quads with their flawless emerald lawns and tucked-away mullioned windows. Imagine studying there, calling one of those windows your own. Turning back to the cobbled alleyways, we ventured into tiny bookshops, gazed at glittering window displays and picked our way through the marketplace. This was the picture-postcard version of Cambridge I'd envisioned, and I allowed myself to pretend I was a student there, riding my bike, working in the library, hanging out in cafés as a customer rather than an employee.

At Em's request, we went to look at the Corpus Clock, on King's Parade – an extraordinary mechanism that sat behind glass outside Corpus Christi College. It was an enormous golden disc with a metal sculpture of a locust sitting above, and, as the concentric circles of the clock rotated, the creature moved with it, as if stuck pushing an endless hamster wheel. The movement wasn't entirely regular, and seemed to catch occasionally, which in turn made me twitch uncomfortably. The whole effect was eerie and unnerving, but somehow hypnotic – the locust erratically, unstoppably eating away the seconds. Time slipping away, reminding you to make the most of it before you too were gobbled up.

Gazing at the contraption, surrounded by hustling crowds, I didn't notice Em disappear, and it was only when someone shoved me as they tried to take a photograph that I realized she wasn't there. I felt a rising panic – not that she'd got lost or been abducted, but simply that there was one place she might have gone; the one place I didn't want her to go. After racing back and forth down the Parade without finding her, I found myself veering off towards King's College, slipping past the porter who was arguing with a group of tourists, making my way across the quad as if I knew where I was going. It took a few wrong turns before I found myself in front of an intricately carved oak door, and there it was: the name-plate I'd spent so long thinking about, wondering if he ever thought of me, of us, what he left behind. I stood rooted, remembering that last night, swaying as the deluge hit and swirled around me. His face as I backed away, the resignation, waiting for him to call me back but hearing nothing, and then . . . *nothing, nothing, nothing . . .*

I shook my head to clear it. All at once, I was terrified: what was I *doing* there? Only a door between us. He might come out and see me – he might come out at any moment. I had to leave immediately. I turned and ran, back down the corridor, cannoning through the stone archway and round the sprawling quad, stumbling on the flagstones, back out onto King's Parade, breathing hard, thoroughly overwhelmed.

'Oh, good, I was hoping to bump into you.'

Roz was standing in front of me, holding several bags. 'Martin Bishop is such an old fuddy-duddy. He insisted on marching the kids round each college giving a potted history – "St Benedict laid this foundation stone in 1346" – Jesus Christ. I sneaked off to do some shopping. What's wrong?'

'I've lost Em,' I gasped. 'We were looking at the Corpus Clock and she just . . . vanished.'

'Oh.' A furrow appeared on Roz's brow. 'She can't have got far, surely? Can you call her?'

'She doesn't have a phone.' A mobile for an eleven-year-old had seemed an extravagance; now it felt like a necessity. I'd get her one, as soon as I found her.

Roz rubbed her forehead. 'What we should do, then . . .' she began, and jumped as her own phone buzzed in her bag. As she answered it, her brow cleared.

'Fabbo, tell her we'll see you at Queens'. Martin's got her,' she added, as she finished the call. 'She caught up with them and is going to join in for a bit. Said she'd see us after lunch.'

Sinking onto the low wall that flanked the college entrance, I took a sagging breath of relief, though I couldn't throw off my unease, the sense that Em was playing a deep game. But how much trouble could she get in under the beady gaze of Mr Bishop?

We went to a pub Roz knew, all dark wood and cosy corners, found a table by the fire, and I tried to relax. Em was a law unto herself, and who knew what she was up to with her five pounds and almighty brain? Trying to ignore my worries, I absorbed the warmth of the place and ate a shepherd's pie, as Roz made me laugh, telling me how she'd overheard two students in the street discussing the structure of DNA: 'Go and get laid, for God's sake!' Then she had another go at me about quitting the A level, saying it was a waste of my talents, and hers.

'I'm a brilliant teacher,' she announced, waving a chunk of Yorkshire pudding. 'Much better teacher than actress.'

I tried to distract her. 'You said you regretted dropping out of uni to do the film?'

Roz wiped her lips on a napkin. 'Yes, of course. It was mad. One minute I was in Manchester having a great time, the next I was in LA being told to get my teeth fixed.'

'I guess you thought you were going on to bigger and better things.'

'Hmm.' She chewed and swallowed. 'They were bigger, but not necessarily better. I've spent the last ten years trying to change course. But I still wonder . . .'

'What?'

Roz looked troubled. 'I used to do photoshoots. Now I do photocopying. It's hard to know, isn't it – what's the best choice? I'm never sure I made it. But the work dried up, and I had the kids to think of. Wouldn't get to see them if I was going off to Vancouver to film a sitcom for three months. Now and then I get offered an audition, and I've always turned it down. But sometimes I wonder if I should . . . seize the opportunity. Go for it, one last time.'

'I'm sure you make the best choices for you and the kids,' I said quietly, sipping my water.

'You make the best choices for you and Em, too,' she replied, clinking her glass against mine.

After lunch, we went to meet Mr Bishop and Em and found the group standing outside Queens' College, dodging cyclists.

'Where did you go?' I demanded. 'I was worried.'

She shrugged. 'I couldn't see you. But I saw Mr Bishop, so it was fine.'

'It was a shame you couldn't join us,' said Mr Bishop. 'You missed a treat at the Fitzwilliam Museum.'

I eyed my daughter suspiciously. 'What did you do about lunch?'

She avoided my gaze. 'I had a baked potato in the café, with the others.'

About to quiz her further, I reasoned she didn't have the look of a child who'd gone looking for her father in her lunch hour, so decided not to press it. Should I talk to her about him, stop it in its tracks? The truth was, I felt ill-equipped to deal with that conversation, the kind of questions it might throw up. Some of them would be unanswerable. Instead, after looking round Queens' with the others, we went for scones in a little tea shop opposite Peterhouse College, and I scrutinized her face, trying to work out who she looked like. Was it me, or Adam, or someone else entirely? Though just as curly, her hair was lighter than mine, a dull mouse, and her eyes were rounder. I thought there was a trace of JoJo in the flecks of gold around her pupils, but couldn't be sure.

At five o'clock, we all met back where we'd started on St Andrew's Street. Roz arrived marshalling her group, hair unravelling from its topknot, breathless and sweating, Mr Bishop still carrying his clipboard.

'I've got an idea,' said Roz. 'Something to round off the trip. Follow me.'

She led us all back into the centre of town, bustling down the narrow streets, her shopping bags bumping against her legs. Now it was dark, the decorated shop windows glowed brighter, Christmas lights twinkling as we emerged on King's Parade. Roz headed towards the college, its mighty chapel looming like a giant sarsen stone, whisking us through the porter's lodge and out into the great square beyond. I kept my head down, my scarf over the lower half of my face. After all this, it would be a disaster to run into him now.

'You have to be here early to be sure of getting in,' she said, leading us to a small queue that had formed alongside the chapel wall.

My heart sank. Evensong. Nothing wrong with Roz's plan, a free and fitting conclusion to our day. She wasn't to know I'd been here before, one of my last memories of being in a proper family.

'Sorry, but don't you think . . . ?' I wanted to make an excuse, say it was getting late, escape. But my words were lost in the crowd as we were pulled into the chapel, as inexorably as the locust eating time, Em hopping from one foot to the other in excitement. I kept my head down, didn't look around as we entered the building, didn't gaze up at those dizzying feathered vaults, or at the glorious stained-glass windows, or the dozens of candles that flickered in the holy gloom. I couldn't allow myself to see or feel any of this, because it was too much, the memory of both my parents there all those years ago.

Even as the voices of the world-famous choir soared into the rafters again, I didn't let them lift me up, staring resolutely at the stone-cold floor and praying for it to be over. But those pure tones filtered in, and the '*Alleluia*' refrain began to reverberate in my head – '*natus virgine*', a maiden mother and no earthly father. Just like Em. And then, just like mine in Maman's, I felt her hand creep into my own, looked down at my daughter's tremulous face with a film of tears in my eyes, and everything came full circle. A full golden circle, ticking around, eerie and beautiful. Together, we gave ourselves up to the music; gripping Em's hand, I smiled at her. Like Miss Challoner said, you passed on the baton, and had to trust it was going the right way.

Afterwards, we got the bus back to the station and, when we were all on the train, scuttling its way into London, Em leant against the window, and drew the omega sign again, her thin finger squeaking against the glass. It loomed stark and black in the harsh light of the carriage. But now, instead of seeing death, I saw a line drawn, maybe the beginning of something better – a new start. That name-plate might always be there on the door, but it would fade in my mind, along with everything else. Maybe I could stop dwelling on my mistakes and try to remember the good things – evensong, stories, and sitting in trees.

I turned to Roz, who was dozing in her seat.

'Maybe,' I said.

She opened one eye.

'Maybe I won't give up,' I said. 'Maybe I can do it after all.'

She smiled sleepily. 'Of course you can. I always knew you would.'

Chapter 32

We squeezed in a last lesson before Christmas, after one of my shifts at Merhaba. Selassie had decorated the restaurant with an abundance of fairy lights, hanging enormous baubles from the ceiling and sprinkling fake snow on the shelves that I kept sweeping up along with cake crumbs. Roz came straight from school, settled herself in her usual seat, and fixed me with her hard stare.

'This is better,' she said, waving my latest essay which I'd finished before work that morning. 'You actually have a point to make. Some of it is verging on original.'

I'd slaved over it, comparing *Jane Eyre* with *Rebecca*, exploring jealousy and obsessive love via Mrs Reed and Mrs Danvers. I was pleased with it, and tried not to be cast down by Roz's faint praise – she'd clearly been taking pointers from Mrs Boleyn. There was something buoyant about her, bouncing in her seat as she circled and underlined.

'You're getting there,' she said, pushing the papers back to me, liberally scribbled with green pen. 'You just need to loosen up a bit. Have some fun. Like Em.' She nodded at my daughter, who'd just arrived with her rucksack over her shoulder. 'Her essays are *wicked*.'

I often invited Em to join us, because she liked Selassie's lemonades, and listening to us talk – mostly listening to *Roz* talk. Just as I'd worshipped Miss Challoner, Em adored Mrs Gill, and I loved watching her little face light up as Roz took us both through a new poem, or staged one of her literary quizzes. Something was different today though. Roz was cheery but distracted, checking her phone and messing with her hair, which was blonder, cascading around her shoulders. She also didn't eat, whereas usually she would tuck into a slice of Abrihet's cake and talk with her mouth full. After discussing my written work, we looked at an unfamiliar sonnet by Thomas Wyatt, but she kept fiddling with her phone like she was waiting for a message. Something was afoot, and Em noticed it too, her eyes narrowing as she watched us.

'Is anything wrong?' I asked, finally.

Roz jumped, looking defensive. 'Nothing, what? Nothing, why?'

'You seem like you're on edge. What is it?'

She twirled a sachet of sugar around her fingers. 'Oh, I don't know. I was thinking about how I gave it all up. My degree. For the film. Obviously wanted that more, at the time.'

'Do you regret giving it up?' asked Em.

'The degree? Yes, all the time. I wonder where I'd be if I'd carried on. Maybe a professor somewhere, writing impenetrable books.'

'No,' Em said. 'I meant, do you regret giving up acting?'

'Oh.' Roz seemed nonplussed. 'Well, maybe I didn't. Just . . . put it to one side, while I was teaching.'

'Past participle,' I said. 'Aren't you still teaching?'

'Yes, of course.' Roz tugged at her hair, flustered. 'I've got an audition,' she blurted.

'Really? What for?'

'A big BBC drama. The lead role.' She was trying to sound casual but it was clear she was bursting to tell someone.

'What's it about?'

She put her elbows on the table and whispered as if confiding a state secret. 'It's called *Emma, After*. It's about Emma Woodhouse, twenty years after her marriage to Mr Knightley. He dies, and it's about what she does next.'

'Wow. That sounds . . . great.' I tried to inject some enthusiasm into my voice but mostly felt disappointment and irritation. Why had she bothered persuading me to take my A level if she was going off to star in a TV show?

'Don't worry,' Roz added, seeing my expression. 'I wouldn't leave you in the lurch. We'd get you through your exams.'

'What would you do about school?' asked Em, with an air of disapproval.

'Oh, I don't know – take a sabbatical?'

'Put it to one side?' fired back Em.

There was an uncomfortable silence, Em kicking her heels and sucking on her paper straw. She was being a brat, but I felt sorry for her – she was clearly devastated by the news.

'Anyway, enough about me,' said Roz, putting her phone face down on the table. 'Delphine, let's go back to that sonnet. We were getting somewhere.'

Em carried on kicking, and I could feel her bristling next to me as we talked.

'It's not second-best,' she said suddenly, cutting across us. We both turned to her, noting the knitted brow and sullen mouth. 'Teaching.'

'I know it's not,' said Roz, but she sounded half-hearted.

'Mr Griffiths cried,' said Em fiercely. 'At the school show. When Hannah played the violin. He spent hours with her practising. He didn't have to. Mrs Boleyn doesn't have to dress up as Professor McGonagall for Halloween. You don't have to help Mum do her exams. But you all do it. Why?'

'Because . . .' faltered Roz. 'Because . . . it matters.'

'But not as much as being on telly?'

'Em, that's enough.' Though I kind of agreed with her.

'Probably won't get the part, anyway,' muttered Roz. She pushed the phone further away. 'Anyway, let's finish up – I told Jay I'd be back to make the kids' dinner.'

Em stared at the floor as we said our goodbyes and didn't say another word until we were outside the door, ready to go our separate ways. Then, as Roz was digging around in her bag, she handed her the mobile she'd left on the table.

'You're making a mistake,' she said.

Roz looked up, her forehead wrinkling. 'Nothing's even happened yet.'

'Mr Gill loved you because you weren't Selina Sands,' said Em. 'He wanted something real.'

Roz stepped back, dropping her bag. 'W-what? How . . . how do you know about that?'

'Em-Jo,' I murmured, pulling her away. 'Sorry,' I added, as Roz shook her head in disbelief.

'What's up with you?' I asked, as we walked towards the bus stop. 'Who's Selina Sands?'

Em kicked a stone, hands in her coat pockets. 'Her husband's ex-girlfriend. She's an actress in LA. Mrs Gill thinks he still loves her, sometimes.'

'How on earth do you know that?'

'Heard them talking, at the school show, and looked her up.'

So Selina Sands was Roz's Rebecca de Winter. 'Well, you were out of order. You're too nosy. It will get you into trouble one day.'

'She's wrong,' said Em. 'About taking that acting job. She's the first teacher who's ever . . .' She tailed off, and I grabbed her shoulder to make her face me.

'The first teacher who . . . what?'

She studied the pavement, trailing the line of the flagstone with her shoe. When she spoke, I had to lean forwards to hear her.

'Sometimes I hate being clever,' she muttered. 'It's like I see in three dimensions, and everyone else is in two. And I just want things to be simple, just go along with everyone else. Not to see everything, all the time. It's exhausting. Before Mrs Gill, I used to stay quiet in class, keep my head down, but she has this way of making me want to . . .'

'To what?'

She raised her face, her eyes bright, feverish. 'To show the world what I can do.'

I sighed, thinking of Miss Challoner. 'Oh, Em. I'm glad she's done that for you, and I can't wait for you to show the world what you can do. But that doesn't mean you get to tell her what *she* can do. You can't interfere with people's choices.'

'I do it all the time,' Em replied. 'You can make people do almost anything if you know what button to push.'

'But you didn't know. You were just jabbing at them.'

Her lips thinned. 'I'll work it out.'

Going home for dinner felt like a dismal prospect after the warmth and fairy lights of Merhaba but, when we arrived, Dad wasn't sitting in his usual position in front of the television. Picking up Maman's blanket from the floor, I arranged it on the arm of his chair while Em went to look for him. When I entered the kitchen, he was standing there with a tea towel over his shoulder, a pot of pasta bubbling over on the hob, trying to open a jar of pesto. Em was already grating cheese, so I turned the heat down and went over to help him prise the lid off. As I handed him the open jar, he said: 'You get the cake, Em-Jo?'

'I put it in the fridge.'

Intercepting the little glance between the co-conspirators, I went to the fridge and wrenched it open. Alongside a pint of milk and a tub of margarine was a dented box of Victoria sponge.

'Where did you get this?'

'The supermarket, on the way from school,' said Em. 'Granddad gave me the money. I've had it in my rucksack though, it's a bit squashed.'

'Nearly Christmas,' said Dad. 'Thought it might be nice.'

'Did you . . . what did . . .' I was lost for words, and Em had to take over.

'Why don't we set the table?'

We ate together, Em chatting away while Dad listened, nodding and occasionally murmuring sounds of approval. I watched them, heads bent towards each other, and wondered which had come first: had he asked her to buy the cake, or had she suggested it?

Maybe you couldn't interfere with people's choices, but you could make it easier for them to make the right ones.

Chapter 33

On Christmas Eve, I finished my shift at Merhaba, clearing the table of a rowdy office party who'd been exchanging wacky Secret Santa presents and left wrapping all over the floor. Picking up a discarded ribbon and some glittery, holly-covered paper, I smoothed it out and used it to wrap my tiny gift for Selassie and Abrihet. In my few short months there, they'd made me so welcome, sending me home every week with containers full of leftover stews, teaching me to cook them, letting me arrange my shifts around Em and my studies. It felt like too much good fortune, the kind that angers the gods, so I was preparing an offering.

As I was fetching my coat and bag from the little room off the kitchen, Abrihet stopped me, as she often did, pressing a warm container into my hands.

'Doro Wat,' she said, the dimples deepening in her cheeks. 'Chicken.'

'*Yekena'lay.*' I stammered out my thank you, making her chuckle. Putting the container in my bag, I held out my parcel. 'For you both.'

She took it from me, her fingers tracing the glitter. 'Sisi!' she called. 'Here.' Selassie came bustling through, wiping his hands on a towel, and Abrihet held out the gift.

'From our Delphine,' she said, using it to beckon him over.

They unwrapped it as I stood holding my box of stew, feeling embarrassed and worried they would be somehow offended by what Em and I had done. For a second, they stared down at the small wooden frame that emerged from the paper. Eventually Selassie looked up and spoke, his voice strained and hoarse.

'How did you get this?'

'Em found it, on the internet. I hope you don't mind.'

Abrihet clutched the frame to her chest. 'Jamal, Jamal, Jamal,' she sobbed.

I stepped back, overwhelmed by the intensity of her reaction. 'Sorry, I didn't mean to upset you.'

She shook her head, wiping her eyes. 'No, no,' she cried, and held the frame out to her husband.

Selassie took it from her gingerly, as though it was a delicate artefact. 'Come with me,' he said.

He led us through to the café, to one of the bare brick walls dotted with black and white photos of famous jazz singers. Taking down one of a young Frank Sinatra, he hung the little frame in its place and stepped back to admire it.

'Perfect,' he said, and wiped his eyes with his towel.

It was a photo of their jazz club, Tesfay's, taken in 2004 before they left Asmara. Selassie and Abrihet were standing outside, with their teenage son Jamal in front of them, shading their eyes against the sun, their faces smoothed out and shiny, like the paper I'd retrieved from under the table.

Em had discovered it online, trawling through an archive website until she found what she was searching for, and we'd had it printed and framed, wondering if they knew such a picture existed. It seemed from their reaction that they didn't. They gazed at it, their arms around each other, heads together, hearts beating as one, and I felt a sudden drop in my stomach watching them, wishing I had a partner so attuned to me, so in sync. Someone to lean on, like that. I started to back away, feeling out of place, but Abrihet turned, smiling, her hand held out, black eyes glistening.

'Blessings,' she said. 'You have brought our past back to us.'

I squeezed her hand. 'I'm glad you like it.'

Selassie blew his nose on his towel. 'Our business here will be a success,' he said. 'Because we have this watching over us.' He gestured to the photo. 'Thank you, Delphine. And Merry Christmas, *fiori*.'

As I stepped out into the icy December night, Dylan was standing there, hands shoved into his pockets, collar up against the cold, Bernadette at his heels. I nearly stumbled, astonished to see him, and instantly self-conscious. We hadn't spoken since the school show, when I'd rushed off in an agony of embarrassment and hacking coughs. He sent me a text after that said, Guess we're moving to New Zealand then, and I hadn't replied. Everyone else seemed to find our performance funny apart from me.

'Why didn't you come in?' I wrapped my scarf up around my face to hide my flushed cheeks.

'The three of you seemed to be having a moment,' he said. 'Thought I'd wait.'

'What are you doing here?' If I'd known he was coming I could have done something about my scraped-back hair and bare face.

'Dog walk.' He pointed at Bernadette, who wagged obligingly. 'Thought I'd stop by and say Merry Christmas. Are you heading home?'

'I'm on my way to Letty's, the old lady I see.' I'd made a panettone for her, and wanted to drop it off.

'We'll walk with you.'

We set off, our breath ahead of us, and I tried to think of something to say. 'Where are you spending tomorrow?'

He grimaced. 'At my mother's, in Crickhowell. She's preparing the fatted calf. What about you?'

'We're just at home with my dad.'

'You said he was a piano tuner?'

I was gratified he remembered a passing comment. 'Well, not any more. He doesn't . . . he doesn't do much now. He wasn't very well after my mum died, and . . .' I tailed off, unsure what or why I was telling him. But Dylan nodded.

'It's hard, isn't it. My dad died when I was twenty. Mam pretends she's fine, but I know she's not. It's the pretending that's worse, I think.'

But it wasn't. It was Dad who was worse, unable to pretend, unable to do anything. Was that what true love did to people?

'Anyway, it's better than if Mam comes to mine – she always moans about the furniture, says I live like a student.'

I laughed, thinking of his bare living room. 'Your crates are lovely.'

He grinned. 'My ex-girlfriend took all our stuff when she moved out.'

'Oh. I'm sorry.'

'Don't be. She bought it all, and I never liked that IKEA shit. I just wanted the piano, and Bernie.'

His dog was trotting along beside us, gazing up at him adoringly, tongue out. 'Well, you got the best deal.'

'Obviously. Anyway, I wanted to tell you that Brownswood made five hundred pounds from ticket sales, and a thousand pounds from the bar. So, you know, the show wasn't a disaster.'

'Really?' I thought of all those parents milling around with glasses of wine. 'Well, that's nice.'

'I think we should carry on.'

I stopped, because we had reached Letty's, but also because I didn't understand what he was talking about. 'Carry on what?'

The puffs of our breath met in the middle as we stared at each other. I didn't know what he meant, and I didn't know what I wanted us to be – friends, or something else; something more.

'The band. I think we should carry on.'

'What do you mean? What for?'

'For fun. You enjoyed it, didn't you? At least, until you coughed up your innards. You were getting better, Jay's writing songs again, I'm still looking for a gig. It might keep us going, until . . .' He hesitated. 'Until something better comes along.'

For fun. *Pour se détendre.* I was going to say I didn't have time, but then remembered singing in the back room of the pub, feeling fine and mellow, part of a gang. I didn't want to say no, but wasn't ready to say yes, either.

'I'd better get to Letty.' I lifted my cake tin.

'Think about it.' Dylan clicked his fingers to Bernadette, who scampered round his legs. '*Iechyd da,*' he said, and walked away with his dog, gradually fading until he was swallowed up by the darkness.

'Merry Christmas,' I called out, but he'd gone.

Chapter 34

*I*t was a low-key day, watching *It's a Wonderful Life* and pretending not to see the silent tears rolling down Dad's cheeks. I'd got hold of a cheap chicken to roast, and we ate in front of the telly, watching George Bailey search for Zuzu's petals, toasting the day with lemonade. I'd saved enough of Letty's money to buy Em a mobile phone – just a cheap one, but it felt essential after losing her in Cambridge that day – and a copy of *Wolf Hall*, which she immediately buried her nose in, and from then on was dead to the world. Feeling flush with the prospect of future Letty visits, I'd bought myself a new dress from a vintage shop in Stoke Newington – a festive red wraparound, with a V-neckline and a flared skirt. It probably wasn't as useful as a winter coat, but it was cheaper and much more fun. *Il faut se détendre.* I told myself I definitely didn't imagine Dylan seeing me in it, and definitely wasn't reminded of him when George Bailey passionately kissed Mary in her mother's hallway.

I gave Dad a DVD of *Cinema Paradiso*, one of his favourite films. It was a strange choice, given he didn't speak Italian and found it hard to follow the subtitles, but he'd always loved it, although the kissing montage at the end provoked many silent tears. When he opened it, he fingered the corners of the case and murmured the name of the composer who wrote the soundtrack. I figured it was one of those instances when he relied on his ears rather than his eyes. Em gave Dad a scarf – rather optimistically, I thought, given he hardly ever went out. I couldn't imagine when he would get to wear it but, when he tore off the wrapping, his face lit up and he reached out to grab his granddaughter's hand. 'You're a good girl, Em-Jo,' he said. She looked up from *Wolf Hall* and beamed.

Later on, in the evening, when we were in the kitchen clearing up, he called us back, fumbling down the sides of his chair. We watched as he dug out two tiny packages, which he offered up with shaking hands.

'FiFi, Em-Jo,' he said, tapping each one.

We opened them slowly, taking care not to tear the paper. Inside mine, I found a little necklace, a delicate silver chain with a tiny star charm. Em stood, for once dumbfounded, holding an identical chain.

'My two stars,' said Dad softly.

I held it up to the light. 'Where did you get these?' Then worried that my response sounded accusatory. 'Sorry, I mean . . . Where did you buy them?'

He shifted in his seat. 'There's a shop. Next to the tube station. A lady there helped me.'

'You went to a shop?'

He nodded, pleased and embarrassed. Em bent forward to allow him to fix the clasp, while I fastened mine on along with my crucifix, and we both paraded in front of him, as he surveyed us with something approaching pride.

'Beautiful,' he said.

'Thank you,' I replied, wiping away my own silent tears.

'Gave JoJo a necklace like that, once,' he whispered. All at once, there was a memory surge – eating trifle as Dad secured a glinting silver chain round Maman's neck. I opened my mouth to ask him about it, but sensed the shutters closing. As though the effort had been too much, he turned back to the television, pulling his blanket over his knees.

'Thank you, Daddy,' I said again, putting my hand on his shoulder. He lifted his hand to cover mine.

'My pleasure,' he said.

Back in the kitchen, up to my elbows in soapy water, I began to scrub the greasy roasting tin. 'Well, that was unexpected. Who knew Granddad was going out again?'

'He's had extra DVDs,' observed Em, who noticed everything. 'Ones we didn't get.'

'Wonder what's changed,' I mused, looking out the window at the starlit sky. 'It's like he's waking up.'

'I've been reading to him,' said Em, as she took the tin off me to dry it. 'In the evenings, since you've been at Merhaba. We started with *Animal Farm*, because we were doing it in class, but now we're on *Emma*, because Mrs Gill . . . Anyway, I couldn't tell if he was enjoying it, but the other day he said, "That Frank Churchill is no good."'

'You are the sweetest and best of all creatures,' I said, reaching over to squeeze her arm.

She wiped away the drips, smiling wryly. 'In spite of all my faults.'

Em & Me

'Faultless,' I said, dabbing a washing-up sud on her nose.

'It's not me though,' she continued, taking a wet plate. 'It's you.'

'Me what?'

'You're what's changed. You're different lately. Reading, writing, singing. Maybe it's rubbing off on him.'

My hands stilled in the water. 'You think so?'

'Like you're a bit more in tune. And you know he's got perfect pitch.'

Was it the books, the music, or something else? I thought of Dylan's suggestion, that we carry on the band, carry on our gang. Drying my hands, I nodded towards our treat cupboard, fully stocked for Christmas.

'Come on, let's have a hot chocolate. Extra marshmallows for all.'

'OK,' said Em. 'You make the drinks and I'll set up the board. Maybe we can persuade Granddad to join in.'

He didn't, but he watched us play, and when Em won, he told her she was a clever girl, switched the TV off and opened up his old record player, a turntable that usually sat in the corner gathering dust, to put on an Ella Fitzgerald album. As he sat in his chair, swaying to the music in a cockeyed paper crown, I thought that maybe the petals were still there somewhere, tucked away, waiting to be rediscovered. Not his old self, but a new, different one, who could find joy and wonder in life again, tune himself up. We just had to help him find his way there.

Chapter 35

On the dying days of December, I called Letty to see if she'd had a merry Christmas, even though she didn't celebrate it, saying it was dreadfully common. The thought of her sitting at home with her *porto* had made me uncomfortable, despite her daughter living in the house above. There was a recipe in Jean-Luc's book for *galette des rois*, French Epiphany cake, which I was planning on making her as a surprise.

The first time she didn't pick up, so I tried again just before lunch, and this time she answered immediately.

'I don't want to speak to you until you've returned it.'

For a second, I thought she'd mistaken me for someone else, a salesman or those computer people who kept ringing her to tell her she'd been hacked.

'It's me, Delphine.'

'Yes, I know quite well who it is. I'm not entirely senile, although you obviously appear to think so.'

'I'm sorry?'

'Perhaps you thought I wouldn't notice? I am a dotty old bat after all.'

'What on earth are you talking about?'

'Don't play the innocent with me, missy. I want it back.'

'What?'

'Jean-Luc's book!' Her rasping voice sounded close to tears. 'I know you took it.'

I fell silent, torn between confusion, regret and embarrassment. When I'd gone round on Christmas Eve, I'd seen the book in the kitchen and on a whim had slipped it into my bag, intending to return it along with the Epiphany cake in the New Year. There wasn't time to find and take a photo of the recipe, and I thought she wouldn't miss it.

'I . . . I . . .'

'Nothing to say? Aphra got your tongue?'

'Letty. I only borrowed it, because—'

She cut me off. 'You didn't ask. You just took it, as though I'm some sort of lending library. It's my only copy. He gave it to me, he wrote in it. I sleep with it by my bedside. And you just took it without asking. *C'est vulgaire.*'

I gripped the phone, horrified, never imagining my impulsive gesture could have had such repercussions. My gift for Selassie and Abrihet had been so well-received, I'd felt puffed up, thrilled with my enterprise, and wanted to recreate that feeling, plan another surprise.

'I'm so sorry, Letty. I truly didn't think you—'

'No excuses! Just give it back. Unless you've already sold it on eBay? A signed first edition would fetch quite a sum. Perhaps you've already pocketed it?'

'I didn't! Of course, I didn't! Why would I do that when you pay me every week? When . . . when we're friends?'

There was a pause, and then she sniffed. 'I don't need a

friend. I just need someone to speak French with. I'll find someone else. Your services are no longer required. Please don't call again. Just return the book.' She hung up.

Staring at my phone, I willed her to call me back and say it had all been a mistake. It *had* all been a mistake. I was mortified that she could think I would steal from her, and brooded on it all day, shifting Selassie's fairy lights to dust the fake snow away, feeling that the decorations were garish and incongruous, now it was all over. On the way home from work, I stopped by Letty's house and knocked on the door, hoping to apologize in person, but, despite seeing a light on inside, no one answered. I walked home in sporadic flurries of real snow, the flakes melting on my cheeks like tears. It wasn't the money, though that was bad enough. It was that I'd lost a friend. *Tu*, not *vous*. The bungee rope hadn't pulled me back; it had snapped.

Spring Term

Chapter 36

Sometimes it was easier to ignore a problem instead of facing it.

Adam didn't like Mr North helping me research Oxbridge but never actually said so — I could tell by the set look on his face when he left Clit Class, and I stayed behind to read brochures and talk about entrance exams. Maybe it wasn't fair that I was getting the attention, but he had his private tutors, and his dad had gone to Trinity, so he was already ahead in the race. Adam wasn't quite as relaxed and laidback as he made out — underneath that amiability was an iron thread of ambition. When we walked in the park during our lunch hours, he talked about how his parents were going to take him on a tour of colleges in the summer holidays, and my hands curled to fists in my pockets. What if he got in and I didn't? We hadn't even started sixth-form and already I was worrying about our university careers forcing us apart. More than that — I couldn't bear the idea of him being the only one to have the opportunity. I'd grasped that iron thread and was pulling on it along with him.

'Would you like to come to dinner on Friday?' he asked one afternoon, as we wandered past the lakes.

I felt a stirring of excitement. 'Are your parents going away again?' We'd managed several nights in his loft room over the past few months – plus one hurried evening when his mum and dad were at the Globe, quaffing fizz with the other theatre-goers who just adored Mark Rylance. We were both eager for a repeat performance.

To my surprise, he looked embarrassed. 'I meant, actual dinner. With my parents.'

I was silent. Up till now, I'd never met them, even in passing, and had never dared mention the possibility. Obviously, he hadn't met Dad either, because that would have been too fraught an introduction for all of us. But meeting Adam's loving, supportive and functional parents would be a normal and welcome occurrence, wouldn't it? The fact it hadn't happened yet was just due to circumstance – them being off watching plays, staying in their converted barn in Norfolk and skiing in Meribel.

'Well?'

'I should be revising.'

'They'd really like to meet you.'

'That would be . . . nice.'

Having been desperate to meet them, now I didn't want to at all, and spent the rest of the week hoping they'd decide to slope off to Holkham so I didn't have to face them and pretend to be the perfect girlfriend. I was painfully aware of my shabby background, estuary accent and charity-shop clothes, though of course I didn't mention any of this to Adam because I didn't want *him* to notice these things, and feel he had to cover up for them. So, I borrowed a sundress from Sheba, and got Marni to lend me her hair straighteners. On Friday, after putting tinned soup out for Dad, I walked across the park because it was a lovely evening and better to save the bus money. It was warm though, and sweat was pooling under my arms, trickling down my ribs. I worried it would soak through the thin material of the dress and I'd have to greet Adam's parents with damp patches. I should be studying in my room, not sucking up to Mr and Mrs Terris in someone else's outfit.

Arriving on the dot of seven-thirty, I spent five minutes hanging around behind a bush to avoid being unfashionably prompt, frantically fanning under my arms and dabbing at the beads on my brow. How I wished they'd gone to the barn, and Adam and I could hide out in his loft getting unapologetically sweaty. I knocked on the door, gripping the cellophane wrapping of the flowers I'd brought and shifting my feet out of my sandals to air them.

Adam opened it, grinning and holding a corkscrew. 'Hi, there. Nice hair.' He kissed me and led me towards the kitchen while I willed myself to look like I'd never been there before, hadn't thumbed the cookery books and eaten postcoital pasta at the table. They had to believe this was new to me – new, but not unfamiliar, and not at all intimidating. I could be part of this world, if I played my part.

When we entered the room, I was so busy making a show of gazing around that I almost didn't notice Virginia Terris come towards me, hand outstretched. She was petite and attractive, ash-blonde hair swept up in a ponytail, wearing white jeans and a vest top that showed impressively sculpted arms.

'Delphine! Wonderful to meet you.' She held my shoulders and kissed me on the cheek. I reared away as she leaned in for the second kiss and had to duck back, blushing furiously.

'Sorry. These are for you.' I thrust out the flowers, realizing too late how cheap and nasty they were; livid pink chrysanthemums, still dripping from the bargain bucket.

'How delightful, I must go and arrange them. Clem will be down in a jiffy, he's just finishing *The Archers*.'

The kitchen table had been laid, with a linen tablecloth and heavy cutlery. Radio 4 might have been playing upstairs in Clement's study, but downstairs it was Radio 3, some opera I didn't recognize, though Virginia obviously did, humming away as she unwrapped the flowers in the sink.

'So, Adam says you live on the other side of the park?' She chopped the stems with her back to me, which meant I could massage the truth without feeling too scrutinized.

'That's right, towards Highbury.' Our dank, poky flat on a housing estate in Finsbury Park, a world away from leafy Stoke Newington.

'Such marvellous transport links, we're out in the sticks here. Darling, would you get a vase? The top cupboard. No, not that one; the Denby one.'

Adam reached up and passed it to her, then ambled towards me, picking up a bowl from the table. 'Olive?'

I took one, hoping the skin wouldn't get stuck between my teeth, then remembered brushing them in Adam's ensuite to get rid of the garlic smell before we had sex, and looked down at the floor in case such sordid thoughts showed on my face.

'Your kitchen is lovely.'

Virginia turned, kohled blue eyes flicking around the room. 'We haven't had a chance to change anything yet, but it'll do for now. At least it's south-facing. Ah, Clem is here. This is Delphine, Clem. You know, Adam told you about her.'

A tall, greying, bespectacled man wandered in, carrying a newspaper. 'Delphine, yes. Hello. Adam, did you see this? Peter Bradshaw reviewing that *Da Vinci Code* film. Bloody funny.' He passed the paper to his son and picked up the corkscrew from the table. 'Shall I do the honours?'

It felt too awkward and unsophisticated to tell them I didn't drink, so I accepted a glass of white wine and sat down as instructed, while Virginia – or Ginny, as they all called her – served up salmon and potatoes. Clement ate with a fork, still reading the paper. Adam hoovered his up like a Labrador, but Ginny didn't eat at all, just sipped at her wine and pushed the fish around her plate.

'So, Delphine,' she said, patting her lips with a serviette – *napkin* – that matched the tablecloth. 'Adam tells me you're an English scholar.'

Swallowing a mouthful of potato, I nodded. 'It's my favourite subject.'

Clement peered at me over his spectacles. 'What are you reading at the moment?'

'Well, we're reading *Of Mice and Men* . . .'

He waved impatiently. 'I don't mean set texts. What are *you* reading?'

I considered committing intellectual suicide by saying the latest in the *Twilight* series, but Adam was gazing at me hopefully. 'A biography of the Mitford sisters.'

'Ah, yes.' Clement nodded, glasses slipping down his nose.

'Not much literary merit, of course, but a fascinating family nonetheless. I know Debo slightly, formidable woman.'

Risking a glance at Adam, I saw he was grinning, so relaxed a bit, feeling like I'd passed a test.

'And you're half-French?' Ginny cut up a potato and held it to her mouth but didn't eat it.

'Yes.' I pleated my napkin, wishing I could cover my face with it. 'My mother was French.'

'There's a lovely little *gîte* we go to in the Ardennes. We try to get out there as much as we can, be among the trees. Have you ever been?'

'Not recently, no. This salmon is delicious.'

'Thank you, there's a wonderful new fishmonger just opened on Church Street.'

Adam was sniggering now, looking between his mother and me, helping himself to seconds.

Ginny glanced at him. 'Stop it, Addy, we're only making conversation.'

'I'm sure Delphine will be rushing to change her seafood supplier,' observed Clement, not looking up from his paper.

I couldn't think what to say, unsure how to fit in with this tight threesome, contribute to their banter, make them love me as a possible daughter-in-law. Maybe we would get married in the Ardennes, wherever that was, wildflowers in my hair, Clement reading Yeats during the ceremony, watching me fondly over his glasses. Obviously, we'd have salmon for the wedding breakfast, and it would be a family joke by then, referenced in the groom's speech, as his friends from King's roared with laughter. Transfixed by the image, I barely noticed my future mother-in-law clearing our plates and coming back with a lemon tart. They'd started talking about politics, something to do with Sir Menzies Campbell. I'd been pronouncing the name wrong in my head, all this time. Clement knew him, as well as Deborah Mitford.

'Do you like the tarte au citron?' Ginny asked, although she hadn't touched her own slice.

'It's divine,' I managed, brushing crumbs off my chin.

'Tell her which *pâtisserie* on Church Street it's from,' said Adam with his mouth full, and his father hit him with the paper, smiling.

'What subjects are you taking for your A levels?' Clement asked, turning back to me.

'Um . . . English, French, Music and History.' Mr North had recommended History over Drama, as a more academic subject that would be viewed favourably by Oxbridge colleges.

'Adam's taking English, French, Spanish and History of Art,' said Ginny.

'I didn't know you could take History of Art at Brownswood,' I said, puzzled. 'Who's the teacher?'

Adam frowned at his mother. 'I haven't decided yet. We haven't even taken our exams.'

She looked down at her untouched plate. 'Of course. Plenty of time, darling.'

There was something I was missing, but I felt overwhelmed by it all; fishmongers and vase libraries and knives with ivory handles. We finished the dinner and went into the front room – living room, drawing room, whatever – where Ginny sat at the piano by the bay window. There was no television to be seen. She played Chopin, which was a bit too much for her little fingers, and I couldn't help comparing her, thumping away, to my own mother, who got more warmth and joy out of our battered old upright than Ginny could ever manage with that gleaming baby grand. It felt suddenly ridiculous, perching on the chaise longue next to Adam, who was lounging and chatting to his father about the cricket. Brownswood didn't offer History of Art as a subject. Maybe it was just wishful thinking on Ginny's part. I held the thin stem of my glass and inhaled the citrussy scent of the wine, pretending to sip occasionally, swirling it round and wondering when I could leave.

At nine-thirty, I excused myself, apologizing, saying Dad was expecting me back. They offered to call me a cab but I said it was fine and I'd enjoy the walk. Ginny fretted about young women wandering out alone at night and told me not to go through the park. Adam escorted me to the door, squeezing my shoulders from behind and briefly reaching round to do the same with my breasts.

'You did great, they loved you,' he said, beaming down at me.

'You think?'

'Definitely.' He nodded. 'If only for giving Dad the opportunity to tell everyone he knows the Duchess of Devonshire.'

'Dowager Duchess, she's been downgraded.'

It was better now we were on our own, but the question remained. Had I really played my part and, even if I had, was it a role I could continue to inhabit? I opened my mouth to ask him about History of Art, then closed it again.

'What?'

'Nothing.'

For some reason, I didn't want to ask him. Better to just

forget it. So I kissed him and walked home, trying to ignore the conclusions I'd drawn.

Adam was the gleaming grand piano to my battered old upright, and it didn't really matter how we played; we were both working with very different instruments.

Chapter 37

As soon as I could, I returned Jean-Luc's book, along with the *galette des rois*, baked carefully, reverently, as if the perfectly risen puff pastry could make the apology on my behalf. Letty took the cake and the book without a word, shutting the door in my face. I had a speech all prepared, in my best French, but it was lost to the harsh January wind, left unsaid, like so many things. With both her and Dylan, it felt easier to forget them for the time being. I missed the money, and I missed the fun, but tackling either of those problems felt too difficult, so I focused on my remaining work, my studies, making time for Em and Dad. It was more than enough to be going on with.

One problem I couldn't ignore was that my cleaning job had become a source of stress. Every time I'd been round to Elise's flat, I'd felt a sense of dread, wondering if Albert would be there. I hadn't seen him since that afternoon before Christmas, but there were signs of his presence – in fact, there seemed to be more mess than ever, as if he was deliberately leaving a tip for me to clear up. One Friday,

I went over after a lunchtime shift at Merhaba, thinking that if he was there then I'd make an excuse and go back later. But the flat was empty, so I started hoovering the bedroom slightly feverishly, noting the rumpled sheets and pants on the floor. If I worked quickly, it should only take a couple of hours.

I worked quickly, but it took longer than that to wipe away the evidence of Albert's activities, and I was red-faced and breathless by the time I gave the kitchen worktop a final polish and plumped the cushions on Elise's corner sofa. All done. After loading the cleaning products back on their shelves, I put on my coat and hurried to the door, pausing to remove a wilting lily from the flower arrangement on the dining table. As I swung my bag onto my shoulder, I had a smile on my face – £50 better off, and home in time to make dinner for Em and Dad. Perhaps a risotto, then we could watch something together, maybe have a game of cards. Em could look at my latest essay, she was so good at spotting spelling mistakes, and then we could—

'You brought me flowers!'

Barrelling out, still carrying the dead lily, I walked straight into Albert's arms. He was holding a key, swaying in the hallway outside, his hair askew. Catching me by the elbows, he plucked the stem from my hand.

'Well, if it isn't Cinderella,' he said, smelling the withered petals. 'My little Cinders, sweeping up after me.'

I jerked away, back into the flat. 'I've just finished.'

'Don't rush off.' He closed the door behind him, dropping his key and the flower on the side table. 'Stay and have a drink.'

'No, thank you. I've got to get home.'

He shrugged off his coat and flung it on the sofa. 'Come on, don't leave me all by myself. Just one drink.'

It was never just one drink, but I didn't know how to say no without being rude. Or how to say yes without it seeming like I was saying yes to something else as well. So I just stood there as he moved to the kitchen.

'Take it off, and we can be comfy.'

He nodded at my old puffer jacket. It was frayed at the wrists, and I wanted to replace it with a new winter coat, only I didn't have the money. Even with this job, I didn't have enough, not quite. I was waiting till the end of the sales, for a really good bargain.

'I'm fine, thanks.'

He handed me an inch of amber liquid in a crystal tumbler. I took it but didn't drink, simply clutched the glass, staring at him, wondering what to do. Maybe nothing. Maybe I was worrying for no reason. He was just my employer's son, being friendly. No need to get all het up.

'So, do you do extras?'

'What?'

Albert settled himself on the sofa, crossing his legs, swilling his drink. 'Additional services.'

Sidling towards the kitchen, I put my glass on the counter. 'What do you mean?'

He took a gulp, hissing through his teeth. 'Cooking, that sort of thing. If we want to have a dinner party. What did you think I meant?'

I exhaled a shaky breath. 'Oh. No. Sorry, I'm not a very good cook.'

He squinted at me over his glass. 'I bet you're good at other things.'

Writing about Mrs Danvers, singing Billie Holiday songs, speaking French, playing chess with Em.

'I really have to go.'

'I'm only joking, there's no need to look so terrified.' As I moved towards the door, he jumped to his feet, putting his hand on my arm as I reached for the latch.

'I'm not terrified.' My fingers groped for the catch.

'You are,' he murmured, his thumb sliding inside the ragged wristband, feeling for my pulse. 'You're all of a flutter.'

A cat dabbing at a mouse, waiting for it to run away. He would have been good-looking had he not been so vile. But that monstrous sense of entitlement lay on him like a sweaty sheen, shape-shifting Prince Charming into Grendel. Everything about him was repellent – the loosened tie with some sort of club insignia, the immaculately pressed shirt, shiny shoes he didn't shine. He wasn't anything like Sid – they were from very different worlds – but he was still Sid, on some base level, in the end. And I thought of that day, in Sid's flat, when I didn't say anything, just snuck out like a thief, ignoring the *l'esprit de l'escalier*, snuffing out my staircase wit. Never again.

'You need to let go of me right now. Because I'm leaving.'

He made a mock-sad face. 'You look all cross. When will you be back?'

Pulling on the latch, I opened the door and jammed one foot in the gap. 'I won't be.'

'What will I tell Ma? That she's lost her Mrs Mop?'

I turned and looked him in the eye. 'Tell her I don't need

the money. Tell her her son needs to work on his manners. Tell her her son can clean up his own cocaine.'

His mouth dropped a little, before he regained his composure. 'Feisty,' he murmured. 'I like it.'

'Fuck you,' I said, and slammed the door.

Running along the corridor and jabbing at the lift buttons, I cast glances back, but the door stayed closed. He was probably already sleeping it off. Downstairs in the lobby, feeling reassured by the presence of the porter, I got out my phone. Elise received a very short text telling her I could no longer work for her. It was an effort, but I managed not to say sorry.

On the bus home, I thought I was certainly good at some things, losing jobs being one of them. The puffer jacket would have to make it through another winter, but that was preferable, all things considered. My phone buzzed in my bag, and I dug it out, tucking it between my ear and my shoulder as I picked at the loose cotton.

'Hello?'

'Darling, it's Elise. What was that about?'

I was surprised she'd called. Despite our history, we weren't close, had barely seen or talked to each other in years. 'I'm . . . I have another job. And I'm studying now. I don't have time.'

'It's only a couple of hours a week. Can't you squeeze it in?'

'No. I'm afraid I can't.'

'It's just . . . There's not another reason, is there?'

'What do you mean?' The bus jerked and rolled past Sadler's Wells, the dance theatre. Maman took me there once, just before she died. We watched some modern ballet, which I didn't enjoy. Just a lot of people leaping about, twisting this way and that.

'Ah . . . um . . . Has Albert been round recently? He sometimes stays over.'

'Yes. Yes, he has.'

'And . . . How's he been? All right?'

'Why wouldn't he be?'

'I just . . . He hasn't been *naughty*, has he?'

I was bored of this dance. 'I wouldn't put it like that, no.'

'Oh good, because for a second I thought—'

'Mrs de Trafford, your son is a complete arsehole.'

There was a silence for a second, then she sighed. 'I know. He's just like Hugo, his father.'

'I don't want to see him again, or be there any more.'

'Darling, I feel terrible. I could have a word with him, then you could—'

'No. I couldn't.'

'I tried to help, you know, when Josephine – your mother – died.'

'You did. Thank you.'

'Oh, well. Good luck with your new things. *Adieu.*'

'Goodbye.' I put my phone back in my bag and stared out the window as the bus rumbled past the shops on Upper Street, then got it out again and scrolled for a number I'd stored in my contacts but never called before.

'Hi, it's Delphine.'

'Hello.' Dylan sounded distracted; I hoped I hadn't interrupted one of his lessons. 'How are you?'

'I think we should carry on with the band.' I wanted to say it quickly, before I lost courage. What if he'd changed his mind?

'Great. Why the change of heart?'

219

'You were right. I need to have some fun.'

'You could start right now. I'm at Jay's, we're playing a few tunes.'

I heard Roz in the background, shrieking, 'You're not playing, you're drinking!' and laughed, thinking it would be nice to go and unwind with them, forget about everything that had happened that afternoon.

'Sorry, I've got to get back to Em and my dad. But maybe we could have a session, soon?'

'Sure thing.'

There were the Hugos and Alberts of this world, and then there were the Dylans and Sanjays. I knew whose side I wanted to be on.

Chapter 38

The following week, when Em had gone over to Halima's for the evening, I settled Dad in front of the TV with a pizza. I'd got him a new selection of DVDs from the library, and left him choosing between *Contact* and *Shakespeare in Love*. As I prepared to slip out into the night, he turned and looked at me quizzically.

'You off somewhere nice, FiFi?'

I immediately felt guilty and embarrassed. Was it OK to leave him on his own? He'd seemed better lately, more talkative; perhaps he wanted company.

'Just going to a rehearsal. I won't be long.'

'For your band?' He frowned. 'But Em said you did the show already. You had a cough.'

My minx of a daughter, telling me it was fine, then sneaking to Dad. 'Yes, well. We thought we'd try again.'

He nodded. 'That's good, Fi. I'm proud of you.'

'Oh, Dad.'

'You have fun now.' He turned back to his DVDs.

'Do you want me to start the film? What have you chosen?'

'*Contact*,' he said, and settled himself deeper into his chair.

In the back room of the Highbury pub, limp tinsel still decorated the grubby mirrors, even though it was the end of January. When I arrived, Dylan and Sanjay were sitting at a table surrounded by empty crisp packets, Bernadette huffing patiently at their feet.

'I'm telling you, you can't tell the difference.'

'Bloody can.'

'Can't. They taste the same.'

'Bloody don't.'

I took off my coat and sat down with them. 'What?'

Sanjay turned to me, holding out his hands in appeal. 'Greggs. The new sausage roll.'

'The *vegan* one.' Dylan snarled it like an expletive.

'I haven't tried it.'

'You should.' Sanjay leaned forwards conspiratorially. 'I'm thinking of adopting a plant-based diet. For the planet.'

Dylan snorted. 'Then why'd you just inhale a load of smoky bacon crisps?'

We didn't achieve much in that rehearsal. Sanjay and Dylan were larking about, but I still felt uptight after the school show, worried my throat would never open up again. We ran through a few songs and, after watching me struggle with a held note, Dylan taught me a breathing exercise.

'Normal breathing is shallow,' he said. 'You only use about five to ten per cent of your lung capacity in an average breath. But when you're singing that goes up to fifty per cent. So if you don't use your diaphragm properly, you'll mess up. You need to strengthen it.'

At his direction, I put a hand on my stomach and began to pant in a way that made my abdomen push against my hand. With each downward push of air, I had to imagine sighing out a phrase, and engage every one of my muscles, the sound coming from deep within my body. With both of them watching, I felt silly.

'You need to use the full potential of your lungs,' said Dylan. 'Stand straight, make it come from right down in your belly.'

Catching sight of Bernadette panting along with me, I began to giggle. Dylan followed my gaze.

'She always sings from the diaphragm,' he said. 'Great breath control, though it doesn't smell great.'

'I need a lamb rogan josh,' said Sanjay.

'What happened to your plant-based diet?'

'Starts next month. Come on.'

They'd mentioned getting a takeaway when we'd arranged to meet up but, although it sounded nice, I couldn't justify the cost since I'd left my cleaning job.

'Actually, I'd better be going. I've got to get back to Em.'

'No, you haven't,' Dylan replied, hooking his dog on her lead. He smiled at my dropped jaw. 'You forget I teach at your daughter's school. Her friend Halima is one of my students. If she practised as much as she talks then she'd play like Liberace. She told me today that Em was coming over to watch *Sabrina*.'

'Em said they were doing a history project.'

'Maybe it has something to do with witches.'

Caught out in my own lie, and discovering my daughter's, I was so distracted that, before I knew it, we were in an Uber. When we arrived, Roz was already unloading foil trays and rattling cutlery.

'I'm doing Dry January,' she said, as we went into the kitchen. 'I want to kill myself.'

Sanjay cracked open a beer. 'I'm not.'

She shot him a dirty look and turned back to me. 'Don't let me eat anything. I can't have any rice.'

Piling poppadoms on a plate, Roz told me the producer of her BBC series had taken her to dinner at the Ivy, and said they wouldn't be filming until early summer, which would give her plenty of time to get into shape, if she got the part. She grimaced at my intake of breath. 'That's what it's like. I'll have to shift at least a stone.'

'But you don't need to.'

'If we want to convert the loft, then I *do* need to.'

She already seemed thinner, her faded jeans sagging, cheekbones a little more pronounced. Along with the blonder hair pinned up with a chopstick, she was starting to look more like Rosalie Murray in *Agnes Grey*, winding back to the days when she was a film star and had the world at her feet. Could she do it all again? She obviously wanted to try. While Dylan, Sanjay and I ate rogan josh with pilau rice and peshwari naan, Roz nibbled on a leg of chicken tandoori and threw us resentful glances.

'How'd it go this evening?' she asked, licking her fingers.

'Great,' said Sanjay.

'OK,' said Dylan.

Maybe I was the reason for his lukewarm response. Did he

still think I was holding something back? I felt tired and unsettled, thinking of Em and Halima watching *Sabrina*. She was growing up. My breathing went shallow just thinking about it. If only I could talk to Letty about it, and let her tell me '*Il faut se détendre.*'

Idly scratching under Bernadette's ear with one hand, I listened to Roz tell us outrageous stories of being on set with soap stars, watching Sanjay's eyes soften as they rested on her. I was envious of their easy, jokey intimacy, their love evident in the relentless mockery, the tag-team parenting, one of them picking up where the other left off. Sanjay might never unload the dishwasher, according to Roz, but he shouldered her burdens in other ways. Not for the first time, I felt desperately sad for Em that she'd never had a father to share her secrets with; never had a dad ruffle her hair, help with her homework, carry her to bed on his back.

As we were stacking empty containers, their daughter Izzy appeared in the doorway in her pyjamas, bug-eyed with sleep, clutching her toy horse.

'Daddy, are you and Mummy going to get a divorce?'

Roz hastily wiped her hands on a tea towel as Sanjay shifted round in his seat and opened his arms.

'Of course not, sweetheart. Whatever gave you that idea?'

'Mummy was talking about people having affairs. And you're drinking. Like *EastEnders*,' sniffled Izzy into his shoulder.

'Oh, darling.' Roz knelt by her daughter to stroke her dark, fluffy hair. 'We're nothing like *EastEnders*. We're more like . . . *The Simpsons*.'

Sanjay stood and took his daughter's hand. 'I'll take you

back upstairs, Izz-Bizz.' As he led her down the corridor, we could hear her saying, 'I saw *EastEnders* once. A man strangled someone and then married her. What's bigamy?'

Roz clutched her head. 'She's a liability.'

I harvested a leftover shard of poppadom. 'Does Izzy get on with her brother?'

'Christ, no,' replied Roz, winding a finger around her plate and licking it. 'They fight like cat and dog. The other day Izzy whacked Joe with that bloody horse and took a chunk out of his arm. Thought we'd have to go to A&E but I patched it up with Steri-Strips and he was OK.'

'Right.' I reassessed my worry that Em was an only child.

'Of course, they *love* each other,' continued Roz. 'Joe will ignore her all day, and then I'll go up to check on them at night and find he's climbed in bed with her and they've fallen asleep holding hands.'

My worry came crashing back. Em didn't have anyone to do that with but me. No father, and no sibling. Chalked outlines of a missing family. I got to my feet and started taking plates to the sink.

'Oh, don't bother with that,' said Roz, waving me away. 'I'll do it tomorrow morning. At least I won't have a hangover. Go home and read something from your course.'

'OK, thanks.' Gathering up my coat and bag, I rummaged in my purse, calculating in my head. 'Here, for the takeaway.' I offered my last ten-pound note.

She shook her head. 'Don't bother about that either, we can stand you a curry.'

'But . . .' I held it out, embarrassed and unsure what to say.

She pressed the note back into my hand. 'Seriously. Keep it. Spend it on a book. Preferably one of your set texts.'

'Does that mean I don't have to give you any money either?' asked Dylan.

She snorted. 'You can give Sanjay beer money. You drink enough of it.'

'That's why I'm so chilled out,' he replied, tipping his chair back, catching the tea towel she threw at him. His teeth were neat and white, the only neat thing about him.

'Roz, can I ask you a favour?' I hadn't meant to say anything, certainly not in front of Dylan, but suddenly felt the urge, maybe because I'd chilled out too.

'Sure thing, what?' Roz leaned forwards, palms on the table.

'Will you . . . talk to your friend Sylvie for me?'

'Sylvie? Why?'

'Letty . . . er . . . fired me. Because she thinks I stole from her.'

Roz's eyebrows disappeared into her wavy fringe. '*What?*'

'I took a copy of her husband's book.' Aware of Dylan's narrowed eyes, I found myself stammering. 'It was a misunderstanding, I gave it back. But Sylvie might, I don't know, talk to her for me. Or ask her to let me go round and explain.'

Roz whistled. 'That's a bit of a lime pickle, isn't it.' She drummed her fingers, then nodded. 'Leave it with me. I played a marriage counsellor in *Midsomer Murders*, and have experience in delicate negotiation.'

Dylan smirked. 'Didn't you get killed in that episode?'

She stuck her tongue out at him. 'Didn't know you'd watched it. Are you a fan?'

'Thank you,' I said. 'And if you see her, tell Letty . . . I'm sorry.'

She stared at me. 'You didn't really steal this book, right?'

'Of course not! But . . . I'm sorry she thinks I did.'

Roz huffed. 'It's her who should be sorry, throwing out accusations without waiting for an explanation.' She reached across and patted my arm. 'Don't worry, I'll speak to Sylvie.'

'Thanks. I'd better get going, got an early shift tomorrow.' And another essay to finish.

Dylan clicked his fingers at Bernadette. 'I'll come with you.'

The dog came shuffling out from under the table, where she'd been hoovering up grains of rice, and I told myself I didn't feel nervous or excited about the prospect of being alone with her owner.

Out in the cold, Dylan blew on his hands. 'How are you getting home?'

I pointed down the road. 'The number 19.'

'I'll walk you to the bus stop.'

We strolled in silence for a while, before he said, 'You like this Letty, then? She's the woman you go and speak French to, right?'

'Yes. She's lovely. Well, not lovely – she's rude and eccentric and bossy, but . . .' I looked up at the stars, visible despite the city lights. 'She's interested in me, in what I have to say. And sometimes it's easier to say things in French than English.'

He didn't reply for a second. 'There's a word in Welsh,' he said eventually, his voice slightly croaky. '*Hiraeth*. People describe it as homesickness, but it's not really translatable. It means longing, missing something. It might be your home, but it might be a person, or a time in your past. It's a good word.' He smiled at me. 'Sometimes we need another language.'

He didn't say anything else until the number 19 pulled up, and I started digging in my bag for my card. As I boarded the bus, he raised his hand in farewell.

'*Hwyl*,' he said. Which was obviously goodbye but, the way he said it, I could tell it meant something else, too.

And he and Bernadette stood watching as the bus drove away.

Chapter 39

*O*n the way home, I kept thinking about *hiraeth*, that sense of longing, of something being missing. Em's father, Maman, Dad. My childhood, after the age of thirteen. Before he gave up on everything, my dad was a piano tuner, and the story of how he met my mother was one I'd told Em many times. She couldn't hear the story of how her parents met, so I told her the tale of her grandparents instead.

As a teenager, Nathan Jones was apprenticed to a blind tuner in Stoke Newington, who trained him in exchange for Nathan being his eyes, when he needed them. Elmore Humphreys was partial to a tin of Quality Street, and wanted someone to separate the Dairy Fresh Toffees, which he liked, from the Montelimarts, which he didn't. So Nathan picked out the correct chocolates, passing them to Elmore as he tightened the tuning pins, and a partnership developed. When Elmore died, Dad took over the business, though he never had an official qualification.

One day, he arrived at Josephine Colbert's flat to tune her upright. He was nearly forty by then, and not much of a ladies' man, but as soon as he heard her husky, lilting voice, he was lost. He nudged her strings into place and, when the piano was at a perfect pitch, she played and sang for him – a Gershwin song – and he listened with his eyes closed. Love was here to stay.

Once they were settled in their little flat in Finsbury Park, with me in the cot, Josephine Jones went back to work, teaching the piano to the children of Islington's most ambitious parents. Nathan did his rounds, servicing Elmore's clients and occasionally adding a new one. There was one in particular, Hortense Smith, who lived in a shambling old house in Barnsbury, with a Steinway in the drawing room. Twice a year, Dad would go to tune it, while she made him weak tea and talked to her parakeets. Afterwards, twice a year, she would hand him an envelope with three hundred pounds in it. Of course, this was way above his rate, but she wouldn't listen to his protests. That was what she'd decided his skills were worth.

Twice a year, on the Hortense days, Dad would bring his envelope home to JoJo, who, in honour of the occasion, would provide a celebratory English afternoon tea. As a Frenchwoman, she had a fascination for it, making scones from scratch and brewing tea with proper leaves. But, as a Frenchwoman, she was slightly off-key – she always produced a magnificent trifle rather than the classic Victoria sponge. Dad never told her because, as far as he was concerned, she always struck exactly the right note. So they toasted each other and ate her trifle, scattered with hundreds and thousands, as I toddled around them, dipping fat fingers into the whipped cream.

Hortense's money paid for my school trips, our holiday to the B&B in Whitstable, the star necklace Dad bought for Maman, lovingly fastened around her neck as I swirled the jelly and custard with my spoon. Now, as I thought about *hiraeth*, fingering the silver cross and star that swirled at my throat, I wondered where JoJo's star had gone, why it had never come to me, like her crucifix. It would have been another memento, a reminder of the heavens; the hope that somewhere she was nestled in a celestial branch, looking down on me. But, like so many things, it was missing.

When I got home that night, the lights in the living room were on but the TV was off. Dad was sitting in his chair with a book in his lap, tenderly turning the pages, a greasy empty plate on the little table next to him. He looked up and smiled as I came in, then bent his head back to his task.

'Is Em in bed?'

He nodded, still turning. 'Halima and her father brought her back in the car. Mo. Nice man.'

'Good.' Was *Sabrina* suitable viewing for two not-quite-twelve-year-olds? Presumably Mo must have approved. I leaned down to pick up the plate, then stopped. 'What's that you're reading?'

He held it up. 'Recipes.'

The plate was forgotten. It was Maman's notebook, pasted with cutouts from magazines, along with her scribbled additions, the looping cursive spiralling across each page. All the dishes I remembered from my childhood – the yoghurt cake we made together; her version of onion soup, with an extra dollop of cream; a slow-cooked pork and potato stew we used to have on Sundays; the layered trifle she produced whenever Dad tuned Hortense's piano. They were all there, with others I didn't remember but must have eaten, at one time or another. Holding the tattered pages in my hand, breathing the scent of them from deep in my diaphragm, I remembered Letty's devotion to Jean-Luc's memoir.

'I haven't seen this in years.' The cover was faded and mottled, 'Recettes' written in careful capitals with a smudged cloud drawn around them. 'Where did you find it?'

'It wasn't lost. It was always here.'

I didn't know what he meant, but assumed it must have been in their bedroom somewhere, along with the other things he kept pristine, as if she would come back one day, ready to write in it again.

'It's lovely.' I handed the notebook back to him and he pressed it gently against his heart.

'Did you have a nice night?'

'Yes.' I took the plate. 'It was fun.'

Stacking the washing-up, I smiled to myself. Dad reading, asking me about my evening. Outside it was dark and cold, but it felt warm and bright in here. I turned the light off and said good night, edging quietly into the bedroom in case Em was already asleep. But she was sitting up in bed, reading *Wolf Hall*.

'Hi.' She didn't look up. 'You had some post. I put it over there.' She gestured towards a pile of books stacked on a chair.

'How was *Sabrina*?' I picked up a thick cream envelope resting on top of *Emma*.

The pirate smile appeared. 'How do you know?'

'Halima told Dyl— Mr Taylor.'

'She's such a chatterbox. Mr Abdullah got Netflix. I thought

233

you wouldn't let me go on a school night if we weren't doing homework.'

I sank onto the bed. 'Of course I would have. I'm not . . . a *witch*. Just tell me.'

'OK. Can I go and watch *Stranger Things* next week?'

'No way.'

I ripped the envelope open. Inside was a personalized note-card, with the letters 'EdT' embossed at the top, followed by an address I didn't recognize. Somewhere called Great Tew. Where was that? It was a handwritten note, something familiar about the writing. The same flowing script as Maman's, only this wasn't my mother's writing – it was Elise de Trafford's. They went to the same school in France together, as children.

> My dear Delphine,
>   Thank you for the work you've done over the years. Stay in touch.
>   Sincerely,
>   Elise

Loitering inside the envelope was a cheque for three hundred pounds. Payment for Albert's misdemeanours. I sniffed the scent of blood money; maybe I should tear it up, throw it away. But she could afford it, and Albert had been extra work in more ways than one. Three hundred pounds, just like that, all in one go. That's what she'd decided I was worth. I imagined her dashing off the note, signing the cheque, stuffing it all in the envelope, heading off for some lunch party without a second thought. It didn't mean much to her, but I could make that money count.

My brain began to bubble and fizz, plans taking shape – ideas, schemes, enterprises. I could get Em a proper birthday present, buy some books, DVDs for Dad, maybe save for a new laptop that didn't stall every time I tried to open a document. A new winter coat, for me *and* Em. So many possibilities.

But first, Letty.

Chapter 40

'You'll have to railroad her,' Sylvie had warned me on the phone. 'She'll moan and groan, and you'll have to ignore her, bully her more than she bullies you. My father, Jean-Luc, always said, *"Qui n'avance pas, recule!"* What isn't an advance is a retreat. So just keep barrelling on.'

Wearing my new red dress under my coat, hair scraped back into a chignon, hooped earrings and high heels, I was dressed for my date – my date with Madame Riche. Arriving at her little courtyard, I knocked tentatively and waited, shivering in the cold. After a moment, the door opened and she regarded me, unsmiling, Aphra weaving around her legs. But she was wearing a nice dress herself – a chiffon number that wouldn't have been out of place on a dowager in *Downton Abbey*. Her nails were painted a subtle mauve. Taking heart from that, I held out my arm, gallantly.

'Are you ready? Shall we set off?'

'Haven't got my outer clothes,' she grumbled, shuffling backwards into the kitchen. I followed her, gathering her bag, helping her into her coat, handing over her hat, while she chuntered and fussed.

'Where are my keys? I must leave a light on for burglars. Gloves! Not those, the other ones. Damned cat.'

By the time we made it up the steps to the street, we were both breathless, and I was starting to think this had been a bad idea, not to mention an expensive one. But to give up now would waste Sylvie's advice, Em's research, and my chance at forgiveness. The grand gesture must go ahead. Flagging down a passing cab, I helped Letty into it and we settled ourselves as Canonbury's fine Georgian houses flashed by.

'Are you going to tell me where we're going?' With finicky precision, Letty pulled off her gloves, finger by finger, glaring at me.

'It's a surprise.'

'Let me tell you, your last surprise did not go down well. Don't know why you would think another one would make up for it.'

'Did you like the galette?'

Her lips thinned. 'The pastry was soggy. And in the south, we prefer brioche.'

I sighed. 'I'll remember next time.'

The streets thickened as we edged deeper into central London, and I kept my eye on the meter. When we reached Wardour Street, it was registering just under twenty pounds. It was fine, Elise's cheque would cover it. The sky was dark and heavy, although it was only midday. Pedestrians hustled their way along the pavement, heads bent as if anticipating rain.

'Stop here, please.'

Letty put her gloves back on infuriatingly slowly, and peered around for her bag.

'I've got it.'

Her dark eyes snapped. 'Stealing again, are you?'

'For God's sake, Letty, give it a rest.'

The eyes widened, but there was the hint of a grudging smile on her face as I handed over the bag.

'Where are we?' she said, looking up and down the dingy street. 'Some godawful place.'

'Just along here.' I led her through a narrow alleyway and, as we reached our destination, her step faltered.

'Have I been here before?' she demanded, her hand tight on my arm.

'Yes. Years ago.' I pointed to the sign above our heads: 'La Poire Dorée', with a painted golden pear hanging from the 'L'.

There was a slight but discernible catch in her breath. 'La Poire,' she whispered.

'We're booked in for lunch,' I said.

Downstairs, the restaurant was a tucked-away bunker that resembled a luxurious air-raid shelter, dotted with candles, linen napkins bright white on ebony tables. Letty gazed around wonderingly, gnarled hands shaking as she took off her coat.

'Madame? Let me help you,' said our waiter, whipping off one of the napkins and laying it on her lap.

'How did you know?' she asked in a low voice, as he went away to get our drinks.

I hesitated. Letty didn't like to be pitied. 'Your daughter said there were a few places Jean-Luc reviewed in London. Em looked them up. This was the last. And the best.'

'The best.' She blinked rapidly. 'Jean-Luc said it was "an adequate attempt to recreate Saint-Germain in Soho". They were thrilled.'

'They *are* thrilled,' I replied. 'The owner remembered you. He's delighted you're coming today.'

She passed a hand across her face, then rallied as the waiter brought her glass of champagne. 'In that case, we'd better do justice to the menu.'

I'd never been anywhere like this before in my life, not even with Sid. Trying to forget about money, I ordered pâté, then salmon with puy lentils, while Letty pointed and issued a series of demands to the waiter, who departed hastily.

For a second, we both stared at the shiny black table. 'Letty,' I began. 'I just wanted to say—'

'*En français*,' she barked. Then glared at a picture of Edith Piaf on the wall as I spoke.

'I just wanted to say . . . I'm sorry I took *Les Carottes*. I should have asked, and had no idea that copy was so important to you. I just wanted to cook the galette and give it to you on Epiphany as a surprise, and I got carried away.'

For a while she didn't say anything, just studied Edith, who was leaning towards the microphone, arms stretched out in supplication. 'That crucifix you wear,' she said eventually, still not looking at me. 'Whose is it?'

Startled, I fingered the two necklaces tangled at my throat, my star and cross. 'My mother's.'

'You see,' she said, finally turning to me. 'When those we love are gone, we cling to what remains of them. Jean-Luc didn't wear jewellery, didn't give me jewellery. He gave me books. He wrote them, he wrote *in* them, and that is what

I cling to, all I have left. When you took that book, you took a part of me.'

I stared down at my napkin, stark white against the black. 'I'm sorry.' Then looked back up again. 'But you've got to move on. I'm your friend, I wanted to do something nice for you. It went wrong, but you're blowing this out of proportion.'

'How dare you? You stole my book!'

'No, I didn't, and I don't believe you thought that, really. There was never any danger you wouldn't get it back.'

She opened her mouth to argue, but the waiter reappeared with our food and for a while we busied ourselves arranging plates. Letty had ordered *les escargots*, the shells nestled in a sizzling sauce dotted with parsley.

'*Où est le pain?*'

The waiter hurried off again to fetch the bread, as Letty began ruthlessly prising snails out of their cocoons.

'I'm so angry,' she spat. 'So angry with him. For leaving me.'

The tables seemed to recede around us, as I remembered that day in hospital when my mother died. The grief was incandescent. How *dare* she? Nothing but a poxy cross to remember her by. Not nearly enough.

'Me too,' I said, and she looked up, smiling through the tears trembling on her lashes.

'*Eh, bien,*' she said. '*En marche.*'

'*En marche,*' I said, raising my glass.

'Have some snail.' Letty held out her fork.

I frowned at the impaled grub, which didn't look particularly appetizing.

'Go on,' said Letty. 'It will broaden your palate. It's just garlic, really.'

Taking a bite, then chewing more vigorously, I decided this was a culinary branching out – one small morsel for a man; one giant mouthful for Delphine Jones. As the texture hit the back of my throat, I retched, groping for my napkin and glass of water.

'Ugh!' The snail slid down like a pill. 'It's like eating rubber bands!'

Letty threw her head back, amethyst earrings glinting in the candlelight. 'It's an acquired taste,' she cackled. 'One you're not yet sophisticated enough to appreciate.' I made a mental note of '*raffinée*': sophisticated. 'But you'll get there.'

'Not sure I want to,' I replied, gulping my water.

'What are we but a series of evolutions?' she said, gaily, spearing another shell. 'Each one a better incarnation. One day you'll be a person who eats snails.'

For a second, I pictured another Delphine – an older one, with more expensive tastes, a degree, a mortgage. *Raffinée*, *détendue* . . . what was the word? *Avisée* – wise. But imagining her enjoying *les escargots* was too much of a stretch.

Snails aside, the food was delicious – full of rich, precise flavours, elegantly presented on the plate. When the owner of the restaurant – a short, rotund man with red cheeks and a fairly obvious wig – brought out our desserts, Letty was enchanted.

'Michel, *mon ami*,' she rasped. 'You look so much older.'

'But you do not look a day over twenty-five,' he replied, setting her crème brûlée in front of her.

'You rascal,' she chuckled. 'I was so drunk last time.'

'My dear, your inebriation only served to make you even more entertaining. And this is your friend, Ms Jones? I am honoured to nourish you with my meagre cooking.' He nodded in Letty's direction. 'Did Madame tell you about her husband, the famous Monsieur Riche? His review had everyone flocking here. We had to turn people away. I never forgot it.'

I nodded, sipping my water, watching as they teased each other, the years falling away from them both. The waiter brought us coffee, and Michel went away to get the bill.

Letty looked at me over the rim of her cup. 'You're quite devious, you know.'

'I get it from my daughter.'

'Yes, my daughter is also *très sournoise*.' She was talking about Sylvie, obviously, but for a second it felt as if she meant me too.

Michel returned, placing a folded piece of paper on the table between us. Letty reached out, but I put my hand over hers.

'No, this is my treat.'

She tutted. 'Don't be ridiculous. This lunch would cost everything I've ever paid you.'

'It's not about the money.'

She used her other hand to rap mine. 'You're as big a rascal as Michel.'

'No,' he interrupted. 'I am a much bigger rascal.' He twitched the paper from under us both and opened it. It was blank apart from one word: '*Merci.*' 'And I have something else for you.' From behind his back, he produced a brown leather book. 'Our visitors' record. From 1997.'

Letty took the volume from him and flicked through it, slowly, eyes roving the pages. Finally, she stopped.

'*Jean-Luc et Lettice Riche*,' she murmured. 'We both signed it. I had quite forgotten.'

'Well, you were very drunk,' said Michel.

Despite feeling dizzy with relief that there was no bill to pay, I worried that meant my grand gesture didn't count. But as we went back up the steps of the restaurant, Letty leaning on my arm, she squeezed it and pulled my head towards her ear.

'You are a very clever girl,' she whispered. 'Very clever.'

'The cleverest of them all,' I replied.

'You were right,' Letty added, and there was the glint of an unshed tear. 'Once I'd calmed down, I knew you didn't steal it. *Nous sommes amies, n'est-ce pas?*' She switched to French again, our shared language, which felt like a secret we kept. Sometimes you needed another language, to say the things you couldn't say otherwise.

'*Oui, bien sûr*,' I said, looking down at the steps so she couldn't see my own eyes.

'*Une taxi, maintenant*,' she said, as we reached the pavement. '*Tu peux m'aider?*' She held out her arm.

'*Oui, bien sûr*,' I said, taking it.

'*Le Gallois. Qui est aussi pas raffiné . . .*' The Welshman who is also not sophisticated . . . '*Mais il est craquant, non?*' For a second, I struggled to remember the meaning of '*craquant*', then recalled our very first meeting, Letty lusting after Emmanuel Macron.

'*Oui, bien sûr*,' I said, and led her out into the street, to find a cab home.

Chapter 41

With Elise's money cushioning us, I was able to give Em a proper birthday treat, taking her to see a candlelit production of Shakespeare's Scottish play. She was entranced, but teased me all the way home, because I was uncomfortable saying his name. 'It's not bad luck,' she kept telling me. 'There's no such thing.' But I couldn't take the risk, smiling at her glowing face, bouncing in her seat on the tube carriage, wishing we could always be like this, without the toil and trouble, nothing wicked coming our way.

Spring blossomed, and the pace of life went up another notch. Now we were friends again, I loved my sessions with Letty, a constant source of amusement and fascination. We made dishes from Jean-Luc's cookbook – a hearty cassoulet, tarte tatin, galettes Bretonnes, quatre-quarts – dishes Maman would have showed me how to make, if she'd lived long enough. We ate our creations while Letty entertained me with tales of her life in France, enriching my vocabulary as Aphra purred on her lap, delicately licking morsels off her knees.

There were hours spent with Roz, preparing for my exams, going over my essays in her chaotic kitchen, discussing Austen and Eliot, studying unfamiliar poems, listening to Roz read out play dialogue with her perfect diction, occasionally throwing in a swear word to make me laugh. My mind was opening up, a budding shoot emerging from the ground after the cold of winter. I began to miss playing the piano, something I hadn't done since I was a teenager, apart from playing 'Solitude' with Dad that terrible day. The upright was almost unplayable, as he hadn't touched it since JoJo died, and I kept thinking of Dylan's beautiful Bechstein, smooth ebony and perfectly pitched. One afternoon, when Sanjay and I were at Dylan's flat for a rehearsal, I sat down at it, running my fingers over the keys and tracing the golden lettering on the lid.

'Do you play?'

I looked up to see Dylan holding out a cup of coffee and took it, shaking my head.

'Used to. Haven't played in years, I've forgotten how.'

'It'll still be in there somewhere.' He nodded at the keyboard. 'Give it a go.'

Clutching my cup, I pictured myself sitting in our living room, my mother behind me, her hair tickling my shoulders as she turned the pages, humming along as I stumbled over Scarlatti. Later, she encouraged me to play by ear, listening to Dad's records and picking out the tune, showing me how to add the chords underneath. I passed the cup back to Dylan and rested my hands on the keys. Could I remember anything?

'Try it,' said Dylan. 'It'll come to you. Just let it happen.'

In the end, my fingers remembered, a muscle memory,

moving of their own volition, settling into a gentle G major chord like they were glad to come home. At first, I didn't even know what I was playing, but gradually the tune emerged. With Dylan and Sanjay leaning against the gleaming lid of the baby grand, I picked out 'Dream a Little Dream of Me', my fingers responding more fluently as it came back to me. When I finished, I put the lid down, feeling embarrassed, but they both looked serious, intent on the performance.

'That was great,' said Sanjay. 'I didn't know you could play.'

'You could do with some practice,' said Dylan. 'You're a bit rusty.' But he smiled, softening the blow. *Rouillée*. I'd got better at French, maybe I could get better at the piano too. Flexing my fingers, which felt stiff and cold, unused to the exercise, Dylan pressed the still-warm cup of coffee back into them. We had our rehearsal, trying out a few more experimental pieces, then Sanjay and I got ready to go, him loading his guitar in its case while I put on my coat, ready to face the chilly March winds. But when we were both halfway down the stairs, about to push through the beaded curtain into the ever-unoccupied shop, Dylan called me back. I looked up at him leaning in the doorway of his flat, and now it was his turn to be embarrassed.

'I could teach you,' he said. 'If you wanted me to.'

The blood rushed to my cheeks as we stared at each other. 'Sorry,' I said. 'That's a really kind offer, but I don't have the money for that sort of thing.'

He ran a hand through his hair and shifted his feet uncomfortably. 'Wasn't asking for money. I'd do it for free. Because you're, you know . . . a mate.'

It would have been impossible for my face to go any redder, my mind and body closing down, unwilling to let me do anything other than gape up at him, as half-formed thoughts and feelings churned around uselessly. Gradually, one clear image solidified in my muddy brain: me sitting at the piano with Dylan, playing together. And suddenly I wanted that more than anything else in the world.

'That would be . . . nice. Thank you.'

'*Pleser*,' he said, giving me a salute, and closed the door.

Outside, I let the cold air cool my cheeks and tried to ignore Sanjay's curious glance as I joined him on the street.

'What was that about?'

I did my best to look unconcerned. 'Dylan's going to teach me the piano.'

He stared at me incredulously for a second, then guffawed. '*Teach* you? The piano? Hahahaha! Will you call him Mr Taylor and let him put you in for your grades?'

'Shut up.'

'Please, sir, can you help me with my arpeggios?'

'Pack it in.'

He snorted. 'You could just go for a drink like normal people.'

I ignored him, marching off to the bus stop, waiting for my heart to stop beating so fast. Sanjay was wrong. It wasn't a stupid idea. And there was no way we could go for a drink like normal people. A drink together would tip us into something; something I wasn't sure I was ready for. Not after Adam, and Sid, and what happened in between.

But . . . learning the piano. That would be fine.

Chapter 42

One of the last times I'd played the piano properly was back at Brownswood, aged sixteen, in one of the school music rooms. We were in the middle of exams, gruelling mornings and afternoons spent in the hall, sweating and scribing, all our lives up to that point and beyond riding on what we wrote in that echoing sports hall. I loved it, relishing that focus, unloading everything onto those blank white sheets, setting my pen down at the end, pleasantly sated and washed out. But that day I'd taken an English Literature paper and been distracted from a question about Maggie in *The Mill on the Floss* by the sound of Olive O'Leary sobbing at her desk behind me. She'd been led out after five minutes, but it took me a while to get back into my rhythm afterwards, thinking of her hiccupping breaths, and the fact the space behind me was now empty. One of the things I liked about those exams was the shared industry, all of us scratching away together, and I felt her absence, even though she was a terrible student who always referred to George Eliot as 'he'.

After we'd finished, we all streamed out into the pulsing June daylight but, feeling disjointed and in need of some peace, I went back inside, wandering down corridors until I arrived at one of the music rooms used for private lessons with the peripatetic teachers who visited. It was empty, so I went in, closing the door behind me. For a while I sat at the piano, reliving the questions, wondering if I could have done more, musing on what had happened to Olive. Without really thinking, I began to play; to soothe myself with one of my mother's favourite tunes – 'Comes Love'.

I barely noticed the door opening and closing again, and didn't realize there was anyone else in the room until I felt warm hands on my shoulders and a kiss on the back of my neck.

'I missed you on the hill. What are you doing here?'

'Playing.'

Adam reached across and struck a chord with his huge right hand. 'I can see that. I didn't know you played. You should have told my mother.'

I laughed. 'Didn't want to interrupt her.'

Although I hadn't been invited round officially again, as Adam's parents had been busy doing work on their barn in Norfolk, he'd told me his mother thought I was 'fascinating' and that his father had said there was 'something of *La Gioconda*' about me. Adam seemed to think that signified approval.

'I wanted to tell you,' he murmured, his lips an inch from mine. 'That they're going away again on Friday. The house will be empty.'

'We've got to study,' I breathed back.

'We *will* study,' he promised. 'There'll be a lot of studying. I might even use a magnifying glass.'

We were both laughing as we kissed, but the door opening again broke us apart. Mr North stood on the threshold, scowling.

'What are you two doing here?'

Adam shuffled his feet, looking at the floor, but I met my teacher's gaze. 'Sorry. I was playing the piano. Adam came in to listen.'

Mr North raised his eyebrows. 'Really? I didn't know you could play.' It was a challenge rather than an interested comment. He didn't believe me, which was annoying, because there was no particular reason why I wouldn't be able to play the piano. I wasn't one of those posh Lucindas who paid for lessons, sure, but his assumption irritated me. So I turned back to the piano and began to play again, but this time my fingers didn't settle into a gentle jazz standard. Instead, they tackled a fiendish Bach fugue, my heart thumping as I remembered my mother going over the fingering again and again: '*It must become second nature.*' And it had, because here I was, more than three years later, playing it like that moment was yesterday.

Finishing the piece, I felt triumphant but also despondent, because in losing my mother I'd also lost my piano teacher, and one day would forget how to play that fugue, and there would be no one to help me remember it. I looked up at Mr North, hollow-eyed and defiant, and he backed away saying, 'As you were,' nodding to Adam to go. Adam left, squeezing my shoulder, and I sat in the music room on my own until the next exam.

Chapter 43

I handed in my coursework to Roz in mid-March, crossing my fingers that it was good enough. Slaved over late into the night, it was a 2500-word essay comparing class and culture in *Howards End* and *Middlemarch*. I'd showed it to Em, who read it with a shuttered expression while I waited nervously. Eventually, she raised her eyes to mine, still impassive.

'It's good,' she said. 'Brutal. Funny.'

I exhaled, weak with relief.

'You spelled "syncretism" wrong,' she continued, going back to the pages.

'No!'

She looked up again, her stern face breaking into a smile. 'Gotcha.'

Only a few weeks before, Roz's teaching technique had included whipping me over the head with another of my essays as she yelled, 'Virginia Woolf wrote *The Waves*, not Iris Murdoch!' But when I emailed her the document, she replied, 'Can't wait to read this. I'm sure it will be brilliant.

Now go and relax.' It was as if Miss Challoner had given me one of her rare compliments. Roz was still waiting to hear if she'd got the part in the BBC drama, and I found myself hoping they'd cast someone else as Mrs Knightley of Donwell Abbey, so she could stay as Mrs Gill of Brownswood Academy.

My next session with Letty had been rescheduled for early on Saturday morning and, unusually, she had asked me to come to St Pancras. I left the flat early, shouting goodbye to the Em-shaped mound in our bed, wondering why Letty wanted to meet at a train station. I hoped she didn't intend for me to accost travellers arriving from France to practise my conversational French. It was the kind of crazy thing she would do.

It turned out Letty had a very different though equally crazy idea. Arriving outside Fortnum & Mason at 8 a.m., as instructed, I dodged suitcases while Letty delved into her enormous vintage Hermès bag and pulled out some cards, brandishing them in my face.

'We're going to Paris, Mademoiselle Jones!' shrieked Letty, waving her stick and narrowly missing a family of four. 'Day trip!'

She handed one of the cards to me. It was a return ticket, valid that day. I rotated it in my hands, letting it sink in. *Paris.* I had never been abroad in my life. Imagined it; walking down the Champs-Élysées with a miniature dog and smoking Gauloises in a café, the Eiffel Tower looming above. An impossible dream.

'I'm sorry, I can't go to Paris.'

'Nonsense,' replied Letty briskly. 'One has no idea how

broad one's vocabulary truly is until one has quibbled with a surly waiter on the Boulevard Saint-Germain.'

'I'd love to go.' I handed back the ticket. 'But I don't have my passport.'

'Yes, you do,' cackled Letty triumphantly, digging back in her bag. She produced my passport, unstamped; the one I'd renewed to register for my exams.

'How did you . . .' I began, tailing off as Letty winked.

'Your delightful daughter gave it to me, last week. Marvellous gal. Rosalind says she's some sort of genius, but she seemed perfectly normal to me.'

My *très sournoise* daughter. 'I feel bad about leaving her for the whole day.'

'Don't. She said she was going to see her friend. What was her name? Hilda? Helen? Something more exotic.'

'Halima?'

'Ah yes, that was it. Capital of Peru. Shall we get on?'

Em was fine. I'd handed in my essay. Roz had told me to relax. *Il faut se détendre.* I was going to Paris. Trying to banish a sudden dizziness, I smiled at my travelling companion.

'*Oui, bien sûr.*'

We headed towards the Eurostar check-in, Letty's stick clacking as she chattered away.

'We've got to go before that blasted Brexit thing, while we still can. Heaven knows what will happen after, maybe they'll build a wall or something. I haven't been to Paris in years, you know. Bloody hip. And my bloody husband dying. I'll never forgive him.'

'I'm sorry.' I risked a touch of her hand, but Letty waved me away.

'No need, it's not your fault. It's his, for giving himself diabetes. Silly man.'

We queued, and were searched, and went through things that beeped, and Letty argued with almost everyone we encountered.

'I thought we might get a free upgrade if I complained,' she whispered, as we sat down to wait for boarding.

'I don't think that's an option,' I whispered back.

'Always worth a shot,' replied Letty, getting a lipstick out of her bag and applying a dash of scarlet.

On the train, we had airline seats. 'Thank God we don't have to sit opposite some dreadful plebeians! Wine gum? Your ears will pop when we go into the tunnel.'

I accepted a sweet, putting my bag under my seat and wriggling my way to comfort with an extra breath of excitement. I was going to France, to the City of Light! *Quelle merveille.*

Letty ordered a glass of champagne, I had an orange juice, and we clinked our glasses to toast our trip, settling back to enjoy the views. We went into the tunnel surprisingly quickly, the train racketing into the ground and down under the sea. I gazed at my reflection in the window, imagining the sights at the other side. The Louvre and the Palace of Versailles and Napoleon's tomb and the Notre-Dame and the Arc de Triomphe . . .

'The Galeries Lafayette,' mused Letty. 'We should start there.'

'An art gallery?'

'No, a shop. A very nice shop. I need some new gloves. I have Raynaud's disease and I find Maison Fabre are the only ones that are any good.'

'Oh.'

'Don't worry. You can see that Pompidou claptrap if you want to. But it's not enough just to look at things. Gawping at the Eiffel Tower isn't going to help you speak French. Trying on a ridiculous dress and asking a snooty assistant if they have a size smaller is the way forward, trust me. Ah, here we are. *La France!*'

We emerged from the tunnel and Letty immediately switched to French as I pressed my face to the window.

'Don't expect anything yet. The countryside round here is very boring,' she said. Then she donned an enormous pair of sunglasses and appeared to snooze for the rest of the journey. I spent it staring at the (fairly dull) scenery, reminding myself that this was *ennui* and therefore more sophisticated than British boredom. Our surroundings began to thicken and darken as buildings – definitely Gallic – appeared. Letty took off her glasses and sniffed as we pulled into the Gare du Nord.

'We'll have to get a cab. I can't abide the *Métro*.'

In the taxi, the driver raised his eyebrows in the mirror and Letty barked, 'Boulevard Haussmann,' then continued in English to me. 'You'll find you have to be rather rude, I'm afraid. Any hint of apology and they'll despise you. Luckily, I have a natural inclination towards incivility. Perhaps that's why I've always got on well here.'

On the journey to Letty's shop, my eyes couldn't open wide enough to take in the sweeping boulevards, narrow side streets and shuttered windows, elderly ladies in tottering heels and café tables on every corner. It was everything I'd imagined; the film-set version.

'It's terribly dirty,' observed Letty. 'And no green spaces

like in London. Just odd little clay courts. But it's Paris, so it's better than anywhere else. *Arrêtez-vous ici!*'

Letty paid the driver, while I gazed up at the imposing triangular building. Inside it was even more magnificent, a gigantic theatre, with its huge steel-and-stained-glass dome, ornate balconies and Art Deco staircase. The faint sense of disappointment that my first visit to France's capital should start with a department store disappeared, as I watched impossibly chic women browsing the perfume counters. This *was* Paris.

'Womenswear is on the first floor,' announced Letty, leading the way. Even the mannequins had an attitude, like they should have been holding cigarettes.

'Here is your first challenge,' she continued. 'I want you to choose three smart dresses you like. But get them in the wrong size. Go and try them on. Ask the assistants for the right size. Ask them for their opinion on what suits you. If they suggest something different, accept their advice. Come back to me here with the dress you end up with.'

'But I couldn't possibly afford to buy a dress here.' I thought of the designer names we'd seen – Dior and Balenciaga, not exactly my usual market stall purchases.

'Who said you were buying one? It's not against the law to try things on. Chop-chop. Off you go. I'll see you in half an hour.'

Obediently, I walked towards a rack of dresses and started to sort through them, then looked at the price of one and dropped it like it had just come out of the oven. But, as Letty said, there was no law against trying things on. Particularly things this *élégante*.

Thirty minutes later, I arrived back holding an Agnès B grey gingham crepe dress with a maroon belt, which the severe-looking assistant with slicked-back hair had assured me was *'flatteuse et parfaite'*. It was 230 euros, but that didn't matter. This was just an experiment. I felt bereft though, as I recounted my efforts, and Letty nodded and hung it back on a rack. Looking in the mirror while wearing it had been something of a revelation.

'Bien. Maintenant.' She held out her hand. 'Here are ten euros. I want you to meet me at the Polidor. It's a restaurant. You have three-quarters of an hour.'

'But . . . where is it?' I whimpered, clutching the banknote.

'Well, you'll have to find that out, won't you? And don't use your phone! *A bientôt!'*

Two minutes later, I emerged on the corner of the Chaussée d'Antin, my heart beating hard. I was alone in a foreign city where I knew no one, and my grasp of the language felt suddenly chiffon-flimsy. It was one thing to sit in Letty's living room and chat, listening to Aphra's purring, quite another to stand on a street corner trying to find a restaurant you'd never heard of.

Hesitantly, I approached a pallid, languid-looking man holding a tiny coffee cup as he stared at his phone. *'Excusez-moi. Pardon, pour aller au Polidor? C'est un restaurant.'*

'Je sais pas.' He turned away. I remembered Letty's directive: 'Any hint of apology and they'll despise you.'

There was a taxi driver leaning against his cab, reading a newspaper. I marched up to him.

'I need to find the Polidor restaurant. It's a matter of urgency.'

He curled his lip. 'A matter of urgency? For you to eat steak?'

'It is an assignation. He said he would only wait half an hour, and then he would go forever.'

The taxi driver's face lit up, and he folded his paper. 'In that case, you will need to hurry. The *Métro* is quicker – the nearest station is that way. Line 9, Saint-Denis. But you'll have to change. You need the Odéon. Good luck!'

Forty minutes, two lines, eleven stops and three people later, I turned the corner into Rue Monsieur-le-Prince. Crémerie-Restaurant Polidor was almost cartoonishly French with its brown wooden frontage, gold lettering offering '*Vins Fins*'. Inside, Letty was sitting bolt upright at one of the long tables. When she saw me, she clapped her hands.

'Well done!' she said. 'You're just in time. Hemingway ate here, you know.'

'I know. I'm having the boeuf bourguignon. Apparently, we should avoid the bathroom.'

'Splendid!' Letty saluted me. 'You did your homework.'

Sitting down at the red and white chequered table, I nodded thanks to the waiter who filled my water glass. 'Did you get your gloves?'

Letty was surrounded by bags, though I had no idea how she'd managed to do so much shopping en route. She reached into one and pulled out a purple leather pair. 'Cost me a fortune of course, but I'm rich as Croesus, you know, thanks to Jean-Luc.' She looked around. 'He loved this place, even though the food is only so-so. Said you could taste the history.' Her gaze fell to the tiled floor, trodden by so many luminaries.

'You must miss him.'

'I miss arguing with him. And making up afterwards.' She grinned wickedly. 'You should really have red wine with beef, you know. Particularly here. Why don't you drink?'

I took a sip of my water. 'When I was thirteen, my mother was knocked off her bicycle and killed. The driver didn't stop, but the police caught him and breathalysed him. He was over the limit. I didn't want to drink after that.' I had drunk, once, but didn't want to remember that time. Couldn't.

For several seconds, Letty just looked at me, her rheumy eyes filling. 'Well, she would have been very proud of your excellent French,' she said, finally. 'That was faultless.'

'It was easier to say in French,' I admitted. 'I've never told anyone in English.'

'No need to go shouting your problems from the rooftops,' observed Letty, picking up the menu. 'Young folk are far too open these days. Always sharing things on Facespace. Where's the mystery?'

I had the boeuf, recommended to me by a garrulous old man on the *Métro* at Saint-Denis. Letty had confit de canard, Jean-Luc's favourite, washed down with a carafe of red wine. I took a sip, in the end, to be able to say I'd drunk where Hemingway drank, and because after my confession it felt like I'd let go of something. *Il faut se détendre.* So I had my mouthful, like communion wine, and it slipped down easily, pulling my shoulders with it, easing me back in my chair. As Letty began chatting to the couple next to us, I found myself joining in the animated discussion, debating the merits of British cheese, then let the conversation drift around me like smoke as I took a moment to absorb just being there, where Victor Hugo and Rimbaud were regulars, where James Joyce had lunch. Delphine Jones, sitting in Paris with a glass of wine, speaking French to the locals. Like the Agnès B dress, it was a revelation.

We finished our meal with a dark, sticky tarte tatin and strong coffee that rivalled Merhaba's.

Letty signalled to the waiter to bring the bill. 'Where do you want to go next? You may choose one heinous tourist destination before I have my *chocolat.*'

I pondered. So many places I wanted to visit, enough to fill a month of sightseeing. My eyes could never get enough of it all. But I thought of what Letty had said – 'Where's the mystery?' – and remembered Adam's father's comment – 'something of *La Gioconda*' – and decided there was one thing I wanted to see more than anything else.

'It's probably a terrible cliché. But there is somewhere I'd like to go.'

'Well, then,' said Letty, clicking her stick on the tiled floor. 'Lead the way.'

Chapter 44

The Friday after the music room incident, I went round to Adam's after school. I had just two more exams to take the following week, then we could relax and let our hair down at the prom. Remembering last year's event, kissing Adam for the first time by the library, I gloried in how far we'd come. My teachers were confident I would get top marks, I'd chosen my A levels, Mr North would be helping me with my Cambridge application, and, of course, I had Adam. A bright future beckoned.

When he opened the door, he was holding a magnifying glass to one eye, making it look huge and distorted.

'Ready to study?'

I laughed as he led me to the kitchen, where he'd already prepared a huge bowl of pasta for dinner. Adam had a hearty appetite, particularly before and after sex, and had been known to pad down naked from his loft room in search of snacks.

'How did you find the French paper?'

'*Comme ci comme ça.*' I settled myself at the big oak table and picked up an old copy of *Le Monde*. There was an article about student riots, and I barely noticed Adam gathering together the glossy-looking brochures that had been stacked underneath, shoving them on a shelf to clear the space for us. We ate there, listening to the Buena Vista Social Club, and I felt perfectly happy, imagining it was our house, rather than Ginny and Clement's.

After dinner, Adam took my hand and led me upstairs, his thumb rubbing my palm as we made our way to his garret. It was as neat as ever, and I'd understood he hadn't tidied the room for me that first time; it was always immaculate. Perhaps Ginny kept it that way. But there was nothing neat about us as we fell onto the bed, sloppy and frenzied. With practice, it had become second nature for me to know what to do, where he liked to be touched, how to breathe along his neck and then down, down. It was only afterwards we realized what a mess we were in. Because we forgot the condom. They were there, in the bedside drawer, but somehow neither of our hands found their way in to fish one out. We lay on our backs, breathing heavily, and the air was also heavy with the weight of what we'd done.

Staring at the ceiling, Adam said: 'Oops.'

The kind of thing you say when you accidentally bump into someone in a shop doorway.

'Sorry,' I said.

'S'OK,' he mumbled. 'You can get the morning-after pill.'

'Right.'

I'd never done that before. I thought of Marni, who'd finally got it together with Dan Edwards after they'd both had their teeth fixed. Their condom had broken, and after a snotty-sobbing conversation with an unsympathetic Sheba, whose father was a doctor, she'd sorted it. Adam and I curled up together and I fell into an uneasy sleep, dreaming of trying to swallow enormous tablets, choking on them, my teeth falling out as I crunched.

The next morning, I gathered my clothes, making sure not to leave any errant underwear, and we went downstairs to Ginny's south-facing kitchen. Adam made me toast, which I ate dry, already feeling queasy. Was that the first sign? I munched away, standing by the sliding doors, thinking about all the chemists on my way home. Plenty of choices.

'Will you go and get it today?'

Adam was holding his piece of toast, lavishly buttered, looking concerned, like he hadn't slept. But he had, because I'd heard him snoring.

'What?'

'The pill.' He folded the toast in half and took a bite. 'Do you know how to get it?'

'Yes,' I said. 'I know how to get it.'

'Cool.'

He gave me a greasy kiss and I walked towards the front door, catching sight of the magnifying glass winking on the little shelf above the radiator. If he'd looked through it, he might have seen my enigmatic expression, neither one thing nor the other. *La Gioconda.*

I went straight home. Didn't go to Marni's, didn't go to Sheba's, didn't go to the chemist. Just went back to Dad, and sat on the arm of his chair as he watched *Father of the Bride*.

Chapter 45

I couldn't believe I was in the 1st arrondissement, standing in front of the Louvre Palace, looking at the pyramid. Having asked directions from a fellow diner in the Polidor, watched by a hawk-eyed Letty, she then ignored them, insisting on getting a cab from the restaurant instead.

'Can't be hobbling down side streets at my age.'

I spent the journey with my face pressed to the window, gorging on the views. On the Rue de Rivoli, Letty told the driver to stop, and we got out. She handed some folded notes to me: my next challenge.

'Go into that shopping centre. There's a tobacconist on the ground floor. You can buy tickets for the Louvre there. I'm not queuing with all those tourists.'

Having secured our tickets, we walked the short distance to the Palace, me hugging myself as I glimpsed a few bonus sights. There were the Tuileries, and the Arc de Triomphe and the Eiffel Tower in the distance. But it was the pyramid that jolted me the most, snagging my attention when I was trying to appreciate the Renaissance architecture behind it.

'I don't like it.' Letty sniffed dismissively. 'A symbol of death. And vulgar besides.'

But I thought it was beautiful, the panes of glass catching spikes of spring sunlight – and also menacing; the megalith with its smaller companions either side blocked the view, but also somehow completed it. The past behind, and the future in front. You could maybe try to forget the past, but you couldn't ignore what lay ahead, the leaps that would be required to navigate the path.

'We can't go in that way anyway,' said Letty. 'Terrible queues. There's a much quicker entrance round the side. Follow me.'

We got in via Letty's 'secret' entrance in the south wing and, after passing through security, made our way to the first floor. Jostled by tourists, I could barely see any of the art, could hear Letty panting alongside, leaning heavily on her stick. We shouldn't have come. It was too busy, Letty was old and tired, and it had already been a long day. We should go back. But then I caught sight of her, in the distance, behind glass, and forgot about everything else. Partially obscured by heads and waving phones, the bustling activity around only served to highlight the quiet composure of the *Mona Lisa*. I dropped Letty's arm and moved forwards, weaving my way through the crowds until I was close enough to look her in the eye.

She was smaller than I had imagined, entirely protected, enigmatic, remote. The protection was necessary – over the years she'd been stolen, had acid, a rock, paint and crockery thrown at her. But she remained serene, with that knowing side-eye. She rose above it all, and kept on, commanding attention despite the slings and arrows. In that moment, surrounded by selfie-taking tourists, Lisa and I exchanged glances, recognizing each other as kindred spirits, past and future, trapped in our glass cases, refusing to reveal our secrets. I stood rooted, drinking her in, until my arm was jiggled and a voice barked in my ear.

'Have you finished gawping yet?'

Letty was glaring up at me. 'Honestly, I'd forgotten how odious this place is, absolutely riddled with idiots. It's just a lot of men's daubings. No need for this hysteria.'

'Sorry,' I said, coming back down to earth. 'Do you want to go for your *chocolat*?'

'Yes,' she said. 'I want the finest *chocolat* in Paris, and I want you to find it for me.'

I smiled. 'Where else but the Café de Flore?'

'*Naturellement.*'

After one last look, I could feel the *Mona*'s eyes on me as I turned my back, that sidelong gaze lingering even as we made our way downstairs again, pushing against the hordes determined to capture her on camera.

We went back to Saint-Germain and ordered hot chocolate in one of Paris's oldest coffee houses. It arrived, soupy-thick and delicious, and we drank crammed side by side at a tiny round table. Two elderly men along the row were playing chess, and I was suddenly poleaxed with longing for Em, who would have adored and embraced all this. My Em, who had a pirate smile to rival *La Gioconda*'s, and guarded her own secrets as serenely.

'Ah,' sighed Letty. 'England does the best tea, but France does the best *chocolat*. It's one of the things I miss most about living here. That, and undiluted pastis.'

'I might risk the bathroom,' I said.

'*Bonne chance, mon amie.*'

We got yet another cab to the Gare du Nord, and by that point I was fretting about money as we caught our final glimpses of the city. Letty must have spent a fortune, and even if she was rich, it was still a terrible imposition. My hostess had another glass of champagne on the train, but I stuck to water. I'd drunk wine with Hemingway, and would leave it at that.

Back on the concourse at St Pancras, I marvelled that we'd only been away a day. It felt like a lifetime. Not even seven o'clock; I could be back in time to make Em dinner and tell her all about it. Impulsively, I stepped forwards and hugged Letty, kissing her wrinkled cheek.

'Thank you so much. That was wonderful. I'll never forget it.'

'Pah.' Letty pushed me away, but her eyes were full. 'Here. I got you a little something to commemorate the trip.' She held out one of the shopping bags.

'You shouldn't have.' I took it and peeked inside. Wrapped in tissue paper was the Agnès B dress I'd tried on in the Galeries Lafayette. I gasped. 'You *really* shouldn't have! That's far too much.'

'Pish. I told you, this is just pocket money. Besides, every gal needs a decent dress. I used to wear nothing but Balmain. Always had very expensive tastes, even before Jean-Luc bankrolled them.'

'You're so kind. I love it. I got you something, too. It's not much.' I reached into my own bag and pulled out a small packet. 'The waiter at Café de Flore made it up for me. It's the chocolate they use.'

Letty didn't speak for a moment, turning the parcel over in her hands.

'You . . . got this for me?' she said, her voice slightly croaky. 'They don't sell this.'

'No, I persuaded him. It was my final challenge. My very best French.'

'*Ma chèrie*,' said Letty, reaching up to touch my cheek, eyes brimming. 'I think one day you will be almost as dashing and outrageous as *me*.'

'*Cela est impossible!*' I laughed. 'Come on, let's get you another cab home.'

But as we walked along, my phone rang and Letty watched my face fall as the high, frightened voice came through at the other end.

'Oh, Mummy,' sobbed Em. 'I'm sorry. I'm sorry. I've ruined it all.'

Chapter 46

By seven-thirty, I was on a train again, going north rather than south, a wad of cash in my pocket given to me by Letty. Didn't even try to refuse. All that mattered was getting to Em.

I thought about what she'd said, and how it made me feel. Horrified, enraged, and desperately, desperately sad. And then: *contrite*. When you spilt something in the café, you had to clear it up and apologize. Even if the spillage was caused by someone else. So I was going to clear things up, and my instinct was to say sorry – to go to Adam and say sorry. Sorry for inconveniencing you, sorry for making a mess, sorry for ruining it all. And the more I thought about it, that was the thing that enraged me the most. As Letty said, apologizing didn't work; sometimes it made them despise you.

Are you OK? Are you still there? Don't move, don't go anywhere, just wait. I'm coming. I texted her the whole way there, desperate to keep up the contact. Thank God I'd bought her the mobile phone for Christmas. She'd never sounded like that before. My Em was buoyant, resilient, in control, but on the phone she'd sounded lost and adrift, sobbing hysterically and babbling about a lost train ticket. My whole body burnt with the urge to get there, see her, make it all right, even though I knew that was beyond my powers. *Come on, come on.* I leaned forwards in my seat as if it would make the train go faster, and caught sight of my reflection in the window, the tension in my jaw, shoulders taut, hair on end like it was charged with electricity.

The train pulled up in Cambridge at 8.33 p.m., exactly on time. I erupted out of it, barrelling down the platform to find my daughter. Em was standing by a vending machine, looking smaller and more forlorn than I'd ever seen her. I ran towards her and gathered her up.

'This is not on you, you hear me? This is not on you.'

Em's face was pressed to my shoulder, but I felt the answering shudder and clutched her closer. We stood like that for a while, as her breathing returned to normal, and then I bought her another ticket and we waited for the next train home.

In the warmth of the train carriage, Em seemed to deflate even more, sinking into the seat as if she wanted to disappear, and I could tell my reassurance hadn't hit home. She had that same urge to apologize, to claim responsibility and wipe away the spillage. I groped for better words, ones that would find their mark, but there didn't seem to be anything to say, so I just held her hand tightly and looked out of the window without really seeing anything.

Eventually she gave a sniff and wiped her nose with the back of her hand.

'You OK?' I said, squeezing the other one I held.

She nodded but pulled away.

'What happened?'

Em stared at the black window, and there was a vacancy in her gaze that disturbed me. 'I've been saving up,' she murmured. 'For a train ticket.' She said it idly, as if she'd planned a trip to the seaside. 'Then I gave Letty your passport and she gave me twenty pounds.'

'And you *took* it?'

She shook her head, irritably, like she was waving away a fly. 'She insisted. Told me to spend it on cider in the park, or whatever the young folk do nowadays.'

'How did you know . . . where he was?'

Em flicked me a sidelong glance. 'I've known for ages. Someone put an old photo of you both on Instagram, and I googled him, found his office at King's when we were there at Christmas. Couldn't see him then though, because you were hanging round.'

I winced, picturing us both circling the college that day. 'So . . . you went back to the college.'

She nodded. 'Had a clipboard. Was going to pretend I was at a local school and that we were doing a project on studying at university. It was pretty stupid, and he might not even be there on a Saturday, but I thought maybe I'd get lucky, might get five minutes with him and . . .' She tailed off, tracing the grubby grey floor of the carriage with her shoe.

'And what? What exactly were you hoping to achieve?' I tried to stop the anger creeping into my voice. It was misplaced, but if ever a plan had been doomed to failure it was this one.

Em's eyes filled with tears. 'I thought it might help me understand. Why I am . . . like this.' She gestured to her head, and my heart contracted with the pity of it.

'Like what?'

There was a catch in her voice. 'Mrs Gill said I was special. She makes me feel special, most of the time. But other times, I just feel . . . weird. Thought meeting him might make sense of it. Like the missing piece of a jigsaw puzzle.'

'You should have asked me. I would have told you anything you wanted to know about him.' Even as I said it, I could hear the weakness in my voice, the lameness of that claim.

'But you didn't, did you?' The words sliced straight through me. 'Anyway, it wasn't just that. I wanted to see for myself. To see whether . . . I felt like his daughter.'

'And did you?' I wasn't sure what answer I wanted to hear.

'It felt . . . like I was a wasp in the room he needed to get rid of. He didn't want to know. Just wanted me to leave. Couldn't wait for me to go. Kept looking at the clock on his wall and arranging his papers and asking if I needed money.' She put her head in her hands and started to cry in earnest. 'But when I was leaving he called me back and I thought . . . I thought . . .'

'Shhh, sweetheart, it's not your fault.'

'I thought he was going to say something, you know, *nice*. But he just said, "If you go that way you can avoid the porter's lodge." All he cared about was that no one saw me. I ran so fast out the college, that must have been when I lost my train ticket.' She looked up, finally, and I flinched at the ferocity of her expression. 'Why didn't you just *tell* me? Why didn't you tell *him*?'

I grabbed her hand again, fuelled by her rage, feeling the fires build against Adam, who turned and ran, just as he did all those years ago, leaving me to clear up the mess. But also a dark, shameful fury, directed at myself. When Em was born, I knew something would be missing, that I'd have to be both mother and father to my little girl. It was like planting a tree, but not bothering to fill the hole in properly, so it was lopsided, couldn't take root, couldn't grow, until the gaps were filled on both sides. I hadn't given her the foundations she needed, had let her down, just as Adam had.

'We used to walk past each other in the school corridor,' I whispered. 'There's people you just don't notice, and then people you deliberately ignore, to make a point. That's what we did. In the beginning, we ignored each other.'

Em wiped her nose on her sleeve. 'Why?'

'I'm not sure, that was just the way it was. We couldn't let on that we were interested. But we both knew anyway. I liked him because he was just so sure of himself. Sure of what he wanted. I think I wanted some of the . . . surety. Felt very unsure, myself.'

'He sounds a bit of a . . . jerk, to be honest.'

'He probably was. Teenage boys are, aren't they?'

She sniffed. 'He wears glasses, but I think they're just for show. And he had one of those jackets with patches, like you see academics wear in films. It looked like he was playing a part.'

'That figures. When we were going out, he used to buy the *Socialist Worker* and talk about how New Labour had sold out. I found a Che Guevara beret in his room once, but then he decided he really admired David Cameron. So it didn't run very deep. He had phases. I guess I was a phase, though it didn't feel that way at the time.'

Em's eyes were still moist and red, but they began to gleam. 'A *beret*?'

I snorted. 'It seemed cool, back then.'

'A beret . . . with a *star*?'

'Citizen Terris,' I sniggered.

We didn't speak for a while, as the tears and laughter subsided. Then I reached for her chin and turned her face towards me.

'You *are* special,' I said softly. 'In the best, most perfect way. I'm sorry if I didn't make you feel like that was a good thing. Sorry I didn't give you a better dad. And, most of all, I'm sorry I never spoke to you about him. I should have told you, but . . . I didn't know what to say, or how to say it.'

Em looked away again, out of the window. 'He . . . he has another child, you know. There's a photo on his desk of him and a woman holding a baby boy. Is that my brother?'

Swallowing painfully, I stroked her hair. 'I . . . don't know. Maybe. It doesn't matter. He's never been a dad to you, not really. You've got me, and Granddad.' That seemed like a very fragile house of cards. Em deserved so much more. How could Adam, having had a child, deny another?

Back at the flat, we climbed into bed and she fell asleep holding my hand, as she had as an infant. I thought of that time, nestled together in the night, drowsy fingers reaching out for mine. As she grew older, she stopped reaching out, started doing things for herself, and I had been so tired and ground down by life that I'd let her get on with it, left her to her own devices. That brain of hers made me forget how young she was, and I resolved then and there that I would not forget again – I'd be the stake that propped up Em's tree. I would prop up Em, and stand up for myself. That night I slept more deeply than I had in months.

The next morning, Em went to spend the day at Halima's for real, and I used the last of Letty's cash to buy another return ticket. The resolve had grown and hardened as I thought about Adam's frantic dismissal, while the photo of the baby on his desk signified the devoted father. My rage simmered throughout the journey, and I slapped the arm of my seat as I brooded and fumed. How dare he? Swanning off to Cambridge without a care in the world, first-class degree, setting himself up as an academic with his elbow patches, everything falling into his lap like it always did. But there was that darker, latent fury – I'd put Em in this position, because I'd never told her, directly, who her father was. Just left her to assume, like I assumed. *Hiraeth*; missing things, longing. She missed and longed for a father, a homesickness she couldn't shake, and I was responsible for that gap in her knowledge.

At the station, I queued for the bus, tapping my foot as the old lady in front of me fumbled for her purse. Getting out my phone, I checked the address. Sheba Hughes had given it to me the last time we had coffee together. On my way out, I couldn't resist asking if she knew.

'He's got a girlfriend, you know,' she'd said, as she texted me the details. One of the nicest roads, of course, near Jesus Green. 'I think they're engaged.'

'I know.' I'd looked at the photos on his Instagram page, which included a picture of the advert in *The Times*.

The Honourable Sophie Clifford. Ginny and Clement must have been thrilled.

'Might be best to leave it.'

'I know.' And I intended to. But what if Em had had some sort of genetic illness, or I died? I justified it with all sorts of sensible reasons, but deep down I knew that one day I'd want to find out, for sure. And seeing him was the only way I could do that.

I got off the bus and walked to De Freville Avenue, bristling at all the big bay-windowed houses until I arrived at one of the biggest of all, a redbrick Victorian pile, with an extremely neat front garden and ruthlessly pruned wisteria around the front door. Marching up the flagstone path, I knocked firmly, and waited for my first love to answer it.

Chapter 47

*A*fter a few seconds, the door was opened by a pretty blonde. I recognized the Honourable Sophie from the engagement photos, and smiled brightly.

'Hi! I'm Fi. Fi Colbert. Used to go to school with Adam, and was in the area, so thought I'd look him up. Is he in?'

Before she could reply, Adam appeared at her shoulder, eyes widening in alarm.

'Hi, Adam! How are you? It's been ages.'

He looked much as I remembered, but in a different costume. Red-setter hair, broad shoulders in his corduroy jacket. The teenager in me felt a tweak of longing. Pushing past Sophie, he came to stand on the doorstep, putting himself between us.

I felt like I had pins and needles all over my skin, but carried on. 'Don't suppose you've got time for a coffee? It would be so great to catch up.'

'I'm not . . . I . . .' He looked from his fiancée to me, and back again. 'Darling, do you mind? Just five minutes. Haven't seen . . . er, Fi . . . in years. Good to catch up.'

He hustled me down the path and I heard the door slam shut behind us.

'Why did you come here?' he muttered, as we walked away.

'To settle some scores,' I replied.

He marched me to a café around the corner and ordered two coffees, carrying them to a table at the back. Taking off my coat as we sat down, I revealed the Agnès B dress underneath – its first outing. Adam's eyes flicked up and down, before sliding to my left hand.

'You can't do this,' he began in an undertone, emptying sugar into his coffee and sweeping the dropped grains off the table. 'Barging into my home like that. Doorstepping my future wife.' I twitched at that, but he was building up a head of steam, fuelled by self-righteous outrage. 'What are you playing at?'

'Let me stop you right there,' I said. 'I'm not playing at anything. And that's not how this conversation is going to go. You don't get to lecture me, or tell me what *I've* done wrong.'

'She came to my office,' he spluttered. 'Just turned up, out of the blue. What was I supposed to do?'

'Maybe not be a total shit?' I retorted. 'Maybe have an ounce of compassion for a twelve-year-old girl? Who might be your own child?'

He stared at me like I was insane. 'She's not my child.'

I glared at him. 'How can you be so sure?'

He shook his head. 'She's not my child.'

That total denial. Something murky and unspeakable began to unfold in me, curling up into my chest, making me feel like I was suffocating very slowly. I couldn't decide if it was rage or fear, but had come this far, and had to finish it. He was always so sure of himself, but he couldn't possibly be sure of this. I leaned forwards, fingers gripping the table until they turned white.

'I was sixteen. Sixteen and pregnant. I never told you because . . .' I swallowed. 'You'd made it quite clear you were moving on. But you must have known . . . You must have known when you met Em that there was the possibility.' Tell me, I thought. Tell me there's the possibility.

He wouldn't meet my eye, twirling another packet of sugar. 'I had no idea about any of this. You never told me. That one time . . . You said you'd get the morning-after pill.'

'No, I didn't. You told me to, then never mentioned it again.' I kept my voice tight and controlled. 'Because it was all my responsibility, wasn't it? To deal with it.'

For a few seconds he was silent, but when he finally raised his face to mine there was something about his expression that made me afraid of what would come next.

'I'm very sorry for . . . whatever happened,' he said. 'But . . . she can't possibly be my daughter.'

'Why not? How can you be so sure?' I hissed, but something was deflating in me. I could feel it. I wasn't sure. But he was.

'Because I'm . . . infertile,' he said, very quietly. He uttered the words as if they were a terrible admission, as if there was *anything* he would rather say than that.

The fires spluttered out. 'But . . . you . . . Em said there was a photo of a baby in your office?'

Adam shook his head and, in that moment, I saw it. Looking more closely, he seemed smaller, less golden, than I

279

remembered, the beginning of lines either side of his mouth. Everything had always come so easily to him. Apart from this. Undone by this one thing.

'We couldn't get pregnant. Sophie's five years older than me. She's desperate for a baby. We had tests. Lucas is . . . her sister's son. The photo is of us and him.'

There was a long, long silence. The sugar packet he was fiddling with broke, scattering grains everywhere. He didn't brush them away, just stared at the granules littering the table. I closed my eyes, absorbing the seeping horror. All these years. I thought I knew. *Hoped* I did. But it was just wishful thinking.

'Sorry,' I managed, finally, trying to shift the thorny blockage in my throat, rising like bile. 'I didn't . . . know.' I pushed my chair back and got to my feet, my tears blinding me.

He looked up and smiled bitterly. 'We all have our demons.'

And now my demon, latent for so long, reared his head, lips pulled back in a snarl. Why had I ignored that little voice? The little voice that said, 'You can't be sure.' I pretended that Em's father could only be one person, the one person I wanted it to be. Anything else was unthinkable.

In a daze, I put on my coat and stumbled out of the café, leaving him sitting there surrounded by spilt sugar. I walked down side streets, hardly aware of where I was going, ignoring sideways looks from passers-by, until I found myself back on King's Parade. Slipping past the officials who manned the entrance, I strode on, round the huge lawned quad, until I reached the door of the chapel. I didn't expect it to be open, but it was, so I carried on inside. A woman was cleaning, sweeping at the far end of the aisle, but she barely registered my presence, so I sat down on one of the benches and bent my head as if I was praying. Praying what I'd just heard was somehow not true, that my greatest fear had not been realized. Praying that I could forget it all and carry on as normal. Praying that Em would never find out what happened. I sat with my head down, listening to the relentless strokes of the broom, then got up and left, praying I could leave the knowledge back there in the chapel, locked away forever, like a confession.

Chapter 48

*M*emories of that last prom night came back to me in flashes, lightning bolts, each one sending me skittering in another direction. I didn't want to remember anything, but now and then an image seared its way into my brain and I couldn't ignore it.

It all began so well, meeting Adam outside the school gates, just like the year before. He looked so handsome in his suit, and this time he was carrying a rose, which we'd joked about, for our 'anniversary'. He kissed me and led me inside, where the hall was set up with banners and balloons. It was all for us, and we were meant to be there, but it felt like a rerun, like that film I'd watched with Dad – *Groundhog Day*. We'd done this before, and there was a strange dreamlike quality to the evening, everything in soft focus. But then it turned into a nightmare.

Flash. Adam hands me a lemonade, leaning in to make an observation about Marni and Dan Edwards, who've just arrived, looking self-conscious.

Flash. We're dancing, my arms around his neck, his around my waist, grinding against each other in time to the music.

Flash. We bump into Miss Challoner. She congratulates us on finishing our exams, on the great grades we'll surely get. Then Sheba's talking to me, so I don't quite hear what Miss Challoner says to Adam.

Flash. Outside on the hill, smoking weed. As it hits, a moment of clarity. I did hear what Miss Challoner said to Adam.

Flash. Shouting outside the library. Sobbing, leaning against the wall, as Adam tries to explain. It's no good.

Flash. Running away, back indoors, through the heaving crowds, grimly telling Lee Enright to give me whatever alcohol he's selling.

Flash. Drinking, drinking, drinking. Nothing, nothing, nothing.

And then it goes dark and I can't remember any more. Won't.

Chapter 49

I got back from Cambridge in the early evening, and headed from the station towards home. Didn't relish the prospect of sitting in our dismal living room eating claggy pasta off my knees, but Em would be home, and I had to be with her. On the way, I stopped at a fish and chip shop – at least it would save us cooking – and caught sight of myself reflected in the mirror behind the counter. My coat dragged off at the shoulder by my bag, my hair ruffled by the breeze, face pale and drawn.

It was nearly dark by the time I arrived at our block and, as I made my way down to the flat, the door opened, a shaft of light hitting the path. My daughter's pirate smile was a beacon in the dusk.

'Hi, Em-Jo, baby.' I wanted to collapse on her, draw her into my arms, confess everything. But I couldn't.

'Where have you been?'

I shifted my bag on my shoulder. 'Just went to visit . . . a friend.'

She looked at me intently, the cogs of her brain whirring, and I brandished my greasy cartons to distract her.

'Cod and chips. Thought it would make a change from pasta. Shall we go inside?'

As we went into the hallway, something was different, but I couldn't work out what it was, busy passing the food to Em, taking off my coat, hanging it up. But as I licked oil off my fingers, I realized. The television wasn't on. There was music playing, but it sounded scratchy and forlorn, the faded crackle and hiss of old vinyl. Dad must have got the record player out again.

'Billie Holiday,' I murmured, frowning. 'What's going on?'

'Come and see,' said Em.

We went through to the living room, where Dad stood waiting for us. He was smiling shyly and, as we entered the room, he nodded towards the hatch that led to the kitchen. The leaves of the table underneath had been propped up, a white tablecloth laid across with a couple of flickering tea lights. There, alongside a bunch of daffodils, was a trifle in a glass bowl, scattered with hundreds and thousands.

I gasped, my hand flying to my mouth, staring at the dish as if it was a crystal ball. But this one was telling a tale of past pleasures, once-upon-a-time celebrations when Dad came home with his pockets stuffed, and my mother waited with her confections. Very slowly, I walked over to the table, inhaling the faint scent of the flowers, noting the tiny chip on the rim of the bowl, where Maman caught it on the tap when she was washing up. Her exclamation: '*Ah, mon Dieu, si maladroite!*' I traced one finger carefully, reverently, along the flaw, before gently dipping it into the cream and lifting it to my lips. Then turned to my father, who was nodding and smiling.

'Dad,' I said. 'Oh, *Daddy*.'

'Thought we could have a party,' he said. 'Now you've handed in your essay.'

A single tear rolled down my cheek. I'd almost forgotten my essay. It felt like an irrelevance, harking back to an innocent, carefree time before the horror of today's discovery. 'I don't even know what mark I'll get.'

'You'll do well,' he said. 'I know my queen. You'll do well.' He opened his arms and I fell into them, clutching his cardigan and holding out my hand to Em, who joined the three-way embrace, awkwardly, because she wasn't a tactile soul.

'Did Em help you?'

'We made it together,' said my dad, pinching her cheek. 'Followed the recipe. From JoJo's book.' He pointed back to the table, where my mother's old notebook lay, stuffed with her magazine recipes. I picked it up and clasped it to my chest as if I could absorb the warmth and industry of the pages.

'Let's have the fish before it gets cold,' said Em.

We sat on stools around the little table, eating straight from the cartons, and the white tablecloth got oily but I could take it to the laundrette another day. Em went to the kitchen to get bowls, and we ladled out huge helpings of their creation, the layers as clumpy and haphazard as the hundreds and thousands on top. The candles cast a warm glow across the table and, when I cleared away the crockery, I thought of what I'd said to Em, that she didn't need a dad because she had me and Granddad. At the time it seemed inadequate, but maybe it was OK. Maybe it was enough. Maybe if I could forget that conversation with Adam, we could all move on, and everything would be fine.

Chapter 50

As a distraction, I threw myself into my work, studying late into the night after shifts, preparing for my exams with a single-minded determination. Roz helped when she could, but there was no doubt her own mind was elsewhere, now the BBC had officially offered her the part in their drama. She was going to take a sabbatical from teaching, said Mrs Boleyn had been very understanding, that she'd come back when filming was over. But we both knew it wasn't true; she'd be doing publicity for the series, and other acting jobs would come along off the back of it. Who would really turn any of that down in favour of staying at a struggling school that sold raffle tickets so they could buy pens? We were both moving on, in our own ways. I wondered what I would do once my exams were over. What next? The truth was, I couldn't think beyond them, just like I couldn't quite banish the thought of what Adam had told me that day. A fog lingered on the horizon, and no amount of sweeping or studying could disperse it.

One of the more successful distractions was my piano

lessons with Dylan. We didn't find the time very often, but occasionally I would go over to his flat and painstakingly pick over a piece he'd chosen, and then he'd take me through it again, correcting my fingering, improving my technique. I had the tendency to let my wrists drop as I played, which he didn't like, and he would hook a hand under mine to lift them up. I found myself letting my wrists fall on purpose, sometimes, then berating myself for doing it, for encouraging that mild proximity, when I still wasn't sure where I wanted it to go. Afterwards he'd make me a coffee and we'd chat as Bernadette weaved between our legs, wanting affection.

'My mother breeds spaniels,' he said, smiling down as he scratched her neck. 'That's why I have Bernie. Mam has eleven dogs. She sleeps with them. One day she'll be eaten by them.'

I couldn't help laughing. 'Don't say that! Eleven dogs is a bit much though.'

'She's kept dogs since my dad died,' he continued. 'They're his replacement. Says they're just as messy and annoying. I probably take after him.'

'Well, Bernadette is lovely. So maybe your dad would have been pleased.'

'Like I said, I take after him,' replied Dylan, straight-faced, and I blushed, backed into the corner of the compliment. Why did he affect me this way? He often annoyed me, unnerved me, and yet, somehow, I always looked forward to being in his flat, playing the piano and drinking coffee with him. Or singing alongside him as he played. I peeked under my lashes as he fondled his dog, watching his fingers sink into her fur, racking my brain for other ways we could be together without going for a drink like normal people.

'Em asked me to ask you something . . .' I began, setting my coffee cup down on the crate.

'What?' Releasing Bernadette, Dylan pulled a packet of tobacco and some Rizlas from his pocket and began rolling up.

'It's just . . . She says you put an advert in the staff room at school. For a dog walker.'

He raised his eyebrows. 'Yes. I could do with someone to walk Bernie occasionally. How did she see it in the staff room?'

'Em sees everything. Anyway, she wondered . . . Why is she called Bernadette?' I found myself putting off asking the real question.

'Oh.' Dylan hesitated, embarrassed. 'It's a Four Tops song. "In her arms I find peace of mind." Is that really what she wanted to know?'

'No . . . She wondered if you would let her walk Bernadette?'

Since the terrible trip to Cambridge, I was eager to do anything that might comfort Em, and dogs were high on her list. She walked Colin, our next-door neighbour's chihuahua, sometimes, but found him yappy and aggressive. Bernadette was a more restful presence. Maybe Em could find peace of mind with her too.

Dylan sat back, amused. 'Your daughter wants to be my dog walker?'

I took a gulp of coffee. 'She's always wanted a dog, but we can't have one, in our flat. So, she thought she could maybe borrow yours.'

'I was expecting to pay someone.'

'You don't charge me for my piano lessons. Think of it as payment in kind.'

'OK,' he said. 'Tell her to come over on Saturday morning and she can give it a go.' He tucked the perfectly rolled cigarette behind his ear.

'You never smoke them,' I said, pointing to his home-made accessory. 'You only ever roll them.'

'Just like having something to do with my hands.'

'But isn't it a waste of money?'

Dylan shrugged. 'Not a waste of time though. Calms me down.'

'Doesn't Bernadette do that?'

He looked down at his dog, still panting at his feet. 'She gives me peace of mind. They give me peace of body.'

Dylan gave me neither, and yet I was envious of the attention he gave Bernadette, and his cigarette. I'd finished my coffee and it would have looked desperate to stay for another, so I said I'd better get to Letty's, and got my things together while the dog danced around as if it was me who'd begged to be her walker. As I got to the door, my hand on the latch, Dylan suddenly reached out and caught my wrist, not just nudging it up, but encircling it firmly. His fingers were long and sinewy. I'd watched them reach well over an octave on the piano keys, and now they closed around my arm, warm and strong. I looked up at him enquiringly, my heart thudding.

'Just . . .' He paused, frowning. 'Just . . . you did well today. On the, er, piano. You're improving.'

That was obviously not what he had intended to say, but it was all I was going to get. All I could cope with, for now. I ducked my head and he released my hand.

'Thank you,' I stuttered. 'And thanks for the lessons. It's . . . good of you to . . . take the trouble.'

He smiled. '*Pleser, cariad.*'

I unlocked the door and left, running through the deserted shop and out towards the bus stop. Didn't let myself look until I was on the bus. As soon as I was in my seat, I got out my phone and googled, just to check.

Darling. He called me darling.

Chapter 51

My visits to Canonbury were now conducted almost entirely in French, Letty rapping out orders and queries, banging her stick in counterpoint, while I raced to keep up. Occasionally Aphra would deign to leap onto my lap and needle my knees before settling, thrumming as I tickled her neck. The words were coming more easily; I was barely having to think before a sentence was formed.

'It was there all along, thanks to your mother,' she remarked. 'You just had to learn to unlock it. It's a good thing I'm here, or you'd still be *rouillée*.'

It felt like I'd forged a link with Maman who, as the years passed, had faded in my mind. Speaking French warmed her into clarity again, a Polaroid taking shape. For Letty too, it made her feel closer to Jean-Luc.

'My daughter is fluent, of course, but we don't speak it to each other – that would be terribly pretentious of us. Jean-Luc and I only ever spoke French at home, and I miss it. I'm sure being bilingual is the only reason I'm not completely senile.' She picked up her china cup with gnarled fingers. 'Anyway, enough about me. How's your dashing Welsh pianist?'

My cup clattered into its saucer, Aphra's ears twitching in irritation. 'He's not . . . We're just . . .'

Letty cackled. 'Not so fluent now, are you? Get on with it and pin him down, before some other *pouffiasse* snaps him up.'

'*Pouffiasse?*'

'Floozy,' said Letty, revealing an uneven row of yellow teeth.

That was when I found myself telling Letty about what happened with Adam, and with Sid. Maybe it was because we were speaking French, which made it easier, like the day in Paris when I'd told her about Maman's death. While I talked, Aphra moved away, as if in disapproval, jumping delicately back on Letty's bony knees. Letty said nothing, but let me run on, stroking the cat's downy head.

'Because it all went so wrong,' I concluded. 'I just don't think I'm ready to . . . make the leap.'

Letty tutted impatiently. 'So. Because you've had two failed relationships – one when you were a teenager – you've decided you're unlucky in love?'

'Well . . .'

'And also,' she continued, banging her stick. 'What are you expecting from this Dylan? That you'll go for a drink, and get married?'

'I don't . . .'

'I have had sexual relations with at least seventeen persons,' announced Letty. 'Sixteen of them were not The One. At least three of them were bounders. One of them was a woman. *Je ne regrette rien.* It might be love. It might not. But you have to at least open yourself to the possibility. If it's not love, it might just be fun!' She winked at my astonished face.

'I had an affair once, with a painter,' Letty continued, leaning back with a faraway look in her eye. 'Before Jean-Luc and I were married. I wanted him to propose, but he wouldn't, so I went off and met this artist. He was quite old, but terribly sexy. We had a passionate few months, and he painted me, which I must admit was rather boring, all that sitting around, and then Jean-Luc found out and was furious. But he proposed, which was what I wanted, so it served its purpose.'

'Wow,' I said, in English. 'Was the artist upset?'

Letty shrugged. 'No, he was relieved, I think, to have it over with. He gave me a painting to remember him by – it's there, above the desk.'

She pointed with her stick, and I got up to look. It was a small painting, abstract in style, and vaguely familiar. I peered at the signature.

'Letty,' I whispered. 'This is a Picasso.'

'Yes,' she replied. 'I imagine it's worth something now.'

'Well, thank you.' I cleared my throat. 'That's certainly put my own situation in perspective.'

'Happy to be of service.' Letty leaned on her stick to struggle to her feet. 'I suppose what I'm saying is . . .' She switched to English. 'Suck it and see!' She cackled as she led me to the back door and I could still hear her sniggering as it closed.

I laughed too, but felt a chill as I went up the steps. Letty might have had sexual relations with seventeen persons, but she hadn't had Em to consider. I wanted to open myself to possibilities – love, fun, whatever came my way – but the fallout could be much worse than a priceless painting.

Much later, lying in bed with my daughter, listening to her soft breath in the dark, I wondered again if I should tell her about Adam and what happened that night. That night that wasn't love, and wasn't fun. For the first time in years, I thought about why I had gone ahead with the pregnancy, why I hadn't just dealt with it, like Annabel Lloyd had in the spring term of Year Ten – unrepentantly heading for the clinic, telling anyone who gave her a look after to fuck off. I believed in a woman's right to choose, and my choice, in the end, was to have a baby. Because of my mother singing in church, gazing up at the Virgin Mary, genuflecting, lighting candles. She described herself as a lapsed Catholic, but said the religion ran deep in her roots, and, wearing her crucifix, it was hard to deny my own. Because of my father, whose love and fun had been switched off, the day she died. And because of Adam, who had gone, but had left something of himself with me. Probably. Hopefully. I had been open to that possibility, at least.

Summer Term

Chapter 52

'*I*s it always Christmas in here?' Sanjay fingered the threadbare tinsel that still hung from the mirror in our pub rehearsal room.

Dylan looked up from the piano. 'Frank says it saves him a job.'

'The queen leaves her decorations up till the sixth of February,' observed Em.

'We're way past that,' said Dylan. 'And Frank's no fan of the queen.'

'A re-publican,' I said, arranging my lyrics sheets, and was gratified by Dylan's smile.

'Right, let's make a start,' he said.

I'd invited Em to our rehearsal, to cheer her up. She'd been quiet and withdrawn recently, both of us still recovering from our respective Cambridge trips, and I thought an evening out might make a welcome change, even if Em was, to all intents and purposes, tone-deaf. Her grandparents' musicality might have skipped a generation, but she'd enjoyed listening to the choir in King's Chapel, so I brought her along, gave her a bag of crisps and settled her in the corner with her book. She glanced up occasionally, contributing to our chat, sharing her crisps with Bernadette, and I felt better with her there.

Dylan took me through my breathing exercises, and we worked our way through our growing playlist of jazz standards and more experimental pieces. Em swung her legs and smiled during our interpretation of Ariana Grande's 'thank u, next', but mostly remained absorbed in her copy of *Little Dorrit*. Eventually, her presence receded in my mind as I concentrated on singing from deep in my belly, getting my phrasing right, obeying Dylan's occasional instruction, keeping to Sanjay's strummed beat and enjoying the lulls when I stopped singing and just listened to them play together. We were beginning to sound tighter, and more professional, although there was no real goal to all this, apart from having fun.

When we'd finished and were packing up, Em raised her head, looking slightly dazed, and put her book back in her rucksack. As usual, the men stayed for a pint, but I wanted to get home for dinner, so we said goodbye and set off back towards Finsbury Park.

'You were really good,' she said, as we walked together.

'Really?' Despite her lack of expertise, I was delighted. 'Thank you.'

She nodded. 'Much better than the school show.'

'We couldn't really be worse.'

'No, you couldn't,' she agreed, and giggled when I hit her. We linked arms, and got home to find Dad had made a terrible mess in the kitchen trying to cook fish fingers and chips, but if the chips were burnt and the fish fingers soggy, no matter, because there he was, eating with us at the table and asking Em if she enjoyed listening to my band. After a dinner drenched in ketchup, Em and I did our homework together and, when we went to bed, I thought what a lovely Sunday it had been – somehow just falling into place easily and simply.

The first sign that things were more complicated than they appeared was when I went into work the next morning.

Selassie greeted me with a beaming smile. 'So, *bisrat*, your rehearsal went well?'

Taking off my jacket, I nodded warily, wondering how he was so well-informed on my weekend.

'Yes, thank you, but how . . .'

'I asked Emily to help me with a little detective work.'

At the time, it seemed like it had been my idea to invite Em to the rehearsal. It *seemed* that way. Looking back, I could see how she turned the conversation, how the seed was planted. As my boss held up his mobile and played me a recording of last night's session, my first thought was the sound quality was very good, considering it had been recorded on the very basic smartphone I'd bought Em for Christmas. 'Bewitched, Bothered and Bewildered', 'But Not for Me', 'It Was Just One of Those Things', 'thank u, next' . . . She'd captured a good chunk of our playlist. We'd been played, good and proper. Similarly, Selassie seemed to think he'd set the whole thing up, persuading Em to tag along, spy on us for him. He'd 'taught' her how to record on her phone, he said, elated by his enterprise. I pictured my daughter swinging her legs in his café, sucking on her lemonade as she sucked him in. *Très, très sournoise.*

'So now,' he exclaimed, 'you have had your audition! Consider The Tiny Pennies booked.'

He wanted us to play at his inaugural Jazz Night, the following week. A new monthly event, to push Merhaba closer to his beloved Asmara club, Tesfay's. I began to protest, but he shut me down.

'You must do this for me, *fiori*,' he said, firmly. 'My business depends on it.'

I was about to object again, then thought of calling Dylan, telling him we had a gig. The temptation was too great, so I succumbed, said we'd be glad to do it, then tried not to go and throw up in the toilet. What had I done? The school show had been a disaster, but at least a fairly private one. This time, my failure could be witnessed by the paying public. Unless no one turned up, which would be even worse.

When Em got home from school later that day, I was waiting for her.

'Pleased with yourself, are you?'

She smiled her pirate smile.

'It was just supposed to be pleasure,' I said. 'Now it's business. What if it goes wrong?'

Em plucked an apple from the fruit bowl. '*Macbeth*,' she said. '*Macbeth*.'

'Don't!'

'I should think you've had your bad luck, when it comes to performing,' she said, taking a bite. 'May as well take advantage of the good karma coming your way.'

When I called Dylan later, he laughed and said something that sounded like '*bendigedig*'.

'What does that mean?'

'It's Welsh,' he said, 'for fan-fucking-tastic.'

Chapter 53

'You look like death,' Roz announced. 'Those eye bags!' Wielding a concealer stick like a weapon, she bore down on me, looking incredibly glamorous – thinner than ever, her hair layered and highlighted, skin honey-gold. I knew she'd been having screen tests that week. No one would take her for a schoolteacher now.

'You look like you haven't slept in a week. Also, that practice paper you sent was brilliant but it wasn't finished.'

'Sorry. Didn't have time,' I mumbled, as her fingers gripped my chin.

'Well, finish it, then I can mark it properly. Right, you'll do. That's a nice frock,' she added, as I moved away. 'Pipe down, you two!' she bellowed, as Izzy's screams clashed with Joe's howls.

My red Christmas dress, the only vibrant thing about me. All I could think was that we were going to perform in front of all those people, and they'd be disappointed. What if I dried again, like last time? Forcing my trembling legs to go downstairs, I found Dylan and Sanjay in the kitchen forking up pasta, Bernadette panting and drooling under the table.

'Lining our stomachs,' Sanjay mumbled, as my own turned. 'Want some?' He pushed the pot towards me.

I shook my head. If I ate anything, it would come straight back up again. Instead, I wandered round the kitchen, looking at the paintings and Post-it notes plastered across their fridge. One of the notes read, 'BUY SOME SODDING MILK, YOU BASTARD'. Hopefully it was too high up for either of the children to read.

'Come on, then,' said Dylan, heading towards the living room. By the time I arrived, he was already sitting at the piano. Sanjay ambled in, holding his guitar. Taking a gulp of air, I smoothed my hands down my dress, tried to straighten my spine and open up my lungs. Everything felt tight, like I was wearing a corset. We ran through a couple of the intros, and Dylan's set brow told me that he thought I was holding back, not singing from my diaphragm, but there wasn't time to do anything about it.

'Come on, the Uber's here.'

We left, waving to Joe and Karina, the babysitter. Roz blew kisses to Izzy, who was hugging her horse at the top of the stairs. 'I'm going to cut my hair!' Izzy yelled, as we closed the door. 'Then you'll be sorry.'

Roz rolled her eyes. 'She doesn't like us going anywhere.'

Squashed into the car, with the dog in the footwell, I moved as far away from Dylan as possible and concentrated on the view, using the shifting landscape to distract myself. My phone beeped to announce a text message, and I squinted at it in the half-light of the cab: See you later, stranger. It was from an unrecognized number. Who was it? I felt spooked, my heart hammering an uneven beat. For some reason, I had the crazy idea it might be Adam. Maybe, after that day in Cambridge, he'd been thinking about me, decided it was time to . . . The cab lurched, stopping at a traffic light, and the jolt brought me to my senses. Dylan's hand was on my knee, stopping me falling forwards. He withdrew it hastily, and I looked out of the window again, my cheeks on fire.

'Do you think anyone will actually come?' asked Sanjay. 'Or will it just be us performing into a vacuum?'

'Not sure,' replied Roz, getting her lipstick out and haphazardly applying it. 'They put an ad in the *Gazette*, but does anyone actually read that? Poor Selassie.'

'Poor us,' said Dylan. 'We'll look like a right trio of twats.'

But when we arrived, Merhaba was packed. Abrihet was bustling about serving stew, and the new waitress they'd hired to fill in for me was looking harassed as she hurried backwards and forwards with bottles of wine. I couldn't decide whether to be pleased or appalled. Selassie was delighted, bustling round rubbing his hands together as he contemplated his profits. A small blackboard had been set up advertising the event. 'The Tiny Pennies', it said. 'Thursday Jazz Night. All welcome.' How had that bald announcement drawn in all these people? Looking around, I saw several of them were parents and teachers who'd been at the school show. Sarah Boleyn was there with her son, who Roz said was back from Cardiff University. Dom Seddon, our drummer, was there with his mum and dad. I felt tears prickle at seeing them, and took another gulp of air. It was probably better not to check out the audience, it just made things worse. Sanjay was greeted by a couple of his old bandmates who'd come to support him and was borne off to their table, while Roz waved at colleagues.

We found Em sitting in a corner, nose buried in her Charles Dickens, an empty lemonade glass in front of her. She raised her head as we arrived, and gestured to the crowds.

'You're famous.'

Roz beckoned the new waitress. 'Another lemonade. And a bottle of Pinot Grigio, please.' Evidently, her movie star diet was on pause.

Dylan slumped at the table, ushering Bernadette under it and nodding a greeting to Em, his new dog walker.

'Bernie!' Em bent to tickle her and she immediately rolled over in supplication, paws in the air. 'You know, in *Lady and the Tramp*, Lady is a cocker spaniel.'

'That makes you the tramp!' Roz hooted, pointing at Dylan, who scowled and poured himself a glass of her wine. 'Why don't you have one?' She nodded to me. 'Might calm you down.'

'No.' I hugged myself, shivering. 'Won't be able to concentrate.'

'We'd better set up,' said Dylan. 'Can I leave Lady with you?' He nodded to Em, who flushed with pleasure, holding out her hand for the lead.

'Give my regards to Broadway,' drawled Roz, smirking as Dylan shot her a filthy look. He stalked off and I followed, my legs leaden, mouthing the words of our first song.

A space had been cleared towards the back of the restaurant, where a piano and a microphone had been set up. Briefly allowing my eyes to dart over the audience, I thought there must be at least fifty people there, huddled round tables or perched at the tiny bar that ran along one wall. Plenty to witness my comeback, or total collapse. I was glad I'd forbidden Letty from coming, to avoid any further humiliation. I wondered about that strange text, and what it meant. *See you later, stranger.* For some reason, it sounded familiar, but I couldn't work out why. Dylan had a face like thunder, sitting down at the piano and adjusting the stool's height, savagely winding round the wooden knobs. He was in a bad mood, considering he'd been the one looking for a gig in the first place.

Sanjay came over, holding a beer, his guitar over his shoulder. Seeing us together, the diners quietened. I adjusted the microphone with shaking hands and glanced at the playlist Dylan had taped to a music stand. I couldn't remember the first song. Or any of the others. Maybe I should go and be sick again.

Selassie marched over and clapped for attention. 'My friends, welcome! Tonight, I am proud and heartened to introduce you to Merhaba's first Jazz Night, the first of many. Please big it up and make a loud noise for . . . The Tiny Pennies!'

There was enthusiastic applause, probably thanks to the numerous bottles that littered the tables. I pushed my hair out of my eyes, trying to control my erratic heartbeat as the crowd blurred in front of me. Dylan played the intro to the first song and I breathed in, fingers tightening on the microphone stand to stop myself falling. I took another breath, but couldn't get air into my lungs, crushed like a rusty squeezebox. Deep from the diaphragm. *See you later, stranger.* Stranger. There's an opposite to déjà vu: *jamais vu* – never seen. It's the sense that, even though you're somewhere familiar, you've never seen it before. Everything is the first time. Everything is strange. Everyone a stranger.

'*All of me,*' I croaked. '*Why not . . . take . . .*' Grinding to a halt, I brought my hands to my hot cheeks. Dylan looked up in alarm, fingers stumbling over the keys. He leaned forwards and spoke softly over the uneasy hum of the crowd, as Sanjay started gently strumming a riff on his guitar, like holding music on a telephone line.

'It's OK,' he said. 'Just breathe. Deep down, from your core.'

Nadine, the new waitress, came out of the kitchen bearing a loaded tray, her eyes on the floor. Someone in the audience whooped in encouragement and she flinched, tripping over the mic's lead and sending the tray flying.

As if in slow motion, one of the glasses flew in a perfect arc towards me. My lovely new dress, perfect make-up, wild curls for once coaxed into casual waves. Everything, in an instant, drenched in red wine. It went everywhere; all over my hair, across my face and dress, dripping down my legs. As the blood-red drops trickled down my cheeks like tears, you could have heard a pin drop, had it not been for the glasses shattering as they hit the floor. Nadine stood rooted to the spot, her face blanched in shock. For a second no one did or said anything; then, from the back, a voice spoke up, slicing through the silence like a boiling knife through butter.

'Looking good, Jones!'

I blinked out into the audience, their faces fogging and refocusing, my eyes roving backwards until I saw two women wedged behind a wicker table. A bottle of wine, already half-drunk, sat between them, and they were both doubled over with laughter.

Sheba and Marni.

See you later, stranger. Not strangers. Friends. My old friends from Brownswood. Sheba stood, swaying slightly, and held her glass aloft, saluting me, while Marni carried on hooting. Merhaba's crowd faded like an old photo ebbing at the edges, and for a second it was just us, the Weird Sisters, in perfect clarity.

When I found out I was pregnant, I'd been too sick and scared to say anything about it, even to them. I retreated, pulling up the rope ladder behind me, leaving no route in. They carried on at school, taking their A levels, and occasionally I'd see them in the park, heads together, but when they saw me and my pram, they'd stop and make conversation, pinching Em's cheek and saying things like 'Hasn't she grown!' We never discussed my baby's father, though the unspoken question hovered in the breeze. Eventually I started looking out for them, ducking behind a hedge until I was sure they'd passed.

Years later, when Sheba had become a doctor and moved back to London to work at a hospital on Euston Road, she looked me up again: 'Hey stranger, fancy a catch-up?' We met for a coffee, and she told me Marni lived in Scotland with her boyfriend, that occasionally she would go up to Edinburgh and they'd sink a bottle of wine and talk about the Brownswood days. I felt so envious then, imagining them knocking back like normal people who did everything in the right order, at the right time. Since then, she'd given me news of Marni, who worked in a bookshop in Marchmont, and sent the odd message via Instagram. But there was always a distance between us, between our experiences. Sheba joked, but we *were* strangers, and I'd resigned myself to the fact that the three of us would never be friends again, not like we were. Just another missing thing.

But now, here they were. I stared at them sitting there, toasting me, and in that moment felt a strange sense of inflation, as something broke, or fixed, inside me. Licking the wine around my lips, I spotted another full glass at a nearby table. Leaning forwards, I picked it up, raised it in a toast to Sheba and Marni, and downed the lot, as they clapped and cheered.

'Let's try again.'

Dylan was staring at me in astonishment, Sanjay in growing amusement, as I turned towards our audience, bringing the microphone up to the correct height with a steady hand. When I sang the first line, clear as a bell, it came from right down in my diaphragm, from my core, all the way up through my heart.

Dylan had to hustle to keep up, his eyes never leaving me as I swayed behind the microphone, tucking bedraggled wine-wet hair behind my ear. And they both had to keep up all evening, as I segued from song to song, lazing behind the beat and speeding up, keeping them on the hop as I nuzzled each note, owned every phrase. My 'Bewitched, Bothered and Bewildered' was languorous and lingering; my 'Just One of Those Things' fierce and flippant; my 'Don't Explain' ravaged and heartfelt. 'Say you're good and get on with it,' Letty had said. A demon let loose that night; I felt unhinged, unravelled, unrepentant, the wine unwinding me like it had in Paris. When we finished, and the storm of applause broke out, my eyes met Dylan's and he nodded. It was all I needed.

We were mobbed afterwards. Someone asked us to play at their wedding; someone else said we should get a recording contract; one of Brownswood's teachers said we were 'much less shit than the school show'. As I attempted to mop my dress with a napkin, Dylan brought over a glass of water.

'Here you go,' he said. 'For your throat. And to counteract all that booze you just necked.'

'Thanks.' I sipped it, feeling dazed, while he watched me, hands in his pockets, rocking back and forth on his heels.

'I'm sorry,' he said. 'I've been a miserable bugger. I was nervous.'

'*You* were nervous?'

'Yeah. After what happened at the school show. I wanted us to do well. Wanted *you* to do well. Knew you had it in you.'

I opened my mouth to say something but Selassie interrupted us. 'A token, my dears, of my appreciation.'

He slipped some banknotes into my hand, then turned and did the same to Dylan and Sanjay. I clutched mine, stunned and sticky.

'I didn't realize . . .' I faltered.

He winked. 'Neither did I, but we all did very well tonight, *fiori*, so we all share the bounty.'

Dylan and Sanjay were jubilant, high-fiving each other and discussing taking their earnings to a nearby pub to 'get wrecked', but I had other plans. Leaving Em reading in her corner, I made my way to the back to see two women still laughing and talking, their empty bottle of wine between them. As I approached, they both stood and held out their arms.

'Jones!'

Hugging them, one by one, Sheba was as tall and elegant as ever, and Marni was pregnant.

'Congratulations.' I gestured to her belly, and sat with them at their table.

'I'm so wasted,' said Sheba. 'She wouldn't even have a taste.'

'But you're here,' I said. 'All the way from Edinburgh.'

Marni nodded, rubbing her back. 'I'm down for a book fair and Sheba told me about it. You were always a great singer. I remember from assembly.' She started to warble, '*Morning has brooooo-ken!*' and we all sniggered.

'And now a *professional* singer,' said Sheba. 'So mad, my mum saw an advert in the *Gazette*: "*Chanteuse Delphine Jones.*" It's fantastic, well done.'

'*Chanteuse?*' I scoffed. 'Selassie's such a drama queen.' He was rushing around clearing up and I watched him fondly, then caught sight of Em looking tired, and got to my feet.

'Listen, I've got to take my daughter home, but . . . can we do this again? Catch up properly. I've got so much to ask you. Thank you for coming, it's good to see you.'

'Good to see you too, Jones,' said Sheba, draining her glass. 'Don't be a stranger.'

'I won't,' I replied. Not any more.

On the bus home with Em, I peeked in my purse to check the notes I'd stuffed there – my fee for tonight's performance. My fingers shook as I counted. Fifty pounds. I flicked through again, just to be sure. Selassie was hoping to do this every month. It wouldn't be us every time – he would book other performers, but had made it clear we were his 'house band'. Em's frizzy head was lolling, her eyes heavy as she stared out of the window, but they widened when I handed her the cash.

'Here.'

'What's this?'

'Selassie gave it to me. But you were responsible for everything that happened tonight, so I think you should have it.'

'What should I do with it?'

'Whatever you want. It's up to you.'

Em looked thoughtful. 'I might invest it. I've been reading about geothermal energy, there are some really interesting companies . . .'

'Right.' Each to their own.

'Or I might just spend it on books.'

I savoured her little face; the sharp, beloved lines of her firm chin, the round wise-owl eyes of my girl. 'That sounds perfect.'

Chapter 54

After the heady thrill of a live gig, it was time to come back down to earth and prepare for a performance of another kind. I felt like I'd ducked underwater, swept away in a restless current of revision notes – Post-it scribbles pasted all over the flat, reminding me of this and that. My exams loomed, like the kraken in the deep, and I had to be battle-ready.

I re-read my set texts in the kitchen of Merhaba while making coffee, mumbled quotes to myself as I took orders, recited Shakespeare as I swept the floor, looked at practice papers while cooking dinner. When I closed my eyes, lines of poetry marched across my lids, and I dreamed of taking exams naked or oversleeping and missing them altogether. Jerking awake in bed to check the time and date, then lying, twitching and fretting, that hoped-for grade reverberating in my head like a jeer: *A, A, eh, eh* . . . To be so close, the culmination of months of work within reach, was exhilarating, but what if I sank or got eaten up just as I reached the shore?

'You should do yoga or something.' Roz watched my legs jiggling as we shared a coffee and a pep talk in Merhaba on the day of my first paper. 'Might calm you down.'

'Ran ten K this morning.' I recalled my unhinged sprint around the park, startling the deer as I pounded past.

'Jesus. Maybe I should come with you, might help me lose the weight.' Roz pinched her midriff glumly.

'You're quite thin enough. When do you start filming?'

'In the summer, apparently. The BBC's wrangling over the budget.' She didn't sound particularly excited.

I felt ambivalent about Roz's big break. Em strongly disapproved, and was making sure her class showered their teacher in praise and on-time homework in an attempt to persuade her that staying at Brownswood Academy was preferable to the lead role in a BBC drama. But I could only imagine the potential amount of money on offer, and didn't think anyone could reasonably be expected to turn that down. I could use that kind of windfall myself. Who were we to tell Roz to stick with teaching – that she was already living her best life?

But it was dismal to imagine the Brownswood kids going to school and not being taught by Mrs Gill any more. Mrs Gill, who sent Em home every week with essays covered in glowing comments, which in turn made Em glow. Mrs Gill, who'd bullied and enlightened me, restored my confidence and made me feel that anything was possible. Teachers like her and Sarah Boleyn were precious, should be fêted and put in magazines like Hollywood stars. Maybe then they wouldn't want to do other things.

'Delphine, *sweet'ay*, your first exam is this afternoon?'

Selassie came over to refill our coffees, unashamedly reading the notes on the table between us.

'Two o'clock.' I wiped my damp palms on a napkin. 'Love Through the Ages. Then Post-1945 next week.' My legs started jiggling again.

'Don't worry,' said Roz. 'You'll ace them.'

'Just worried it'll go wrong,' I muttered. 'Don't want to let anyone down.'

'You won't,' promised Roz. 'You'll make us all proud, and after your exams you can storm Selassie's Summer Jazz Night, and have a rest before your results.'

Selassie had been working to transform Merhaba's back garden into an oasis, and was planning a launch night in June featuring The Tiny Pennies. Every shift recently had been punctuated by him going back and forth carrying Moroccan tiles and huge pots for the olive trees he'd bought. I couldn't bring myself to think about it, because the time when my exams were over seemed immeasurably far away. All through my shift that morning, as Selassie and the builders toiled away out the back, I manned the front, allowing my body to do the work of serving drinks, clearing tables and taking orders, while my mind steadied, readying itself. After lunch, I grabbed my bag, waving goodbye as Selassie shouted blessings, and set off.

Roz had registered me through the Academy, so I was taking my exams in the school hall along with the other students. I felt awkward, wondering if they would stare at me, the 'mature' candidate who'd obviously messed it up first time round. But no one seemed to notice, their own nerves etched on their faces as we filed into the room. The invigilators walked round handing out the papers before that charged silence settled, provoking a familiar spark of excitement. Back where I belonged, where I should have been ten years ago. Reaching for the paper, I read the first question – 'Compare how the authors of two texts you have studied present barriers to love' – and picked up my pen, feeling thoughts bubble and flow from my brain to my fingers . . .

Three hours later, I emerged into the sunshine, the earlier twitchiness banished. Sated, satisfied and—

There was Dylan, at the school gates. Seeing him there made me catch my breath. Of course, I was wearing my exam uniform, jeans and a T-shirt, chosen for comfort rather than style, my hair scraped back.

'Hi.' Studiously, I looked down at my scuffed trainers.

'Wondered if you fancied a walk? You know, to wind down or something.'

'OK.' I followed him, as he headed towards Highbury Fields.

'How did it go?'

'OK.' Why couldn't I think of anything to say? Get a grip, Jones. We were like two teenagers.

After walking through the park for a few minutes in silence, we reached the tennis courts. For a while, we just watched the players hitting their balls back and forth, and the rhythm of it calmed me. Eventually, Dylan cleared his throat.

'Em's been walking Bernie,' he said. 'Twice a week after school. She's very responsible . . . Scrupulous.' He sounded like he was giving her a reference.

'Great.' Em had made several observations about his flat that I'd pretended not to be interested in. 'I asked where the dog's bed was, and he said she just slept on his.' 'He collects vinyl, like Granddad used to.' 'There's a photo of his ex-girlfriend next to the piano. They split up because she went back to Wales, but they're still friends.' She reported that Bernadette was sweet and affectionate, but liked rolling in unspeakable things. Apparently, this was preferable to Colin, Mrs Munroe's dog, who liked eating them.

'Have you seen Anne Frank's tree?' Dylan grasped my elbow.

I shook my head, distracted by his touch. 'What do you mean?'

He pointed. 'Over there. It's a sapling from the original horse chestnut that grew outside her hiding place in Amsterdam.'

We walked over and stood by the young daughter-tree, which was protected by a wire fence decorated with paper butterflies made by local schoolchildren.

'Grown from one of the last chestnuts left of the original,' said Dylan, but his hand on my elbow made it hard to concentrate on the tree. Small, in an innocuous location, it had a history, and was destined for greater things. I reached out with my free hand, to touch one of the butterflies.

'Roots and wings,' I whispered. 'Life goes on. Thank you for coming to meet me.'

'*Pleser*,' said Dylan, still staring at the sapling, leaves and paper wings waving in the breeze. '*Pleser . . . cariad.*'

And then, somehow, we were kissing, my barriers swept away as I gave myself up to a moment so instinctive that all other considerations faded into oblivion. Being together in this way felt right, a natural chord progression, totally in tune. But as we drew apart, everything came flooding back, along with the blood to my face.

'Sorry.' Dylan backed off, stuffing both hands in his pockets. 'Just got carried away . . .'

'No, it's fine.' I sneezed violently, lurching on the yellowing grass. 'It's nothing . . .' Couldn't find any words, my vocabulary recoiling like the tide going out. I'd learnt to speak French; now I was forgetting English.

He started forwards. 'I didn't mean . . . It's not . . . Dammit.' He ran his fingers through his hair distractedly, muttering something that sounded like '*tupsin.*'

'What's that?'

He gave me a wry grin. '*Twpsyn.* Stupid idiot.' Seeing my face, he added, 'Me not you.'

Like the tree, there was a wire fence around me. He obviously thought it was a mistake. We were both stupid idiots, pushing our friendship, tugging too hard on the rope.

'OK. Well. I'll see you . . . around.'

The only thing to do was walk away, head up, to stop the tears from falling. He hadn't meant any of it, he regretted it. I kept walking and didn't look back, even as he called my name, didn't think about the kiss, which, although it had felt so right, was obviously stupid and wrong, and would never happen again.

'Just breathe . . .' I told myself as I walked off, rubbing my eyes. Breathe, and leave, while your roots and wings are still intact.

Chapter 55

*M*y second English Literature paper was scheduled for a Wednesday afternoon at the end of May and, in the morning, there was a text from Roz – a photo of her, Joe and Izzy holding a picture Izzy had drawn of a rainbow, with the words: GOOD LUK!!!

Feeling twitchy again, I went for a head-clearing run to banish doubts and creeping thoughts. That kiss. Dylan's expression before I walked away. I hadn't contacted him, because I couldn't believe that he'd really meant to do it, or that I should have done it, with Em and everything else that was going on. I could imagine Letty scoffing at me, saying, 'Get on with it,' but I felt like a rabbit in the headlights, unsure which way to run.

Pounding on, past the playground, early sunshine warming the climbing frames and gleaming slide. Once again, I pictured Em there, perched at the top, shouting down for me to watch. What Adam had told me in Cambridge still haunted me, and every day I woke up wondering if I should tell her, if it was right to keep something so monumental to myself. The story of who she was, how she came about. But every time I was on the cusp, poised and ready to push myself off, I couldn't go there. Couldn't bear to revisit that moment, that fulcrum that sent me in a different direction, hellbent on ruining everything. Couldn't ruin it again now.

Back at the flat, I showered, dressed and managed half a sandwich before nerves got the better of me. My phone pinged again and Dylan's name flashed up on screen. Grabbing it, I stared at the text message: Pob Lwc. I could guess the gist, but checked to be sure, just in case it meant: 'I want to kiss you again.' At least he was thinking of me, remembered it was my exam day. I typed, Diolch, but deleted it without sending. Stupid idiot to start up a Welsh text-banter – what did I think was going to happen? That he was going to turn up with a rose on my doorstep and Celtic declarations of love? Feeling rattled and annoyed, I set off towards Brownswood, trying to focus.

Arriving early, I signed in to get my pass and wandered through reception into a little courtyard that looked out on a grassy stretch of land, exactly the same as it had been in my day. It was still lunchtime and the students were milling round, standing in groups, talking, some of the younger kids shoving each other in a flirty game of tag. I sat on a bench and watched them, wondering if I'd see Em there, how she interacted with her peers when I wasn't around. It took me back, the self-consciousness of the school yard, all of us eyeing one another and establishing the pecking order. Fittest, funniest, most popular . . . You got grades in school, you got grades out of it, too. Getting pregnant aged sixteen made me flunk the lot. Stupid idiot.

Once again, we filed into the hall and sat down as the invigilators handed out papers. I took mine and read the first question: 'In *Cat on a Hot Tin Roof*, contrast Maggie's childlessness with Mae's fertility to explore the role of women in the 1950s.' That slide in the playground, burning the back of Em's legs as she shuttled down. I twiddled my pen around my fingers like a majorette, feeling a shaft of sunlight scorch the back of my neck, turning it to hot tin, too hot to handle, too hot not to cool down . . . *Il faut se détendre. Détends-toi. Come on, Delphine, twpsyn, sort yourself out.* I rested my forehead on the desk, feeling dizzy, hot, stupid. All this pushing, it was too much, too much when in the end you just got pulled back . . .

Feeling a firm hand on my shoulder, I looked up to see Mrs Boleyn. She would always be Miss Challoner to me, sitting on the desk in Clit Class with her feet on a chair, making us laugh at Shakespeare. If only that prom night hadn't happened, she would have taken me through my A level all those years ago, and I wouldn't be here now, confused and distracted, in danger of messing up again.

She leaned towards me and murmured in my ear. 'Remember, whatever happens, you are a star. No matter what the outcome, I'm proud to be in the race with you.'

The same thing she said all those years ago. I felt a lump in my throat, an inflation in my chest. She patted my shoulder and moved on, down the line of desks. Picking up my pen again, I stared at the blank white paper for a second; the endless possibilities it offered. I began to write, feeling that familiar bubble in my brain as thoughts were born. Heard Letty's voice in my head: 'Say you're good and get on with it,' and smiled as I scribbled. Not stupid; brilliant. As my pen flew faster and faster, it seemed like someone else had taken control of it, an alter ego who knew exactly what to write, the right thing to say. That same electric charge I'd felt at Merhaba's Jazz Night – unhinged, like I could do anything.

When the time was up, I pushed my paper away, breathing hard like I'd been on a run. That same purged, cleansed feeling – unburdened, with a leftover buzz. On the way out, I headed for Mrs Boleyn, who was sorting through papers. She saw me coming and smiled.

'How did it go?'

I hesitated. It was hard to describe what had happened, how the seesaw had gone one way, then the other; how I felt in my bones I'd written something vital and true.

'Good, I think. I wanted to say thank you, anyway. For getting me through it. Now . . . and all those years ago.'

She dropped the papers and put both palms on the table. 'I meant it, you know. You were my star pupil. Not Adam Terris. I'm glad you've come back.'

I flinched at the name, but met her gaze. 'Me too.'

She walked around the desk. 'Are you heading out? Can I walk with you?'

We began to trace our way back through the corridors towards reception, buffeted by dashing students.

'Dulcie Norris, sort yourself out!' she barked, to an unkempt teen who'd knotted her tie round her head, then continued, to me. 'This A level. What do you see yourself doing with it?'

Make my mark, my fortune, show the world what I could do. 'I don't know. Just thought I should start somewhere.'

'What would you like to do? What would you like to be?'

I pictured Roz, a Bic in her hair, scrawling questions on the whiteboard, giving Em her A-plus, unpicking a love sonnet. 'I think . . . I'd like to be a teacher.'

Mrs Boleyn sighed, like she'd finished a good meal. 'I was hoping you'd say that. Because I have a proposition for you . . .'

Coming out of the school, I was fired up, by the exam, and my conversation with Sarah Boleyn. Triumph, surging inside me. I wanted to tell someone about it, someone who would listen with their head on one side, dark eyes snapping, clap their hands and say, '*Formidable! Maintenant, va chercher le Gallois!*' Walking briskly through squares and side streets, I was fizzing with anticipation, with potential. Anything was possible, if I put my mind to it. Em, Dad, Dylan – I could align my stars, make it all work out.

Letty's daughter's house looked lovely, bathed in late afternoon sunlight, and I took a moment to appreciate the graceful Georgian symmetry – pruned parterre, golden flagstones lined with shingle. Imagine owning such a house, and having the time to keep it like this. It was a different kind of neatness to Adam Terris's speckless lawn – more artless, stylish. English order versus French *soigné*. Maybe one day, Em and I would have a place as elegant and homely as this house. I walked round the back to the stone steps, the courtyard littered with pots. Lavender, and jasmine, miniature acers, thyme, marigolds and an enormous sunflower that had come out of nowhere, according to Letty: 'It just sprang up one day, like Jack's beanstalk.'

The door was open, as usual, so I let myself in, stopping on my way through the tiny kitchen to switch on the kettle. We'd share a pot of tea and a gossip, and I'd tell her about the exam, how I wasn't stupid, but brilliant, dazzling, on fire. I would tell her what Sarah Boleyn said to me, the opportunity she'd just offered. I would tell her about Dylan, our kiss. And I would tell her what really happened on the night of the prom. I had no mother to tell, so I would tell her. Time to get it all out, and move on. *'En marche,'* as Letty liked to say.

'Bonjour, madame.' I opened the door to the living room. *'J'arrive!'* She was asleep in her armchair, Aphra purring in her lap. As she dozed, I took the opportunity to tiptoe over to the Picasso and take a closer look. Was it really an original? Had Letty's story been true? She'd been known to embellish her anecdotes occasionally. Maybe Jean-Luc had simply bought the painting, years ago. Was the woman in the portrait Letty? If it *was* a woman – it wasn't clear. The mismatched eyes appeared to be closed; asleep, like Letty. I turned back to the real thing, still snoozing with the cat on her lap. Moving closer, I whispered, 'Letty! *C'est moi.'* It didn't do any good, so I stepped forwards and gently grasped her shoulder.

'Letty . . . *Réveille-toi.'*

The grey head slumped sideways. Something about the sagging face, the mouth drooping slightly, was unsettling. A fractal chill began in the nape of my neck, circling down my spine as I shook the bony shoulder and heard the click of the kettle coming to the boil in the kitchen.

'Letty! Wake up!'

Something wicked this way comes . . . I grabbed her wrist, not quite sure what I was feeling for. Was there a pulse? Would I even register it if there was? Maybe old ladies' pulses were barely discernible anyway. My own heart was beating so hard I could hear the blood pounding in my ears. Please no, let it not be this. Not now. As I held the frail, birdlike arm, Aphra stretched and needled, settling herself more comfortably on Letty's lap. Noting my proximity, her tail flicked irritably.

'Oh, Letty . . .'

But Letty couldn't hear me. She was with Jean-Luc, finally, enjoying a fiery sunset on their veranda in Provence, cooled by the mistral. Dying and living, warm and cold, there and not there, all at the same time. I'd never seen a dead body before, much less one I loved. Dad identified Maman, the last thing he did before he retreated into the seclusion of our flat, obliterated by the furies. I sank into the other armchair, breathing hard, vision blackening at the edges. Letty couldn't be dead. It wasn't possible, because I'd invited her to the Summer Jazz Night next month, and she'd promised she would come. No, not Letty, who'd reunited me with my mother's language, taken me to Paris, helped me get to Cambridge to defend my daughter, lived the rich and enriching kind of life that I wanted for myself. Rich, in every sense, all the time.

Had to do something, tell someone. Her daughter, up-stairs. I staggered to my feet and stumbled out, through the kitchen, the courtyard, up the steps, clinging to the iron railing. Round the front, through the gate and along the shingled path to the lacquered black front door. I pressed the doorbell and banged the knocker but, despite dogs barking inside, no one answered. Feeling desperate, I got out my phone and dialled 999.

'What service do you require?'

'Ambulance. No, police. My friend is . . . dead.' My breath snagged on the word and I started to cry, staggering back down the path, choking, still holding the phone to my ear.

'Right. I know it's hard, but can you stay on the line, please. We need to get some details . . .'

I provided the information they needed, wiping my mouth on my sleeve and making my way back down to the living room. Had to keep her company, along with Aphra. I gave the address, using one hand to stack some books that had tumbled to the floor when I'd backed away from Letty's body. The place should be neat when the police arrived – *soigné*-neat.

As soon as I'd finished the call, I went over and sat at Letty's feet, leaning against the knobbly knees and clasping the cold hand that lay along the arm of the chair. Her nails were painted a deep ruby-red. The cat's tail flicked again, warning me away, but I stayed, holding the limp fingers, resting my cheek against the prickly wool of her skirt.

'*Détends-toi, mon amie. En marche.*'

We sat like that, Aphra's tail flicking away, until the police arrived.

Chapter 56

*F*or three days after that, I called in sick and sat with Dad in the flat, watching films. Could see why he liked them. Every now and then I'd slide out of consciousness, immersed in the action, forgetting everything but the astronaut fixing a transmitter, in a race against time; the schoolgirl walking home alone at night, watched by a predator; the troubled artist infatuated with his muse, who loved another. They all had bigger problems than me, and I abandoned myself, letting the screen lull me into a stupor. So much easier to do that than think about Letty's cold, sagging body, Adam's hollow eyes as he told me he wasn't the father, or the spinning wheels of my mother's bicycle, the cake intact in the basket.

Em tiptoed around us, making tea, suggesting we come to the table to eat the dinner she'd cooked. It was wrong, but I found myself smiling vaguely and patting her arm, just as my father did to me. Simpler not to engage, not to dig any deeper, but to exist, on the surface, waiting for the storm below to pass. And if it didn't, then I would just stay, tucked up in Maman's blanket, idly winding down the days.

But on the fourth day, in the morning, when I'd settled to watch *Mission: Impossible* and Em had gone to school, leaving us with toast curling on the fold-down table, my father turned to me with that new light in his eyes.

'Delphine,' he said. Like that day with the daffodils. I knew what needed saying, and was only vaguely surprised it was coming from him. Someone had to do it, shake me out of the torpor. And who better than someone who'd endured it himself for years?

'Delphine,' he said again. 'You've got to get out. Before it becomes a habit.'

I gazed at him through a well of tears. 'You didn't though.'

He passed a hand across his forehead. 'I know,' he said. 'But I'm trying.'

My tears began to flow, drizzling down until I could feel them trickling around my neck, dribbling towards the crucifix. 'Why did you not try before?'

He kept his head lowered, staring at his own bony knees. 'It was too hard. Didn't just feel my pain. Felt yours too. Too heavy for me to get up. It's been easier lately. Now and then, it's lighter.'

I wiped my eyes, and held out my hand. 'Could we get up together, do you think?'

We went out to the grassy bank alongside the flat, and stood under the trees for a while. Dad closed his eyes, holding up his face to the sun. When he got tired and went indoors, I stayed, sitting on a wall, staring at the swaying leaves like I'd stared at the TV screen, scraping the moss on the brick with my fingernail. My phone buzzed in my pocket, and I answered it with a muddy finger.

'Delphine? Where are you? Why haven't you returned my calls?'

'I just . . . couldn't talk.'

'Where are you?'

'Home.'

'I'm worried about you. I've been calling for days. Ever since Sylvie phoned.'

'Letty's dead.'

'I know.'

'I found her.'

'I know. Delphine, I'm so sorry.'

The grass was shorter. The council must have mowed it. I picked up a shiny little shard of glass poking out of a patch of soil. It cut my finger, and I sucked at the blood and mud.

'Delphine? Are you still there? Can you get to Merhaba? I'll meet you there. Are you listening? Get to Merhaba.'

Putting my phone away, I stood, contemplating my grimy fingernails. I guessed I could get as far as Merhaba. Maybe a coffee would be nice. Hearing a buzzing in my ears, which might have been bees, or just buzzing, I moved slowly away from the flat, dropping the glass back into the grass. One day, Em and I would have a lovely garden. Like Letty's courtyard, or Selassie's, gradually emerging from the wasteland behind the restaurant. Creating something beautiful from the mess. It had a Mediterranean feel. Letty would have liked it.

Somehow my feet took me there and, seeing the blue and gold sign, I began to cry, like I'd arrived home after months away. I stumbled in, to see Selassie's worried face, Abrihet behind him wiping her hands on her skirt. He was carrying the jebena pot, usually brought out for a celebration, but as he set it down on the table and led me there, the ceremony of it seemed right. He poured me a tiny cup and I held it, absorbing the warmth, inhaling it.

Roz barrelled in, sweeping me into a hug. 'Hi, love, how are you feeling?'

I took a sip, wiping my mouth with the back of my hand. 'She had an affair with Picasso. Or at least, she told me she did. She has a painting on her wall. *Had*. Past participle.'

Roz's eyes met Selassie's, and he pulled a face. She nodded to him. 'Come on, finish your drink.'

She sat down beside me, hesitating as if trying to find the right words. 'Listen, what happened is awful. Horrible. But Sylvie told me that Letty had a heart condition. Plus, she had a minor stroke, out in Provence, and that was how she fell and hurt her hip. So she wasn't well. I know it feels like a terrible shock, but she was very old. She had a wonderful life, and it was all the more wonderful, these last few months, because of you. I know, because she phoned to tell me. Said that trip to Paris was the best day out she'd had in years.' Roz grinned. '"Marvellous gel, if I was fifty years younger, and one of those sapphic types, I'd go for it myself."' Her impersonation of Letty was so accurate that I couldn't help a choke of laughter.

'I wish I spoke like that,' I muttered, gulping my coffee. 'I wanted to be like Letty, all posh and outrageous, daring to do anything. But I'm not. It's not worth it, pushing like this, hoping for something more. Sometimes I think I'd be better off back in my old job, the one I got fired from. You get one good thing, you want another, and another and another, until nothing is good enough. And then this happens. Better not to get anything in the first place. Stay where you are, in your box.' The cup clattered against the saucer as I put it down.

'Bullshit,' replied Roz. 'Letty, posh? She was an Essex girl! Sylvie says she started talking like that at Oxford, because she wanted to marry a lord.' She put her hand on mine. 'We're all just trying to get on. What would Letty want? Would she want you to sit here crying over her, or would she want you to get up, go and make something of yourself? Show the world what you can do?'

She waited, as I stared at the black curves of the jebena, the base decorated with bold red lines and white dots that danced before my eyes. '*Les carottes sont cuites . . .*' But they never were. That was the point.

'Well?'

I put down my cup. 'She'd want me to press on.'

'Exactly.'

'But I don't know how. Don't know where I'm supposed to go, what I'm supposed to do. You have exams at school to show how you're getting on, if you're doing well or not. But there's nothing to show you how well you're doing in real life. Talking to Letty, telling her what I was up to . . . it made me feel like I was doing OK, like I had something to report. She was interested, she cared, she told me off. I haven't had that since my mother . . . since . . .'

Roz squeezed my hand. 'Then keep talking to her. Keep talking to them both. Who knows, they might be up there together, listening. It's worth a try.'

It was worth a try. I heaved myself to my feet, pushing my straggly hair back, wiping the drying tears from my cheeks.

'I should go and pick Em up from school. Apologize.'

'Do. See her, talk, rest. Everything else will come.'

'Thanks, Roz. You're . . .' She had the usual pen in her hair, an ink stain on her white shirt. 'Wiser than you look.'

She batted away the compliment. 'Played a psychiatrist in an ITV crime drama once. Know what I'm talking about.'

Hugging her, Selassie and Abrihet, with promises of calls and catch-ups, I walked out of Merhaba and headed for the bus stop, plucking my phone from my pocket. I had to go and see Em. 'See her, talk, rest. Everything else will come.'

En marche.

Chapter 57

$\mathcal{W}$hen I arrived at the gates of the park, the sun was still blazing – no clouds to herald Letty's passing. Em was waiting there, rucksack over one shoulder, a paper bag clutched in her hand.

'I got your text. Why did you want to meet here? Are you all right?'

'Sort of. There's something I want to show you.'

She held out the bag. 'Granddad gave me money for marshmallows. Letty liked hot chocolate too, didn't she? You said you had one in Paris.'

'Oh, Em-Jo.' I looked inside the bag, and back to my daughter, my heart melting. 'You always know.'

'Thought we could toast her later. If you want to.'

'Yes. I think she would have liked that. But first, I wanted to say I'm sorry. For these last few days. I've been a mess, and you've had to clear up, and that's not on.'

Em shrugged. 'That's OK. I knew you'd come out of it.'

'I will. But there's something I have to tell you.'

You could try to keep it all buried away, but sometimes the

334

shard of glass still poked out of the soil, waiting to cut you. Em deserved more than a mother who kept secrets from her, and, young as she was, she was – hopefully – brave enough to cope with this one. I couldn't tell my mother, I couldn't tell Letty, but I could tell my daughter, before it was too late. Taking her hand, I started walking, pulling her along with me.

'Is that why you wanted to meet here? Where are we going?'

'This way.'

The park was wide and welcoming that summer afternoon, with dog walkers and joggers and mothers pushing prams. It wasn't raining like it had been that day with Maman, but the tree was still there, arching invitingly out of the ground, offering us a view of everything below. Dropping the bag of marshmallows on a grassy knoll by the trunk, I put my foot on the first branch and grabbed another above.

'What are you doing?' Em looked up at me in alarm.

'I did this with your grandmother a long time ago. It's time I did it again. Will you come with me?'

She frowned, but put down her rucksack. 'OK.'

Together we climbed, branch after branch, until we were settled in the highest limbs of the tree, and the patchwork of the park emerged below, lakes glittering in the sunshine, little figures running and playing, the green fringed with grey buildings all around. An oasis. I took Em's hand and turned it over in my own, tracing the lines on the soft palm.

'You always wanted to know about your dad, and I never said anything. I'm sorry about that. But the truth was it was complicated, I was ashamed of the mess I'd made. And in the end . . . In the end, I just wasn't sure . . .'

Em stared at me, her eyes huge. 'Not sure of what?'

I took a deep breath. 'Who your father was. But now I know. And I'm going to tell you how it happened, and hope that you can understand, and forgive me.'

She gave a tiny nod, and I let myself go back. Back to that night, nearly thirteen years ago, when it all went so wrong.

Chapter 58

*I*t was prom night. My exams were finished, they'd gone brilliantly, I had Adam. After what happened with Maman, and all the difficulties with Dad, it finally felt like my life was getting back on track, that I might be able to make something of myself and move on. Get my A levels, apply to university, maybe try for Cambridge. It felt like I was on the cusp of something, full of hope and expectation. It all began so well . . .

He met me, holding the rose. 'It's fake,' he said, as I accepted it, laughing and curtseying. 'Made of plastic. Happy anniversary.'

We got our drinks and stood at one side for a while, watching the others. Marni and Dan arrived, looking adorably self-conscious. Adam leaned towards me and I felt his breath on my neck.

'Look at them both. The straightest teeth in school.'

I laughed, though was glad he'd said it only to me. Adam could be thoughtless sometimes. So laidback and sure of himself, it didn't occur to him that others might be less so.

We danced for a while, entirely in the moment, and I relished leaning against him, gyrating to Gnarls Barkley, the music throbbing through me, aware of his arms draped around me, how perfectly we fitted together, with a familiarity born of those long nights in his loft room. I hadn't really thought about that one night much, the one when we forgot the condom. Or afterwards, when I never did anything about it. The morning-after pill had to be taken within seventy-two hours, a short window, and I found myself busy with all sorts of jobs during that time – grocery shopping, fixing the boiler water pressure, trying to kill the ants in the kitchen, last-minute revision. When the time had passed, I couldn't decide if the distraction had been deliberate or not.

Anyway, Sheba always said it was actually quite difficult to get pregnant, that most couples trying for a baby had to do it over and over again during the brief fertile phase, until they got sick of it. We'd only done it once, and I wasn't sure where I was in my cycle, but it would probably be fine. And if it wasn't . . . well, maybe it was a sign. That it was meant to be. That Adam and I should be together, bound by that moment.

Obviously, that was ridiculous, but I was sixteen, and in love. Could think a hundred contradictory thoughts all at once and be passionate about every single one of them. I wanted to take my A levels, go to Cambridge, travel the world, but I also wanted Adam, to have a family around me, someone to cherish. So in the end, I just let nature take its course, allowed my body to dictate the consequences, my mind in the back seat.

Eyes closed, head leaning against his chest, I wondered

if there was a life unfurling within me, whether a baby of ours would have his eyes. But then Brownswood's resident DJ – Mr Donaldson, one of the Geography teachers – followed 'Crazy' with Shayne Ward's 'That's My Goal', sending everyone streaming off the dancefloor in disgust. Adam and I headed outside for some fresh air, and that was when we bumped into Miss Challoner.

'Hello, you two,' she said, hands clasped behind her back in a mannish way. 'Enjoying yourselves?'

'Yes.' We grinned at her, feeling a sense of camaraderie now our exams were over, as if we were friends rather than teacher and students.

'Delphine!' Sheba's voice distracted me and I turned to see her looking harassed, tucking long blonde hair behind her ear as she pulled me away. 'You have to help me.' She lowered her voice. 'I've got my period.'

Sheba was wearing a white halterneck dress, her long brown limbs contrasting with its crisp lines. I could also see the whites of her eyes as she bent towards me.

'Have you got anything?' she whispered.

Adam and Miss Challoner were still talking, and a few words poked through my consciousness as I shook my head at my friend.

'No, sorry, have you asked Marni?'

'Albemarle Academy . . . my parents . . . a better fit . . .'

'Already asked. Nothing. What am I going to do?'

'What about the toilets? The machine?'

'It's a shame . . . We'll miss you . . .'

'It's fucking broken.' She was on the point of tears, and I forced myself to stop listening to the other conversation.

339

'Here.' I was wearing a backless black dress, borrowed from Marni. At the last minute, self-conscious about the amount of flesh on show, I'd added a long silver-grey cardigan. I took it off and handed it to her. 'Put this on, and ask Miss Challoner if she's got anything.'

Sheba did as she was told, and soon had Miss Challoner rooting around in her bag, while Adam and I headed off to the hill, his hand on my bare skin. Marni and Dan were already there with some others, chatting and rolling up. She nodded at me as I arrived.

'Much better, why were you wearing that thing?'

I shrugged and sat down, the words I'd overheard still tugging at me. *'We'll miss you . . . Albemarle Academy . . . a better fit . . .'* What had they been talking about? I lay down on the grass, the blades tickling my back as I gazed up at the deepening summer sky. Marni handed me the joint Dan had been rolling and I inhaled, breathing in the bittersweet fumes, relaxing into the hit. Adam was next to me, talking to Gus Grayson about the Premier League. He sounded as if he was really into it, when he didn't care about football at all, just like he wasn't really a socialist. I remembered the brochures on his kitchen table. School brochures. Sixth-form colleges. Albemarle.

'I was sorry to hear you'll be leaving us next term.'

'Yeah, it was all a bit sudden.'

'Where is it you're going again?'

'Albemarle Academy, in Hertfordshire. My parents thought it would be a better fit, for the subjects I want to do.'

'Well, it's a shame. We'll miss you.'

Adam was leaving. He was quitting Brownswood to go

to another school, a posh private school that taught History of Art and prepared you for Oxbridge if you could pay for it and play the part. Adam's parents could pay for it, and he could play the part.

I sat bolt upright, the joint falling from my fingers into the dry grass.

'What are you doing?'

Various voices crowding in, chastising me, but I didn't care, struggling to my feet, caught up in the skirt of the dress, and striding away, without a backward glance, heart pounding, blood rushing in my ears.

He caught up with me outside the library, a hand on my elbow pulling me round.

'What's going on? Why did you go off like that?'

I glared up at him, pushing my hair out of my eyes. 'When were you going to tell me?'

A flicker of guilt flashed across his face. 'About what?'

'Albemarle.'

He grimaced. 'So you heard.'

'I heard. Nice of you to fill Miss Challoner in. Were you just going to let me work it out for myself when you didn't turn up next term?'

'Of course not. I just . . . wanted us to get past our exams, have some fun, before . . .'

'What?' I demanded. 'Before you broke up with me?'

The thing was, in that moment, I didn't really think he was going to break up with me. I was just being dramatic. It was upsetting, of course, that he was going to another school and leaving me behind, but I assumed we'd stay together, be at different schools but see each other outside them. I'd go round to Ginny and Clement's for dinner, stay in his room when they were away. We'd carry on. But spitting out the accusation, I saw it in his face: the truth of it. He *was* going to break up with me. A fresh start at his posh new school, without his not-very-posh girlfriend. Different personas sat easily with Adam. He could pretend to be left-wing when he wasn't; pretend to like football when he didn't; pretend to love me when he wasn't really that bothered at all. Everything was easy for him; easy come, easy go, his path greased by Daddy's Amex.

I began to cry, retreating until my back was against the wall of the library, where we'd first kissed a year ago. It was rough against my skin and I slid down it, relishing the pain.

'Delphine, come on. It's not that bad.'

'What do you know?' Salty tears on my lips, what a waste of make-up.

'Don't ruin it. We can still have a nice evening.'

'Don't let me stop you. Go on, off you go.' I huddled against the brick, my knees against my chest.

He argued for a bit, justifying himself, while I ignored him, my back against the wall. Finally, he stared at me for a second, then sighed, raising his palms as if in defeat. 'OK, have it your own way.' He walked off, a resigned set to his shoulders as if there was nothing he could do about any of it. Out of his hands.

Such an ignominious ending. Along with the dejection and anger, I felt let down. It felt like a damp squib of a break-up, rather than the fireworks our relationship demanded. I wanted fireworks. When he'd gone, I cried for a bit, then ran back into the hall, punching my way through the dry-humping hordes until I found Lee Enright chatting up Stacey Turner, who seemed distinctly unimpressed.

'What have you got?'

He looked around, briefly irritated, then intrigued. 'What do you want?'

'Whatever you've got.'

Lee usually charged for this sort of thing, but as a known non-drinker, he was probably keen to break me in, secure a new client. He took me to his locker.

'Here.' He filled a plastic cup with what looked like a fruit punch. It would pack one. We all remembered Ceci Barlow last year, vomiting over the wall by the science block, her friend Alison holding her hair. All that rage and bile inside me; I wanted it out.

I drank it in a few gulps, wincing at the strength, and visited him twice more within the hour. By 10 p.m. I couldn't see straight, existing in another dimension, and feeling much better about everything. The dress was fine, condoms didn't matter, Adam didn't matter, nothing mattered. There were no consequences, to anything. You just did what you liked, when you felt like it, in the moment.

Barrelling down a random corridor, cannoning from one wall to the other, I arrived outside one of the practice rooms, the same room I'd been playing in when Adam found me. It was open, so I went in and sat down at the piano, leaning my foggy head against the wood. When the whirling receded, I began to play, my fingers clumsy on the keys, but a tune emerging. So much about that night was a blur, but I remembered the song I played was 'It Could Happen to You'.

The door opened behind my bare back, and I felt his

eyes on me, but carried on, watching him out of the corner of my eye. So drunk. Could almost imagine it was anyone, almost imagine it was Adam, come to say sorry, it was all a mistake. Taken up with my storyline, the what-might-have-been, I barely noticed when he gently closed the lid and took my hand.

'Are you OK?'

I nodded, leaning towards him, desperate for comfort, validation. His hand slid to my back, fingers running along the scratches there, tracing the path of the evening to this point.

'Did he break up with you?'

I nodded, and he rubbed away my tears with his thumbs.

'Oh, Delphine,' he said. 'I'm sorry. You deserve so much better.'

I looked up at him, thinking he wasn't that much older than me, and it didn't matter anyway. Nothing mattered. I put one hand up, cupping the back of his neck.

'Ms Jones,' he murmured, as a kind of warning.

'You said I was beautiful and clever,' I mumbled, pulling his face down.

'Both,' he breathed, before his lips met mine.

Chapter 59

'*Your teacher?*' Em spoke in a low voice, her eyes on the skyline.

I blinked back my tears. 'Mr North.'

We were both whispering, though no one could hear us, up there in the tree. I'd spent so long burying the knowledge, trying to forget that night, that sometimes it felt like it hadn't even happened, like it might have been a bad dream. When I found out I was pregnant, I was so sure it was Adam's, because I couldn't really remember that half-hour in the music room, exactly who did what. Afterwards, I never saw James North again – he never went back to the school, was never heard from, like he never existed. So I pretended he didn't, as it was easier that way. Everything was so difficult; for once I just wanted the easy way out, like Adam. When I discovered I was pregnant, when I gave birth, I was certain Em was his – my teenage sweetheart's. That was that.

'Did you tell him?'

Em's voice was a tiny thread, and I had to keep hold of it, before it was severed.

'No. I never saw him again. I didn't want to. It was . . . wrong, obviously. Very wrong. But . . .' I looked down at my hands. My red, cracked hands, worn down by years of washing up and wiping.

'But what?' Her eyes fixed on me, round like his.

I took a deep breath, knowing what I said next could tip things one way or the other. 'It's really important that you know . . . I thought what happened with Mr North was a mistake. For all those years. A terrible, terrible mistake. One that I wanted to forget, pretend it never happened. And on one level, that's what it was. But on another . . .' I reached out to caress her cheek. 'It was the best thing that ever happened to me. Because it gave me you. Now, I know it gave me you. Something good came out of it all.' I carried on, louder and fiercer. 'Having a baby wasn't a mistake. It gave me another – *better* – life, as your mother. It gave me you. I wouldn't change a thing. I would always – *always* – choose you.'

For a while there was silence, apart from the swishing of the leaves, ruffled by the breeze.

'Is that why I am the way I am?' she asked, finally.

'What are you?'

She dashed a hand against the corner of her eye. 'Weird.'

I grabbed the hand and held it firmly. 'You are not weird. You are wonderful, and you are mine.'

'But what happened to him? To . . . to my father?'

I closed my eyes. I'd done my own detective work, reluctantly, after I went to see Adam. Just to know everything, for sure.

'He died. In a car crash, in Spain. A few years after you were born.'

Em would never know James North and, given the circumstances of her conception, perhaps that was for the best. Like the song in King's College Chapel – *'natus virgine'*, a maiden mother and no earthly father. I didn't want there to be any more uncertainty, any more wishful thinking. Nothing missing from the jigsaw puzzle. Em was silent, picking a piece of bark off the branch she was sitting on. Eventually she sniffed, and shifted her legs over.

'Where are you going?'

'It's uncomfortable up here. And I said I'd go to Halima's.'

'But . . .' I was bewildered by the about-turn. I'd bared my soul, and she was off to her friend's for tea. 'Are you OK? How do you feel? Do you want to talk about it some more? Ask me anything?'

She shook her head, shimmying down, slipping from my grasp. 'I want to think about it. How I feel. What I want to say.'

'What about the marshmallows?' I started to slide after her, scratching my legs on the branch in my desperation. 'Please . . . come back. Don't run away. Let me explain . . .'

But she jumped to the ground, shouldered her rucksack and ran off, her skinny legs carrying her away from the green, towards the grey.

Chapter 60

The following Friday, I got ready for Merhaba's Summer Jazz Night, putting on my red dress, which I'd hand-washed in the bath, and pinning up my hair with a white gardenia I'd found in the street, languishing in the summer heat. Dressing for Dylan, perhaps, unable to let go of the memory of that kiss, whatever it had meant. But also for Letty, to give her a good send-off. Her daughter Sylvie had rung during the week to tell me about the funeral – or at least, the lack of one. Letty hadn't wanted a ceremony – 'She always said funerals were terribly common' – preferring her ashes to be scattered to the mistral while the thrower shouted, 'Bollocks to Brexit.' I had laughed down the phone, then clapped my hand to my mouth in horror, but Sylvie had laughed too.

'It's awful, I'm so desperately upset but I keep chuckling at things she said. Do you know, she saw Boris Johnson in the street a few weeks after she moved back from France, and she threw her handbag at him and called him a *connard*. I can't stop thinking about it.'

Em had avoided me all week, and I couldn't stop thinking about that. She wasn't angry, hadn't shouted, wasn't ignoring me as such, but there had been a retreat, and it felt as if a cold wind had blown through the flat, leaving me shivering and exposed. At night, she lay still in our bed as I stared up at the ceiling, trying to make out darkened shapes in the mould. I wished I could go to Letty's, confide in her, get some of her robust advice, but she was gone, without even a headstone to visit.

When I reached Merhaba, people were already arriving, Selassie having set up his blackboard outside the front: 'The Tiny Pennies – Summer Jazz Night in the Garden'. Striding through the double doors that led out onto the back, I stopped in amazement. During my shifts, Selassie had been working on the wasteland behind the restaurant, smuggling in builders outside opening hours, struggling through carrying plant pots and bags of compost. Now I could appreciate the full transformation. Mud and rubble had made way for terracotta tiles warmed by evening sunshine. The space was a riot of bougainvilleas and camellias, solar lights and lanterns strung across between hooks and branches, wooden tables and chairs set up with candles in wine bottles, plus little jam jars full of sweet peas.

At the far end in the corner, between two fig trees, Selassie had set up a microphone and wheeled the piano out, where Dylan was already sitting, hitting one note repeatedly. He looked up as I arrived and my heart thumped in response, his finger lingering on the key as he took in the dress and the gardenia. Then he seemed to check himself, and removed his hand from the keyboard. I tried not to think about the feeling of that hand around my wrist, or his lips on mine. *Twpsyn.* Stupid idiot, stop.

'We could do with your dad to tune this. I think Selassie buggered it, moving it outside.'

I was touched that he still remembered what Dad used to do for a living. Putting my folder of lyrics on a nearby table, I began to check the microphone. Selassie had run a lead from inside, which should be fine.

'How are you feeling?'

'OK.' It wasn't true, but I had to believe it might be, one day.

Sanjay arrived with his guitar, and the audience started to filter into the garden – the usual crowd, plus several new additions. There was Roz near the front, beckoning the new waitress over to take her wine order; Sarah Boleyn with a group of teachers from the school; Dom Seddon, with his mum and dad; other parents I vaguely recognized. Em's friend Halima's parents came in, hissing at each other as if they were having a row. Em wasn't there. She'd said she was going stay with Dad and do her homework, and I'd tried not to feel too rejected. She would come back to me when she was ready. Probably. Hopefully. I was open to that possibility.

By eight o'clock, there were at least fifty or sixty people there, with more crowding in the doorway, Selassie rushing back and forth while Abrihet settled herself next to Halima's mother.

Dylan caught my eye, nodded, and I bent towards the microphone. This time, I had no doubts as I opened my mouth – this wasn't about me; it was about Letty, singing her to the other side. We opened with 'Summertime', then

'Blue Skies', segueing into 'On the Sunny Side of the Street' and 'Fly Me to the Moon'. As the sun's rays sank, the solar lights began to glow, Selassie switched on the lanterns and lit candles as the diners ate, drank and swayed to the music. I rarely spoke in between songs but, as the applause died down after our cover of Norah Jones's 'Don't Know Why', I took a sip of water and made an exception.

'This song is for a dear friend of mine who can't be with us tonight. But I hope she's up there somewhere, listening. This is Letty's Lullaby.'

> Silver feathers, eagle eyes,
> Scarlet-painted claws,
> She rears up, spreads her wings and flies
> To dear and distant shores.
> *Au revoir et bon voyage, ma chère,*
> *Je t'ai tout dit sur moi,*
> *Mon amie et autre mère,*
> *Letty, détends-toi.*

I wrote the lyrics, and Sanjay the tune, working together one evening in Frank's dingy pub where it was always Christmas, and sending Dylan our scribbled notes to arrange. As the song went on, my voice floated up into the sky, where sister-winds could carry it to be picked up by the Provençal mistral. Who knew where it would end up?

We finished with 'At Last', and afterwards the applause was so thunderous and prolonged that Dylan and Sanjay came out to the front to join me, and we bowed and waved until people were distracted by Selassie bringing out free limoncellos. While Dylan knocked back at least three shots, I collected my denim jacket and bag, thinking I should make a quick exit, not hang round waiting for . . . for what? What was I waiting for? What did I want to happen? The spirit of Letty was telling me to get on with it, just ask him if he wanted to go for a drink, but I felt like I'd lost my voice again.

'That was bloody marvellous,' said Roz, coming over to give me a hug. 'You did Letty proud.'

'Thanks.' Certain I would start to cry, I tried to change the subject. 'Have you got your filming schedule yet?'

To my surprise, she looked away and bit her lip. 'Told them I didn't want the part.'

'What?' I tried not to let the relief show on my face. 'But you wanted it so much, and lost all that weight . . .'

Roz grimaced. 'Yes, I was miserable, and the producer was a total knob, suggesting I get a skin peel, and the schedule would have meant weeks away from the kids and . . . I just don't need that shit in my life any more.' She lifted her palms and gave me a faint smile. 'Thought being an actress again would be a step up, but it felt like a step back. Emily's class made me a Bruce Bogtrotter chocolate cake as a send-off, and I broke down in tears in the staff room because I realized I didn't want to go. I like where I am now. It's what I'm good at.'

Sanjay slung an arm around her, kissing her cheek. 'I prefer Mrs Gill to Rosalind Cartwright.'

She poked him. 'Misogynist prick.'

'Delphine, *shikor'ay*, what a triumph! Here is a little gesture of my appreciation.' Selassie tucked a roll of notes into my hand and pinched my cheek, before passing one to Dylan and another to Sanjay. Abrihet came over, beaming.

'You look thin, Delphine. I will make you some stew. Don't you think she looks thin, Mr Taylor?'

Dylan shrugged. 'It's none of my business.'

'Hahaha!' Selassie guffawed, slapping him on the shoulder. 'None of your business! Very good joke!'

Abrihet frowned at her husband, and patted Dylan on his arm. 'Make sure she gets home safe.'

Dylan led the way out of the restaurant, both of us accepting congratulations from lingering customers on the way. When we got outside, he turned to me, hands jammed in his pockets. *Ask him. Ask him for a drink.* I said nothing.

'Where do you live?'

'Near the mosque. It's a bit of a trek.' Come on Delphine, *twpsyn*. 'Do you . . . do you want to come with me?'

'Sure. I need to walk off the booze.' He turned and set off.

He didn't talk much on the way, which was good, because I couldn't think of anything to say. It was still warm and the moon was bright and, despite our silence, I hoped that somehow our block of flats would retreat further and further away as we approached, so that we never got there and could just carry on walking forever. Eventually we reached the turn-off.

'It's this road.' I pointed.

'How was your last exam?'

We spoke at the same time. I took a moment to consider, because everything that had happened since had made it fade in my mind, and I wasn't sure if that euphoria in the exam room had been real.

'It was good, really good . . . I think.'

He didn't look at me, kicking a stone on the pavement. 'I bet you aced it.'

'Maybe. At least I gave it my all.'

'Yes. You gave it your all,' he said, smiling. 'Now that your exams have finished . . .' He held out a hand and pulled me towards him.

I didn't resist, allowing myself to be tugged forwards, heart jumping, Letty's voice in my head – 'Just get on with it' – no going back, just pressing on, open to the possibility . . . But as he bent his head, a voice cut through the darkness.

'Delphine, is that you?'

We both turned in shock as Adam Terris emerged from the communal entrance of the block – assured, potent; a seasoned version of the confident teenager I remembered striding down Brownswood's corridors. The streetlamp caught the red in his hair, shooting off sparks, as if fired up by the sun. Beside him, Dylan seemed to have deflated, shrinking into the shadows, fading to grey.

I hugged my arms around myself as if to ward them both off, glaring at Adam. 'What are you doing here?'

'We need to talk. It's important.' Adam raked a hand through his russet hair. The elbows of his corduroy jacket had patches on, just like Em said, even though he was only my age. 'I'm Delphine's ex-boyfriend,' he added, to Dylan, and for a second there was the hint of a smirk, a smidgeon of complacency, as if he was returning to reclaim his crown. Dylan's own expression was shuttered and blank, his hands back in his pockets.

'Right,' he replied. 'I see.' And without another word, he spun on his heel and walked away. I watched him, feeling the unfurling roots between us ripping apart, then turned back to my first love, one-time father of my child.

Chapter 61

'*H*ow did you know where I live?'

We were sitting in a late-night café in Finsbury Park, next to the railway station. I was clutching a coffee in a paper cup, blowing through the little hole in the lid. If I did it at a certain angle, it made a fluting noise, a sound I was experimenting with. I could tell it irked him.

He gave me a rueful smile. 'Sheba. She wasn't keen on telling me, but I said I wanted to apologize. She thought I was going to send you a letter.'

'Oh.' I took a sip of my drink. 'Go on, then.'

'What?'

I blew through the hole. 'Apologize.'

'Ah, er . . . well.' He shifted uncomfortably in his seat. Adam was clearly not a man used to saying sorry. 'I *did* want to say . . . that is, I could have gone about it all a little better, been a bit more . . .'

'Considerate? Empathetic? Thoughtful?'

'As I said before, it was very unexpected. I didn't react in the way I should have, and I regret that. But . . . seeing

Emily made me realize . . .' He stopped, twirling a wooden stirrer between his fingers.

'What did it make you realize?'

To my surprise, he dropped the stirrer and took off his glasses, pinching the bridge of his nose as if he was about to cry. 'It made me realize that there was a time when I would have believed she was mine. That she *could* have been mine. That, in a way . . . I wish she was mine.'

I took the lid off the cup. 'But she isn't.'

'No.' He swallowed, staring at the steam billowing from his drink. Then, still not looking at me: 'Whose is she?'

The lid went back on. 'That's none of your business.'

'No, of course. It's just . . .' He sat back, putting on his glasses again, and risking a sideways glance. 'I wondered . . . Do you know who . . . Have you found him?'

'He's not a part of our lives.' I didn't want to give anything away. 'We're better off without him.'

We were both silent for a second, listening to the faint announcements coming from the station. The last train back to Cambridge was in two minutes.

'If you like,' said Adam, almost casually, 'we could pretend she's mine.'

I jumped, spilling some of my coffee on the table. 'What do you mean?'

He leaned forwards, as if to take my hand, but I wrenched it away. 'She could have been mine. Why not let people believe it? I know I messed up when we met, but I'm ready to . . . get to know her. We could be a family. Kind of.'

Dabbing at the spillage with a napkin, I stared at him in disbelief. 'What on earth are you talking about? One minute you're marching her out of your office, the next you're ready to play daddy? What's going on?'

He slumped in his seat. 'Sophie and I have split up. The engagement's off.'

There was a time, even recently, when I dreamed of this moment. The crawling-back, it-was-all-a-mistake moment when he would beg for forgiveness, say he'd found out about Em and was ready to be a father. Now it was here, and it felt like I was going to be sick. So many emotions, memories, retorts, a pile-up in my head, along with one, very strong, urge to say yes. Yes, let's get back together, and you can step up and be Em's dad, carry her up the stairs, ruffle her hair, help her with her homework, support me, and we can live happily ever after.

But we didn't have any stairs, Em didn't like people ruffling her hair, didn't need help with her homework, I didn't need his support, and wasn't sure I believed in happy ever after anyway. Happy ever after wasn't necessarily a good thing. It was a bit too . . . *simple*.

Roz and Sanjay weren't happy ever after. They squabbled, struggled, argued about money, and housework, and their careers, and sometimes he was depressed, and sometimes she was angry, but they still loved each other enough to carry on. The fact they were still together when they hadn't always been happy was more important. Letty and Jean-Luc weren't happy ever after. They had huge arguments, and occasionally lived apart when they were really irritating each other, and then he died, but she carried on because, while he was one of the best things in her life, he wasn't the *only* thing.

Looking at Adam across the table, it would have been easy

to say yes, to go for the simple option, both of us pretending to everyone, pretending to each other. But I'd pretended to myself for years that he was Em's dad, and it was time to stop. I reached for his hand across the table.

'Are you sure that it's over between you and Sophie?'

He looked utterly wretched. 'She really wants a baby.'

I squeezed his fingers. 'I'm so sorry. Have you looked into other options?'

'Yes, she wanted us to talk about getting a donor but I just couldn't . . .' He tailed off.

'So,' I said. 'You're prepared to pretend Emily is yours, but you couldn't countenance a sperm donor?'

He reddened, pulling his hand away. 'It's different. Because . . .'

'You love Sophie.'

'Yes. I can't stand the idea.'

'But you can stand being without her?'

He shook his head, tipping his chair back with one foot. 'I don't know what to do.'

I drained the last of my coffee. 'Here's a suggestion. Go and talk to her. Try to make it work. Then, when you feel a bit more settled, come back and see us again. Not as Em's dad, or my ex. Just as . . . our friend.'

When he looked up, his eyes were puffy and red. 'Why?'

I thought back to those days in the park, lying on the grass. The bad memories were receding, as better ones pushed to the front. Adam wasn't Em's father; he was just my first boyfriend – a fumbling romance I could look back on fondly.

'Because there was a time when I really enjoyed hanging out with you. It was fun.'

A hint of a smile played around his lips. 'Discussing *Richard III*?'

'Exactly. My daughter and I are both in need of a study partner.'

When he grabbed both my hands, I didn't resist.

'I'm sorry I left you,' he said, abruptly. 'It was unforgivable, to just . . . go off like that.'

'It's OK,' I said, discovering that it was. 'You were very young. And no doubt your parents were very persuasive.'

He sighed. 'Dad's a Sir now.'

'Your mother must be so proud.'

We both laughed and, when we stopped, I felt the teenager in me let go of a balloon and watch it drift away above the trees.

'It's late. I'd better be going,' he said, getting to his feet.

'Did you miss the train?'

'No, I drove. Will you be OK getting back? Do you want a lift?'

I shook my head. 'It's only over the road.'

'Right. Well. Goodbye, then. And thank you. I'll . . . see you around.'

Watching him walk away, out onto the pavement, the streetlights caught that lovely fiery hair of his, hair that was so different to my daughter's mousy frizz. Whose side was I on? No contest – I was on Em's side. She would always come first.

It was a warm night, drinkers spilling out of the pubs, kebab shops doing a roaring trade, sirens wailing in the distance. A typical Finsbury Park Friday night. I walked slowly home, feeling the beginnings of blisters, and quietly let myself in, stopping in the hallway to ease off my shoes. It was after midnight but there was a chink of light under the door of the living room. Dad must have left it on when he went to bed. Or maybe he'd fallen asleep in his chair. Tiptoeing forwards, wincing as the carpet scraped my rubbed-raw flesh, I pushed open the door. The heels dropped from my hand.

Dad wasn't asleep, wasn't in his armchair. He was standing by the piano, in his Sunday-best suit, the one he used to wear to church.

'I've been waiting up for you.'

'Oh, Dad, I'm sorry, it's been a long night.'

'Not to worry, you're home now. And I've been busy.'

Leaning towards the keyboard, he tapped middle C. It should have sounded tinny and flat, but it didn't; it was fine and mellow as the richest Yirgacheffe coffee.

I caught my breath. 'You . . . *tuned* it?'

My father nodded. 'Started this morning. Finished this afternoon. Took a while, but I think it's good. In case you want to play, now you're studying again.'

At some point, while I had been trying to turn my life around, often making a mess of it, my dad had been enjoying his own quiet renaissance – a gentle progression towards the light, nudging his strings, semitone by semitone, along with me. I felt tears rise up, threatening to overcome me as I looked at him, standing there so proudly. Forgetting Adam, and Dylan, Letty, and my guilt about Em, I sat down at the piano, and began to pick out a tune, softly, Dad humming along, his hand on my shoulder.

Sometimes you just had to leave your worries on the doorstep. For the duration of the song, at least.

Chapter 62

'*Y*ou all set?'

Phone pressed against my ear, I hooked myself into my sandals. 'Yes.'

'Good. Back straight, look her in the eye, give it all you've got. You'll nail it.'

'Yes, miss.'

'Sarky! And remember – next week, you're going to see that new place. I think it'll be perfect, lovely attic flat with two bedrooms. And you'll *love* your new landlady, she's an absolute treasure. Em might have to walk her dog though, she's getting on a bit. But the rent is a steal.'

'Yes, but Roz—'

'Don't forget, I'll text you the address.'

'I won't forget, but—'

'Maybe take her some flowers, it'll make you look—'

'Roz, I've got to go, I'm going to be late!'

'OK, OK, good luck!'

I was wearing the dress Letty bought me – the Agnès B from Paris. It was chic and smart and, peering at myself

361

in the thin mirror in our hallway, I thought of the French store assistant who'd said it was '*flatteuse et parfaite*'. I needed it to be perfect, needed everything to be perfect, so I could get this job.

Mrs Boleyn set it all up, after my final exam. 'There's an old colleague of mine,' she'd said, as we walked through the school towards reception. 'She's headteacher at a primary in Woodberry Down now. They're looking for a new teaching assistant, and I thought of you.'

I'd gaped at her, and she'd laughed. 'Why not? You have all the necessary qualifications. You'd do an excellent job. Would you like me to recommend you for the position?'

Being recommended was one thing, but I'd never been interviewed like this before, for any kind of position. Roz had sent me a list of questions I might get asked, and Em had read them out, lips pursing in disapproval whenever she thought my answers were too vague or clichéd. Rather than make me feel well-prepared, the practising made me more nervous, so we ended up getting a takeaway the night before instead, eating it on our knees in front of the TV. Afterwards, Em and Dad played chess while I watched them, thinking how much better he looked – Maman's blanket draped on the back of his chair instead of wrapped around him, and when Em won the game, he laughed and said, 'Em-Jo, you've got a computer instead of a brain in that head of yours.'

Maybe in the end, that was the best preparation of all, because when I arrived at my interview there was a smile on my face, and my hand forgot to shake as I held it out to Mrs McCleod. My nails were painted a defiant scarlet.

'Welcome to St Kilda's.'

It was a school like any other – red brick with tall, white-framed windows, black tarmacked playground, echoes of chattering children, the smell of floor cleaner and baked potatoes. Mrs McCleod – Elspeth – was a gentle, slightly scatty woman in her mid-fifties who Sarah Boleyn had told me was as sharp as a tack. 'Think of her as a young Miss Marple,' she'd said. 'Under all those scarves, she's ruthless.'

After fussing while she found the right pen, she squinted at me over her spectacles, shook out my CV and asked her first question.

'Why did you leave Brownswood without doing your A levels?'

'I was pregnant.'

'Ah.' She sat back. 'That explains it.'

That didn't explain the half of it. 'I've just taken my English A level. Get the results next month. And I plan to study for more. French, and Music. Then I want to get my degree.'

'Good, good.' She nodded. 'Why do you want to be a teaching assistant?'

'I don't,' I said, smiling as her brow furrowed. 'I want to be a teacher, eventually. This is the first step.'

She beamed. 'It is indeed! An excellent step, if I may say. And what makes you think you will be a *good* teacher?'

Em had asked me the same question, and screwed up her face when I said I wanted to give something back.

I pointed at my CV, still in Elspeth's hand. 'I didn't do things the usual way. Got things wrong, made mistakes, messed up. But I carried on, tried again, and hopefully now I'm starting to get things right. Maybe if it had all come too easily, I wouldn't have made a good teacher. When you fight for something, you want it more. And you get better at fighting.'

Elspeth stared at me over the rims of her glasses. 'Well, we teachers certainly have to do a lot of fighting.'

I thought of Sarah Boleyn struggling to raise funds for the leaking library, dressing as Professor McGonagall for Halloween; Roz painting the backdrop for the talent show, taking head lice treatment in for the kids. 'I know.'

She gave me the job then and there, subject to necessary checks. From the moment I walked in, I'd experienced a sense of calm, like sinking into a hot bath after a long trip away. I left with the promise of a contract starting in September, a part-time position that would allow me to do the occasional shift at Merhaba and, more importantly, get on with studying. I had work to do.

When I got back to Dad's that evening, loaded with shopping, I peeled off my clothes, kicked off my sandals and put on my running gear. Full tilt from now on, no half-measures. Scraping back my hair and pulling on a pair of trainers, I let myself out and set off. Down Blackstock Road, towards the park, the last of the late-evening sunshine caressing my face, warming my muscles as they stretched and flexed.

The carrots *weren't* cooked. I was rich, and it had nothing to do with money. I had a wonderful father who was starting to put himself back together again, and an amazing daughter who, one day, would show the world what she could do. There was the prospect of a new career, which excited me the more I thought about it. There was this new flat, owned by a friend of Sylvie's, which Roz said could be perfect for us. Sheba, Marni and I were meeting the following week for dinner, to talk about a possible weekend in Edinburgh. Letty might be gone, but I had the memory of her, an example of the kind of life I wanted to live – bold, ambitious, joyful.

But there was one thing I didn't have. My step faltered as I ran around the curve of the playground, picturing the children playing, climbing, digging, swinging there. I'd always imagined Em would be my only child, but now, there was a sense of loss, the Ghost of Christmas Yet to Come, showing me what might have been. Christmas Day would probably always be just me, Dad and Em, drinking lemonade in the flat. Something missing. Someone. 'Everything else will come,' Roz said. But sometimes it didn't. Sometimes you had to go and get it.

And I found my feet were carrying me out of the park – not the usual exit – past the church and the library and on, down the winding street to an empty music shop. I looked up to the flat above and saw a light was on, and, without thinking about it, without pausing to consider, carried on running, full tilt, pushing open the door of the shop, charging past the cellos, through the bead curtain, up the concrete stairs. As my feet pounded, I could hear a piano being played – more pounding, someone angrily punching the keys like a punishment. I didn't bother knocking, because the momentum was carrying me and it was too late; I was erupting into the room, breathless and sweating, hair escaping from its ponytail, face shiny and hot.

The music stopped abruptly. Dylan was sitting at the Bechstein, an empty bottle and a glass of red wine next to him, Bernadette panting below. Both of them jumped up as I arrived, Dylan half-rising from the piano stool before slumping down again, picking up his glass and swigging. Bernadette trotted over and sniffed me, licking the sweat off my hand when I bent to scratch her neck.

'Rachmaninoff,' I gasped. 'The neighbours will complain.'

Dylan didn't smile. 'What are you doing here?'

My hands were braced against my knees, getting my breath back, but I straightened up, looking him squarely in the eye.

'I came to say something I should have said months ago. I really like you, but was scared to do anything about it, because I made such a mess of things in the past, and I was sure it would happen again.'

I paused to catch my breath again and Dylan said nothing, his eyes back on the keyboard.

'I made myself a promise I would stop saying sorry. And I'm *not* sorry. I've made some shitty choices, muddled through as best I could with Em and my dad, and everything else. I'm not sorry. But I wish . . . I wish . . .' My voice broke and I bent again to stroke Bernadette, so I didn't have to look at him.

'What do you wish?' Dylan's voice was so low I could barely hear it. He was still staring down at the keys, his fingers resting on the black notes.

'I wish I could go back, and do it differently.'

'What would you do?'

'I would have got on with it, ages ago. Asked you for a drink or something. My first boyfriend was only interested in me because he thought I was clever. My last was only interested because he thought I was beautiful. You . . . You made me feel I might be both, at the same time.'

My breath had come back. I held it, and waited.

There was a long silence, broken only by Bernadette panting. Dylan didn't say anything, still stroking the keys, lost in thought.

'Dylan?'

He picked up his glass again, knocked back the last of his wine, set it down on the piano and looked at me properly for the first time.

'I was never interested in you because I thought you were beautiful or clever,' he said quietly, and closed the lid.

Bernadette nudged my leg, wanting more, but I ignored her. I'd gone for it, leapt off the cliff, and hit rock bottom. Only myself to blame.

'I'm . . . Never mind.' Before he could say anything else, I turned, wrenched open the door and ran, back down the stairs, out of the empty shop and onto the streets of Stoke Newington. Ignoring the bus stop, I started to trudge back home, all the energy and positivity seeping out of me. What an idiotic thing to do, barging in like that, thinking that I could fix things, that he even cared. My arms were cold but my cheeks were still hot as I brooded over my humiliation, the sheer stupidity of thinking that he could ever, *ever*—

'*Delphine!*'

Dylan, standing behind me, out of breath, dishevelled. I stared at him, rubbing my arms, unable to think of anything to say. I'd already said too much.

'Wait. Please. I wanted to say something.'

'What?'

His hair was on end, red wine on the neck of his T-shirt. He looked a complete wreck.

'Came to say I'm sorry. Made a cock-up of that. Didn't expect to see you, and I was drunk and . . . and angry, because I thought you'd gone off with that professor bloke. You turned up with your speech, and I wasn't prepared. It came out wrong. That's not what I meant to say.'

'What did you mean to say?'

He stepped forwards, taking my hand in his own. 'I was never interested in you because I thought you were beautiful or clever. You are those things, but I never cared about that.' He cupped my cheek with his other hand. 'I was interested in you because I thought you were strong, and kind, and funny. I was interested in the way you looked after Em, how you seemed to be working all the time, always rushing off. The way you were studying. The way you talked about Letty, like you'd known her for years. The way you sang, like you meant it; the way you played the piano; the expression on your face as it all came back to you. The way you have no idea how lovely you are.'

He took my other hand and pulled me towards him. 'I was interested in all of that, but I'm such a grumpy bastard I didn't know how to say it.'

'You should have said it weeks ago.'

'I meant to, but I didn't want to get in the way of your exams. Roz said we should just go for a drink like normal people.'

'That's what Sanjay said.'

'He said it to me as well. Jay's a big cheese now, because he sent Universal some of his songs, and they've offered him a recording contract.'

'*Really?*'

'Really. Roz is livid. She hates any evidence that he isn't useless. But he's been feeling a lot better since we set up the band. It made him believe he could do it again.'

'Wow.' I squeezed his fingers. 'We did that.'

'Yes, we did that, when we should have been going for a drink like normal people. So how about it?'

'How about what?'

He smiled down at me. Such neat white teeth. 'We could go to the pub. Roz told me you had an interview. We could celebrate.'

I bit my lip. 'How do you know we're celebrating?'

He shook his head, still smiling. 'We're celebrating, I promise. So, Delphine Jones, will you go for a drink with me?'

'Do you like hot chocolate?'

'I do,' he said, stepping back and offering me his elbow. There was no patch on his jumper, just a ragged hole, open to possibilities. '*Dewch ymlaen, cariad.*' I didn't need to speak Welsh to know he was saying '*En marche.*'

'Come on then,' I said, taking his arm. 'Let's get on with it.'

Chapter 63

It was a really beautiful spot. Sunlight dappled on springy tufts of grass, wiry trails of ivy curled over the clean granite curves, while wildflowers – cowslips and harebells, dandelions and daisies – sprang up around the base. Although it was a place for the dead, it felt lush and vibrant, lurching gravestones displaced by rich and fertile earth. Life goes on.

Em, clutching our offering, tentatively stepped forward.

'Hello, JoJo,' she whispered, and bent to place her bunch at the foot of her grandmother's headstone. Daffodils weren't in season, so we'd gone for ruby-red gerberas. Em traced the elegant grooves, her finger pale against the black tablet.

JOSEPHINE JONES
T'AIMER TOUJOURS, T'OUBLIER JAMAIS

'Good girl,' said Dad, rubbing her shoulder as she shuffled back. He knelt, brushing away tendrils, busily patting down moss, making things neat. Then stilled, head bent, to commune with his wife.

'We'll see you later, Dad.'

Em and I moved away, and began to stroll through the cemetery, stopping to read epitaphs, stare into the worn faces of angels, spy a fox ahead, its plumy brush weaving through the ferns.

'It's nice here,' she said, crouching to right an upended stag beetle. 'Like being in the countryside.'

'Yes. We were lucky to get the space.' One of the few things Dad had managed to do during that terrible time, but neither of us ever visited, because the reality of it, the solid undeniability of that stone, was too much to bear.

Em watched the beetle scurry away into the undergrowth. 'Do you know where my . . . my dad is buried?'

I stumbled on the path, kicking up dust. She hadn't mentioned her father since that day in the park, and I'd been unable to broach it, wanting to reach out to her, but worried about saying the wrong thing, pushing her away.

'No,' I said finally. 'Do you want me to find out?'

She gave me a look, the ghost of her pirate smile. 'I could find out for myself, don't you think?'

'Probably, but . . . do you want to?'

Em hesitated, rubbing her palm along the arch of a tombstone. It read, 'Doreen Flint, may the earth lie light upon thee'. Someone else's beloved.

'I've always liked knowing things,' she mused. 'Felt like the more I knew, the better. There's part of me that wants to find out everything about him . . .'

'And the other part?' I held my breath.

To my surprise, she sidled over and took my hand. My daughter wasn't physically affectionate, resisting my attempts at cuddles even when she was a toddler, rearing away from the most casual hair-muss. She tolerated contact, never pursued it. I cradled her paw like a new-born skull.

'The other part,' Em said, 'a bigger part . . . feels like this is enough.' She squeezed.

My breath slid out and sailed up into the trees. Still holding hands, we set off again.

'I always felt like something was missing,' continued Em. 'But it was here all along.' She swung her arm back, pulling mine with it.

Lacing her fingers, I swung my arm forwards. 'There's nothing missing,' I said. 'We have everything we need.'

She smiled, looking at the path ahead, brought her arm down and up again, my hand with it. Propping each other up, propelling each other along. I looked up at the overarching sky, infinite potential in the deep blue. The world was wide open, calling out, making space for my next leap, wherever I landed. Wherever *we* landed. Me, and Em.

Hands swinging back and forth, we carried on.

Acknowledgements

$\mathcal{S}$econd time around it's been a steep learning curve, and I'm very grateful to the following people for their invaluable help, time, expertise and support:

Harriet Truscott and the staff at Newnham College, Cambridge. Newnham is basically my muse, so it's lucky that the people there are incredibly friendly and helpful, and don't mind me hanging around all the time.

Kate Coghlan and Victoria Harvey at Lucy Cavendish College, Cambridge. When this book was going in a slightly different direction, I had a wonderful tour of the college, met the guinea pigs and mined the staff for information. The whole experience was delightful and the knowledge didn't go to waste.

Ross Sellwood, for musical advice, and helping me craft an imaginary recording career.

Alex Hutchinson, for quality Quality Street history, a piece of research I found very useful and hugely enjoyable.

George, Agnes and the staff at Butler & Booth, a café that sadly is no more, but remains my favourite writing place. Both Missy and Delphine were born there, and I remember it fondly.

Audrey Price, for unpicking my terrible French and sorting it out. Any mistakes that remain are my own, or maybe I'll just blame Letty.

Dan Thomas, Ruta Soquar, Robin French, John Lake, and my neighbour Matteo, for further translation assistance in Welsh, Italian and Tigrinya.

Geneviève Rich, for language and law help, particularly obscure points of 2004 legislation.

The D20 Authors group. Launching in lockdown isn't a barrel of laughs, particularly for a debut, but you lot lifted the whole process, providing comfort, wisdom and gossip. And you all write bloody good books.

I owe a huge debt of gratitude to teachers. Don't we all? Not just my own teachers, who inspired me and set me on this path, or my children's teachers, who amaze me every day with their dedication and spirit, but teachers everywhere. I agree with Delphine – they are precious, should be fêted and put in magazines like Hollywood stars. More importantly, they should be funded and remunerated properly, acknowledged and championed as a linchpin of our society. Next time you see a teacher dressed up for World Book Day (or any day for that matter), give them an elbow bump and tell them they're ace. Specifically, with regards to this book, I would like to thank the following magnificent educators: Nell Rufey, Quentin Hughes, and Rosa Aers, for providing crucial insights into the logistics of teaching, exams, and school life. And most of all, Lydia Aers, for being my sensitivity reader and also cheerleader, happily fielding my queries to the staff at Hills Road Sixth Form College, who responded cheerfully and patiently. A-stars to every one of you.

My agent Madeleine Milburn and all the wonderful people at the MM Agency, who have provided such constant support, in difficult circumstances. I'm truly grateful that I have such a strong, kind team to help me navigate this exciting but bewildering new career.

Martha Ashby at HarperCollins and Tara Singh Carlson at Putnam. You know I like teachers, and that's how I see you – I learnt so much writing this book and that's because you both pushed me in the best possible way. And to Lynne Drew at HarperCollins, who stepped into Martha's shoes so gracefully and calmly, providing a steady flow of encouragement – maybe one day you'll commission me to write that Georgette Heyer fan fic? In addition, to the brilliant, talented teams at HarperCollins and Putnam – assistants, publicists, marketeers, copy editors, illustrators, designers, the sales teams, and many others who pitch in to create a book. You're all wonders.

My family – my mum and dad, who let me witter on about writing angst and then ask how the boys are, reminding me what's important. To the boys, Wilfred and Edmund, my roots and wings, the finest and funniest boys – this book is for you, even though I know you'd both prefer an iPad. To my girl, Polly, for constantly occupying my writing chair, and providing distracting smells and snores when I'm trying to get on.

And to my husband Tom: thank you for sheltering me from the storm.

'A touching, deftly written debut that celebrates community and kindness' *Sunday Times*

'A thought-provoking, uplifting read that is far from predictable' *The Independent*

'Bittersweet, tender, thoughtful and uplifting' **Nina Stibbe**

'A beautiful story about love, loss, guilt and the power of friendship' **Jill Mansell**

'A fabulously enjoyable book' **Sarah Haywood**

'A hymn to the power of basic human kindness' **Rosie Walsh**

'Tender, funny and thoughtful' *Daily Express*

'Will delight readers right up to the very last page' *Stylist*

'One to savour' *Woman & Home*

'[A] glorious debut . . . simply stunning' *Woman's Weekly*

EXCLUSIVE ADDITIONAL CONTENT

Includes an author Q&A and details
of how to get involved in *Fern's Picks*

Dear lovely readers,

I am delighted to introduce you to Em and Delphine, the stars of this month's pick *Em & Me*, whose story will lift you up and remind you it's never too late for a second chance! Get ready for a new beginning this spring with a glorious story of mothers and daughters and learning to be brave.

Delphine is a struggling single mother who has always wanted more for her daughter, Em, while mourning the loss of her own dreams and carefully guarding a secret which might break everything apart. When Delphine is offered an opportunity to change things for the better, she has to learn how to let help in – as well as how to spread her own wings again.

Deliciously warm and hugely life-affirming, this is a book that will make you laugh, cry and hug your loved ones tighter, while also reminding us all to step out of our comfort zones once in a while.

I hope you enjoy it and I can't wait to hear what you think.

With love
Fern x

Fern Britton Picks

Exclusively for TESCO

Fern's Picks

Look out for more books, coming soon!

For more information on the book club, exclusive Q&As with the authors and reading group questions, visit Fern's website **www.fern-britton.com/fernspicks**

We'd love you to join in the conversation, so don't forget to share your thoughts using **#FernsPicks**

A Q&A with
Beth Morrey

Can you tell us what inspired you to write *Em & Me*?

It's hard to pin it down to one thing, but I had an idea about a little girl who was eerily intelligent – I wanted her cleverness to be a bit unnerving. I was thinking about the hardships she might face, sometimes hiding her intelligence, sometimes using it and getting into trouble. I wanted to write a kind of homage/update to *Matilda*, by Roald Dahl – 'Em', as in 'M' for Matilda. But then I got interested in Em's mother, and what it took to raise a child like that – and I imagined how much more difficult it would be to raise her alone. So that became *Em & Me*.

Motherhood and mother–daughter relationships are at the heart of this novel, and explored in different ways. What is it about these relationships that makes you want to write about them?

It was probably becoming a mother myself – I found it so tough! I also write a lot of short stories, and all of them seem to centre around motherhood. I can't let it go, worrying at it like a dog with a rope. So much about parenting baffles me and I think I'm trying to crack it, write about it until I understand it and am better at it. Of course, that time will never come…

With both of your novels, *Em & Me* and *Saving Missy*, you've written about kindness, generosity and warmth from friends

and strangers – was it an active choice to explore these
themes? And why?

My natural state is anxious melancholy. I'm a terrible worrier with
an inclination towards pessimism, so I think in my writing I'm
trying to fight it and teach myself to believe in good things, and
trust in them. But also, the world feels scary right now, for all sorts
of reasons, so it's nice to try to provide a bit of light, to try to cheer
people up.

**Teaching and learning are powerful themes throughout the
book – who have been the teachers who changed your life?
And why did you want to celebrate them in this book?**

I am very passionate about the brilliance and worth of teachers.
In the book, Delphine says they ought to be fêted and put in
magazines like celebrities, and I agree. It's such hard work, and
they're not paid enough, don't have enough resources, yet are doing
one of society's most vital jobs. During lockdown when we were all
home-schooling, I felt even more acutely that teachers are heroes.
I had wonderful teachers as a child – the primary school teacher
who taught me to read gets a namecheck in *Em & Me*, at the
beginning of Chapter 16. I also had a beloved piano teacher who
was like Miss Marple – gentle and ruthless. I wanted to honour
the profession in this book, and hoped that it might help readers
remember the teachers who changed *their* lives for the better.

What do you want the reader to take away from *Em & Me*?

There was a viral YouTube clip that showed young people running
a race, but runners were allowed a head start if they fulfilled
certain criteria – for example, if they were privately educated,
had never been hungry, or had always been healthy. They were
staging the race of life, literally. I'd like readers to remember the

people who might be behind them, struggling, but also know that wherever they are in the line-up, it's still possible to finish – and maybe even win. I'd also like them to come away from *Em & Me* knowing a few new French words, and perhaps even the odd Welsh one! 'Hiraeth' is a particular favourite – it's a sense of longing, a kind of homesickness, and I think it's such a beautiful, enriching word.

Can you tell us a bit about what you're writing next?

I've just finished my third book, about a busy TV executive called Clover Hendry who goes a bit crazy and tries to take the day off, but her quest for me-time keeps getting scuppered by other people. However, there's a deeper reason she desperately needs some time out, and that reason is gradually revealed. It's a perimenopausal *Ferris Bueller's Day Off*. I've really enjoyed writing it – it's funnier and fiercer than my previous books, and I hope readers enjoy Clover's journey. Maybe it could inspire others to take a day just for themselves…

Questions for your Book Club

Warning: contains spoilers

- Did you enjoy *Em & Me* and why?

- Delphine keeps a big secret from her daughter, Em. Do you think she was right to keep the secret for so long? Could you understand why she did it? And what do you think you would do in that situation?

- Delphine is lucky enough to come across several influential teachers in the book who have powerful transformative influence over her. Sarah Boleyn, who taught her at school and believed in her when no one else did; Roz, who teaches her how to let people in again; Letty, who teaches her French and a certain *je ne sais quoi*; perhaps even Dylan, who teaches her to open her heart again. Who have been the influential 'teachers' (either academic or otherwise) in your life and why?

- Did any of Delphine's experience of job insecurity/housing insecurity resonate with you and why?

- What do you think the main themes of the book were? What did you take away from them?

- What do you think the future holds for Delphine and Em?

- What's the one thing you'd say about this book if you pressed it into a friend's hands?

An exclusive extract from Fern's new novel

The Good Servant

March 1932

Marion Crawford was not able to sleep on the train, or to eat the carefully packed sandwiches her mother had insisted on giving her. Anxiety, and a sudden bout of homesickness, prohibited both.

What on earth was she doing? Leaving Scotland, leaving everything she knew? And all on the whim of the Duchess of York, who had decided that her two girls needed a governess exactly like Miss Crawford.

Marion couldn't quite remember how or when she had agreed to the sudden change. Before she knew it, it was all arranged. The Duchess of York was hardly a woman you said no to.

Once her mother came round to the idea, she was in a state of high excitement and condemnation. 'Why would they want *you?*' she had asked, 'A girl from a good, working class family? What do you know about how these people live?' She had stared at Marion, almost in reverence. 'Working for the royal family . . . They must have seen something in you. My daughter.'

On arrival at King's Cross, Marion took the underground to Paddington. She found the right platform for the Windsor train and, as she had a little time to wait, ordered a cup of tea, a scone and a magazine from the station café.

She tried to imagine what her mother and stepfather were doing right now. They'd have eaten their tea and have the wireless on, tuned to news most likely. Her mother would have her mending basket by her side, telling her husband all about Marion's send off. She imagined her mother rambling on as the fire in the grate hissed and burned.

The train was rather full, but Marion found a seat and settled down to flick through her magazine. Her mind couldn't settle. Through the dusk she watched the alien landscape and houses spool out beside her. Dear God, what was she doing here, so far away from family and home? What was she walking into?

When the conductor walked through the carriage announcing that Windsor would be the next stop, she began to breathe deeply and calmly, as she had been taught to do before her exams. She took from her bag, for the umpteenth time, the letter from her new employers. The instructions were clear: she was to leave the station and look for a uniformed driver with a dark car.

She gazed out of the window as the train began to slow. She took a deep breath, stood up and collected her case and coat. *Come on, Marion. It's only for a few months. You can do this.*

Available now!

The No.1 Sunday Times bestselling author returns

1932. Dunfermline, Scotland.

Marion Crawford, a bright, ambitious young teacher, is ready to make her mark on the world. Until a twist of fate changes the course of her life forever…

1936. Windsor Castle.

At first this ordinary woman is in a new world, working as the governess to two young princesses, in a household she calls home but where everyone is at a distance. As the course of history changes, she finds herself companion to the future Queen, and indispensable to the crown. And slowly their needs become her needs. Their lives become hers.

It's then she meets George, and falls in love for the first time. Now Marion faces an impossible choice: her sense of duty or the love of her life.

Available now!

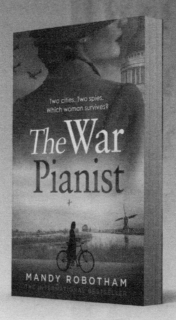

Two cities. Two spies. Which woman survives?

The War Pianist

MANDY ROBOTHAM

THE INTERNATIONAL BESTSELLER

Pianist: NOUN. Informal. A person who operates or controls a radio transmitter – often in code.

July, 1940

Blitz-ridden London: Marnie Fern's life is torn apart when her grandfather is killed in an air raid. But once she discovers that he'd been working undercover as a radio operative – or pianist – for the Dutch resistance, Marnie knows she must complete his mission – no matter the cost…

Nazi-occupied Amsterdam: At the other end of the wireless, fellow pianist Corrie Bakker is caught in a dangerous game of cat-and-mouse as she desperately tries to keep her loved ones out of the line of fire – even if it means sacrificing herself…

Bound together by the invisible wires of their radios, the two women lead parallel lives in their home cities, as both are betrayed by those they trust the most. But when the Nazis close in on one of them, only the other can save her…

Two cities. Two spies. Which woman survives?